Praise for the works of E. J. Noyes

Loyalty, the latest... on Series, is just another sh... prowess. Her exhilarating narr... master writer and queen of sapphic r...

-*Women Using Words*

Loyalty is equal p... ...ing, thrilling, suspenseful, angsty, romantic, and funny–it's perfect and exceeded my expectations, and believe me, my expectations were high.

-*The Lesbian Review*

Leverage

It's clever, funny, and sweet. It deals with hard topics, but the author does a brilliant job of lightening the mood through witty dialogue, and humorous anecdotes.

-*The Lesbian Review*

It's pure Noyes storytelling, and fans won't want it to end!

-*Women Using Words*

Ms. Noyes once again delivers us a balanced storyline that contributes to a winning reading experience that will appeal to fans of both romance and suspense genres.

-Carol C., *NetGalley*

Integrity

Noyes writes in first-person point of view like no other. This author made me see and feel everything through Lexie's eyes. Noyes' writing is beautiful and real, I loved getting lost in the main character's head and re-read several paragraphs because they were so poignant.

Noyes always writes witty, funny heartfelt dialogue and this book has all of that in bucket loads.

-*The Lesbian Review*

Noyes never fails to impress me with her talent. She is fearless in her storytelling, never hesitating to flesh it out and let the story take her where it will. Because she does, it feels organic to the reader. ... Book one of the Halcyon Division Series is a fantastic beginning; I have no doubt readers are going to enjoy this journey and sign up for more. This is heart-pumping, non-stop, page-flipping fun, and one heck of a ride! My recommendation: don't miss out!

-*Women Using Words*

Schuss

This is an absolutely charming first-love, new-adult romance between characters that I had already bonded with. Seeing how they have grown and matured in the four years is a treat and watching the two struggle with their feelings for each other just melted my heart... *Schuss* could be read as a standalone novel, but honestly, I think you should read both books together. They are wonderful stories, and I highly recommend them.

-Betty H., *NetGalley*

E. J. Noyes has this way of writing characters that you get completely absorbed into. When we were left with the Gemma and Stacey cliffhanger in *Gold*, I was hoping we'd get their story and it was phenomenal.

-Les Bereading, *NetGalley*

If I Don't Ask

If I Don't Ask adds a profound depth to Sabine and Rebecca's story, and slots in perfectly with what we already knew about the characters and their motivations.

-Kaylee K., *NetGalley*

Overall, another winner by E. J. Noyes. An absolute pleasure to read. 5 stars.

-*Lez Review Books*

Go Around

Noyes excels at writing both romance and intrigue and it shows in this book. Her characters might as well be real they are so well-written. I'm a pretty big fan of second-chance love stories, and I love the way this one is done. You get the angst you expect from the two women trying to get past the pain of their separation and work their way back to being a couple in love. …E.J. Noyes' works always get my highest praise and recommendation, and this novel is no different. You really need to read this book.

-Betty H., *NetGalley*

In *Go Around*, E.J. Noyes has dipped her toes in the second-chance romance pool and was masterful in blending angst, enduring love and suspense in it. The chemistry and dynamics between the pair were thick and palpable but what stood out for me throughout the book was the type of love everyone wished they had; fierce and protective, grounded in loyalty, passionate yet to be able to just be when you are with the other. Noyes also made Bennet, Avery's dog, another highlight for me. He was the tension breaker and a giant darling.

-Nutmeg, *NetGalley*

Pas de deux

Pas de deux doesn't disappoint: the writing is excellent, the pace is ideal, the characters are layered and, yes, relatable, including the secondary characters, from Caitlyn's groom Wren, to Addie's friend Teresa and, of course, Dewey the horse. One of the many things I loved in this book is the way the MCs deal with problems. They do this very adult and very rare-in-lesfic thing: they talk to each other. This book is proof that miscommunication isn't required for drama. Neither is a breakup. Well-fleshed characters with very human hang-ups bring all the angst and drama necessary. It's all the more interesting here as *Pas de deux* is part enemies-to-lovers romance, part second chance, depending on whose point of view is playing.

-*Les Rêveur*

This story is not the traditional enemies-to-lovers romance, and I love that. Noyes really puts emphasis on how skewed memories can become as you get older, and how an experience may appear different to another person who had the exact same one. Even if you are unfamiliar with dressage, Noyes' writing is still spot-on and delivers the same compelling, fun, and intriguing story with loveable characters of both the two-legged and four-legged kind. This love letter to a sport she obviously has a passion for is so evident, and I felt honored to have her share her passion with me and every reader who picks it up. If you love horses, enemies-to-lovers, or even just Noyes' stories in general, this one will definitely be a favorite on your list.

-*The Lesbian Review*

Reaping the Benefits

The story is quite eccentric with its paranormal context but in fact is a pure romance at heart with a nice dose of humor. The book is written in third person, from the point of view of both protagonists, which is not common for Noyes, but it is executed perfectly. With all main elements done well, this makes an awesome read which I could easily recommend to all romance fans.

-Pin's Reviews, *goodreads*

It's fresh and original. It's everything you crave when you want to dig into a great romance. I highly recommend it.

-Deb M., *NetGalley*

If you're looking for a lesbian romance, but with a twist of something different, I recommend *Reaping the Benefits*. It's sweet, sexy, and fun.

-*The Lesbian Review*

If the Shoe Fits

When we pick up an E.J. Noyes book we expect intensity, characters with issues (circumstantial and/or internal), and a romance that builds believably. Considering this is *Ask, Tell* #3 we expected all of the above

layered with epic seriousness. We were pleasantly surprised and totally floored by the humor in addition to what was already expected!
-*Best Lesfic Reviews*

Alone

E. J. Noyes is easily one of the most gifted writers pulling us into whatever world she creates making us live and feel every emotion with her characters. Definitely, loudly, vehemently recommended.
-Reviewer@Large, *NetGalley*

Alone is an absolutely stunning book. This book is not a 5-star, it is well above that. You don't see books like this one very often. Truly a treasure and one that will stay with you long after the final page.
-Tiff's Reviews, *goodreads*

There are only a few books out there so compelling they seem to take control of you and force you to read them as quickly as possible. You can't put them down. You just want the world to go away and leave you alone until you can finish this story. *Alone* by E. J. Noyes is that book for me. This novel is absolutely wonderful.
-Betty H., *NetGalley*

Ask Me Again

Not every story needs a sequel. *Ask, Tell* demanded it, and Noyes delivers in spectacular fashion. Sabine and Rebecca show us their fortitude and their strength in their love for each other…Thank you, Noyes, for giving us a great story, a great series, and amazing women that teach us the best things in life are worth fighting for.

There really is only one way to tell this story, and Noyes executes it perfectly. She gives us events from the first-person perspective. However, she alternates each chapter between Sabine's point of view and Rebecca's point of view. You're able to get the full perspective of their inner feelings and turmoil they hide from one another. In addition, you're able to get the complete picture of the unconditional love Sabine and Rebecca have for each other. It's this little light of love that propels the reader to keep going and hope these women will finally reach the end of the darkness.

-The Lesbian Review

Gold

This is Noyes' third book, and her writing just keeps getting better and better with each release. She gives us such amazing characters that are easy for anyone to relate to. And she makes them so endearing that you can't help but want them to overcome the past and move forward toward their happily ever after.

-The Lesbian Review

This book is exactly the way I wish romance authors would get back to writing romance. This is what I want to read. If you are a Noyes fan, get this book. If you are a romance fan, get this book. I didn't even talk about the skiing… if you are a skiing fan, get this book.

-Lex Kent's Reviews, goodreads

Turbulence

Wow… and when I say 'wow' I mean… WOW. After the author's debut novel *Ask, Tell* got to my list of best books of 2017, I was wondering if that was just a fluke. Fortunately for us lesfic readers, now it's confirmed: E. J. Noyes CAN write. Not only that, she can write different genres…

-Gaby, goodreads

The entire story just flowed from the first page! E. J. Noyes did a superb job of bringing out Isabelle's and Audrey's personalities, faults, erratic emotions, and the burning passion they shared. The chemistry between both women was so palpable! I felt as though the writer drizzled every word she wrote with love, combustible desire, and intense longing.

-The Lesbian Review

Ask, Tell

This is a book with everything I love about top-quality lesbian fiction: a fantastic romance between two wonderful women I can relate to, a location that really made me think again about something I thought I knew well, and brilliant pacing and scene-setting. I cannot recommend this novel highly enough.

-*Rainbow Book Reviews*

Noyes totally blew my mind from the first sentence. I went in timidly, and I came away awaiting her next release with bated breath. I really love how Noyes is able to get below the surface of the DADT legislation. She really captures the longing, the heartbreak, and especially the isolation that LGBTQ soldiers had to endure because the alternative was being deemed unfit to serve by their own government. I applaud Noyes for getting to the heart of the matter and giving a very important representation of what living and serving under this legislation truly meant for LGBTQ men and women of service.

-*The Lesbian Review*

E. J. Noyes was able to deliver on so many levels… This book is going to take you on a roller-coaster ride of ups and downs that you won't expect but it's so unbelievably worth it.

-*Les Rêveur*

Noyes clearly undertook a mammoth amount of research. I was totally engrossed. I'm not usually a reader of romance novels, but this one gripped me. The personal growth of the main character, the rich development of her fabulous best friend, Mitch, and the well-handled tension between Sabine and her love interest were all fantastic. This one definitely deserves five stars.

-*CELEStial books Reviews*

Merry Weihnachten

Other Bella Books by E. J. Noyes

Ask, Tell
Turbulence
Gold
Ask Me Again
Alone
If the Shoe Fits
Reaping the Benefits
Pas de deux
Go Around
If I Don't Ask
Schuss
Integrity
Leverage
Loyalty

About the Author

E. J. Noyes is an Australian transplanted to New Zealand, which may be the awesomest thing to happen to her. She lives in the South Island with her wife and the world's best and neediest cat, and is enjoying the change of temperature from her hot, humid homeland.

An avid but mediocre gamer, E. J. lives for skiing (which she is also mediocre at), enjoys arguing with her hair, pretending to be good at things, and working the fact she's a best-selling and award-winning author into casual conversation.

Merry Weihnachten

E. J. Noyes

Copyright © 2024 by E. J. Noyes

Bella Books, Inc.
P.O. Box 10543
Tallahassee, FL 32302

All rights reserved. No part of this book may be reproduced or transmitted in any form or by any means, electronic or mechanical, including photocopying, without permission in writing from the publisher.

This is a work of fiction. Names, characters, businesses, places, events and incidents are either the products of the author's imagination or used in a fictitious manner. Any resemblance to actual persons, living or dead, or actual events is purely coincidental. The publisher does not have any control over and does not assume any responsibility for author or third-party websites or their content.

First Edition - 2024

Editor: Cath Walker
Cover Designer: Kayla Mancuso

ISBN: 978-1-64247-610-1

PUBLISHER'S NOTE

The scanning, uploading, and distribution of this book via the Internet or via any other means without the permission of the publisher is illegal and punishable by law. Please purchase only authorized print or electronic editions, and do not participate in or encourage electronic piracy of copyrighted materials. Your support of the author's rights is appreciated.

Acknowledgments

I wouldn't call myself a Christmas Grinch, but the holiday season has never held much appeal for me, and writing a Christmas story has been an interesting experience. But of course, because I'm E. J. Noyes, I couldn't make it easy. I just *had* to write a Christmas story that features main characters from America and Germany, with their own personal and broad Christmas traditions that I had no experience with. So! I needed help.

To everyone on Twitter (X, bah) who gave me your American and German (and sometimes Austrian!) Christmas traditions when I asked a while back – thank you for sharing.

Grandma, thank you for making our Christmases as special as you could. You've always given me everything you had, and I'm not talking about material things. That said, I still really want that remote-control hovercraft I begged you for every year for many years.

Chris, you have my eternal gratitude, not only for being my Pocket German but also for your keen eye and thoughtful comments throughout the manuscript. Thanks for curing me of my ähm addiction…

Christina, much thanks for the Boston insider info.

Abby, thank you for showing me the way forward when I was feeling a little bit lost recently. Sorry about all the German and accent and stuff.

My friends and found fam. You all exist in varying stages of my consciousness—some in the periphery, some close, some midway. But no matter where you are in my sphere, I hope you know how important you are to me.

Kate, thank you so effing much for setting aside a portion of your busy life for me, and for doing it when I came rushing at you with a changed (i.e. waaaay shortened) deadline. Beyond book shit, thanks for just being you and hanging out with me.

Cath! Fifteen books together. How can I find a new way to express how much I love working with you? I can't. Thank you so much for your quick work on this one – it's so appreciated. Up, down, or across the hall?

Bella Books family. You're fab. Go team.

Pheebs, my darling coriander (cilantro) hater. I would gladly pick the Devil's herb out of your food for you any day, or drink your beer so you could stay in a German beer hall this time instead of being asked to leave (I shouldn't laugh, but I am). Thanks for letting us not make a big deal of Christmas. You're the only gift I need. I know, corny, I'm sorry.

CHAPTER ONE

Evie

I was so absorbed in imagining dialogue for Harper and Thea's sexy goodbye scene that when I opened the front door of my building it took me a few moments to realize there was a strange woman going up the internal stairs to my condo. After a second of confused anxiety, logic reminded me that to get inside the building, you needed a key, or a serious set of lockpicking skills. If she was a lock-picking thief, she was a gorgeous and well-dressed one.

I knew she was gorgeous because she'd glanced back at me. In those few seconds of us staring at one another, I added to the mental list I'd started about her. She had a great butt, snugly ensconced in a pair of tight, faded blue jeans. It wasn't a pervy observation, more just a reasonable thing to notice given that great butt was on the stairs just above my eye level. She was clearly coordinated, as evidenced by her expert juggling of a medium-sized cardboard box, a handbag, two canvas tote bags, a paper takeout bag, a bottle of wine, and her keys. And, she had the most adorable expression—part amused, part expectant, and part curious—that just made her more attractive, if that were possible.

Thankfully her gorgeousness wasn't that scary "you're so hot I'm too scared to talk to you" kind, more just a regular "you're so hot

I almost forgot to breathe for a moment" kind. It took another few seconds for my brain to move out of admiration territory and into chivalry territory. I pushed the door closed behind me, yanked out my AirPods, and rushed through the small foyer to help with her armloads. "Here, let me grab that for you," I said breathlessly.

I wasn't exactly sure what *that* was, but I figured she'd tell me what she needed me to help with. Assuming she even needed help. Shit. She'd been managing just fine before my clumsy offer. What if she didn't need help?

My sudden football-rush approach was apparently more alarming than chivalrous, and she dropped the box—thankfully nothing inside sounded shattery as it bounced down two stairs to land at my feet— and we both moved to retrieve it. I won the retrieval contest and the moment I'd stood up again, I found her watching me. Not unexpected given a stranger had just invaded her space. Technically *she* was the stranger invading *my* space, though on second thought, she could be my new neighbor.

Her greenish eyes held a hint of amusement, and maybe a little pity. Amused-slash-pitying was a fair reaction. I closed the gap between us, still at the lower-stair disadvantage. "Shit. I'm *so* sorry. I didn't mean to scare you. I'm harmless, I promise."

After offering her the box, I realized she had no way of taking it from me with everything else she was holding. Doing really well on the social interaction and good-impressions scale here. This small respite while we figured out how to deal with the box gave me a moment to take a close-up look at her. I studied her in my not-creepy, I'm-an-artist-who-notices-faces way. Artist aside, I was interested in the woman who I was apparently going to be sharing the second floor with.

Wavy, light-brunette hair streaked with blond, brushing her shoulders. Full, bow-shaped mouth. Sloping, angular jaw with a strong chin. Now that I was closer, I changed my mind about the color of her eyes. Not green, but hazel flecked with brown, wide and curious, with laugh lines at the corners. Yes, she was undeniably attractive. But beyond being gorgeous, she had an interesting face, with a magnificent bone structure that my fingers itched to draw.

Realizing I'd been staring instead of remembering my manners, I tucked the box against my side and the wall and held out my hand. Then retracted it almost immediately when it twigged, again, that her hands were full and mine—along with the rest of me—were probably sweaty after my middle-of-the-day run. I brought that hand back to indicate myself. "Seems I'm your neighbor at number four, right next door. Oh, that rhymed. And I'm not really next door, I'm technically up the hall. Or down the hall, depending on which way you're going. Actually, I guess I'm *across* the hall but our doors are at opposite ends, so…" I coughed out a nervous laugh, wishing a meteor would descend from space and squash me, saving me from myself. No such luck—the universe was fresh out of meteors.

Better introduce myself. "I'm Evie. Evangeline. Phillips." Okay, maybe I *was* stuck in a mix of hotness reactions and had landed on "so hot I forgot how to talk to you."

She tucked the takeout bag under her arm and reached down to offer her hand, and a smile that made my knees feel wobbly. "Hallo, I'm—"

Not only hot with a low, mellow voice, but also German. The accent wasn't thick, but it was definitely there. And it was definitely sexy. I swallowed hard, hoping my mental gymnastics about this woman's sexy face and sexy voice weren't obvious.

"—Annika. Annika Mayer." Her lips worked as if she was mouthing my name before she added, "It's nice to meet you, Evie-Evangeline."

Laughing, I corrected her, "Sorry. My name is Evangeline, but most people call me Evie."

She laughed with me. "Oh, that makes a lot more sense. You have a beautiful name, both versions of it."

I blinked. Wow. Smooth. Do you give lessons on flirty pickups, Annika Mayer?

"Which version do you prefer?" she asked before I could make my mouth form words that weren't just blathering in response to her flirtation. It *was* flirtation, right? But who flirted with someone they'd only just met? Hot, confident women, apparently.

My response squeaked out. "Either or. Whatever. I don't mind."

"Good. Then I will think about which one I think suits you."

I let myself imagine the unspoken *and let you know the next time we talk*. "Sounds good." I flailed for small talk that didn't feel quite so intimate, but ended up with boring and super-obvious and not-flirty (because I was not as adept at flirtation as she was). "You're new to the building?"

Annika nodded, and thankfully she didn't say something like "No shit, dumbass." Instead, she answered cheerfully, "Ja, new to this building. This city. New to this country, too."

"Right. When did you move in? Aside from recently, that is. And where from?" Obviously, from the place of really hot people.

"Just today. And I moved from München. Munich. That's in Germany," she added, with a smile of encouragement as if talking to a small child. Given my impersonation of someone with limited mental capacity and vocabulary, I understood why she felt I needed a little hand-holding.

My return smile was patient and a little smug. I'd seen a lot of Europe, hence my picking her accent. "Oh, yep, I know where it is. I've been there. To Munich. And Germany. Obviously, if I've been to Munich I've been to Germany." Keep rambling and she might think you have more than one brain cell, Evie. I wouldn't class myself as smooth around women, but I could usually string a more coherent and intelligent sentence together. But there was something about her that completely frazzled my ability to put thoughts into words. I didn't know if it was her appearance or her accent or that freckle underneath her lower lip or the way she looked at me, but *something* was getting under my skin, in a very pleasant way. "I've been to other places in Germany too."

Her mouth had twitched throughout my monologue, but the amusement was quickly overtaken by pleasure when I confirmed I'd been to Germany. "Really? That is amazing. Did you enjoy your visit? Or…visits?" Her voice rose at the end of the question.

"Mhmm, I did. Very much. Munich is a beautiful city. But my enduring memory is of getting kicked out of a beer hall for not drinking beer," I said ruefully. "Kicked out very politely, obviously." Heather had laughed and laughed. And only once she'd finished her massive beer, then a second massive beer (of course), had she come to find me a few blocks away where I was sulking in a café.

Annika nodded sagely. "Oh, ja. They'll do that. So, you don't like beer?"

"Not really, and I was taking the seat of a person who would pay for beer." I cleared my throat. "And now that you have part of my life story, I'm going to let you get back to…whatever it is you're doing. Moving in, it seems." Time for an exit, and it was not going to be a smooth or suave one at all. I extended a forefinger to point vaguely past her. "I, uh, need to get up the stairs."

"So do I," she said, leaning forward, a conspiratorial tone lacing her words.

"Great. After you." She was ahead of me. Obviously she'd go first. God, what was wrong with me? When had I become an idiotic Captain Obvious?

Annika flashed me another bright smile, adjusted her arm cargo, turned around, and started walking upstairs again. I kept my attention on the stairs in front of me for the walk up to the second floor. Not staring at a stranger's ass, no siree, not me. She slowed down once she reached the top of stairs and the space widened slightly into the hallway. I had to either commit to walking beside her or lagging behind. Behind was where her ass was, so I settled for to the side and a little behind but not behind enough where I'd seem creepy.

Annika paused by my door, staring expectantly at me. Right. Time to say bye. Pointing over my shoulder, I said unnecessarily, "So, I'm just here, the only other one on this floor, if you need anything." Cup of sugar, make-out session, you know, just normal friendly neighbor things. "I work from home, so I'm around a lot. Feel free to knock on my door and give me an excuse to procrastinate."

She laughed—a loud, kind of snorty, unashamed guffaw that seemed almost incongruous with her put-together appearance. At least she thought I was funny, or was polite enough to fake it. "I will remember that. Thank you."

"Great. Then I guess I'll talk to you…sometime."

The genuine warmth in her smile made my stomach flutter. "I hope so," Annika said smoothly, her voice tinged with an inflection I couldn't quite place, but that I thought was anticipation. I hoped it was anticipation.

I fought the urge to respond with something inane like "Great" or "Okay then" that would just prolong the back-and-forth into indefinite politeness, and turned away to unlock my door, while Annika continued up the hall to hers. I'd just inserted the key when I realized I was still holding her box. I hastily walked up the hall, feeling like an idiot for adding to her armloads. But offering to take it into her apartment only minutes after meeting her felt more than a little weird. And I'd been weird enough already. "Here. Sorry. Inadvertently stealing your stuff isn't a great first impression."

Annika grinned. "No, it isn't." She ducked down and managed to slip an arm under the box and balance it on her forearm without endangering the other things she held. The seeming ease of it made me feel slightly better about passing the baton, so to speak. "But you stealing my box *would* mean I'd see you again soon when I came to request it from you."

Wow, and smooth again. "That's true," I agreed, pleased when I sounded casually musing rather than hyperventilate-y. "Okay, I'll just,

I'll see you later then. Maybe soon. Without the theft." With a fingers-twinkling wave, I walked away and slipped through my door before I could dig myself deeper into my hole of bad first impressions. I'd like to think I was charmingly awkward. But Annika Mayer? Now she was downright charming, period.

I dumped my keys, phone, and AirPods on the floating Caesarstone kitchen island and instead of beelining for the shower, I rushed upstairs to my office. After a habitual glance at the storyboarding whiteboard that took up an entire wall of my office, and my desk with my iPad and MacBook, each connected to a forty-inch monitor, I confirmed the main screen still held evidence of my artist's apathy. I'd hoped that abandoning my lack of work to move my body for an hour might magically fix this block, but it hadn't. It *had* given me another idea though, so I supposed it hadn't been entirely pointless.

I grabbed a sketchbook and the Caran d'Ache Grafwood graphite pencils I preferred for pencil-and-paper sketching. I didn't think, I just started drawing Annika's face, still standing up and leaning over my desk. I drew her as I'd seen her, totally unembellished. This was the kind of drawing I loved, the kind of drawing that was why I'd never used my MBA. No thought as to composition, just raw art from memory or recognition, and one of the best things I'd found to overcome creative burnouts. It took a little over fifteen minutes to shade in the lines and shadows fully and when I was done, I held the sketchbook at arm's length, trying to reconcile the woman I'd just met with what I'd drawn. Yes, this was her. Seeing her rendered in graphite strengthened my original assessment of *hot*.

At the bottom of the page I wrote *Aphrodite/Artemis?* My new neighbor had the perfect face for either: the Goddess of Love's beauty and mischievousness, or the Goddess of the Moon's (or of the Hunt, or of Chastity—Artemis filled a lot of shoes) strength. I drew a few different expressions like that wry smile, the eyebrows-raised interest, the curious attentiveness. When I'd exhausted my need to get that face on paper, I pondered Annika Mayer and our disastrous first meeting.

Okay, maybe *disastrous* was a little strong, but I certainly hadn't showcased my best character traits. I didn't get out much anymore and it had been a while—okay, a *long* while—since I'd tried to impress a woman. And I didn't recall it being so…hard. Annika, on the other hand, was one of those people who was effortlessly friendly and even flirtatious, if I'd been reading the situation correctly. Shit, what if I hadn't been? What if I'd just been wishful-thinking projecting onto her? I mean, she'd said my name was beautiful. That…wasn't really flirting, just complimenting my parents' ability to name their offspring. I flipped the book over, because staring at the drawings just made me feel like an idiot. More of an idiot.

After a quick shower to wash away my run, I made myself a smoothie and drank it while staring out one of the living room windows to the street below. Nothing like people-watching for more motivation to brush away the ol' "don't feel like working" cobwebs. Non-creepy people-watching, of course.

By the time I'd finished my smoothie, I'd drawn an animated conversation between two women, a most ridiculously ruggedly handsome man who would make an amazing villain (sorry, Stranger Man), and a cute kid trying to help walk a dog.

I turned the pages back to my drawings of my new neighbor. I'd seen dozens of people, and not one of them was as attractive as Annika Mayer.

CHAPTER TWO

Annika

Though I'd begun searching while still in Germany, I'd been concerned about finding somewhere in Boston to live and had resigned myself to staying in an Airbnb while I hunted for an apartment. As it turned out, it had been surprisingly fast and easy, perhaps because I wasn't particularly worried about cost. But now I'd moved into the place that would be my home for the next year, I had a new concern: how to coexist with the attractive woman with whom I shared a hallway, without breaking the only rule I'd set for myself during my temporary, twelve-month reassignment.

No romantic relationships. No casual sex. Prioritize myself and focus on the reason I was here: my job.

I could have laughed at how typical it was of me to be thinking of someone I'd barely interacted with as a potential partner, especially in the face of a resolution I'd made barely ten days ago. And I would have laughed, if I wasn't so frustrated with myself. Well…if nothing else, at least I was predictable.

I'd just set my armloads onto the bare kitchen counter when my phone chimed with a personal email notification. At this time of day, or night in München, it was probably Sascha. His derisive "You don't know how to be alone, Annika" echoed in my head, and had been part of the reason for my resolution. Cutting off my nose to spite my face was one of my less endearing traits, but in this case it was the right choice. I don't know how to be alone, Sascha? Well, we're done, I *can* be alone, and I'm going to be alone instead of with you, you self-centered, whiny man-child. I wished I'd said that instead of just a blandly generic "Long-distance isn't going to work for me, so let's break up."

I didn't even need to look to know what the email would say—the subject of *I miss you* was enough. A wine-soaked essay along the lines of *I love you and I miss you. I want to make this thing between us work. I don't mind the distance. I want you to give us another chance.*

I…I…I…I…

It was such a typical approach from my ex-boyfriend. Our breakup was all about *him*, as if my thoughts and feelings didn't factor into his actions at all. That selfish part of him was one of the reasons why, when I'd been asked to relocate to the Boston office to ensure an important project got over the line on schedule and within budget, I'd agreed almost right away. I indulged in a loud sigh, wishing someone was here to hear my audible annoyance, then, without reading the email, responded as I had to his other emails about wanting to try a long-distance relationship. With a firm *It's over.* This time I added, *Please stop contacting me, unless it's about work.* Direct and to the point, no room for ambiguity.

Fresh country. Fresh start. But I was sure that despite my repeated responses of *no*, he would keep trying to find wiggle room to get back together. He really was deep in the depths of denial about our breakup. If we'd dated for more than a few months and if he was someone I could see myself in a long-term relationship with, then I might have considered long-distance. But knowing him as I did after years of working together and a few months of dating, I knew that within a few weeks without me there, his eye would be wandering. It probably already was. I actually did laugh at that thought. Hadn't *my* eye just wandered, less than a few weeks after the breakup?

I moved the box to the end of the counter, and my mind drifted to what had caught my wandering eye. My new neighbor. Evangeline. The name rolled around my head and I let it roll from my tongue again, whispering, "Evangeline."

Evangeline. Evie.

Whichever version of her name I decided upon, it didn't matter. What *did* matter was that she was incredibly cute, and I wanted to see her again. Seeing her again was a certainty, given we were neighbors, but I wanted more than just moments of bumping into her in the hallway. God knew I needed to expand my Boston friendship circle, which currently consisted of only Rachel. She'd spent eight months in the München office last year as a back-end engineer, and we'd become good friends. I was greatly looking forward to spending time with her again.

But… Evangeline. The moment I saw her, I knew that I wanted more than just a friendship. I hadn't missed the way her eyes had flicked over me before they'd kept disciplined eye contact for the rest of our conversation. I didn't know if she hadn't checked me out again because she hadn't liked what she'd seen, or she *had* liked what she'd seen and was embarrassed that I'd caught her.

It really was a beautiful name, suiting the beautiful woman to whom it belonged. I rolled my eyes at myself. But she *was* beautiful. Perhaps two inches shorter than my five foot nine, dark-blue eyes that held both intensity and softness, lightly curly honey-blond hair pulled back into a ponytail, soft full lips that were quick to smile. About my age, maybe a little bit younger. And she was dressed for a workout of some kind, which meant it'd taken all my willpower to keep my eyes from following her ass into her apartment when she'd walked away after giving me my box.

She reminded me a little bit of the last girlfriend I'd had, Petra, though only physically. Evangeline's charming, almost bumbling introduction and her clumsy attempt to be helpful were as far from the cool, sometimes aloof Petra as Germany felt from the United States. Evangeline Phillips was attractive, and the zing when we'd made eye contact had been undeniable. It wasn't like I'd never had an instant physical attraction to someone before, but this one felt different, more intense somehow. And that felt dangerous.

A text from Mama broke my meandering thoughts, and for just a moment I considered ignoring it. But she'd just keep texting until I answered, or until she grew tired of typing and called. *Have the rest of your belongings arrived yet? Did you remember to pack an Advent calendar? Did you order your wreath? When will it arrive?*

I closed my eyes and summoned some patience. I couldn't bring a wreath with me from Germany because it was made of plant matter and even if it was allowed, it would not enjoy the journey. I'd considered a plastic one but decided the wrath of my mother was not worth it, not to mention my own feelings about a plastic wreath. My being away from my family at Christmas was already a problem and adding to the drama was not on my agenda this year.

I paid for fast shipping for all my belongings, remember? The last update was that everything is waiting official customs clearance, and delivery should be by the end of this week. Yes, I have a wreath. Two wreaths actually, because I wasn't sure which I'd like more, coming from an Etsy store in America, run by a German woman so they will be lovely, and will also be here by the end of this week.

I saw her typing indicator and hurried to appease what I knew was coming, my thumbs moving over the screen with lightning speed. *They will be here in time. It's fine. And if they aren't here, then I'm sure Boston has somewhere for me to buy a wreath, candles, and Advent calendar before the 1st. Or if I miss a few days, it's not the end of the world.*

Not to me it wasn't, though it was close, but it was to my mother. I could almost feel the pursed-lips disapproval in her answer. *I hope you're right. Please let me know they've arrived intact. And send pictures when you've set them up.*

A not-so-subtle hint. I closed my eyes to keep from rolling them. I was thirty-seven years old and sure, I'd never had Christmas away from my parents' place, but I wasn't an idiot and could put a wreath on the table and find somewhere for my calendar. I shook all the sarcastic responses from my fingers and simply typed *Okay, Mama.*

I paced back and forth across my bare living room while I watched the three dots—Mama's usual one-fingered texting style taking an eternity as usual. Eventually the message landed. *Your father wanted me to tell you that he's worried you might not get a good tree close to Christmas Eve because everyone in America buys and decorates in early December. Is there someone who could store a tree for you and keep it alive if you bought it early? Could you ask the building manager? Is there a storage area somewhere?*

Clearly my parents had been Googling "Christmas in America" again. I almost gave in and called her, just to stop this becoming-maddening text-message exchange. But calling her would result in an hour-long conversation where I would mostly just make sounds to agree with her and occasionally elaborate when asked.

I literally just moved into the building, I don't know. I thought about Evangeline, offering to help if I needed anything, and wondered if babysitting a Christmas tree qualified. Ordinarily, my family didn't bring the tree inside until it was time to decorate it, and I had envisioned breaking tradition and keeping the undecorated tree in my apartment until Christmas Eve.

My mother's response was exactly what I'd expected. *Then perhaps you need to make some friends who can keep a tree for you.*

I'm trying!

Sort of. I would be trying. Considering I'd only moved into the apartment this morning, after spending almost a week in an Airbnb, "making new friends" was far down my to-do list. Somewhere below "buy more furniture" and "fully stock refrigerator and pantry." I'd do those two things tomorrow. Friends could go on the list for the day after tomorrow.

How is your new apartment?

I spun in a circle, taking in the space. Eight hundred square feet of modernity nestled in an old building in a prestigious area of Boston. Ten-foot ceilings, polished wood floors, gleaming off-white walls, a galley-style kitchen, and my own tiny private balcony off the master bedroom that would be incredible once it warmed up, even if the view was of other brick structures. When I'd first come to view the apartment, I'd been taken by the red-brick exterior, the towering tree in the small courtyard, and the gorgeous vine climbing up a neighboring building wall.

It's nice. I snapped a few photos on my phone of each room and sent them.

It is nice, Mama agreed. Then just as quickly, *Why haven't you finished unpacking?*

Because I only moved into the apartment today! I'll finish tonight or tomorrow. There were worse things than full suitcases.

Thankfully Mama recognized my exasperation through those words, and let me off the hook with a *Good. I love you, and I miss you already. Talk to you soon.*

I sent back a reciprocal parental love message and a flurry of emojis before tossing my phone onto the counter. I knew she was only trying to help, that she was worried about me being alone for the holiday season, that she was upset the family celebrations would go ahead without me. But there was an undertone of guilting me that set my teeth on edge. Or maybe that guilt was actually my own.

I almost crossed the room to collapse onto my couch when I realized I didn't have one… I didn't even have a bed, but if the young salesman's fervent promises rang true it should arrive, along with the bedding too large to carry home, within a few hours. I hoped it did, otherwise I'd be sleeping on the floor with my backpack as a pillow.

During a confusing jaunt around my new town on Friday, I'd lain down on four mattresses before I became overwhelmed by choice, and just picked the one that seemed least likely to upset my spine. I was only going to be here for a year, and with my resolution to not leap into relationships or casual sex, entertaining anyone in my bed was unlikely.

After my lightning-fast mattress choice, I'd quickly chosen a frame that suited my modern tastes, high-thread-count sheets, pillows, and bedcovers, and had walked out of the store exactly twenty-seven minutes after I'd walked in. Choosing a refrigerator and the rest of my furniture had been done just as fast.

I checked my watch again. If my bed didn't come in time for me to sleep in it tonight, I'd just check into a hotel, or… I bit back a laugh at what would happen if I crossed the hall and knocked on that door. Hallo, Evie-Evangeline, I know we only just met a few hours ago but you said I could come to you for help, so…can I please sleep on your couch? If not, your bed, with you in it too, is fine.

No no no. No casual sex. Oh, yeah, and no relationships. Maybe I needed to put a reminder note on my fridge. When it arrived.

I'd allocated my afternoon to drinking my bottle of wine and assembling somewhere to sleep, so until the bed arrived, I had nothing to do. Hopefully I'd finish the bed before the bottle, or it might be an unstable place to sleep. I'd just unpacked my portable speaker and lain down on the living room floor to wait for the delivery when my phone vibrated with a call. I sat up.

Nathan Mitchell. The last thing I felt like doing was talking to my new manager, but I couldn't ignore him. I answered, "Hallo?"

The sort-of-familiar voice was enthusiastic and warm. "Annika? Hi, it's Nate."

"How are you, Nate?"

"Fan-tas-tic! Now this is just a quick call. I wanted to make sure you've settled in okay and check you're good to come in this week so I can introduce you to everyone, and you can get all your HR stuff organized after the transfer from the Munich office." Okay, so he was a touchy-feely, let's-keep-everyone-happy boss, as evidenced by him calling me himself rather than allocating an assistant to the task. So, I'd have to adjust, but I could work with that. Better than an asshole boss. "Just a reminder," he continued, "the office is closed Thursday for Thanksgiving."

"Thank you for checking in. So far, everything is great." And I meant *everything*, including my neighbor. "And yes, I can come in Friday morning?" I wanted to take the week to familiarize myself with the neighborhood and buy the rest of my household essentials.

"Great! And we're still on track for you to start Monday, right? You don't need any more time to get yourself settled?" It was a polite question, and I was sure if I said "Actually, yes, I need more time to settle in" I'd be accommodated without too much grumbling, but I also knew we needed to get started ASAP. Hence me being here right before Christmas.

"Yes, Monday starting is still fine."

"Fabulous!" Thankfully Nate didn't feel the need to ramble on inanely to pad out the conversation. "I'll see you Friday morning."

"Ja, perfect. I'll see you then." I said goodbye and lay back down. And for the first time since I'd signed my new contract, I had an attack of self-doubt. What the heck was I doing here? There were many lead app designers in the company across three cities—München, Boston, and Paris—but I knew my bilingual abilities made me attractive for this development. I'd be right there in the main production office, able to meet the client face-to-face instead of Zoom or the client having to wait for the München office to respond.

So why *had* I agreed to moving to Boston? Because I'd needed to shake my life up, to reset myself after years of coasting along comfortably. Well, I'd certainly done that, and I'd been excited, almost cavalier about it. But now I was here, exactly a month before Christmas, I felt the sudden and almost overwhelming weight of anxiety. Aside from Rachel, I knew nobody. And I'd be spending Christmas alone, except for FaceTiming with my family. It had been a fit of dissatisfaction, a brief glimpse that perhaps moving countries might kickstart my somewhat stagnant life that had made me dive in headfirst.

So far, all it had kickstarted was a stomach ulcer.

CHAPTER THREE

Evie

The sound of my front door opening and closing, then the thud of bags by the kitchen table broke through my work bubble. I set down my stylus, spun my chair around to face the door, and raised my voice to ask, "Chloe? Is that you?"

"No," came the droll reply from downstairs. "It's Taylor Swift."

"Lucky me," I called back, failing to match the drollness. I didn't know how it had happened, given they'd only had five years together before Heather died, but somehow my sister's smart-assed nature had made its way into my niece. Maybe it'd seeped out of her grave and into Chloe. Stranger things had happened.

Quick footsteps came up the stairs and a few seconds later my twelve-year-old niece came into my periphery, leaning against the doorframe. She rarely came into my office, citing fear of breaking some of my digital drawing equipment. It was a valid fear. Years ago, she'd accidentally spilled juice over my drawing tablet—which was the catalyst for moving to an iPad setup—and had also erased the entire bottom quarter of a storyboarded book on the whiteboard and replaced it with her first-grader writing practice. Her alphabet was excellent—the loss of my work less so.

Chloe narrowed her eyes at me, perfecting the disapproving-parent look. It was disconcerting when your niece felt more like a mom. "I thought you'd be done for the afternoon."

I could have faked a contrite expression, but I knew from experience that it wouldn't make any difference—she knew me well enough to know I was rarely apologetic about work. So, instead, I just wore it, and her disapproval. "Mmm, sorry," I said distractedly as I checked my work had synced to the save places, before pushing my chair back and directing all my focus to her. "I had some ideas while I was out on my run and had to get them down." Inspiration to do the boring stuff like planning the minutia of panels and scenes didn't care what time it was, and I pounced on any bout of enthusiasm.

She crossed her arms, somehow managing to look both interested and withering, like she'd witnessed me have so many ideas that she was now sick of them. This change from bright, bubbly, interested kid toward bored, standoffish preteen had come so quickly I often wondered if I'd been in a coma for a year and missed the metamorphosis. Chloe was still bright and bubbly, but there was an unmistakable hint of "boo, adults" creeping into interactions now. "What idea is it this time?" she asked dutifully.

I stood, reaching my arms above my head to stretch, smothering a yawn as I said, "Harper wants to see Thea before she meets with the leader of the River Queens Gang. Wants time to…uh, connect." Code word for having intense post-apocalyptic sex before she left for maybe-death. "In case she doesn't survive." Spoiler—she does survive. "So I'm just trying to work out how and where, and draft that out." And drafting ideas was more interesting and less hand-cramping than endlessly coloring and shading backgrounds.

My current project, *Chasing Shadows*, was a contracted ten-book graphic novel series that people were calling the "Sexy, snarky, sapphic post-apocalyptic graphic novel we've been waiting our whole lives for." I loved the story and characters, but halfway through working on the eighth volume, I was itching to start a new project.

"That makes sense. Give your readers what they want, but it also gives Harper a reason to come back." Chloe always read a sanitized, blank-pages-inserted-for-intimate-scenes version of all my graphic novels and even though she was just a kid, provided valuable feedback.

I crossed the room to her. "Right? I don't know why I didn't think of it while I was writing my first draft of volume nine." I'd drafted the entire series from start to finish, but left the actual storyboarding and layouts for when I began each new volume. Or…like now, before I'd begun a volume.

Chloe accepted my tight hug, and even squeezed me back—miracle!—as she mumbled, "Because you don't plan well, Aunt Evie."

"You know planning ruins all my creativity." Luckily this new idea I'd had on my run would be in the next volume, which wasn't due for publication until late next year, not the one I was currently working on. Otherwise I would have had a micro meltdown at having to redo panels to fit it in, and then get approvals from my editor and publisher, and then rework everything around it, blah blah.

"I know. Weirdo. I don't know how you work so…" Her face scrunched up as she struggled for a word. In the end, she clearly gave up trying to find something diplomatic, and just said, "Messily."

It wasn't the first time I'd heard a variation of this theme, especially not from family. My niece was Heather 2.0, and that was becoming more apparent every day. Not just physically—in the last six months I'd started seeing more of my older sister in Chloe's face and it still caught me off guard—but also in her personality. As well as the smart-ass streak, both of them were thoughtful and measured, meticulous and careful. From the age of ten, Heather had a planner that mapped her days out to the hour, whereas I was a fly-by-the-seat-of-my-pants kind of person. In everything except my personal life, that is, where I was the planniest planner who ever planned.

"Some days, I don't know either," I said cheerfully. "But it works for me." I kissed the top of Chloe's head and directed her down the stairs to my main living area. "Anything interesting happen at school today?"

"Nope," she said. The answer came back quickly, too quickly, which made me suspect *nope* was actually *yep*. But I knew if she wanted to talk about something exciting or was worried about anything, she'd come to me about it. Whatever had caused her knee-jerk answer was probably something innocuous, just the usual seventh-grade dramas.

"How was basketball practice?"

"Fine." After a pause, during which my expectant stare wore her down, she added, "Made some threes."

Yep, we'd truly begun the slide into mute-or-mumbly almost-teenager territory. "Nice! That's awesome." I pulled her against me for another hug then let her go before she could protest about another PDA—*private* display of affection in this case. "Time to get some fuel into that brain, and those point-scoring arms of yours."

She was more than capable of making herself after-school snacks, and even dinner if necessary, but I loved babying her. Chloe came to my place every day after school and I'd feed her before leaving her to do schoolwork until my brother-in-law, Pete, came by to pick her up.

She stayed for dinner a couple of nights a week so her dad could attend his weekly widower-support group or play tennis or toss a ball around and have a few beers and guy time with his friends, have part of his life that wasn't just "single dad."

"Who's this?" She'd leafed through the sketchbook I'd discarded on the kitchen table, and held it up so the page full of iterations of Annika's face was staring back at me.

"Just a woman I saw today," I said vaguely, not wanting to give away my relationship—wait, no, I didn't have a relationship!—with my new neighbor. "She has an interesting face that stuck in my head." I pulled out things for a PB&J, and veggies with hummus.

Chloe's laugh included a high-pitched squeak. "Yeahhh, I can see why it stuck in your head." The laugh faded as she traced her fingers over the names I'd scrawled on the page. "Are you still thinking about making that Ancient Greece series?"

Saved by myself. "I am. Hence the sketch of possible face claims. And my note about character possibilities." I congratulated myself for sounding appropriately interested but not *too* interested in my new project. New project...the woman I'd drawn. Close enough.

"Riiiight." She brought the sketchbook close to her face. "She's pretty." Chloe looked up, her laser gaze snapping right to me. Her mouth twitched mischievously. "Where'd you go today to see her?"

Chloe had also inherited Heather's razor-sharp perception, and knew that I preferred to build my characters based on real people. I wasn't a hermit exactly, but my social calendar definitely had more free days than full days, and other than a run when weather permitted, my main outing of each week was buying groceries—and that was only so I was out of the house when my cleaner came. I tried not to squirm under Chloe's questioning stare, which was both demanding and amused.

"I, uh—"

As if Annika had somehow been listening to the conversation between my niece and me, and knew I was flailing for a way to escape the interrogation, the faint sound of music came from her apartment. I realized just how quiet my old neighbor had been, and that the soundproofing insulation within this old building wasn't its best feature. Something to look into. Chloe's head swiveled toward the sound so slowly it was like an impersonation from *The Exorcist*. "Didn't they move out?"

"Mhmm." Oh I was so busted.

"So…you got a new floor-neighbor?" She pointed to where the sound of Taylor Swift's "Anti-Hero"—thanks to Chloe, I knew the song—emanated faintly. "With better taste in music too."

"I did." The better music taste was debatable. Thankfully Annika seemed to realize her music might be a little too loud, and it lost enough decibels to become inaudible.

Chloe shook the sketchbook at me. "A new neighbor who looks like this?"

I opened the peanut butter jar. "Maybe."

"You're the worst liar, Aunt Evie. The *worst*." Chloe dropped the sketchbook back to the table and sidled up to the kitchen island, leaning her elbows on it. "So, did you talk to her or just stare creepily while you sketched her?"

"Of course I talked to her," I spluttered. "I'm not some creep drawing strangers in the park." Not this time at least. I had been known to go out and free-draw strangers in the park or on the T to loosen up my brain a little.

"What's her name?"

I swapped peanut butter for the sickly-sweet grape jelly that I only bought for Chloe. "Neighbor Lady," I said. Neighbor Lady was in the hall, arguing with something, if the volume and tone of her voice was any indication. Something thudded to the floor, setting off a fresh round of annoyance. Annoyance in German—muted as it was—was kind of sexy.

Chloe's sigh was so dramatic it was probably heard in California. "Fine. If I see her, I'll tell her you told me to call her Hot Neighbor Lady." She emphasized the *hot*. Not something I wanted my niece thinking about.

I passed her the sandwich. "What makes you think I think she's hot?"

"The way you drew her." Chloe didn't need to add an *obviously*—the "duh" dripped from every word. "Soft. Kind of smudgy. Dreeeeamy. It's the way you draw anything to do with romance."

She shouldn't have seen anything of mine that had "romance" in it. I bit my tongue and concentrated on slicing raw carrot, celery, red pepper, and cauliflower into snack-sized pieces. As Chloe raised one half of her sandwich to her mouth, she said, "Hot Neighbor Lady listens to good music. Nice to have another Swiftie around." I didn't bite on that dig at me. After a few mouthfuls, Chloe shot me a sly look. "Maybe I'll just go knock and ask her what her name is."

"Or you won't. Because a, that's rude, and b, haven't you learned anything about not talking to strangers?" I dolloped a big spoonful of hummus next to the veggies and passed the plate to her. "More eating, less commentary on my social and love life, please."

"What social and love life?" Chloe asked sweetly. "I love you, Aunt Evie, but you're kind of a hot mess."

Hot mess… Kids nowadays. Oh god. I was turning into a fist-shaking "darn you kids" curmudgeon, wasn't I? "Eat," I said flatly.

She opened her mouth as wide was she could and, after smiling facetiously at me, took a huge bite of her sandwich.

I'd made tacos for dinner, helped Chloe with math drama, and had fully figured out the scene I wanted to add to *Chasing Shadows Vol. 9* when Pete arrived to collect his daughter. He bent to kiss the top of Chloe's head—with his six-foot-five height, he had to bend quite a way, even though she was starting to shoot up. "Chloe, honey, I just need to talk to Aunt Evie out in the hall for a moment. Can you pack up your things please?"

She nodded, then shot a look at me before slinking off to put away her homework and wait for us to be done being boring adults. I had no idea how, but that look made me feel like I was in trouble. I followed Pete into the hall, pulled the door mostly closed, and leaned against the wall beside it. "What's up?"

He glanced over my shoulder as if checking whether Chloe was in earshot, before quietly telling me, "She got lunchtime detention today and tomorrow."

My hackles went up. "*What?* Why?"

"Swearing. Apparently she told some boy to 'fuck off all the way to outer space' because he said her mom died because she hated her so much." Pete cupped an elbow in his opposite palm and rubbed his mustache with his forefinger. He'd had that habit for as long as I'd known him, though of course when we'd been in high school and he'd lacked the long, thick beard, he just rubbed his lip.

"You are *shitting* me. Where the fuck did she learn to say that? And what a little prick for saying that to her, fucking little asshole. Hope she kicked him in the balls too. Did *he* get a detention for being a bullying shithead?"

Pete raised his eyebrows, his pointed look boring holes into me.

It took only a moment for realization to whack me over the head. "Ohhh noooo. Shit. I'm sorry." I shook my head. "And sorry for that shit I just said. It's me, isn't it?" Sighing, I said, "*I'm* where she learned to say that."

Pete's answer was very diplomatic. "I think maybe your occasionally colorful language *might* have contributed." He let the implication hang.

It wasn't an implication so much as a reality. Sometimes when I was working on a particularly tricky panel, I swore. Also sometimes when I was driving, cooking, watching television, and…you get the idea, I swore. And given Chloe spent five afternoons a week at my place, she was regularly exposed to my sailor mouth, as much as I tried not to have a sailor mouth. "Right. Gotcha. I am a bad influence."

He brought his forefinger and thumb close together. "Maybe a little. I'm sure she's absorbing some of this stuff through other kids and movies and music and all those terrifying outside things I don't want to think about as a dad. But…she spends a lot of time with you, we both know she adores you and she really takes in what you say." He paused. "And yes, the little asshole got a detention too and has to write an essay about kindness."

"Good." What a dick of a kid. "I think she was very restrained in what she said to him. That was totally uncalled for and just plain cruel."

"I agree," he said tightly.

I gripped his hand. "I'm sorry, Pete. I'll start a swear jar or something and Chloe can have the proceeds to buy a game or clothes or whatever, or we'll go out for burgers or something." I cleared my throat. "Not that there'll be much in the swear jar because I'll try to stop swearing. No, I won't try. I will *do*."

"Thanks, Evie. I'd appreciate it. I hate teacher meetings and the last thing I feel like is having to go in to talk with her if this escalates." Pete grinned, the wonky, kind of shy grin Heather told me had made her fall in love with him. "Plus, of course, I don't want my daughter turning into a degenerate." He did a pretty good imitation of my mother.

I ignored the teasing barb and implication I was a degenerate—my mother's words, not Pete's—and asked, "I thought you liked her teacher? Isn't she single?"

"I do, and I think she is, yes. But I'd prefer an interaction with her where we're not discussing grades and attendance and behavior. Also, how do you even approach asking your daughter's teacher out for coffee? It's creepy."

"I guess. What about that interior designer from last month?" I asked casually.

He shrugged. "No spark."

"Just like the architect from a few months ago?"

He shrugged again.

I hmphed. "You know, I had the weirdest dream the other night. Heather came to me and said, 'Didn't I tell you to make sure Pete moves on after I die, and you haven't, and now I'm going to haunt you.' And you know what? I swear that yesterday, my coffee mug moved all by itself. There's only one explanation for it. My sister is haunting me because you're not dating."

"I *am* dating," he said petulantly.

"No, you're flitting around women sporadically, like a bee who can't figure out which flower he wants to land on so just decides to land on none. Heather wanted you to have companionship, Petey. She was *very* clear on that. So clear that she told both you and me. Repeatedly."

His jaw bunched. "I know. But I'd like to see you move on from your childhood sweetheart. I know what she said, but it's not as easy as saying 'Heather wanted this, so I'll do it.'"

I bit back my "It's been seven years, Pete" and just nodded. I obviously hadn't just moved past my only sibling and best friend dying of breast cancer, but it's not like I could, or had been told to—the way Heather had *insisted* Pete should—grieve and then go out and find myself a new sister. But Pete could move on, had been asked to move forward with his life, while still holding space for Heather.

He ran a hand through his beard. "Also, dating is hard when you have a kid who's not quite ready to be left home alone at night for hours. And she's too old for a babysitter."

I pointed out the obvious solution. "So bring her here and she can hang out with me."

Pete's shoulders sagged. "I know I can, but I hate relying on you so much. I already feel like you do so much. Have done so much," he added in a quiet murmur.

"Well I don't hate it, so get over it. We've been best friends for over twenty years. I'm your kid's godparent and aunt. You're my family. And I love both of you."

"Okay." Then Pete did what he usually did when things got emotional. Changed the subject. "So, speaking of corruption, and hanging out with Chloe, your mother called me at work today."

"Well haven't you had a wonderful day of phone calls," I drawled. "Let me guess. 'Keep my granddaughter away from my daughter so she can't be corrupted by Evangeline's foul mouth and lesbianism'?"

He laughed. "Not quite. She's still pushing me to hire a nanny for Chloe. A *nanny*. For my twelve-year-old child."

I only just held back my snort. Not a snort of disbelief, but a snort of being totally unsurprised that my mother would have suggested that. "Oh yeah. That's her go-to solution for child-rearing. But make sure you get your kids a new nanny every year so they can't bond with the nanny more than you, but also make sure you're a cold, aloof mother so your daughters find it hard to form any fucking attachments with anyone." And in my case, end up in a weird, emotionally stunted gray space. At least Heather had figured out her attachment issues, and had had a fabulous marriage.

Pete adopted a serious expression, though it was obvious he was trying not to laugh. "It's okay, Potty Mouth. I'm not getting Chloe a nanny. She doesn't need one. She's got us."

"Sorry." I squeezed his forearm. "I don't know why you put up with me and my potty mouth. And damned right she does."

"I put up with you because I love you. And so does Chloe."

As I pulled out my phone to make a note to start my swear jar tally—currently at…hmm, let's just say ten bad words for now—I said dryly, "Well that makes two members of my family."

He didn't argue. My estrangement from my parents was old news. I hadn't been disowned or anything like that, just…a mutual ignoring, which was lucky because being a Phillips had benefits, like beyond-ridiculous wealth, and I was a hardcore philanthropist. Philanthropy aside, the obscene amount of money from trusts and investments also allowed me to indulge in my few hobbies—rare bottles of wine and spirits, art (my Pollock, Gauguin, Whiteley, and Saville originals were some of my most prized possessions), and travel. Though travel wasn't really on my agenda much these days.

Pete startled me out of a rare bout of introspection about my family by pulling me into a hug. "Right, I'd best take this delinquent of mine home and figure out what sort of discipline I'm supposed to give her for swearing and getting detentions, even though she was right to stand up for herself." He sighed. "Parenting is so hard."

"I think washing mouths out with soap is out of style now? Grounding?"

He nodded. "Mm, loss of phone privileges and having to do some extra chores is top of my list right now." He sighed again, louder this time. "And I guess we need to have a talk about how to deal with terrible people."

"Better you than me, pal." I loved just being the cool aunt. The cool aunt who taught her niece to swear and got her a detention. Maybe not so cool.

Pete opened the door a fraction to call inside for Chloe to grab her stuff and come out. She appeared, reluctantly, and obviously aware of the conversation that had just taken place, and looking as dejected as I'd ever seen her. Pete took her backpack and basketball bag and slung one over each shoulder, then pulled her to his side until she relaxed against him. The discipline Heather and Pete dished out was worlds away from how my parents had done it.

The door up the hall opened, and Annika's ass appeared before the rest of Annika. Oh. If that's how she went in and out of doors, well…I was all for it. She wedged her body into the open doorway and as she slid through, she dragged some large pieces of cardboard behind her. A huge clear plastic bag filled with more plastic and Styrofoam was thrown into the hallway. Only when she'd locked the door behind her did it seem to register that she had an audience.

She raised her free hand in greeting, a smile following quickly before she gathered her detritus and clumsily made her way past us to the stairs, dragging everything with her. Pete had given my new neighbor no more than a passing glance, but Chloe stared in a way that would have made me tell her to stop if Annika had been aware of it. I pointedly kept my eyes away from the retreating figure and on my niece. The moment she turned back from her reconnaissance, Chloe's eyes went huge. "Hot," she mouthed.

"Hush, you," I whispered, before raising my voice to regular volume. "Okay, see you both tomorrow. Behave yourselves."

Chloe's response to my pointed look was a nose wrinkle. I waved them off and escaped into my condo before Annika came back from ridding herself of trash. I'd had enough of my own fumbling idiocy for one day, but…

Groaning internally, I decided I should really give Annika an apartment-warming gift to welcome her to the building… neighborhood…country?

Tomorrow. I needed to get a handle on my awkwardness first.

CHAPTER FOUR

Annika

I'd just sat down on my newly delivered couch and put my feet up on my newly delivered coffee table after organizing my other newly delivered items when someone knocked at my door. After mentally tallying everything I'd purchased against everything that had been delivered, and confirming my tired brain hadn't ordered food and forgotten about it, I could assure myself it wasn't a delivery. Which left the building manager—who had no reason to knock on my door—or the only person with whom I'd had an actual conversation, unrelated to work or purchasing something, in this city.

Evangeline.

It *was* Evangeline, standing at my door like she couldn't decide if she'd made a good or bad choice by knocking. Her smile was both brilliant and shy, not one of the smiles I'd seen yesterday when she'd been falling over herself with social awkwardness. This smile made her look even cuter than she'd been at our first meeting, and then she was cuter still when she fumbled out, "Hi, sorry to interrupt your afternoon, or, uh, your evening I guess. I'm not sure if you remember me from yesterday, or…"

I leaned against the doorframe, unable to keep from gracing her with my own smile. "Evie-Evangeline. Of course I remember you. It's good to see you." My eyes flicked down to the bottle of red wine in her hand which, logically, was for me. "And with a gift? It's even better to see you."

She looked surprised, but quickly recovered and held out the bottle. "Yes. Just a little something to say welcome. So…welcome. I hope you like red? If you don't, I have white or Champagne."

I assured her, "I do like red wine. Very much, thank you." As I took the bottle, I glanced at the label. 1986 Chateau Lynch Bages Pauillac. A Bordeaux. Seemed like a nice bottle of wine to give someone who was barely an acquaintance. It was older than I was. Just. "It would be rude of me to just take this and say goodbye." I opened the door wider. "Would you like to come in and share it with me?"

A mix of emotions made their way over her face before she seemed to settle on *pleased*. "Sure. I mean, if you'd like the company."

"Ja, I would." The moment I spoke, I realized I had no wineglasses until the rest of my belongings arrived, and I couldn't pour such a nice bottle of wine into a regular glass. "But I have to ask a favor." At Evie's blank look, I sheepishly said, "May I please borrow two wineglasses? And a, ähm…corkscrew? I'm still waiting on some of my things. A lot of my things actually. I only had a refrigerator and most of my furniture delivered today."

A laugh burst out of her, and she was smiling when she assured me, "No problem." She peered past my shoulder, checking out my living area which thankfully now had furniture, except for a kitchen table and chairs, which I had yet to purchase. "Is there anything else you need?"

I ran a mental inventory of my pantry, hoping for something worthy of setting out for a guest. Corn chips and salsa, protein bars, and a jar of olives. Adequate, but hardly the extravagant platter I would have served back home if I were entertaining, and definitely not something I'd pair with a thirty-eight-year-old wine. My refrigerator was still cooling and I'd decided to leave it bare until tomorrow when it'd be fully chilled, to avoid my paranoia about spoiled food. "This is embarrassing, but I don't really have any food. I allocated tomorrow as my 'fill the pantry and refrigerator day.' I've been living on snacks and takeout food since I arrived. But I can order something?"

The transformation of her expression was amazing to witness. It went from amused to almost protective in an instant, and I wasn't sure which of my revelations had triggered that reaction. In an unexpected move, she gripped my hand tightly and squeezed before she released me slowly and with what felt like reluctance. "Gotcha. And…I've gotcha. I'll be right back." She slipped away, leaving me standing in my doorway, totally unsure as to what I should do and what had actually just happened.

I didn't know how long she'd be and decided to take the chance it wouldn't be a great amount of time, so I remained where I was, staring down the hall. Evie had left her door open, but from my position I couldn't see her, just hear her opening and closing doors and throwing things around—or that's what it sounded like. I leaned against the wall and studied the bottle of wine, sliding my thumb over the label.

Evie's brief touch had been friendly, a sort of assurance that she was taking care of things, but it had left me wanting more. Clearly, after ten days apart from people I knew, I was already missing intimate or even just friendly contact. Don't overthink things. Yes, I missed my family and friends. But this? It was me wanting to be touched by this woman I was attracted to, even if it was only platonic touching.

Evie emerged after a few minutes, rushing back down the hall with a bulging cloth bag over her shoulder and holding two wineglasses between her fingers. Winking, she held up her haul and breathlessly told me, "Behold, you're all set with everything one might need to entertain a neighbor who invited themselves over for drinks."

Laughing, I reminded her, "But I invited you, remember? And now I owe you twice, for the bottle of wine and also you supplying everything needed for a get-together. Come in."

Evie showed none of her earlier awkwardness, strolling right into my apartment. She turned back to face me, holding out the bag. "Ask me around again when you've bought groceries, and we'll call it even."

"That is the least I can do to repay you for…" I glanced inside the bag, surprised to see an assortment of foods worthy of a platter, which she'd also supplied. "Providing incredible hospitality in my own home."

Evie laughed. "Sorry, I'm not usually this pushy. I just…thought you should enjoy your first days in the city. And in my opinion, the best way to do that is with good food and good wine."

"I like it. Both your pushiness, and the city."

She cleared her throat and dipped her head a little bit, probably to hide the light flush creeping over her cheeks. Evie extracted a corkscrew from the back pocket of her jeans. "How about I open this bottle to give us all a moment to breathe, then we can put that food together."

I passed her the bottle and began emptying the bag, which held enough food to satisfy a group. "Oh, wow." I glanced over at Evie, who was working on the cork, her tongue peeking out between her front teeth. "Did you invite other people?"

The dull squeak of the cork being pulled free was further smothered by her laugh. "I did not. Most nights I don't feel like cooking, so if I don't have to then I'm kind of a snack-platter-for-dinner gal. My house always has a metric shit-ton of provisions for snack platters. Saves me washing pots and pans and—" She cut herself off, winced, and pulled out her phone, typing something as she mumbled, "Sorry."

"It's fine," I said automatically. "Whatever it is you're apologizing for, because I have no idea."

"It's—" Smiling, she shook her head. "It's nothing important. Shall we get this food set out?"

It took us ten minutes to unpackage and arrange everything onto the platter, which I carried while Evie grabbed the wine and glasses. "Is it okay if we sit on the couch?" I asked.

Evie raised the wineglasses she held by the stem. "Your house, your rules."

"Thank you. As you can see, I still don't have a table. But we can test the ability of my new coffee table to hold food." I was planning a lot of eating solo on the couch while watching movies or shows. Being single had its perks. It also had its downsides. Downsides I was trying not to think about, in case I broke my resolution.

Evie set the bottle on the coffee table then rapped the surface with her knuckles. "Seems like it'll do the job." She poured us each a glass of the wine, and passed one to me, keeping eye contact as I took it. Her gaze was expectant, without being challenging, as she slowly swirled her wine.

I raised my glass, fumbling for something to say in toast. "I suppose…here is to new friends?" I cringed as I said it, aware of not only the cliché, but of the forward implication that we might be friends. We weren't really anything, and that thought sent an unpleasant, unnameable emotion through me. I wanted us to be something.

If Evie was bothered by my accidental forwardness, she didn't seem it. If anything, she seemed pleased. She lifted her glass and echoed, "To new friends."

I swirled my wine too before drinking a small mouthful. "Oh my goodness. That is so good." I leaned forward to turn the bottle around so I could read the label again.

Evie's face softened with a smile, and I tried to ignore the way it made me feel. Excited, nervous, warm, and very attracted. "It is," she agreed. "It'll be even better in twenty minutes. Unfortunately, there's not many bottles of this left in my collection. That's the problem with wine vintages. They're limited. I suppose that's part of the appeal, it makes you enjoy it more because you know it's a fleeting experience." She looked around. "How do you like your apartment?"

I smiled widely. "I like it very much."

"I'm really glad," she said, and it sounded genuine.

I leaned over to cut myself a small wedge of soft cheese. "I wanted to ask, because I'm sure you have a preference, should I call you Evangeline, or Evie? You said either, but…"

"Pretty much everyone calls me Evie." She drank some wine and with a shrug, added, "I don't mind Evangeline, but sometimes it makes me feel like I'm in trouble. It's what my mother calls me." An unreadable expression passed fleetingly over her face, so quickly I wasn't even sure I'd seen it.

"Do you get in trouble a lot?"

"According to my mother, yes." This smile held tension, and I recognized a subject cut-off when I saw one. Evie warded off further travel down this conversational path by pushing the platter closer to me. Once I'd selected an assortment of food, she set it back down and said, "I suppose we should get the 'what do you do?' out of the way right away? What brings you to the States? I'm dying to know why you moved to another country right before Christmas."

"Do you have any theories?" I asked, before slowly sipping my wine. It was such a good bottle, and I wanted to both savor it and gulp it.

"I have a dozen theories. I'm insanely curious. Indulge me?" Evie flashed a winning, pleading smile and any hesitation I might have had—not that I'd had any—would have disappeared the moment she smiled.

"My job. I have…office-swapped. It's a multinational corporation, we work with clients worldwide. This position is for a year, but it *may* be more, depending on how long it takes us to complete the project." I grinned as I added, "But, on time and working as intended is our trademark. Worded more cleverly than that, of course."

"And what multinational business are you in?"

"App development. I'm a senior front-end engineer, but I also handle some of the German-English functionality for multilingual apps. For the past few years, I have been a project manager."

"Wow. Oh, wow. That's…important." She drank another larger mouthful of wine—glad it wasn't just me who wanted to gulp—then cleared her throat. "I'm impressed by anyone who can just pack up their life and move somewhere for a temporary role."

I shrugged. "It was not too difficult." I didn't know this woman and telling her that I needed a life change, a life *reboot* seemed too intense. Laughing, I said, "You look horrified."

"Oh, no. No. I've traveled, a lot. And I love it. But I love coming home." She smiled shyly. "I guess I'm a homebody."

"There is nothing wrong with that. And what do you do? I should have asked earlier. Blame this excellent wine." And the fact I was more interested in who she was than what she did.

Evie paused for a moment before answering. "I'm a graphic novelist."

That wasn't what I'd expected at all. "That sounds amazing. So interesting. How many…novels? Books? Magazines? How many *things* have you produced?"

She raised her glass toward me. "First off, thank you for not saying comics. I know it's a legitimate term, but it makes me feel weird. And I'm currently seven published volumes into a ten-volume series, working on the eighth right now. This is my third published series, I'll have published twenty-three volumes all up when this series is done."

Impressed, I raised my eyebrows. "That's incredible. If you're in awe of me moving to another country, then I'm in awe of your creativity. Would I know your work?"

Evie rubbed the side of her neck, as if trying to rub away the blush that had appeared and was spreading up to her cheeks. "Uh, you might. If you like action adventure fantasy romance-type graphic novels."

"I have never read a graphic novel. Will you tell me your books? Novels. Graphic novels. Tell me your titles so I can read them?"

She looked like she wanted to do anything but share. But she did. "*Behemoth*, *Stark Realities*, and this one is *Chasing Shadows*."

I made a mental note to seek them out. "This is going to sound stupid, but…do you enjoy it?"

Her expression told me she didn't expect that to be the question I'd ask. "I love what I'm doing, I love the creative freedom, the work flexibility. But sometimes it's hard, like, if I'm not feeling creative then I get stuck and it's really hard to force creativity. It's not like knowing you have set, quantifiable tasks, like make a spreadsheet or do some accounting stuff every day. But other than that, it's great." Evie sliced off a chunk of smoked cheddar. "Anyway. Enough about me."

I wanted to hear so much more about her, but I recognized another "let's move on" cue when I saw it. "Tell me about Christmas here. My parents are having a meltdown because I have to organize my own Christmas, and they seem to think I don't know how to organize or celebrate Christmas for myself."

Evie chewed quickly so she could ask, "Christmas is a big deal in Germany?"

"Yes. It's very important to my family. This is my first Christmas away from them." The rush of sadness wasn't unexpected, but it still made me feel like I'd been dropped into a tub of icy water.

"Do you have a big family?"

"No. Just my parents and my younger brother, Markus, and his wife." She didn't ask for it, but I decided to give her a quick overview. "My father is a mechanical engineer, and my mother works in finance. My brother is also an engineer, electrical."

"Wow, so being clever runs in the Mayer family then," Evie said lightheartedly.

"Perhaps it does," I agreed, with the same tone.

"Mm." She peered into her wine. "I'd like to say you get used to being away from your family during the holidays, but in my experience, you don't."

"Your family is also overseas?"

Evie's laugh was like dust. "Oh no. They're here in Massachusetts. But I haven't had Christmas with my parents since I was twenty-one, and even then it was so awful that year that I like to pretend it never happened. Now, I just spend it alone."

I raised the bottle and studied the contents. "I think there is a story here. But perhaps it is one for when we have more left in the bottle."

Evie's smile started slowly, then blossomed into brightness. "Well. I suppose it's a good thing I have a lot of bottles. Next time," she promised.

"I am going to hold you to that."

She looked me right in the eyes, and calmly said, "Good."

CHAPTER FIVE

Evie

I had no idea where my weird awkwardness around Annika had disappeared to, but I hoped it'd found a nice spot to take a permanent vacation. Something about her smile when she'd opened her door to me last night had made my stomach do nervous flipflops and I'd braced myself for more of my fumbling idiocy. But the embarrassment when she'd admitted she was still in the early stages of moving in and had no food or even kitchen basics had made my take-care-of-people trait surge to the forefront. It'd pushed everything else aside, leaving just me behind, sans idiocy. Mostly sans idiocy.

I'd managed a fairly productive workday, even with Chloe hanging out at my place all day due to school being out for the rest of the week because of Thanksgiving. She'd said nothing about her lunchtime detentions, even when I gently prodded her. So I let her be. She'd obviously talked with Pete, and I knew my niece well enough to know that she always came to me if she wanted to talk about something—be it to get an opinion separate from her dad's, or just because I was the only one there.

She didn't want to talk about her lunchtime detentions, but she *did* want to tease me about my new neighbor. I recognized avoidance when I saw it, so I played along. Mostly. She was so like Heather in this way—wouldn't talk about it, wouldn't talk about it, wouldn't talk about it, wanted to talk about it. I just had to be patient.

And it was clear I was going to have to be very patient when she came at me again while I was making her lunch, asking how many more dreeeeamy portraits I'd done of my "Aphrodite/Artemis" since the sketches she'd discovered Monday.

(Two.)

Chloe grabbed the chicken salad sandwich before I'd even set the plate down. "So, have you kissed her yet?"

"Swallow your mouthful before you speak, please. And kissed who?" I asked, so absorbed in planning dinner that I wasn't really concentrating. That was my first mistake.

Thankfully she listened and finished chewing so she could confirm she'd meant, "Hot Neighbor Lady."

"Hot Neighbor Lady has a name," I said as I set another plate with veggie sticks and hummus, and a yogurt in front of her.

Chloe pounced on my second mistake. "Ha! You do think she's hot."

Oh, I was digging myself a wonderful hole here. Of course I thought she was hot. Anyone with eyes and an attraction to humans would think she was hot. "Her name is Annika." It came out way too brightly, which made me cringe internally. Avoiding a topic yourself by any chance, Evie?

"Hot name."

I turned around just in time to catch Chloe bouncing her eyebrows at me. "No comment," I said dryly. "Like I said, less commentary on my love life, please." God, when I was her age, other people's hotness was only just starting to come onto my radar. I didn't think my niece was particularly romantically precocious—or at least she'd never really seemed all that interested in romance, aside from a casual comment here and there. She was just trying to press my buttons. And she was succeeding.

"And like *I* said—"

"Nope. This is not a discussion we're having. Not now or later. Once you've finished the rest of your lunch, you can chill until dinner." Without talking about Annika. "Unless you have more school work to do?"

"A little." She lightly slapped my shoulder as I walked past and when I stopped, leaned against me, squirming under my arm for a hug. I pounced on the opportunity and hugged her tightly for a few seconds. She gave me an extra-hard squeeze before she let me go, mumbling something that sounded like, "Love you."

Whatever, I was going to take it as an "I love you."

Thankfully Chloe took my advice—or my warning, depending on which way you looked at it—and didn't mention anything about my neighbor or my dismal dating life for the rest of the day. Pete arrived after we'd had dinner, and gratefully accepted the container of leftovers, then shouldered Chloe's backpack. "Thanks again, Evie."

"You're welcome. Again."

"Come on, hon, let's give Aunt Evie some breathing room." He checked Chloe had her coat and ushered her into the hall, walking behind her with both hands on her shoulders like he was steering a motorcycle.

After a quick hug with Chloe—two in one day, blessed!—I held on to Pete's bicep, steadying myself as I stretched up to kiss his cheek. As he wrapped an arm around me in a side-on hug, I said, "See you Friday morning. Have a good Thanksgiving tomorrow." They always spent Thanksgiving with Pete's parents, but busy-lawyer Pete worked the days before and after so Chloe was at my place on the days sandwiching Thanksgiving. "Love you guys."

They had just returned my "love you" and started to walk away when Annika appeared at the top of the stairs. She smiled warmly at Pete and Chloe, and the three of them engaged in a little foot shuffling do-si-do to get around each other. Annika paused for a moment to say something, laughed, then continued toward me. Toward her door.

I leaned against my doorframe and waved. I'd expected her to respond in kind then continue up the hallway, but she came right over. She had to pass my door to get to hers, but it still made me feel nice that she wanted a conversation. "Hey," I said, as casually as I could. Awkwardness was peeking around the corner, waiting to see if I needed it. I didn't, thank you. "How's things?"

"Good. Thank you." She shifted the takeout bag and used her now-free hand to gesture toward the stairs. "You seem very close with your ex-husband. That must make things easier."

I almost died choking on my laughter. "My ex…*husband*?" Wheezing made the question pitch up an octave, but I was so busy trying to breathe I couldn't correct her. Pete was going to die laughing too when I told him someone thought we used to be a couple.

"Yes, I…you…share, emm, custody of your daughter? She looks so much like you." Annika's teeth grazed her lower lip. "Have I misunderstood something? You're looking at me like I'm an idiot. Ja, I've definitely misunderstood something."

"Just a little misunderstanding," I assured her, still struggling to regain my composure. "That's my brother-in-law and his daughter. My niece. He works later than school gets out, or has other things to do some nights, so Chloe hangs out with me and does her homework, sometimes has dinner, that sort of thing."

Annika touched her fingertips to her forehead. "Oh my goodness. I'm so sorry. I just assumed. It's, I…never mind. So you're obviously close with them. That's really nice." She glanced toward where Pete and Chloe had disappeared down the stairs a minute ago, and I caught a flash of something that seemed like interest. And that flash of interest sent a flash of discomfort through me.

But…I got it. Even I, with my complete lack of heterosexuality, knew Pete was a good-looking guy—taller than tall, and with the built hipster lumberjack thing down pat, Pete sported a stylish, masculine haircut and full, luxurious beard with a villain-twirling mustache, though he was the furthest thing from a villain you could get. I had no idea how he managed to look both rugged and groomed, but he did. If I were straight, I'd be into it.

And you're being ridiculous, Evie. You have no right to discomfort. You're not dating her. You're nowhere near dating her. Just because you feel some kind of weird zingy connection doesn't mean anything. Possessiveness is not sexy. She'd smiled at Chloe as well as Pete. Smiling means nothing aside from the fact she's polite and nice. And you already know that she's polite and nice.

I dragged myself out of my spiraling thoughts to assure her, "It's no problem, really. I probably would have made the same assumption. It's totally logical."

"That makes me feel a little bit better."

She looked like she still didn't quite understand the dynamic of why my brother-in-law and niece spent so much time at my place, which was understandable. Maybe that was the reason for her look of interest in Pete—it was actually just plain old curiosity, not attraction. Not that that was any of my business, of course. I should probably come clean, but for some reason, it made me feel weird about broadcasting that Pete was single. Still, I came clean.

I leaned against my open doorway, folding my arms over my chest. "Since my sister, Heather, died, I've kind of stepped in as a female parent-type figure. Pete's definitely got the final say for parenting decisions, but there are some things Chloe prefers to talk with me about. I probably baby her a little too much, but…" I shrugged. It wasn't like making Chloe food after school was going to hurt her, but I often wondered if I was overcompensating for my childhood.

Annika's expression softened as she gripped my forearm, squeezing sympathetically. "Oh, Evie. I'm so sorry to hear that." Her thumb lightly stroked my bare skin. "I can't imagine what that is like. I don't know how I would be if my brother died."

"Thanks." I mean, what else do you say? Heather's death was still an open wound, but it was no longer raw and bleeding and I could talk about her without melting down. But I didn't love doing it, and Annika seemed to pick up on my unspoken emotion.

She bit her lower lip. Sexy. Great time to notice that, Evie, while you're talking about your dead sister. Annika said, "I'm glad I caught you. Do you have a minute for talking?"

"Of course. Come on in. Unless you want to have a conversation standing in the hallway?"

She laughed. "No, not particularly."

"Okay then." I backed up, away from her (admittedly nice) touchy-feely hands.

Before I ushered her in, Annika held up her takeout bag. "Just give me a moment to put dinner in the fridge. I got a 'Thanksgiving feast,' whatever that is. Apparently they make it all week so people can enjoy this special food more than just one day a year."

I grinned. "It will be something tasty and plentiful. You can eat dinner first if you want? I can wait."

"No no," she assured me. "I'm not hungry yet. But I needed some fresh air so I went out to buy dinner."

I nodded, then hastily looked around my condo to make sure it was presentable enough for a guest. I waited in my open doorway, wondering if I was being annoying by asking her to hang out with me again.

If she thought I was annoying, she didn't show it. In fact, she came rushing out her door like she couldn't wait to get back. She surreptitiously peered around my living space, and seemed to take a greater-than-normal interest in the stairs up to my second floor where my office, gym, and spare room were. Unless she went up there and poked around, she wouldn't find the sketchbook with the first sketches I'd done of her, and then the others that'd fallen from my fingers in the past few days while I'd been trying to focus on work. But still, I gently guided her away from my potential embarrassment and toward the kitchen. "Do you want coffee? Tea? Something else?" I glanced at the time. "Adult beverage?"

"Were you having something to drink?" She laughed quietly. "Before I intruded, that is."

"I…probably, yes." I tried not to drink every night during the week, but there were some frustrations that could only been soothed by relaxing on my couch with a glass of something alcoholic. "And you're not intruding."

"Then whatever you're having would be great. Adult beverage or not. Thank you."

I grabbed the salt and pepper grinders from the table. "Take a seat wherever. Sorry about the mess. I haven't cleaned up the kitchen after dinner yet."

Annika looked around, widening her eyes in mock surprise. "What mess? And no snack platter for dinner tonight?" she teased. Instead of taking a seat, she followed me to the kitchen and leaned an elbow on the kitchen island.

I laughed, pleased she'd remembered. "Not tonight. On feed-Chloe nights I have to cook an actual meal. Are you sure you don't need to eat something? I can whip up some cheese and crackers."

"I do have food at home." She held up both hands. "And it would make me feel terrible if you had to feed me two nights in a row."

"That's not a no," I pointed out.

Annika raised her chin, and something flashed in her eyes. Not challenge exactly, but she was definitely appraising me. "You're right. It's not."

I backed away from her, not trusting myself to not ruin the moment by saying something stupid. "Red or white wine? Or would you prefer something else? I keep some beer here for Pete and I'm decent with a cocktail shaker."

Instead of hesitating with something polite, like "I don't mind," she came right out and said, "I think I'm in the mood for white wine."

Relieved I didn't have to spend five minutes teasing out what she wanted, I asked, "Any preference?"

"I like all wine."

I crouched in front of the wine fridge in the kitchen and stared into the racks. A New Zealand Chardonnay would do it. I made a mental note to stop by my wine storage unit. If I was going to be entertaining Annika, I'd need to keep a better stock of wine on hand. I presented the bottle like a sommelier. "Does this meet madam's approval?"

She leaned closer, her nose wrinkling as she read the label. "Yes. It does. And there is no way to ask without being strange, so I'm just going to ask. Do you always drink such nice wine?"

I knew "nice" was code for "expensive" and I forcibly ignored the expected discomfort that always came up when someone commented—directly or indirectly—on my economic status. "Mhmm," I said nonchalantly. "What's that saying?" I continued as I rummaged in the drawer for a corkscrew. "Life is too short for bad food, bad wine, and bad women. And I really love good wine."

She raised her eyebrows. "What about good food and good women?"

"Those too," I confirmed, unsurprised by the heat that rose up my spine.

Annika's eye contact was unwavering, her voice almost husky when she said, "That is good to know."

I busied myself opening the bottle, collecting glasses, and something to tide her over until she went home for dinner. The whole time, I was aware of her watching me. Which of course, made me fumble. Crackers spilled out in a fountain of too-many and I hastily tried to gather up some strays. "Ah fuck." And ah fuck again. I grimaced and pulled my phone from my back pocket. "Sorry," I mumbled as I opened my swear jar note. I'd decided the swear jar only applied to spoken expletives, otherwise I was going to be funding Chloe's first car.

"For what?"

"For being rude with my phone. I'm just…making…a note…" I dropped the phone onto the counter. "There, done. Sorry," I said again.

"It's all right. A note about what?"

I puffed out my cheeks. "Swearing. I've promised to try to stop swearing because Chloe seems to be picking it up from me, so if I don't have easy access to my swear jar then I make a note so I'll put a chit in when I get there."

"I see. And…how many *chits* are in there at the moment?"

I opened the pantry, reaching for the jar on the top shelf that was already a quarter full with mostly blue Post-its. It'd been an annoying couple of days of creative frustration. "I only started it a few days ago but I'm already at about eleventy-million, because I have to include derivatives of the words, like if they end in -ed or -ing. It's three dollars, blue, for the F-word; two dollars, green, for the S-word; one dollar, orange, for things like the D-word and B-word; and fifty cents, yellow, for little words I don't even think are technically swearing but Pete does. Like…" I didn't want to risk another yellow note in there, so I spelled. "D-A-M-N."

Annika nodded, and it was obvious she was trying not to laugh. "So if I catch you swearing and you forget to make a note, I should be telling you?"

I grimaced. "Please. If you catch me before I finish saying it and can stop me, even better. I figure I don't have to pay if I don't actually say the word in its entirety."

She glanced at the jar. "That sounds fair. You look like you're on the way to bankrupting yourself."

My laughter burst out and I played along. "Something like that. But the threat of bankrupting myself isn't helping much. I'm still swearing." I exhaled loudly, frustrated with myself.

"Lifelong habits can be hard to break." Her face softened, her eyes creasing at the edges. "But I think it's wonderful, and very sweet that you're trying so hard."

"Thanks." Good thing I managed to stifle my reciprocal "And you're so sweet for saying that" or we'd be stuck in some weird flirty compliment loop.

She looked me up and down. "You know, Evie, I was told that people in New England could be cold toward new people. I was worried. But it's not like that at all. *You're* not like that at all."

Grinning, I told her, "I'm an anomaly."

Her mouth quirked in response, but she didn't say anything.

I finished arranging the food, poured wine, and put the bottle back in the fridge. If tonight was anything like last night, it was going to be finished. I made a second mental note to get myself some liver-support supplements or something if sharing a bottle of wine a night with my neighbor became a regular thing.

Before she sat down, Annika took a quick lap around the living room, pausing first to study my Jenny Saville and then by the mantel where photos of me, Heather, Pete, and Chloe in various configurations clambered for space. She pointed at one of Heather and me on her wedding day. "This is your sister?"

"Yes. Heather," I reminded her, though it felt unnecessary.

"This is a beautiful photograph. You look so similar."

That made me smile. "So I've been told."

Annika took a few more moments to look at the rest of the pictures before coming over. I waited until she'd picked a spot on the couch before I sat down, careful not to sit too close to her. There was some weird energy in the air and I didn't want to add to it. "So, what did you want to talk to me about?"

"Oh, nothing really. I just wanted to thank you for last night. It was…just what I needed. And I wanted to invite you for dinner. Tomorrow is your Thanksgiving, then I have to go to the office Friday, and I start work officially on Monday. So, perhaps next weekend?"

"That's super sweet. Thanks. I will absolutely take you up on that. But we don't have to keep score. You know, I help you, you help me, I have you for dinner, you have me for dinner."

A line appeared between her eyebrows a second before her teeth grazed her lower lip. A naughty smile quirked her mouth. "Have me for dinner? I'm not sure if I like the sound of that or not." After a quick pause, during which her eyes left mine to linger on my mouth, she murmured, "I think I do."

That look made my skin hot and I fumbled out a correction. "Have you *around* for dinner."

"Well, I suppose that sounds good too."

I tried to find an answer to that, and failed. So I redirected. "Did the rest of your furniture arrive?"

"Not yet. I only purchased the table today. Delivery is supposed to be on Friday afternoon." She smiled wryly. "That is why I can't have you…*around* for dinner on Friday—I need to put my table and chairs together first."

I remembered what she'd said about going to the office Friday. "If you need someone to sign for your stuff, I can do it." I pushed the plate of cheese and crackers closer. "Here. You've been eyeballing this ever since I opened the fridge."

She reached out instantly, and as she set a piece of cheese on a cracker, Annika said, "I *do* have food. But I have never been able to pass up an invitation to join someone for a meal."

"I know you have food," I reassured her. "I saw it. Smelled good."

Annika's grin was cheeky. "I mean it, Evie. I'm inviting you for dinner and drinks as soon as I have a table for my guest."

"I know you mean it. And no complaints from me." As I sipped, I stared at her.

She tilted her head. "What is it? Do I have cracker crumbs on my face?"

"No, you don't. I'd tell you if you did. I was just thinking. You speak really good English." Oh, look. Awkwardness has returned from the depths of hell to torture me. Joy.

"I also speak really good German." She winked as she raised the glass to her mouth. "I learned at school and I've mostly worked in multinational companies, and they're generally English-speaking. That makes it easy to become fluent."

"I don't speak German. Except for like, hello, how are you, and do you speak English oh god please tell me you speak English. Oh! I can say 'Bitte ein Glas Wein.' I said that *a lot* during my trip with my sister."

Annika's mouth had been twitching the whole time I'd been going through my list of German phrases, and she finally gave up trying to hold in her laugh, gesturing at me with her free hand. "You already have a glass of wine."

"So I do," I mused. "Sorry about my accent."

"Sorry about mine," she countered instantly.

"Trust me. You do not have to be sorry about that." I'd never considered myself an accentophile, but she might just change my mind. And I couldn't shake the niggling feeling that she might just change my mind about a few things.

CHAPTER SIX

Annika

It wasn't an official work day, but I dressed as if it were in black pants, low-heeled boots, a clingy silk top, and my favorite textured-fabric blazer. I would have loved to just slink into the office in jeans and sneakers, but given I was heading the team for this project, I needed to look like the leader for our first meeting.

Boston in late November was cooler than I'd expected, and when I stepped outside to wait for my Uber, I was grateful I'd brought my heavier coat in my luggage. One of my chores for the weekend was to test the public transport system for travel to work, but today I was spoiling myself with a rideshare. It wasn't worth buying a car—Boston didn't seem very friendly for parking—so I needed to become good friends with rideshare companies and public transport.

I checked my handbag and leather MacBook satchel to make sure I had everything I needed. I didn't expect to do any work today, but one of the hardware techs would supply me with what I needed to use my work laptop in America, and I wanted the opportunity to troubleshoot if needed before Monday.

The sound of the building door closing made me turn around, expecting to see one of the ground-floor occupants, none of whom I'd met yet. Instead of a stranger, it was someone I could see myself calling a friend. Someone, if my libido had any say, I'd like to call much more than that. I reminded myself of my resolution.

My libido was very grateful that Evie was apparently a dedicated runner and I took a few seconds to check her out again before she was close enough to realize what I was doing. I was a legs woman. No, wait, I was a whole-woman woman, but legs were high on my list of "oh yes" body parts, and Evie's legs were sublime. The rest of her was just as sublime and I enjoyed the tingle of excitement that surged through me.

She removed her AirPods when she realized I was there. And I was staring. With an internal sigh, I gave up my admiration of her external attributes. It wasn't hard to find a smile for her, and Evie returned it immediately.

"Hey," she said. Her voice was a little bit gravelly, as if she'd just rolled out of bed and dressed to go running. "What's up?"

Surprised by the question, I raised both eyebrows. "Nothing is up."

Her shoulders dropped. "Oh. Good. You were looking at me like something was wrong."

Something was right would be more accurate. "No, there is nothing wrong," I said, trying to sound cheerful instead of concerned that I'd been caught staring. Caught leering might be a better description. "I didn't expect to see you. It's a nice surprise. A nice start to the morning."

"Mm," she said, and I let myself think the sound was one of agreement.

"Running in the morning today?" As soon as I'd asked it, embarrassment flooded me at the obvious question.

"Pardon?"

"You ran around midday the day we met. Or, that's when you came back." I was mortified that I'd basically just admitted that I'd paid enough attention to her to recognize her running schedule.

If Evie noticed, she didn't show it. "Oh! Yeah, no. The joys of a flexible, work-from-home job. I just go whenever the mood takes me. Need to grab the motivation when I can, and this morning, it was there as soon as I woke up."

"Lucky for you."

"Some days, yes." She smiled fleetingly. "So listen, I just realized I haven't given you my number."

"Why would I need your number?" I asked, trying to be nonchalant. I'd thought about giving her mine, but hadn't found a suitable opening to just say "Let me give you my phone number because I want to spend more time with you." Evie didn't seem to have such a concern.

She faltered, visibly deflating. "Oh, you know, in case you want to borrow a cup of sugar or something and want to check I'm home before making the journey from your door to mine."

"That is a great idea. I don't want to waste time on unnecessary travel," I joked, pulling out my phone. After unlocking it and navigating to a new contact screen, I passed it over.

"Oh. Uh. I'm going to assume the fields are all the same? Now I'm trying to imagine the screen for creating a contact. Um…Vorname. Evie. Nachname…Phillips. Uh…Tele…fon…nummer." She looked up. "That's my phone number, right?"

Smiling, I confirmed, "Yes."

"Great." Her tongue peeked through her lips as she typed. "Right. Okay. Uh…done." With a triumphant grin, she passed my phone back.

I sent a quick *Hi* as a text. "And there's my phone number for you to save."

She pulled her phone from the pocket on the thigh of her running tights and did just that.

Unfortunately, before either of us could say anything more, a silver Audi pulled up to the curb. I checked my app to confirm the license plate. Damn. But also, it was probably for the best that I left before I actually drooled. "This is for me."

"So I see." She glanced at her watch. "And I need to run. Literally. Chloe will be here soon." Evie's nose wrinkled adorably. "Oh to be a kid with a day off school for the holidays. Have a great day. Hope your new office is everything you want in an office."

"You too. Having a great day, not your new office."

Evie laughed. She walked with me to the curb, then paused. "I might see you when you come home."

I opened the back passenger door. "I hope so. Enjoy your run."

Evie saluted lazily. "Shall do." Then, thankfully, she went in the opposite direction so I could clear some of the fog from my brain instead of staring at the back of her in running tights. It was time to get my head in the game. If I wanted my twelve months here to be productive and as stress free as possible, then I needed to focus.

The Boston office of Pyramid Tech Development was a modern, airy, brightly lit loft typical of the tech and software industry. The huge, irregularly shaped space was already decked out with holiday decorations, tinsel and figurines everywhere, and even a tree in the lobby with fake gifts underneath it.

The space was open-plan, but with over a dozen frosted-glass offices set around the perimeter in a horseshoe shape, all clustered up one end. At the other end of the loft was a slightly more enclosed area with two offices. A huge conference table dominated the center of the horseshoe. I counted three people wandering around and seven more seated at the conference table, split in two groups having what looked like deep conversations.

I announced myself to the receptionist, a bright-eyed brunette with a funky sense of style. Within a minute, a stereotypical tech nerd—a midthirties, slightly pudgy, balding guy in a polo and chinos—arrived. "Annika! So wonderful to meet you in person." He offered his hand and though I'd recognized his voice, he introduced himself. "I'm Nate Mitchell!" His enthusiasm was no less intense in person, and his handshake was nicely firm. No limp-wristed light grip for a woman, nor was it dominatingly painful.

"It's great to meet you too. And it's great to be in the Boston office, finally."

"Ah, now that's the enthusiasm we like!" He leaned on the receptionist's waist-high counter. "Kim, do you have Annika's induction packet?"

Kim smiled warmly. "Right here." She hefted a large folder and small envelope onto the desk.

"Thank you kindly." He dragged the items off the counter then turned to me. "Here's the guidebook for this office"—he passed me the folder—"ready for your induction."

"Thank you."

He handed me the envelope. "And here's your keycard. It opens both the front door and your office, and you'll need it in the elevators if you decide to come in after hours. You'll also need to pop by HR to make sure they've got all your transfer paperwork set up and to go through your induction."

"And where is that?" I prompted gently.

Nate actually slapped his forehead. "Right. Sorry." He pointed to the more closed end of the loft. "The big office on the left. It says Human Resources on the door, just in case you're not sure you're at HR." He chuckled at his joke then pivoted toward the conference table. He paused at the head of the table. "Everyone?" They all stopped work and looked to me, all of them smiling encouragingly. "This is Annika Mayer. I know most of you know her from the Munich office, but here she is in person to head up the Global Connect project."

Global Connect was just the working title of the project, and part of our role was to brainstorm names for the app.

They all waved, smiled more, and said some form of hello, which I returned.

Nate turned to me. "Some of your team have taken today off for a Thanksgiving long weekend, so I'll introduce you all properly on Monday," he promised.

"That sounds good, thank you."

He pointed out features of the office. "Break room is through there. Restrooms are up the back there through that door." Nate stopped outside the third door of the horseshoe on the left. "And, here's your office." It already had my name on the door in vinyl lettering. Looked like there was no way out now.

"Thank you." I ran my fingertips over the first few letters of my name.

"I'll leave you to get set up. Ron should be here shortly to make sure your laptop is good to go. Once you're ready to see HR, come find me and I'll introduce you to Stephanie. She'll get everything straightened out for you. And once you're all done with that, I'll take you out for lunch. I'm just down there." Nate pointed back toward the office next to HR.

"That sounds great. Thanks, Nate."

I left the door to my office open and set my satchel and handbag down on the desk. I wandered the five steps to the full-length window that made up half of the back wall. The view out the window was spectacular. I was still figuring out a mental map of Boston, but I knew there was only one big river in the city, so it had to be the Charles River that I could see. Boston was a pretty city. I loved München, the color palette of the old architecture, the way the newer buildings blended in while remaining separate. Boston felt more modern, but held plenty of pockets of "old" like my hometown, which made me feel less like I was in a completely alien place.

"Knock knock," came a familiar voice, and my mood turned instantly from mildly frazzled to joyfully relieved. Last year, Rachel had done the reverse of what I was doing now, and we'd clicked instantly in München.

I moved to the door and walked right into Rachel's hug. "It's so good to see you," I managed. She was squeezing me very tightly.

"Tell me about it." She pulled back and held me at arm's length. "You look amazing. How're you settling in to Boston life?"

"Very well. I think? Ask me again in the new year."

She pulled a sympathetic face. "I know it's shitty timing, with Christmas and all that, but I suppose important projects don't care about the holidays." Rachel settled herself in one of the client chairs in front of my desk and I sat in the other one.

"I know. And it doesn't really bother me," I said, trying to be upbeat. "I'll miss my family at Christmas, but I really needed the change."

Rachel raised an eyebrow but didn't comment. Instead, she asked, "Have you made any friends here yet?"

Laughing, I reminded her, "I've only been in the city for two weeks."

"I know. And for you, that's the equivalent of ten years in friend-finding terms."

She wasn't wrong. I had a…gift? Knack? Whatever you wanted to call it, I never seemed to have trouble meeting people and befriending those with whom I wanted to spend more time. Laughing again, I nodded. "You're right. And yes, I have. My neighbor." Wrinkling my nose, I added, "Sort of a friend. I think. Maybe?"

"Sort of a friend, you think, maybe," Rachel teased. "Well that narrows it down."

"Sorry. I'm honestly not exactly sure what she is. More than an acquaintance for sure, but she is not a I-will-confide-everything-in-her sort of friend." I deliberately left off the part where I wanted to get to that second category of friendship. And beyond.

"Yet." The unspoken "because you've only just met her" was obvious in Rachel's singsong tone.

"Mmm. Ja." I pressed my lips together. Why was it that I constantly felt on the verge of saying something I shouldn't, or saying too much, when I was thinking about Evie?

Rachel frowned, staring at me in the way I knew meant she was trying to figure something out, which she usually did. After almost a minute, she nodded slowly, understanding blossoming on her face. "I see."

I glanced around. "You see what?"

"You've got a really obvious 'I'm into someone' kind of vibe about you when you're…into someone. You had it with Sascha, long before you got together. How is he, by the way?" There wasn't exactly disapproval in the question, but I could tell she was uncomfortable with the fact I was apparently eyeing someone else while in a relationship, even if that relationship was extreme long-distance. I was uncomfortable too—cheating was a no-go for me. Luckily for me and my current attraction to Evie, I was single.

I shrugged, trying to ignore the disquieting sensation crawling over my skin. Was I really so easy to read? "I honestly don't know. But I imagine he is hunting for another girlfriend as we speak."

Her eyebrows rose slowly. "You broke up?" Rachel was doing a great job of seeming both surprised and unsurprised.

I nodded.

"Wow. You okay?"

"Absolutely," I said immediately, smiling because I really was okay.

"So who instigated it?"

"Me. All me. He is not on board with the breakup, which is a pity, because I did just throw him overboard."

She giggled. "I'm sure he'll find himself someone else soon enough."

"I am sure he already has." I shrugged. "And she can be as bored with him as I was." Sascha was definitely a case of the reality being worse than the fantasy.

The giggling ceased. "I know he's boring, but I just figured he was good in bed."

"The sex was—" Frowning, I tried to find the right word. *Tolerable* seemed too mean. *Good* was definitely too nice. "Fine. But…I never thought about it, or about him, when we weren't together, and I did a better job of pleasing myself than he ever could. Am I a horrible, shallow person?" As soon as I'd asked the question, I shook my head. "No. It was the right thing to do. Hopefully he'll see that soon."

"Hopefully." She brightened. "So, in that case. When are you going to ask your new neighbor out?" The fact Rachel had shifted right into moving-on territory made me think she had negative thoughts about my ex-boyfriend, but had been too polite to verbalize them.

"How do you know I want to ask her out?"

"Because you're so easy to read," she said nonchalantly. "Plus, it's what *I'd* do. New city, new hookup." She grinned. "It's what I did do."

"But I don't want a hookup. I'm trying to avoid hookups."

Rachel looked aghast. "Why?"

I leaned back in the chair and crossed my legs. "Because I need to figure out how to just…be myself. I need to learn to be comfortable as a single person, not a codependent person." Of course I'd been single, but if I looked at my adult life and tallied single weeks versus dating weeks, the single weeks were definitely fewer.

"Why?" she asked again. She frowned at me, her stare burning into me. "Did he say you're codependent or something, because this is not the Annika I know." Without waiting for me to answer, Rachel exclaimed, "He is such a narcissistic asshole."

"No arguments from me. "Look. I mean. It's just—" I took a deep breath to stop my spluttering. "Ja, he did say something like that, but it's not like he was wrong. I'm not good at being alone. And some time to sit with myself and grow emotionally isn't exactly a bad thing, is it?"

"Of course it's not. But only if you're doing it because you think it's the right thing for you, and not just because your asshole ex gaslit you into thinking you need to change because he can't handle the fact you broke up with him."

"Why didn't you ever tell me you didn't like him?" I asked, amused at the valve that'd been opened. A valve that had apparently been tightly closed until now.

She shrugged. "Not really my place. If he was abusive or something, then yeah, I'd have stepped in. But haven't we all dated someone that was all wrong?"

I bit my lower lip. "Ja. Too many times to count. Men and women. Some of them have been awful. I don't know why I do it. It's not even about the sex, though most of the time it's good or at least passable. And that's why I think a little bit of alone time isn't a bad thing, and this relocation is the perfect opportunity for me to grow."

"Mmm. Well." She pursed her lips. "If you're sure you're not just doing it because of what he said, then I'm all for it. You know I'm into personal growth. Manifest whatever you need to grow, even if that *is* a hookup or two…or fifty."

What if what I wanted to manifest was casual sex with my gorgeous neighbor? I mentally shook myself out. Thinking like that wasn't going to help my resolution. Neither was the fact I couldn't seem to stop flirting with her. For god's sake, I didn't even know if she was single, or interested in anything more than casual, appraising glances and some teasing flirtation.

"You're right," I agreed. "I shouldn't force myself into something. I'll just be mindful and…see what happens."

Rachel raised a forefinger. "Good plan. And if you need someone to go out with you, let me know. I can be your wingwoman."

"That is the rule," I agreed, nodding thoughtfully. I'd been Rachel's wingwoman in München, and it was logical she should be mine in Boston. Smiling to push aside the discomfort I felt about going out to find a date when I had already found someone I wanted to get to know better, I said, "I lost count of the number of times I said 'Siehst du meine Freundin da drüben? Sie ist aus Amerika zu Besuch.'" Do you see my friend over there? She's visiting from America.

"Oh no, no, no. I spoke German, badly, for almost eight months straight. It's English now, baby." She grinned back at me. "And you were a very good wingwoman…and translator."

I bowed shallowly. "I am always happy to assist."

"Thank you. So, where are you living?"

"Beacon Hill."

She whistled, her eyebrows shooting up. "Wow. I had no idea you were a millionaire."

I laughed. "I know. The price of rent is disgraceful, even more than it is in München, so that is saying something." Luckily my salary was far from disgraceful and I could comfortably afford the neighborhood. "But I needed to find somewhere quickly, and it was available and very nice. You know, there are just so many Mercedes and BMWs and Jaguars, even a Maserati, just parked there on the street, like they don't care if it gets hit or stolen or snowed upon."

"They probably just buy a new one," Rachel said, shrugging.

I smiled in agreement. They probably did. "But it's such a great location. Seems an easy commute and there are cafés and restaurants and bars, and the big park, ähm, the…oh, you know."

She laughed. "Boston Common?"

"That's it. Boston Common. And it's so pretty with the old buildings. And I do not have to buy a house in America, and I don't have a car here. I decided I was worth it, that I deserve to live somewhere nice for a year."

I was aware that I'd been rambling, trying to justify my choice to my friend, even though she'd been far from accusatory. This was the argument I'd used when Mama and Papa had been arguing with me and each other about the frivolity of "wasting" so much per month on rent when I could find something for half that price in a different neighborhood. Of course I could, if I didn't mind living in a less-nice part of the city, or spending more time traveling to work. I tended more toward my mother's spending ways, and the two of us had worn my father down into a place where he'd finally given up arguing.

Rachel held up both hands. "Hey, no judgment here. You don't need to explain yourself to me. Wherever you want to live, it's all more power to you, girl. And hey, maybe one morning while you're putting out the trash or buying coffee you'll meet some hot-as-the-sun, rich-as-sin Bostonian to keep you company for a little while and then you can move to one of the *even more* expensive suburbs together." She laughed. "Assuming people in Beacon Hill even put their own trash out. They probably have a maid or butler to do it."

"*I* put my trash out. And in that case, maybe I'll meet a hot maid or butler."

She grinned. "Why not both. At the same time."

Ah yes, the notion that bisexual people were promiscuous. I knew Rachel wasn't being accusatory; she genuinely thought dating multiple people at once was easy if everyone was on the same page. "I can barely give enough emotional energy to one person at a time. Two would be impossible."

"Shame." Rachel tapped the armrests of the chair. "So, what else are you doing today? You're not starting until Monday, right?"

I sat forward and uncrossed my legs. "I need to see Human Resources, sort out my laptop, and introduce myself properly to those of my team who are here today." I glanced at my watch. "Those tasks should only take a few hours."

"I was going to ask if you needed some help or company for the introductions, and then I remembered who I was talking to. Ms. Social Interactions Goddess herself."

I pretended to dust off my shoulders. "It's a gift. We all need to have one, right?"

"Right," she agreed. "Let me know when you're free for drinks and we can catch up properly."

"Does that mean you're paying for drinks? Living in Beacon Hill is expensive, you know," I deadpanned.

She lightly slapped my shoulder. "Just this once."

Once she'd left, her words about where I was living played upon my mind. It was undoubtedly a nice, expensive part of town. When I'd been in Evie's apartment on Wednesday night, I'd noted that it seemed *really* expensive. It was a strange thing, to recognize that one building could such hold different apartments, even on the same floor, instead of the cookie-cutter buildings in my home city.

My apartment was nice, but Evie's was, for lack of a better description, exquisite. It somehow managed to blend the old-world feel of the building's exterior with a clean modern vibe. She had lots of art—paintings, drawings, small sculptures—and everywhere were small personal touches of photographs and knickknacks. The space looked lived-in without being cluttered. There was only the kitchen, living, and dining rooms that I had been in, but I'd glimpsed a staircase up to another level. Presumably the bedrooms were up there.

Bedrooms.

I bit back my sigh of exasperation. I'd been hoping that spending some more time with her would help douse my raging attraction. It had done anything but. I shook my hands out. Time to concentrate on work for now. Daydreaming about my neighbor could wait.

Organizing my work laptop was thankfully very easy, and after I spent two hours with HR, Nate took me to lunch at a nice café on the ground floor of the building. After he'd checked in again to make sure I was settled, our conversation turned to work. The Global Connect project, a social app for travelers, was one of the bigger developments for which the company had been contracted. It had a lot of interesting and challenging functionality that we'd need to figure out, including the AI aspect the client wanted for text-to-speech translations.

The weather was mild, so I decided to walk home and explore. I enjoyed the stroll, extending the thirty-minute trip by detouring here and there to wander down an enticing-looking street. I stopped into a deli and bought a salad for dinner, walked alongside Boston Common and, noting all the people engaging in physical activity, decided my vacation from exercise while I relocated to another country was over. Tomorrow morning, I'd exercise. Finding a gym was still on my to-do list, but I just didn't have the mental energy to wade through locations, reviews, and membership structures. Maybe I should ask Evie if she had a recommendation.

I'd barely pulled off my coat and hung it on the hook by my front door when my phone rang. Mama. I was close to rejecting the FaceTime call so I could take a shower, and call back when I had shifted my brain from work mode, but she'd just keep trying until I answered. And…I did want to talk to her. I missed my family, even though I only saw my parents and brother in person every four months or so.

Mama was already smiling when I accepted the video call, as if the anticipation of talking to me was enough to bring her joy. "Oh, Anni! I'm so glad I caught you. Is this a good time for you? What time is it there? Are you at work?" She was in the kitchen, and the video shook as she moved around.

"Hallo, Mama. It's just past one p.m. and no, I'm not at work until Monday." It was a small lie, but trying to explain why I'd been at work today but only for a few hours was beyond my mental capacity right now. "How are you?" Asking my mother how she was made me think of Evie, going through her list of German phrases.

"Better than you, it seems. You're still so pale. I thought some sun would help." After a pointed look that conveyed all her disappointment, she bit into an apple—her usual post-dinner snack.

"Mama," I said, mustering every bit of my patience. Sure, I wasn't tanned, but my complexion was nowhere near albino. "It's November. If you still think I'm pale in July, *then* you can worry."

Her "hmm" made me sure she was already committing "Check Annika's complexion in July" to her mental list.

"And if I wanted to be tanned, I'd move to Freiburg. Or Australia."

She made a barely audible sound that conveyed she thought I was being a smart-ass. Which I was. "Have you made any friends yet?"

"Why is everyone asking me that today?"

"Because everyone who cares about you wants you to make friends. And because I'm worried about you being alone. Especially with Christmas approaching."

"Not everyone celebrates Christmas. My new neighbor doesn't."

The pause was long enough that I grew suspicious she was plotting something. I was right. "Then why don't you ask your neighbor to come by and celebrate Christmas with you?"

"I hardly know this woman. I think asking someone who's basically a stranger to celebrate something as intimate as Christmas is a little bit too much."

"You could say that about everyone really, before you get to know them. Your father was a stranger before I met him." God, she had some strange logic. "Why are you so reluctant? Do you think she's a psychopath?"

If Evie was a psychopath, she certainly hid it well. Still, "I get no psychopath vibe from her at all."

"A lot of psychopaths are very good at hiding their psychopathy."

"That's very comforting."

There was a loud crunch as she bit into her apple again and once she'd swallowed the mouthful, Mama mused, "Maybe she thinks you're a psychopath."

"Why are you suddenly obsessed with psychopaths? Did you cheat on your no-crime-show resolution?" Mama had grown obsessed with true crime, and a few months ago we'd had to stage a small intervention to get her to cut back.

"No. It was a podcast."

I mentally rolled my eyes. "Of course. And I don't know. I like her. But what you're suggesting feels strange. And Christmas here is just Christmas Day."

"There's no reason you can't celebrate every Christmas event as you usually would. Why not ask her to join you?" Mama insisted, in a tone I knew all too well but did not expect to hear while I was six thousand kilometers away. "You could merge the two things, do whatever Americans do as well as our traditional celebrations. Wouldn't that be fun?" she asked brightly.

Fun, yes. Weird, also yes. "Are you trying to set me up with a woman I only just met at the beginning of the week, whom you have never met?"

"No," she said, but the protest was a little bit too quick to make me believe her.

Spending more time with Evie wasn't the worst idea in the world, but I'd have to think about it. Inserting myself into her life for something as special as Christmas felt strange, even if I was dreading the thought of spending it alone. Forcing a smile, I assured my mother, "I'm going to make friends. I promise."

At least, I wanted to make friends with one person in particular.

CHAPTER SEVEN

Evie

Seeing Annika in the hallway was starting to feel like a habit. But, I mean, there were worse habits for me to have, right? I could be a drug addict instead of a neighbor addict. And it wasn't like I was purposely going out of my way to see her—she just seemed to come home from whatever she was doing around the times Pete collected Chloe, or, like now, return from grocery shopping at the same time I was returning from my Saturday run. I wasn't changing my routine—it really was a natural, happy coincidence.

Annika shifted the double armload of grocery bags. "You look like you are having some very deep thoughts."

I smiled, though she'd startled me by pausing near my door instead of just waving and disappearing up the hallway and into her place. "Deep? No. Just regular thoughts."

She hmmed, but didn't push further. "How was your Thanksgiving? That's the normal thing to ask, isn't it? I forgot to ask you yesterday morning. The grocery store clerk asked me and I didn't know what to say. I didn't think I had to celebrate Thanksgiving because I'm not American?"

I laughed. "I don't think you have to celebrate anything you don't want to. And yeah, I suppose it is a normal thing to ask. And it was fine, thanks." I didn't want to elaborate on it, because telling her I'd spent Thanksgiving doing what I did most other nights—being alone—was a downer. If I really wanted to, I could tag along with Pete to his parents', but even when Heather was alive, the few times I'd gone with them had felt strange.

"I'm glad." She bent down and set her bags on the floor, pushing them against the wall. "And I'm glad that I caught you. I was going to wait to talk to you about this, but now that you're here, I'll just mention it." She shook her head, laughing softly. "Every time I see you, I want to talk to you."

The feeling was mutual. Smiling, I made a vague gesture. "Then by all means, talk."

"Okay." Annika exhaled as if releasing tension. Tension about what, I had no idea. "The first thing is, do you have a gym nearby that you recommend? As much as I don't want to believe it, I have settled in, and now my exercise vacation is over."

I couldn't help it, the moment she said *gym*, I checked her out. Exercise or not, she looked amazing—slender but not lean, with softness in every place I loved. I realized I'd been staring instead of answering, and fought down the embarrassment, even though Annika was watching me in a way that made me think she knew exactly what I'd been doing and thinking. "Uh…I don't really go to the gym. Not since Heather died." Wrinkling my nose, I forced aside the thought of everything else that I no longer did since my sister died. I cleared my throat. "Did you want a private club or just like…a chain gym? And where? Close to home, or work?" After a deep inhalation, I blew the breath out in a raspberry. "Sorry, I'm rambling. I might need to ask around. Pete probably knows all the gyms in the city. Can I get back to you?"

Annika brushed her fingertips lightly over my forearm. "Of course, that's fine. I can ask people at work, but I thought you might know of somewhere good. And I can walk around the park until I find a gym." She gestured vaguely toward Beacon Street.

"The park?" I said, feigning indignation. "Oh no, it's *Boston Common*, you have to give it the respect it deserves."

She bowed shallowly. "I'm sorry. Boston Common. It's a funny name. Common means…occurring frequently? The Boston Frequently?"

Laughing, I assured her, "You're forgiven. And yeah, common does mean that, and a bunch of other things, but it also means a big green space shared by people. And if you ever need a running partner, let me know."

"Oh…I'm quite a slow runner. And I do not like running outside when the weather is cold." Annika glanced down at my legs, her slow gaze making its way back up again until she met my eyes. The expression conveying enjoyment of what she'd just seen made my skin heat. "But you…You look like you run a lot. I'm not training for marathons or anything like that. I only run because I want to live for a long time, and because I like putting things into my mouth."

Grinning, I agreed, "So do I." I only just held back the rest of the double entendre. "I just like running, any distance, any pace. And I'm not training for any marathons this year either. I'm a free agent, so if you want a partner for any kind of running when the weather warms up, just tell me."

Her eyebrows scrunched. "This year? How many marathons have you done?"

I shrugged. "A handful." I tried to resume marathoning after Heather died, but without my training and race partner, it no longer appealed.

"Well, that is a handful more than me. But I *will* take you up on being running partners in a few months when it's not so cold. If you can make yourself run when you might not feel like it, that is." Annika laughed. "Most of the time, I don't feel like it."

"Absolutely. I look forward to it." The truth felt warm, almost light. Spending time with Annika in any capacity was something to look forward to. I was traipsing merrily toward letting myself fall for someone I shouldn't fall for, and seemed to have no intention of pulling myself up. "If you get stuck finding a gym, I have a treadmill and some other gym equipment upstairs that you can use."

She grinned cheekily. "Then why would I need to find a gym if I can use your exercise things?"

I found myself returning the grin. "That's a good point."

"But thank you for your offer. I might borrow your treadmill until I have a gym, if you are okay with me using it in the morning before I go to the office."

"Sure. No problem."

"I *can* run after work, but I prefer to have all of the things I have to do, that are not work, completed in the morning. Otherwise they…" She gestured over her head. "Dangle on me."

I smiled at her wording. "Any time of the day is fine with me," I assured her. "That's the benefit of working from home and living alone. Except for Chloe in the afternoons during the week, I am flexible as fu—" I caught myself in time and fumbled for a replacement, finally managing, "Fuh-lexxxible can be."

Laughing, Annika wagged a finger. "You almost said it."

"Almost." I glanced down at her groceries. "Do you need to get anything into the fridge?" As much as I could easily continue talking with her for hours, I didn't want her ice cream or whatever to spoil.

"No." Frowning slightly, she bit her lower lip. "Were you telling the truth when you said you spend Christmas alone? No family? Not even your brother-in-law and niece?"

"Yes, of course I was," I said, surprised at the complete one-eighty question and where she might be leading with it. "Why?"

Annika took my hands in her warm, dry ones, and I instinctively squeezed. Her fingertips danced against the backs of my fingers in excitement as she told me, "I had the most brilliant idea. Or, more accurately, my mother had the most brilliant idea."

I could think of plenty of brilliant ideas involving Annika. "And what idea is that?"

"I was telling her about you and that you don't celebrate Christmas with your family." She frowned again. "I'm sorry, it wasn't…sharing something personal but she was asking if I'd met anyone and I told her about you and it just was part of the conversation. And she said that was a shame—you not being with your family at Christmas, not us meeting—and then we talked about me not being able to celebrate with my family. Or not in person. If I'm a little bit upset about not being with my family this Christmas, then my mother is devastated." Annika paused after her long monologue. "So, Mama suggested we share Christmas."

I heard what she suggested, I really did. But I was stuck on the fact my new neighbor had mentioned me to her mother. Mentioned me enough in her conversations that her mom apparently knew enough about me to suggest such a thing. It felt both strange and nice, that Annika seemed to care enough about me to talk about me. I leaned my shoulder against my doorframe. "What do you mean, 'share Christmas'? Like…share custody of it?"

She laughed loudly. "No. Share it like we have Christmas together. I was going to do some of the things my family would do anyway, but doing that alone is going to make me sad. And, perhaps you could do things you used to do with your family. And we'll…" She held her hands up, fingers splayed, and moved her hands together like she was trying to interlock her fingers. "You know…"

She looked so helpless trying to explain her idea that I decided to help out. "Mesh the merry?"

"Yes," she exhaled. "Mesh our Christmas traditions together. "Like…Merry Christmas and Frohe Weihnachten would make a—"

Now her whole face seemed to wrinkle in thought. After a few seconds, Annika blurted, "Merry Weihnachten! Or Frohe Christmas. Actually, no, *not* Frohe Christmas. That sounds very odd."

I bit down on my smile. Because Merry Weihnachten didn't sound odd. I tried not to sound like an idiot with my pronunciation when I asked, "Weihnachten is Christmas?"

Annika nodded enthusiastically. "Ja. But it kind of encompasses Christmas Eve and Day, and the day after Christmas Day." A smile passed over her mouth. "Then there is everything else that happens in December and January for the Christmas season. We Germans like to drag it out. So, if we're being pedantic, mixing English and German doesn't *really* work." Annika grinned and I fought back the excitement at the way that grin made me feel. She held up a forefinger. "But! It does sound fun. And funny."

"It is a fun, and funny, portmanteau," I agreed readily.

Annika's eyebrows came together and I decided that her confused face was one of the best, cutest things I'd ever seen. And if it wasn't so mean to deliberately confuse her with words, I probably would have tried to do so as much as I could. "Portmanteau?" she asked. "What is that? I haven't heard that word."

Oh god. And I'd never had to explain it before. "Um. You know." No, Evie, she doesn't know. "It's, uh…when you take parts from two words to make a new word. Like…Brangelina or Bennifer. Okay, those are really bad examples. But you get what I mean. Brunch is probably a better example of a portmanteau."

She brightened. "Oh, ja, I do know what you mean, and now I know the word for it. And of course I know brunch. I love brunch."

"Good to know."

"So? What do you think about us meshing the merry? We could choose our favorite Christmas traditions, and do them together." She smiled kindly. "It might help us feel less alone for this holiday." Annika's stare seemed to bore into me, her gaze so knowing that I had a sudden and irrational panic that she somehow knew just how much I hated being by myself at a time that was supposed to be about family, blood or chosen.

And though the thought of celebrating Christmas properly for the first time in fifteen years made my whole body clench with dread, it was a no-brainer to spend more time with her. So I agreed with as much enthusiasm as I could muster for Christmas. "I think it sounds like a great idea."

Annika's entire body seemed to scream relief. "Wonderful. That is wonderful." She fumbled in her handbag and produced her phone.

"Why don't we each think of some things that are important to us for Christmas and we can decide how we should proceed. Of course, we'll need a planning meeting." She rolled her lower lip through her teeth as she scrolled through something on her phone.

"Oh, you never said anything about a planning meeting. This sounds…very structured."

Annika glanced up, her face impassive. "I'm German," she deadpanned. "I like structure." After a moment, she grinned hugely and I relaxed.

"So you are. I should warn you though, I'm not really Christmassy."

"Well, it is a good thing German Christmas season is very prolonged. I have enough things to cover for you as well." She folded her arms over her chest. "What about from when you were younger? Before your family trouble?"

"Yes, I suppose there are some traditions that we followed. I don't know that they're 'American' or if it was just what my family did." And my family was not like regular families.

"Great."

"And you don't mind that it's going to be lopsided in favor of German Christmas stuff? If you're looking for an American Christmas cultural experience from me, I'm afraid you're not going to get it."

"No, of course I don't mind." Annika's smile was a little smug, a little naughty. "Unlike you, I am very Christmassy, so that suits me just fine." She waved her phone at me. "When are you available for a meeting?" Annika's eyebrows scrunched. "Not a meeting, but a planning session."

"Any time," I said honestly.

"Tomorrow afternoon? I know it's Sunday, but…"

"Tomorrow afternoon is fine," I cut in. "I'm probably just going to spend most of the day stopping my couch from escaping." Unless I found some creative motivation, which was always a fifty-fifty chance on weekends.

"I don't quite understand what you mean."

My cheeks warmed. "Sorry, stupid joke. I'm going to sit on my couch, and pretending I'm holding it down sounds better than saying I'm going to be lazy." I cleared my throat. "How about around four p.m.? We can have dinner, maybe drinks, afterward," I said casually, while inside I was not-casually hoping she'd agree.

"Tomorrow at four p.m. and then dinner and drinks after sounds wonderful." As soon as she'd finished speaking, she opened her mouth, but closed it again just as quickly.

I nodded. "Sounds great. Can't wait."

"Me neither," Annika murmured. "Okay, I should go and leave you alone." Before I could tell her she didn't need to do that, she crouched to collect her groceries.

I bent over to help. Of course, bending over put me right into her personal space and when Annika looked up, arms full of her groceries again, we were nose-to-nose. We held eye contact for just a moment too long, and I mumbled, "Sorry" and stood up again.

Annika's response was "I'm not sorry" as she stood too. Her eyes left mine for the briefest moment to glance at my lips. "I will see you tomorrow afternoon."

"Mhmm," I managed, though my brain was teeming with thoughts, most of them telling me to just kiss her. She's looking at your mouth, she wants to kiss you, kiss her. *Kiss her.* As soon as I'd acknowledged those thoughts, another bunch moved into my head to push all thoughts of kissing her aside. She's technically your tenant, you're emotionally stunted and relationship-immature, and she's kind of way too hot for you.

Annika smiled knowingly, then left me and my racing heart to calm down. I slipped into my condo before I did something stupid like go after her and kiss her. Because that's exactly what I wanted to do and my willpower was fraying like a rope rubbing over a sharp rock. Hmm. Interesting phrasing.

Once I'd locked myself away from Annika's hotness, I went straight up to my office, opened the document where I stored my random brainstorming ideas, and wrote down the phrase for possible future use. Then I went into my bathroom and took a long shower.

My shower didn't exactly cool my libido, but it did reset my brain enough that I could think more clearly instead of reactively and, sigh… defensively. So, I was seriously attracted to her. Attraction never hurt anyone. And I didn't *have* to act on an attraction. I could just remain in my comfortable little bubble where Annika and I were friends and I had occasional erotic dreams about my neighbor. Totally fine, totally normal.

But this shared Christmas was going to complicate things.

Merry Weihnachten. Why had she asked me? It was an absolutely brilliant idea, even if it had been her mom's and not hers. But it was also…special. Intimate. Far too intimate for mere acquaintances. And yet, I wasn't at all bothered. I already felt some level of intimacy between us, had from our first conversation. So doing something as close as sharing Christmas with a woman I barely knew, but felt I knew, was no big deal.

And it wasn't like I had anything else to do on Christmas. Aside from dinner with Pete and Chloe, and Heather too when she was alive, before they left for the Phillips family holiday obligations, Christmas was a nonstarter for me. Having a December filled with yuletide shit would be strange, but maybe it'd also be fun and interesting. And as I'd already realized—spending time with Annika would be worth putting up with it all.

If nothing else, Heather would be proud of me for not spending the season alone. She'd hated the split in our family and had tried desperately to repair it, but inheriting my parents' stubbornness meant we were deadlocked. At a big ol' impasse.

I was sure Heather would have liked Annika. My sister was full of self-confidence and charisma and was always drawn to other confident, extroverted people. What would Heather have said once she witnessed the vibes between us? She'd tell me to pull my head out of my ass. That the only way I was going to learn to be in a relationship was to be in relationships, to commit to women who made me better, who understood the emotional quirks pressed upon me by my life.

Was Annika that woman though? I didn't think so, as much as I wanted it to be true. Her time in Boston was temporary. And I'd had enough heartbreak in my life to invite more in knowingly. But… maybe someone temporary was just the solution. No expectations. No strings. I could just cut and run when she left, and move on to something permanent after having had a practice run with Annika.

I was so far ahead of myself it was laughable. And also so deluded I could have cried. I was not a casual-attachments person. And treating her like a crash-test dummy for my emotional inadequacy was cruel and stupid. Annika's flirtations were so obvious, so unashamed and certain, and maybe her confidence would give me a little confidence to take the leap. I just didn't know what I was supposed to leap into.

CHAPTER EIGHT

Annika

After knocking twice on Evie's door and receiving no response, I shifted the box I'd brought with me to my other arm and pulled out my phone to double-check I hadn't messed up the time, even though I knew I hadn't. We'd agreed only yesterday to our shared Christmas, and it was right there in my calendar: *December 1st 4:00 p.m. Merry Weihnachten planning session.* Mama had cringed when I'd told her what we'd christened our event, while Papa had laughed until he was red in the face, probably just because he knew his exaggerated mirth would annoy my mother.

When Mama had suggested sharing Christmas with Evie, I'd thought it a ridiculous idea, too much for people who barely knew each other. And I'd decided that I would cope fine with Christmas on my own for the first time. But I remembered what Evie had said about spending Christmas alone, and something inside me broke. I didn't regret asking, but I was slightly worried about spending so much time with Evie when I knew how easy it would be to fall for her.

I was just about to call when she answered the door, wearing a gray Henley shirt unbuttoned to just above her cleavage, sweatpants, and an apologetic smile. "I'm so *so* sorry. I got totally into a shading and coloring zone and haven't come up for air since I sat down. Have to take *that* motivation when it comes up." She dragged the door open, running a hand through her hair which looked like she'd been running her hands through it all day. She glanced at the box, mild panic passing over her face. "Did I miss a gift-giving event?"

Smiling, I assured her, "No. My Adventskranz and Adventskalender arrived. My mother is very relieved. She had been having a nervous breakdown about my Advent wreath and Advent calendar not arriving in time to put out today." Realizing I hadn't actually said what I wanted to, I held up the box, feeling suddenly shy. "I have a wreath for your table too? If you want it. If not, I can just use it for something else."

Evie's face lit up. "Oh? That's great. Thank you. Of course I want it."

"Wonderful." I peered into the box. "And there is also an Advent calendar in there for you. I'm sorry, I only had mine so I had to go out this morning to get some things for yours. I have been on the T today, and visited Target, and I saw the baseball park. And, I also saw a bear playing a…guitar piano near the subway station. It has been a very interesting day."

She smiled indulgently. "Sounds like it. And you met Keytar Bear! You're officially a Bostonian now."

"Who?"

"Keytar Bear. The bear playing the piano guitar. Well, it's actually a person in a bear costume playing a keytar."

"Keytar…" I mouthed the word a few times, trying to connect it to what I'd seen. "Oh! Another portmanteau? Keyboard guitar?"

"You got it! Come on in. We really need to stop having conversations in my doorway."

"I like your doorway," I said as I stepped through it. "I like your house. It's very different to mine. More rooms, fancier. And you have the two levels. How does that work? What about the space above me? Nobody is there?" If they were, they were ghostly quiet and I had no idea how they came and went from their apartment. The apartments on the ground floor were both single level, like mine and I wondered why Evie's was the only two-level apartment in the building, and how it fit like a Tetris piece in the structure.

A flash of unease crossed her features as she closed the door, but it disappeared as quickly as it had appeared. "Directly above you is my private rooftop terrace, and the place where I murder plants through neglect. And yeah, upstairs is my office, gym, spare bedroom and stuff."

"I'd like to see your plant-murdering rooftop sometime. And I would very much like to see your office where you make your graphic novels."

Evie stumbled over her response. "Uh, I…uh, um…" Her reluctance to share didn't surprise me—I knew creative types often didn't like to let people in on their processes—but the downright panic on her face did surprise me.

I took a step back, offering what I hoped was a reassuring smile. "It's fine. Sorry, I shouldn't have asked."

"No, it's okay. Just give me a minute to tidy up some, uh…crappy brainstorming sketches. Come on up." She slipped by me and took the internal stairs two at a time. I set the box on her kitchen counter and followed her upstairs and into another hallway with doors bracketing it on each side. I heard the rustle of paper before Evie's head popped out of the first door on the right. The panic had receded. "Come on in. But I have to warn you that it's not very interesting. Oh, and uh, you might see some spoilery stuff which probably shouldn't be shared."

I pretended to zip my lips. "I am well aware of project confidentiality and shall keep what I see to myself."

"Great. Come on through."

I thought my workspace was complex, but it had nothing on hers. Neatly laid out, the desk had two enormous monitors, one connected to a MacBook, and the other to a big iPad. Four screens seemed excessive but when I looked closer, I realized she really needed all of them. The righthand monitor mirrored what she was drawing on the iPad—a partially finished page depicting two women talking. I hadn't had a chance to look at her published work yet, but Evie's art here was incredible—lifelike, exciting, nuanced. I really needed to buy some of these novels.

The MacBook had a completed drawn page and the left monitor showed some reference pictures of a forest. Despite the mass of electronics, her desk was immaculate. With my hands behind my back like I was afraid to touch something and break it, which I absolutely was, I wandered to the most interesting thing in the room—the full-wall whiteboard, divided into A4-sized segments, each displaying posed stick figures, a rough landscape, or dialogue.

I gestured to the whiteboard. "Have you ever accidentally erased pieces of that?"

Evie laughed and leaned against the edge of her desk. "*I* haven't, no. But Chloe has. When she was six, she erased everything she could reach on the wall, almost a quarter of the third book of *Stark Realities* so she could 'spell some words for me.' I had to redraft everything from memory and my script. So now I take digital photos of the panels for backup. It's better than keeping paper copies. Save the environment and all that."

"Gosh, I can't imagine that. I thought I lost a project once and nearly had a breakdown."

She shrugged. "It's just art, always flexible. Sometimes what comes the second time around is even better than the first time."

I stared at a pencil drawing of a gondola on a snowy mountain, framed and hanging on the wall above Evie's desk. It wasn't…bad exactly, but it was very basic and I wondered about the significance.

Evie followed my gaze, then filled me in. "Heather drew that. Obviously, every bit of artistic talent in our family landed in my body."

"Obviously," I agreed, because she'd already made the joke so it wasn't mean.

Evie pushed herself off her desk, so hard she almost launched herself into me. Laughing, she gripped my bicep for balance. "Sorry. Come on, I'll show you the plant-murder scene and then we can get started? I know about Advent calendars, but how does the German Christmas wreath system work?" she asked over her shoulder as she exited the room.

Wreath system. I held back a laugh, both at her wording and the fact she wasn't far off with her description of Germans and having a system. I followed her down the hall, peeking through an open door into a room which held a treadmill, a spin bike, and masses of free weights and exercise equipment. "There are four candles, and starting on the first Sunday after the twenty-sixth of November, you light one candle. The moment you light the first candle, the Christmas season has begun. Then every Sunday, the next candle is lit until all four are burning."

Evie paused in front of a door at the end of the hall and after opening it, turned around to ask, "Have you already lit yours?" She stepped back to let me through the door. "And here's the terrace."

"Yes, I have," I said as I peeked through the door, receiving a blast of cold air in the face. Evie was right, it was a plant-murder scene. But the space, bordered by a wrought-iron fence would be lovely in warmer weather, even if she couldn't keep plants alive. I pulled my head back inside. "This morning." It had been lonely, sitting by myself at my table, drinking coffee and eating some of the Weihnachtsplätzchen I'd baked. I set that memory aside, and smiled. "Christmas is happening, Evie, nothing can stop it now the first candle is lit. That is the rule."

Evie grinned, hands held up in surrender. "Okay. Then we'd better light mine to doubly make sure Christmas will happen." She closed and locked the door to the terrace, then beckoned me to follow her back downstairs into the kitchen. "Do they stay lit from now until the next one, right through to Christmas?"

"Oh goodness no," I exclaimed. "*That* is a great way to burn down your apartment. I always blow the candles out if I leave the house. Most days I light them again for the evening, just to feel like I'm in the Christmas spirit."

"Got it."

I bit my lip, which was threatening to tremble. "While we light the candles, we would have coffee with cake or Christmas cookies. It's… all about being with family and friends."

Evie watched me, her eyes soft with understanding. "Well. I definitely have coffee. But I definitely don't have cake or Christmas cookies. I do have regular cookies?"

I pulled a plastic container from the box I'd set on the counter. "Then isn't it lucky that I have cookies. I made them this morning before I went on my adventure."

"Will you make them every Sunday for the candle lighting? If coffee and stuff are part of the candle-lighting ritual, then we need the right cookies," Evie said seriously.

"Yes, I will. Or cake."

She nodded slowly. "I think I'm going to like this shared Christmas thing."

"Me too," I said honestly.

Her mouth twitched into a smile. "Let me put the coffee on and we can set up my wreath and calendar."

While the coffee brewed on her gas stovetop, Evie and I set up the wreath in the middle of her kitchen table. Evie expressed surprise that it was made of real greenery, not plastic. The Etsy woman made really nice wreaths. I'd chosen traditional red candles, which thankfully blended in with Evie's décor. I arranged some Weihnachtsplätzchen onto a plate while Evie poured two mugs of coffee. She paused, laughing. "I just realized, I have no idea how you take your coffee. We've only ever had wine."

So we had. "A lot of milk. A little bit of sugar."

"Got it. So…a latte if we're out?"

I nodded. "Ja."

"Good to know." Evie added milk to both mugs, and sugar to one, then passed mine over. She brought the cookies, and we set the plate and our coffees down on the table. But neither of us sat.

Evie produced a box of matches from her pocket. "Do I need to do anything special? Or just…light it? Do we say any special words?"

"You just light it. There is a poem." I paused, then decided to just recite it. "Advent, Advent, ein Lichtlein brennt. Erst eins, dann zwei, dann drei, dann vier, und dann steht Weihnachten vor der Tür."

The edge of her mouth quirked. "What does that mean?" she asked as she struck a match.

Once the candle wick had caught, I answered, "Advent, Advent, a little light is burning. First one, then two, then three, then four, and then there is Christmas at the door. There is a version where it is the Christkind, Christ-child at the door, but not in my house. And then my father would always add 'und wenn das fünfte Lichtlein brennt, dann hast du Weihnachten verpennt.' If the fifth light is burning, you have slept Christmas away." I shook my head, hoping my cheeks weren't as red as they felt. "It...sounds strange in English."

"Nothing sounds strange when you say it."

"If you spend enough time with me, you may change your mind about that," I deadpanned. "Happy first day of Advent, Evie." I took her hand, and after pausing for a moment, leaned in and lightly kissed her cheek, lingering for longer than I should have.

Evie squeezed my hand. "Happy first day of Advent."

I was aware of my breathing coming in short, shallow bursts and of the singular thought pushing in front of all other thoughts. That I wanted to kiss her. On the mouth, not the cheek. And I was certain she would kiss me back. There was still the slightest squeeze on my hand, and I moved closer. Her eyes flashed to my lips.

And then her phone sounded a loud alert. Scheisse!

The moment had been broken and I cursed whoever had decided to interrupt.

Evie cleared her throat, one hand coming up to absently rub at her cheek. "Okay," she whispered tightly. "I think it's time for coffee and cookies."

"Yes," I agreed hoarsely. "I think you're right."

Evie checked her phone, then set it down again, before dropping heavily into the chair in front of her coffee. After a deep breath, I felt more composed and took my place next to her. I'd just sat down when I remembered one more thing, and hopped up again. "I almost forgot, here is your Advent calendar. It's the first of December, which means it's time to start." It was mostly small chocolates and candies, with the occasional pencil or frivolous toy thrown in, that I'd wrapped individually and numbered from 1 to 24, then put in a festive box labeled *Advent Calendar*.

Evie took the box from me, an awed expression passing over her face as she looked inside. "You *made* me an Advent calendar?"

"Ja." It wasn't difficult to create an Advent calendar, and taking the time to create something was a nice gesture.

She blinked hard a few times. "Thank you, that's so special." Once she'd put the box on her bookshelf and unwrapped the gift for today, a KitKat chocolate, she came back and we sat quietly for ten minutes or so, talking about our day, watching the flickering light of the candle, drinking coffee and eating cookies. Evie opened the Advent KitKat and shared it with me. It all was so easy, so normal. After taking another cookie, she said, "These are so good." She bit off a huge mouthful and asked, "Are they always the same kind of cookie for Christmas?"

"No. We have certain types that are Weihnachtsplätzchen. Christmas cookies," I explained at her eyebrow scrunch. I ran my thumbs up and down the outside of the mug. "But I have my favorites which I always make. These Vanillekipferl—vanilla moons. Butterplätzchen—plain butter cookies. Zimtsterne—cinnamon stars. Und Haselnussplätzchen—hazelnut cookies."

"Those all sound like they could be my favorites too."

"That is good to know," I murmured.

She finished the cookie then gripped my arm. "Shall we get started on planning our Merry Weihnachten?" Her pronunciation was pretty good.

Her firm, yet light, grip sent a shudder of goose bumps down my arm. "Ja. Let's plan."

We relocated to the couch, and after grabbing a notepad and pen, Evie put her feet up on the coffee table. "Okay, so, Christmas traditions. I've been thinking about it and honestly? I'm worried things might get a little…smooshy around Christmas Day."

I wrinkled my nose, trying to decipher what she meant. "Smooshy?"

Evie threaded her pen between her forefinger and middle finger, bouncing it a few times, before she began writing…or sketching…or making headings or something. "Trying to fit everything into such a short amount of time," she said as she wrote. "It'll be crammed in, cramped, too many things to do and not enough time." Mostly she looked at me, but every now and then she'd glance down at the page while she spoke. As her hand moved over the paper, I realized she was drawing something, not writing.

I tried unsuccessfully to catch a glimpse. "I think we'll be fine." I'd already resigned myself to the fact that this Christmas wasn't going to be my usual one. The idea of doing something with Evie, even if things weren't "right" was an enticing, exciting thought. "What are your family traditions?"

Evie's mouth twisted, then she returned to the drawing. "Take verbal shots at one another over Christmas dinner until someone snaps and leaves?"

"Jaaaaa…well, we can do that if you want." I leaned forward and rested my hand on her leg, feeling the quick tense and relax of her thigh. "Or we can forget about all of this, if it's something you'd rather just forget."

That stilled her hand. "Oh no, noooo. It's fine, really. Sorry, didn't mean to get all heavy on you there." She cleared her throat and glanced down at the page. Her eyes widened before she quickly flipped to a clean page, but not before I caught a flash of what looked like a face. A face that looked a lot like mine. She'd been drawing me?

Without looking up, Evie said, "My family was pretty boring. Early in December we'd decorate a tree that someone else had collected and manhandled into the house. New pajamas on Christmas Eve ready for the staged present-opening photos the next morning. My mom used to volunteer for the disadvantaged—wearing just her pearls instead of diamonds, of course. Eat a Christmas evening meal prepared by people paid to prepare it, and pretend we liked spending time together."

"Do you even like Christmas?" I asked gently.

Now she looked up, her mouth twisted, changing from a grimace to a grin. The pinkness in her cheeks began to fade. "You know, I actually did. I do. Heather and I used to play pranks, and make bets on what outlandish thing our parents would do. We'd always get each other a totally ridiculous and frivolous gift that my mother would undoubtedly have conniptions over."

"Like what?"

"Remote-control race cars, garish dollar-store jewelry, or costumes that we'd wear all Christmas Day until our mother got annoyed and made us take them off before dinner." She laughed suddenly. "Heather bought me a blow-up doll one year, just to see the look on Mom's face. It was well worth the yelling."

I laughed with her. "That sounds great. Heather sounds great."

"It was. She was. And then I just…stopped being invited for Christmas. Now I have an early one with Pete and Chloe, but otherwise it's an ordinary day for me. So yeah, that's it. Tree, pajamas, gift exchange Christmas morning, meal Christmas evening." She wrote a hasty list, a sly smile tweaking her mouth as she looked up at me. "I think we could leave out the passive-aggression, fights, and all that other stuff from my family?"

"Probably for the best," I agreed, returning her smile. "What about volunteering?" At her slightly blank stare, I elaborated, "Your mother with her best pearls."

"Oh, no, I don't volunteer at Christmas. I prefer quietly giving year-round rather than a performative event for the holidays."

I sensed something deeper behind what she'd just said, but our friendship was far too new for me to be pushing her about something so personal.

Evie glanced at her list before looking back to me. "So what about you?"

"We have a lot more than Americans, but the most important ones for my family are the Christmas wreath and Advent calendar, which we now have. Christmas markets are a very big deal in Germany. It is one of my favorite things. Sometimes I go many times. There is Saint Nikolaus Day on the sixth of December, which is *technically* for children. Children put a boot outside their front door the night before and the good ones receive treats like chocolates, nuts, and fruit but the bad children receive Rute—a bundle of sticks." I smiled, thinking of how I used to line my boot up so perfectly perpendicular to the house.

"Did you ever get sticks?"

"Of course not," I said, feigning indignation. "It's just a threat to make us behave." Laughing, I confessed, "And it works. Even though we're grown-ups now, my parents always send my brother and me a gift for Saint Nikolaus Day. We do our tree decorating on Christmas Eve. There is lots of eating, drinking, and listening to music, singing carols, and then we exchange gifts after dinnertime. And we also have a big a meal on Christmas Day as well. We like to spread things out."

"So you do. It's like having a full week of birthday celebrations, right?"

"That's right," I agreed.

Evie reached for a cookie, studying the list. She'd been hastily taking down notes while I'd been talking and now, she ran her finger down the page. "You know, I think this might actually work. Like, we could fit all this in without overlap. There's pajamas on Christmas Eve but if we're already together giving gifts…" She trailed off, letting a vague hand gesture finish the sentence for her. "We have Christmas markets here, we can just pick a day that suits and go. Oh! And there's this new-ish one at the Seaport, they call it Snowport and it's apparently really fu—n. It's fun, and great. And I suppose I should get a tree soon."

"That sounds like a very good plan. And…about the tree. Can I buy one and store it somewhere? I'm a little bit worried I'll miss out if I don't buy a tree soon, but we don't bring it inside and decorate it until later, remember?" One of the reasons I'd chosen this apartment was because of its "live Christmas tree allowed" rule. Of course the rule had a whole list of subrules associated with it for fire safety and common space cleanliness.

Her eyebrows came together. "Why don't we split the cost of one tree then? I can store it up on my terrace."

"Where all your murdered plants are? Is that wise? Will it survive?"

Evie snorted out a laugh. "Good point, though you'll be here to care for it. If you're worried, it can live inside my place and on Christmas Eve we can take it for a little trip down the hall and it'll become your tree for us to decorate."

I looked at her skeptically. "You really want an undecorated Weihnachtsbaum in your house? Just…sitting there, doing nothing except needing attention and taking up space in your living room?"

"Sure. I mean, I can put an ornament on it or something and call it decorated for the American Christmas." She grinned. "Of course, that means I'll have to purchase an ornament. Do you have decoration stuff?"

"A few things my mother insisted I take from the family stash, plus my own from the small trees I had in my apartment back home. I'll need to buy lights and some more baubles to fill out a full-sized tree."

"I'll buy a few decorations too, if…that's…okay?" Her nose wrinkled. "You look like it's not okay."

"Of course it's okay."

Evie leaned forward, a smile tugging at the corners of her mouth. "You're an aesthetics person, aren't you?"

I made a back-and-forth movement with my hand. "Perhaps a little bit."

Laughing, she held up both hands in a gesture of placation. "Then I hand full decorative control to you. If my decorations work, great, and if not then I won't feel offended."

"I'm sure they will work. And what about food?"

"What about it?"

"Who should be responsible for what? And what if our things do not…" I interlocked my fingers, trying to find the words.

Evie stepped in. "What if it's a culinary clashing disaster trying to mix German and American Christmas cuisines?" she asked, smirking like the idea appealed to her.

"Yes. That."

She shrugged. "Honestly, I would probably just buy whatever I'm supposed to contribute rather than cook it. But I'm excellent at appetizers. And I really love food, so I can't see it being a disaster."

"Yes," I agreed, "you are excellent with appetizers. I am happy to be in charge of the cooking for all of it if you don't know what to make for Christmas, or…" It wasn't just that I was feeling possessive about having the "correct" foods for Christmas—I enjoyed cooking and I really enjoyed cooking for Christmas.

Nodding slowly, she said, "Sure, if that's what you want. Just tell me what you've spent and I'll reimburse you for my half. And I *will* contribute some food, obviously. Or help you cook. It's not fair for you to do all the food labor."

I agreed without hesitation, pleased by her offer to help. Her mention of reimbursement made me decide to address the elephant in the room. "I don't want to be that person, but…what kind of financial commitment are we talking about for gifts? It's just I don't know you well and I'm not sure what you're thinking about it."

Her eyebrows came together in what I was beginning to recognize as her thinking expression. "Well…we've agreed to split the costs for all our shared things like meals and whatnot. Share the tree cost and decorations. And…I don't know, what gift-giving occasions are there again? Sorry, you lost me at Saint Nikolaus."

"Just the two. Boots full of chocolate and trinkets and the like for Nikolaustag—if you're good—and a 'regular' gift on Christmas Eve."

"And regular gift on Christmas morning for us—Santa hasn't visited me in a very long time, so I don't need to hang a stocking for him. Right, so…we have a stocking, or a boot, sorry, each for Saint Nikolaus, and then Christmas Eve and then Christmas Day. Piece of cake. What kind of budget were you thinking?"

"I really don't know." I had no idea how to set a figure for a series of gifts exchanged between new friends. Very new friends. Very new friends who, earlier, had almost kissed.

Evie tore a blank page from the notepad and scribbled something on it. "This is the figure my people have settled on." She folded it and pressed it to her mahogany coffee table, sliding it along the surface toward me like we were in some sort of business deal. "Tell me if you're amenable or if we need to begin negotiations."

Laughing at her pretend business-deal voice, I picked up and unfolded the page. She'd written:

Nick Day $10
Eve $20
Day $20
=$50

And then a question mark and a smiley face.

Evie cleared her throat. "Sorry, I have no idea which is the biggest of your events. I hope I allocated funding correctly. And not too cheaply? Or too…expensively?"

"This looks great. And I think fifty dollars is ample to cover gifts. Not too much for all of this for new friends at all."

Her exhalation was relieved. "Great. And obviously if gifts come in under that, then fabulous, excellent haggling and gift ferreting." She began bouncing the pen between her fore and middle finger again. "I, uh…I might buy my own new pajamas and maybe you do the same? And wrap them ourselves and act totally surprised when we get them. So those aren't part of that gift budget. Or you don't need to do the pajamas thing. We can skip that."

"No skipping family traditions. Unless they're ones you really hate and want to skip."

"I don't hate any of it," she said quietly. "I used to love Christmas. It's just been a while since I celebrated it fully." Evie looked up, and her eyes were soft. "I think I'm looking forward to falling in love with it again."

Falling in love. I bit my lower lip. "I'm looking forward to that too." I looked away from her to hide what felt like a blush and made a few notes on my phone. "Now that it's sorted out, I think we need a day planner to make sure everything runs smoothly. And perhaps we should share a list of proposed food for each meal on Christmas Eve and Christmas Day so we can make sure it all works together."

Evie raised her eyebrows, but she was smiling. "More planning? Do you want to do a shared calendar so we can figure it all out? I'm not great at planning, myself, but I'm really good at following things if someone else makes the plans."

"Yes," I breathed. "Give me a few moments and I'll send you the sharing invite." There was something so comforting about not having to defend my love of planning and organizing—a necessity for my job, but also something I felt necessary in my personal life. For some inexplicable reason, a lot of my partners had scoffed at my ultra-detailed hour-by-hour planning. It was the only way I could organize my days, even if all I'd put in the planner was a block of Free Time. I wondered why I always seemed to choose people who not only didn't understand this part of me, but openly scorned it.

Evie wrote down her email address for me, and while I created our shared calendar, she sat back and ate another cookie. Every time I glanced up, she was watching me. Unashamed, bold, open. The only time she looked away was when her phone sounded the alert from my invitation. She glanced at it then pushed the device aside again. "Got it, thanks. I'll put in some draft things in the morning and we can sort out the rest of the timing in the next few days." Evie relaxed into the couch, her arm slung casually over the back. Her fingers drummed a random beat right next to my shoulder. "Sooo…care to tell me what kind of things you like, to make my gift-hunting a little easier?"

I leaned as close as I dared, wanted to lean even closer. "Now what kind of fun would that be, Evie-Evangeline? You'll have to guess, or get to know me better so you can decide for yourself."

CHAPTER NINE

Evie

I had four days, and a budget of ten dollars for our first Merry Weihnachten (I'd Googled the spelling) gift for Saint Nikolaus Day (I'd Googled that spelling too). There'd been no discussion on using things we already had in our homes as part of the gifting process, and I was going to use that loophole to my full advantage. I'd never paid attention to how much I spent on gifts and I was finding having to do so now incredibly difficult.

But extravagance wasn't an option here, and not only because I didn't really know Annika and going over budget might make her feel weird, but because that would break the rules of Merry Weihnachten. And rules seemed important to her. Another problem with this whole thing was that I really didn't know anything about her, except that she was gorgeous, funny, personable, and worked in app development, so finding personalized gifts was going to be a stretch.

Chloe was actually a huge help. But of course, I'd had to endure my niece's teasing, because when I admitted what Annika and I were up to, her reaction was an incredulous, "You're doing Christmas things with Hot Neighbor this whole month? Laaaawl. From none to heaps. Do you even know *how* to Christmas now, Aunt Evie?"

I paused slicing the tomato for our salad. "I manage to buy you something great every year for Christmas, don't I? Clearly I 'know how to Christmas.' Should I stop those gifts?"

"No thanks," she said instantly, with a hefty dose of cheerfulness and a little dose of facetiousness.

"And I participate in a Christmas meal with you and your dad every year, don't I?"

"Yeah, but—"

"But nothing. I *do* know what Christmas is. Your mom and I used to love Christmas."

She looked dubious. "I know you know what it is. But does Annika know you're kind of a grinch?"

"I am *not* a grinch. I don't dislike the concept of Christmas. I don't want to ruin other people's Christmases. I just…"

"Dislike the concept of Christmas," Chloe said dryly.

"It's not that," I said, exasperated at her for pushing my buttons and at myself for letting her push them. "I just…what's the point when it's just me for the day?"

"You know, it doesn't have to be just you on Christmas Day. You could always crash Grandma and Grandpa's thing. Kick the door in, and yell, 'Surprise, bitches!'"

"First of all, language. And second of all, respect." It was my duty to make sure Chloe turned into a productive member of society and for now, part of that meant respecting my parents. She could choose if she wanted to allocate any of her respect to her grandparents when she was older and realized what kind of people they were. I'd already decided long ago not to elaborate on that whole tangled mess unless Chloe asked me to.

"Sorry," she mumbled.

It wasn't me she should apologize to, and she hadn't actually called my parents "bitches" to their faces, so I decided I'd admonished her enough.

We moved on and brainstormed gift ideas for Annika while I finished the salad and heated the lasagna I'd cooked during the day. Just as she finished adding the minimum amount of salad to her plate, Chloe suggested a "Welcome to Boston" pack. She pointed out I could get menus and loyalty cards, maps, and information pamphlets, all for free, and then just find something to round out the $10, like a gift card for Dunks.

I added more salad to my niece's dinnerplate. "That's a really good idea. But do you think it's maybe a little impersonal?"

"How?" Chloe asked around a mouthful of lasagna.

"Chew, swallow, *then* speak please."

Her eye roll told me exactly what she thought of my manners reminder right in the middle of preteen ravenous eating, but she did as I'd requested. "It's perfect. And not impersonal at all. You're a native Bostonian, you're sharing your eminent knowledge with her, taking time to put together a carefully curated gift to ensure her integration into the city is seamless. That's the very definition of personal and thoughtful."

"Did you eat a thesaurus?" I finally paid some attention to my own dinner and after a huge mouthful of lasagna—no judging, it'd been a busy day and aside from today's Twix from Annika's Advent calendar, I'd barely eaten—I added, "I don't know. Like I said, it's a great idea, sweetie, but it just feels a little…basic."

"There is nothing basic about you, Aunt Evie. You are the most non-basic person I know."

"I think that's a compliment."

"It's totally a compliment."

We ate in merciful silence for a few minutes until Chloe pointed at the wreath occupying the center of the table. "This is cool."

"It is," I agreed, looking at the partially melted candle from yesterday. I'd left it burning until just before I went to bed because Annika was right—it did give me Christmas spirit.

"Did Annika give it to you?"

"She did." I compiled a big forkful of salad in the hopes that the time it would take me to eat it would make some of Chloe's curiosity dissipate. No such luck.

"And what about that cool Advent calendar box? Did she give that to you too?"

I nodded, forking up more salad like a deranged hungry rabbit.

"She took the time to make it? Seems like she likes you, Aunt Evie. Like…*likes* you."

"That's possible," I hedged. "It's equally possible that she just wanted me to have the appropriate Christmas things."

"You're so clueless it'd be funny if it wasn't so sad," Chloe said, not softening her words at all. "Do I need to hang some mistletoe in here for you two idiots?" Before I could think of what to say to that, Chloe barreled on. "I'm finished. Dinner was great, thanks. May I please be excused to finish my homework?"

"Sure," I said, refusing to adhere to my family's response of "you may," always said in a haughty, looking-down-their-nose tone.

Chloe took her plate and cup into the kitchen, rinsed them off and stacked them in the dishwasher. I was still eating, and she went back to where she was set up in the living room, sitting on the floor using the coffee table as a desk. Oh to be young with a flexible spine.

I was the first person to admit that Chloe's idea for Annika's gift had merit, and as I cleaned up after dinner, I made a mental list of things I could collect to make up a Saint Nikolaus gift. Most things would be free, costing only time and gas or foot power. Loopholes for the win.

As if she knew I was thinking about her, Annika texted not long after Pete had collected Chloe. *Are you busy tonight?*

Not at all.

Would you like some company? Because I would.

I answered immediately in the affirmative, and told her to come by whenever. Whenever was in ten minutes. She arrived with a bag of corn chips, a bag of marshmallows, and a bottle of pinot.

After the wine had been poured, I asked, "Have you had dinner? There's a fuc—fairly large amount of lasagna left. Salad too."

Annika pointed to the chips and marshmallows. "This will be my dinner."

"That's not dinner," I said, already fetching a plate to dish up leftovers. Her mouth twisted, and I just knew a "You keep feeding me" speech was incoming, so I cut her off. "It's fine. I like taking care of people, and there's so much left over. Assuming you like lasagna, and salad."

"Ja, I do. Thank you."

"You're welcome."

"You must have had loving, caring parents to teach you to take care of people," Annika ventured.

When I thought I could talk without saying something rude, I answered, "Not at all. My sister and I were raised by nannies for most of our young lives because that's just what my family does. And as we got older, I realized it was probably for the best. The fact I care for people is *despite* my parents." I exhaled loudly, frustrated that I'd allowed some of the annoyance about my parents, that I usually kept boxed away, out in the open.

"Oh," she said quietly. "I'm sorry. You said the other day…about your parents and Christmas. I'm sorry," Annika repeated, more forcefully now.

"It's fine, really, you have nothing to apologize for. When I told them I'm a lesbian, they couldn't or wouldn't accept me for who I am. So after some deep soul-searching, I decided I didn't need their toxicity in my life and gracefully stepped out of the family. Not…out-out, like disowned. I'm still a Phillips and I'm still involved in official family things. But we do *not* communicate other than about those official things." And even then, I only communicated with my father, or one of my mother's assistants. I drank a sacrilegiously large gulp of pinot. "Heather was upset but supportive. My parents were…relieved I think. It's easier to sweep things under the hand-knotted Persian rug than face it and maybe change the type of person you are."

Annika looked genuinely upset. "That's terrible. I'm so sorry."

"I was too." I made myself smile. "Until I realized how much lighter I felt without their constant disapproval hanging over my head."

Her forehead furrowed. "Why do they disapprove of you? Is it just because of your sexuality?"

"Yes. But also, I haven't followed what's expected of me. I have an MBA from Harvard, but it's not a law degree like my father wanted. Not that it matters, because I don't use my degree at all so it wouldn't matter which one I had. They don't approve of me being a 'comic-book artist' at all. Like, I'm a bestseller, I've won awards and stuff. They should be proud, but they aren't."

"And what is expected of you?"

I could tell she wasn't probing for the sake of probing—she really wanted to know. But discomfort about having to explain my life to this woman I was attracted to made my stomach churn.

People within the social set into which I was born didn't care that I'd rejected the family mold, but I didn't spend much time with those people anymore. I'd had girlfriends who could claim ancestry similar to mine, and they were fine, but there was never any deep connection. It felt like everyone was floating from one superficial relationship to another when I wanted a connection, wanted permanence. I tried to move out of that group, tried to be more "normal," but most Bostonians know the implications of my name and it *always* got weird. I'd realized early on that it was just easier to date within my circle—I hated that phrase—and deal with never getting what I wanted, or just not date at all. Eventually, I'd just chosen the latter.

I huffed out a breath, and prepared myself for the moment. The moment everything would change from before she knew to after she knew. I'd had this moment happen so many times that I could almost list the reactions as they'd happen. A few people had strayed from the path, but not many and not by much.

First would be the shock. Then the disbelief. Then the interest. Then the weird, uncomfortable interest.

I *could* lie. But I didn't want to lie to her. So I didn't. "My family is *very* wealthy, Annika. I won't tell you how wealthy, because I honestly don't know the exact amount, and talking about it is gross. But you know my last name, so you can figure it out yourself if you want to spend five minutes on the Internet. I mean, there's even a street, just over there"—I pointed behind myself—"with my last name on it." I wasn't going to bore her with details of my family. If she decided to Google me or my family name, she'd find out everything she wanted to know about the Phillipses.

"Oh! Phillips Street!" she said excitedly. "I did not even connect that with you."

That made something in my chest hurt—she was probably the first person to not do so. "Yeah. Both sides of my family have been in Boston for a very long time. That ancestry, that wealth? It comes with an equal, or greater amount of expectation. Expectations I can't meet. Well, I could, if I didn't want to live authentically and all that. And if my family wasn't so disappointed with who I am."

Realization dawned on her face. "I wondered about—I mean, I'm sure being a graphic novel artist pays well, but…you drink very nice wine and this is an expensive neighborhood and you live in a very nice apartment. I like it here a lot, but I could not afford to buy here and this rent would stretch me if I were here for more than a year."

I agreed, "Yes, it is an expensive neighborhood, but not the most expensive in Boston. Luckily I don't pay rent."

Her eyes widened. "Oh. You…own your apartment?"

I held back a nervous swallow. "I own this building."

"Oh." I could almost see her doing the math, trying to figure out how much this old Beacon Hill building was worth. And then her doing the mental gymnastics of realizing I was technically her landlord.

"Is that weird?" I sighed. "It's weird. I know it's weird." I held back another sigh and waited for the inevitable moment when she decided that either I was too different from her—I wasn't, except for my bank balance—or that she wasn't comfortable with the perceived disparity.

Annika didn't hesitate. "Ja, it is a little bit weird."

"I really don't have anything to do with managing it, or the tenants or anything like that. And I didn't buy it. I inherited it. I think my grandmother wanted to make sure I stayed in Beacon Hill because of the history my family has in the area." I was aware that the more I talked, the faster my heart beat. "My mother hates it, because it's not some thirty-million dollar, too-many-bedrooms-and-bathrooms house like my parents' main residence on Nantucket, or their winter vacation house in Greenwich, or their "just in case" place in Aspen, or their…well, you get the idea." I'd had enough of empty bedrooms as a kid. "And to make it worse for them, I live on the north slope not the south. So that means where I live is absolutely 'beneath a Phillips.'" I forced a laugh. "I love it here. I love seeing my neighbors." But I could still quietly go about my life with relative anonymity. Except, now, I'd let the cat out of the bag, and a not-small part of me worried that I'd just ruined everything with Annika.

"I like it here too," she admitted. "And I don't know anything about Boston, or your family. And honestly, I don't think I need to."

My voice cracked a little when I said, "No?"

She shook her head.

I tried not to look too desperately grateful. "In case you're wondering, or worried about me evicting you, I won't. I can't. Not that I'd want to," I hurriedly added. "Like I said, I have nothing to do with the tenancy arrangements in the buildings I own." When I'd looked at my business account emails and found the one from this property manager about my new tenant, with Annika's application and credit stuff attached, I hadn't even looked at the documents.

"I did just think about that. I never thought you would, but…" She shrugged. "Also, did you just say buildings? That is, you have more than one?"

I nodded. "Real estate is a sound investment, especially in this city. And sound investments fund some of my philanthropic ventures."

Her mouth twitched. "Philanthropic. So…how many hospitals do you have named after you, Evangeline Phillips?"

Thankfully it was obvious she was just teasing, and I went along with the gag, waving dismissively. "Only three."

Annika's eyebrows shot up. "Ah. Then you're not all that important, are you? I thought you needed at least five hospitals and one university named after you to be classed as a true philanthropist."

"Well. I'd better raise the rent so I can get more hospitals named after me." I frowned. "How much *is* rent?" I was embarrassed to ask, but such things were the purview of my real estate managers.

"Four thousand, three hundred dollars per month."

"Oh. Yeah, that's fair for a two-bedroom in Beacon Hill I think."

"Ja, I realized that. And, I'm happy to fund philanthropy through you with my rent. Can we put *my* name on a hospital?"

Laughing, I agreed, "Sure. Just remind me."

She frowned, her teeth briefly finding her lower lip. "When did you...leave your family but not really leave it?"

"I turned twenty-one and got access to a trust fund and my place on the family foundation board, and then I told my parents I was gay. Fifteen years ago. Almost sixteen." I'd always been closer to my dad than my mom and it stung that he'd just gone along with my mother's "disappointment" and not tried to show her it didn't matter who I was in love with. "My mother didn't know me at all. She thought she did, but she didn't. Doesn't. So I guess she felt...wounded by my coming out, by not seeing it. The problem is, when my mother feels wounded, she turns that hurt on everyone else. So instead of support, I got vitriol.

"And I know it was kind of underhanded of me, waiting until I came into the final amount of money from them, but Heather wanted me to be careful. I didn't think they would, *could* deny me that trust money but you never know. I wanted to tell them years before that, when I was thirteen and I knew I didn't like boys, but yeah. I was a coward."

Annika's eyes were soft, understanding. "I don't think it's being a coward. You can do a lot of good with money."

"Thanks. And yeah, you're right. That makes me feel slightly better for selling myself out for it." I laughed dryly. "Heather said I deserved it, that I could be a lazy philanthropist, and if I ever had kids then I'd want to give it to them. I said I wouldn't, have kids that is, and she said she was having kids so I'd need to help her with their trusts, so I *needed* that second trust fund." There was no laugh for that.

"Second trust fund?"

"Yeah," I sighed. "My family is good at holding on to their money. We have trust funds upon trust funds. Building wealth is a skill passed down the generations. That, and being a highly regarded member of society."

"I see," Annika mused. "So...you're a little bit fancy then?"

I laughed so hard I had to make sure I didn't pee. When I could finally talk again, I managed to deadpan, "Oh yeah, totally. You've seen me in my home, all dressed up every day, so you know exactly how fancy I am. Like it's just Champagne and caviar. Everywhere. All the time."

Thankfully she seemed to get the sarcasm. "I've never had it. Caviar. But I have had plenty of Champagne."

"It's disgusting," I said instantly. "And I know this because there really was caviar all the time with my parents. My dad would have it for every meal if he didn't think it was gauche to flaunt wealth." Phillipses didn't need to flaunt our wealth, our name was enough to show who we were. Unless you were a blissfully clueless adorable German. "Personally, I think it tastes like eating the whole ocean, even the dead marine creatures floating around in the sea."

"Interesting. I like seafood, so maybe I'll like something that tastes like dead marine creatures."

"Well, if you like seafood then you're in the right city. Home of lobster rolls and oysters."

"So I have heard. And now I need to add caviar to my list of things I should try while I'm here. Not that I think caviar is exclusive to Boston, but…you told me about it, so now, to me, it is."

I made a mental note to get her some quality caviar to try, though I'd have to talk to a few people because I was the furthest thing from a caviar connoisseur possible. I exhaled loudly. "I know I'm a cliché, the ultra-wealthy woman trying to ignore most of the things her wealth brings."

"I did not think that at all."

"No?" It came out hopeful, almost childishly so.

"No." Annika's eye contact was intense, piercing without being challenging. She took a step forward, right into my personal space. "Do you want to know what I *am* thinking?" she asked, her voice low and with a promise of something delicious.

Swallowing hard, I nodded.

As if she knew exactly what thought had just passed through my head, Annika's mouth quirked. But she didn't say what I'd expected. "I'm thinking that I want to tell you about my first day at work, and I am starving. So. Evie. Are you going to give me some of that lasagna, or am I really having corn chips and marshmallows for my dinner?"

CHAPTER TEN

Annika

After two intensive days at work, trying to acclimate and learn all the moving parts of my team and the project, I was more than ready for some relaxation. To construct a multilingual app, we needed native-level speakers to ensure correctness in each iteration. After a few disastrously incorrect translations in early apps, Pyramid had expanded into the successful multinational, multilingual corporation it was today. The translators worked dual duty, primarily functioning as artists, coders, developers and the like. I wasn't the only person in the Boston office who wasn't American.

But…there was a downside of having people from so many countries working on one project—differing work environment expectations—which was why on this Tuesday as I walked home from the T station, I almost wished it were Friday. Nobody on my team was lazy or insolent, but they all had different ideas about how to approach the project and it was my job to guide them all in the same direction, ensuring their complementary skills remained complementary.

A familiar man had just opened the front door of my building, and when he turned to close it and saw me a few feet away with my keys in hand, held it open until I hurried inside. Evie's brother-in-law was very tall, and very handsome, in the rugged-yet-groomed, ultramasculine way which had always appealed to me. And if I wasn't so fixated on his sister-in-law, I might have examined him a little closer, been open to attraction. But there was nothing when I looked at him, not even the beginnings of a spark, nothing like the instant zing that had hit me the moment I'd first seen Evie.

He smiled. "You're Evie's new neighbor, right?" he asked in a deep voice that matched his appearance. When I nodded, his smile brightened as he introduced himself. "I'm Peter Minogue. Pete. Evie's brother-in-law."

Shaking the offered hand, I smiled at his rambling introduction, which was almost identical to Evie's "Evie-Evangeline" spiel the day we'd met. I backtracked to ask, "Minogue? As in Kylie?"

His expression didn't change when he answered, "Yes, she's my cousin."

My eyebrows shot up. "Really?" I asked.

Pete grinned widely. "No. She's Australian. I'm not. I mean, maybe she's some far-off relative of my family? But I doubt it, and I don't know her."

I waggled a forefinger at him. "Ahh, you got me with your joke. You're funny. And I'm Annika Mayer," I said warmly. "It's nice to meet you, officially, Pete, and I'm so glad I ran into you. Would you like to get coffee, or a drink with me? Sometime soon?" It was perhaps a little bit underhanded, but I had no idea what to give Evie as gifts, and I'd suddenly had the great idea to ask this man who would know her well.

He couldn't hide his surprise—to be fair, a near-stranger asking you out for drinks *was* forward and maybe strange—and his mouth opened and closed before he spluttered, "Uh…sure, yeah. That, um, that sounds great." I detected no hint of attraction toward me, and tried not to seem relieved. Not that I minded people being attracted to me, obviously, but it would be nice to spend time with a guy without worrying about subtext.

"When are you free?" I asked.

He relaxed a little bit, his confidence growing now that he'd apparently moved past my forwardness. "Most nights. I can always ask Evie if she's okay with Chloe staying for a while longer so we can go out."

"Okay, how is tomorrow night?" I wanted it over as soon as possible so I could start planning. With a smile, I added, "But you'll have to pick the place because I'm still very new in town." I knew it was risky going out with a guy I didn't know, but he was Evie's brother-in-law, which made me trust him for that reason alone. And we'd be in public. Plus, it wasn't like he didn't already know where I lived.

"Sure." Pete nodded slowly. "Let me check with Chloe and Evie, and I'll let you know? Do you mind if I knock on your door in ten minutes or so and we can make plans?"

"Of course, that is fine."

"Great." He gestured with a single forefinger toward the stairs leading up to the second floor. "I'll just run on up now and talk to them."

I followed him, thinking it was nice of him to go up first so he wasn't behind me where all I would think about was him staring at my ass, because there were few other places to look when walking behind someone going up stairs. That thought made me think of the first day I'd met Evie, because I'd had that exact same thought as she'd followed me up the stairs, and I hadn't cared. I'd wanted her to check out my ass. I'd wanted to check out hers.

Pete gave me a cheery wave before he knocked on Evie's door, and I returned it as I walked up the hall to mine. I divested myself of my coat, laptop bag, and handbag, and valiantly resisted the overwhelming urge to shed my work clothes in favor of comfortable sweatpants and a hoodie, because Pete would be coming across the hall any moment now. It didn't bother me if Evie saw me so comfortably attired, but I barely knew her brother-in-law and felt like I should make some sort of effort to appear put together.

In less than five minutes, there was a knock on my door. Pete smiled crookedly, shyly. It was a handsome, charming smile, and I could see how he would have women lining up to be with him. But from what I'd gathered from Evie, he was still single after his wife's death.

"So," he began. "Chloe is deep in her homework and wants to keep going, so they suggested we do drinks tonight, now, if that suits you?" He hastened to add, "But tomorrow is also fine. Anything is fine."

It seemed fumbling over decisions ran in Evie's family. Ordinarily, indecision frustrated me, but not in Evie. And not much in Pete.

There was something about his demeanor that made me wonder what exactly Evie and Chloe had said about him going for drinks with me, so I decided to take charge. "Let's go now."

He seemed relieved I'd made a decision right away. "Great. I'll just let them know. See you back here in a few minutes?"

I nodded my assent then ducked back inside and straight into my bathroom to check I looked presentable to go out for drinks. After a quick makeup touch-up, I fluffed out my hair, gathered my handbag and coat, and went into the hall to wait for Pete.

Evie popped her head out of the door and waved when she saw me—it was so nice of her to let me know she knew I was with her brother-in-law. Women looking out for one another and all of that. But I couldn't help the fleeting wish that I was going out for drinks with her.

Pete had removed his tie and suit jacket, and wore his thick wool coat unbuttoned. He held the front door for me. "Have you been out in town much?" he asked.

"Not at all, aside from a little bit of shopping, buying furniture, and going to work."

"Ah. There's a great bar about five minutes' walk from here, called 1928. It shouldn't be too busy on a Tuesday, but if it is, a friend of mine owns it, so I can name-drop to get us a table. Are you hungry?"

"A little bit, yes."

"Great," he enthused. "I think the food is as good as the drinks."

We walked the few blocks to the bar and I could tell he was deliberately slowing his long strides so I could keep up. I pointed at the slightly uneven, worn brick pavement. "I love this."

Pete stood patiently while I studied it. "Yeah," he agreed fondly. "There's plenty of cool old stuff in Boston."

The restaurant was warm and inviting, and we were shown to a seat almost immediately. When the server tried to put us in a darker, more intimate corner near the back, Pete gently rerouted him toward a window seat. I was grateful for his thoughtfulness and also the clear sign that he didn't think this was a date.

The wine list was beyond extensive and as well as the standards, the cocktail selection was fun and interesting. I ordered a French 75 cocktail, and Pete a Reissdorf Kölsch, which I had enjoyed a number of times before moving to München. I smiled to myself, thinking of Evie and her story about her removal from a beer hall.

"Good choice," I said once our drink orders had been taken.

"Did I pronounce it correctly?" he asked, barely suppressing a wince. "I always feel embarrassed speaking other languages, like my accent is all wrong."

Smiling, I asked, "He understood you, didn't he?" At Pete's nod, I continued, "Then you pronounced it just fine. I don't pronounce a lot of words in English correctly, I'm sure, and I have an accent that's all wrong too."

"I suppose that's true," he agreed thoughtfully.

"And if you said that in Germany, they would understand. But… there's an umlaut, so it's pronounced Kölsch, not Kolsch, so not 'ohl' but more like—" I frowned, trying to separate out that one sound and explain it for a person who didn't normally make the sound. I remembered something I'd told Rachel while she was learning some German. "Like you're saying *ay* from day but…with a round mouth so your face will look like an O with an umlaut." I made quotation marks with two fingers, like they were eyes above a round O mouth. Laughing, I said, "I'm sorry, it's hard to explain how to separate a single sound from a word in my own language like that."

He tried it out a few times, copying me, trying to wrap his mouth around the sound.

"You're a natural," I said warmly. "You can now order beer with the aptitude of any German."

Pete laughed. "I can see why Evie likes you."

"The feeling is mutual," I said before I'd policed my thoughts. And because I'd already spoken without moderating myself, and because Pete was obviously Evie's friend, I spoke out again. "She's great. It has been so wonderful to meet someone who felt like an instant friend."

He gave me a slightly quizzical look, but didn't push the issue further—thankfully, because I feared I might crack under his pressure if he started questioning me as to whether I felt more than just friendship for his sister-in-law. Which I did. The problem wasn't that he'd question me—I'd never had an issue standing up under scrutiny. The problem was that I didn't know how to classify what I felt for Evie.

The quizzical look transformed into a warm smile. "I'm glad. Now, anything on the food menu catch your eye?"

"Everything," I said, laughing.

He joined in the laughter. "Me too."

Peter Minogue was quite possibly one of the nicest men I'd ever met. We discovered we shared a common interest in music, which led to an enjoyable conversation. I discovered that my initial feelings were correct and there was no attraction between us, unless he was burying his deep in the ground, which I couldn't imagine because he was so earnest. My attraction was already allocated elsewhere and I didn't need the confusion of having two so close to home, two who were related, even if only by marriage.

We shared a charcuterie board—further proof there was no attraction, because nobody who was expecting anything intimate would eat mounds of sopressa and capicola—as well as crab cakes which were incredible and so fresh I wanted to eat the whole plate, and something called pigs in a blanket which were actually not bad for something so horribly named. He was polite and charming, funny and sweet, and it felt so nice to be out with someone, just getting to know them, but with no romantic expectations at all.

After ordering another drink, I asked, "Has Evie told you about our Christmas mesh-up?"

Pete grinned. "She sure has. I think it sounds amazing."

"I think so too." After popping some prosciutto into my mouth, I chewed thoughtfully. "I have a problem, Pete, and I have to tell you that I invited you here partly for false reasons."

He appeared mildly panicked. "And what reasons might that be?"

"I need you to help me with what to buy Evie for our Christmas celebrations. Saint Nikolaus Day is in a few days, and I don't know what to buy for her. And then there is Christmas Eve, and Christmas Day gifts." I raised my hands, fingers spread wide. "I don't know her well enough to know what to buy, and I do not like giving meaningless gifts."

The panic disappeared, and was replaced by a conspiratorial joy. "Ah, I see."

I turned on my most charming smile. "So, can you help me? You have known her for a long time, so you are clearly the best person to help me."

He nodded around chewing his mouthful. "I suppose I am." Pete leaned his elbows on the table, clasping his hands. "Evie has been my best friend since high school and I know her better than I know anyone. Christmas is…not her favorite time of year. Even when we were kids. Everyone else would be talking about what they wanted, what they were giving their parents, which holiday home they were going to, and Evie would engage superficially, but never share what her family did at the holidays. And then when her parents—" Pete cut himself off abruptly.

"She has told me a little bit about her parents," I said quietly, wanting to reassure him that he wasn't breaking a confidence. I didn't want him to give me any intimate details, but I wanted him to know that I knew, at least on the surface, what had happened.

"Oh. Okay. Well, that's her story to share, but yeah." He huffed out a loud breath. "We've always had her around for a Christmas meal before we leave for family commitments, when Heather was still with us too. But other than that, it's like the whole experience has been expunged from her brain. Christmas just isn't a thing for Evie."

Expunged. I took a few moments to puzzle over the word, and finally worked out the meaning with context clues. "That's very interesting, because she agreed to share Christmas with me immediately."

He looked confused. "Did she?"

I nodded. "Yes. She didn't even think about it."

"That *is* interesting," he mused. Pete brightened, and with a shrug that seemed to throw off whatever he'd been confused about, said, "She must really like you and enjoy spending time with you if she agreed to it." Then, almost to himself, he murmured, "This is excellent."

"I hope so." Scheisse, why couldn't I keep my thoughts inside my head?

Pete paused spearing a little cucumber and looked up. His expression was a curious mix of hope, wariness, and pleasure. "She likes personal things. Like something that you take the time to make. Even if it's simple. Especially if it's simple. Um…" He blew out a breath. "She used to be into rock-climbing, running marathons, she loves skiing way more than a normal person. She loves to travel and find little out of the way places to eat and drink. She loves art, all types of art. She's not huge into music."

I nodded along with his information, some of which I'd gathered up myself during conversations with Evie.

"Mostly, she just likes knowing someone has thought about her, and given her a gift that's not just…generic, you know?"

"Ja, I do know." I felt the same way, preferring someone to have spent their time and effort and thought, rather than money on something that was not meaningful.

"I heard you made her an Advent calendar instead of buying one. She would have really loved that."

"That is good to know," I murmured. "So, you've known her since you were teenagers." I grinned mischievously. "Is she the same now as when she was younger?" The answer would have zero impact on my gifts for her. It was nothing more than intense curiosity about the woman I was attracted to. I'd learned a lot about her, enough to know I wanted to know more, and hearing stories about young Evie would help fill in the gaps. And I'd gained enough of a sense of Pete to recognize that he was protective of Evie and wouldn't share anything she wouldn't be comfortable with people knowing.

He smiled fondly. "Pretty much, yeah. But she was so scrappy in school. Competitive as anything, *with* everything. Annoyingly so." Despite the word *annoying*, he was still smiling and I could tell he wasn't actually annoyed.

I tried to parse a word, and failed. "Scrappy?"

"Um, kind of…not like a fighter, but pushy, determined, feisty. But also so caring and kind. And smart as anything, she had excellent grades, and she also did all the after-school activities, intellectual and sporting—field hockey, lacrosse, soccer. And art, god she was incredible even back then. She always did all the design stuff for any event. And this one time, she got caught in class drawing a portrait of our teacher, because she always has this look when she's drawing so it gives her away. He was furious, and then had to keep pretending to be furious as he confiscated it, even though you could tell he'd realized how amazing it was. He probably took it home."

For some reason, the idea of young Evie indulging in her artistic passions thrilled me. As a young person, I'd had no idea where my working life might lead. I'd studied a broad range of subjects but had been good with computer sciences and thus fell into coding and software. I loved my job, but I'd often wondered if maybe I was a lawyer or doctor or veterinarian or engineer or accountant just waiting for someone to show me exactly what to do. "Ja, I've seen that look. It was so funny when we were planning Christmas and she was drawing."

Pete went still. "She was drawing while talking with you?"

"Yes."

His eyebrows shot up. "It's probably a drawing of you. She likes to sketch from real life. You should ask her to show it to you, she's really good."

I'd suspected that from the brief glimpse, but the confirmation made my skin heat. "I might do that. Can you tell me more about her from your time at school? You said she was kind back then too."

Pete grinned. "She really was. That hasn't changed one bit. So, in ninth grade I think it was, I had these jocks picking on me. I was on the basketball team, because, well…" He gestured at himself. "I was built like a flagpole, all height, no bulk. But I wasn't great at sports. I was uncoordinated and nerdy."

"You were nerdy?" I asked, genuinely shocked.

"Mhmm. I know, right?" he said, chuckling. "And we attended a school that was filled with Boston's wealthiest kids, and a lot of them were just horrible people, but she gave zero fucks about who their parents were. Maybe because she's a Phillips, but mostly it's just Evie. So after a few months, she'd apparently had enough. Probably enough of me complaining about it. She marched right into the boys' locker room before practice—thank god we were all dressed—and just laid into them about being weak-ass bullies."

I grinned, able to imagine her doing just that. "Did they stop bullying you?"

He threw his head back and laughed. "God no. They started teasing me about my little woman having to save me. Kids are *mean*."

"Yes, they are." Smiling, I admitted, "I was very shy as a child, it took me some time to learn confidence, and thankfully the other children mostly just left me alone."

"Ah, you needed an Evie in school then," he said brightly. "She's someone you want on your side. You know, she started this Equality Club, with a whole charter and everything, it was huge. She really should have been a lawyer, much better than me, like she would be saving the world so hard." He shrugged. "She's saving it in a different way, I suppose. She just loves to help people."

"Ja, I've seen that. She was so kind to me when I moved in." Something warm flooded through me at the memory of how she'd arrived with wine and then rushed back to her apartment to feed me too. "I had hardly anything in my house and she just…helped, like it was the most natural thing in the world. But she was almost shy about it? It was very sweet, and very cute."

"Yeah, that's Evie," Pete said fondly. "I wish she'd let someone help her for a change." The look he gave me was pointed and made my heart do a funny little flutter.

We moved on to other topics, though he kept bringing Evie into them, which was fine with me. After what felt like a few hours of easy conversation, Pete glanced at his watch. I took the subtle hint. "Is it time to collect Chloe and go home?"

He grimaced. "Yeah, sorry. And I should probably get a good night's sleep. I have mountains of trial prep to do this week."

The evening had come to a natural, easy conclusion, and I didn't argue. "I wish I were as dedicated about going to bed early."

He laughed. "Dad life…it's not glamorous. Thanks for asking me to come out for a drink, Annika. This has been really great. If you ever feel like another friendly evening, or coffee during the week, then *please* contact me."

I agreed readily, then insisted on paying because I'd invited him out. Pete gently insisted on splitting the cost, even though I'd had two drinks and he'd only had one. So we split it. We walked home, still talking easily, and exchanged numbers while standing outside Evie's door. And I was grateful I'd found myself another friend. Because while his sister-in-law was certainly a friend, I knew, deep down, that I wanted more than just friendship with her.

CHAPTER ELEVEN

Evie

    I spent most of the day shirking off work so I could organize Annika's Saint Nikolaus things. I visited local food places—even the ones I thought were horrible, because who knew what food Annika liked—and collected menus and any free loyalty cards. I used my charming smile and wit, and maybe a little begging, to nab a few tea and coffee samples from Silver Dove and Gracenote.
    I flexed my tourist muscles to get her a map of the Freedom Trail, pamphlets on stuff like the *USS Constitution*, the Museum of Fine Arts, the Boston Public Library, and Castle Island. By the time I was done, I had a two-inch stack of pamphlets and menus, enough loyalty cards to fill any wallet, and information on gyms offering free trials. She still hadn't used my treadmill, but I hadn't heard her leaving for a gym before work in the mornings either. I stopped for mediocre coffee and a delicious Boston kreme at Dunks, which I consumed after ordering a gift card with a $10 balance to get Annika started. Dunks was a Boston institution and she should be indoctrinated. I mentally cracked my knuckles. Done and done.
    Christmas Eve and Day were going to be a little harder. I still had no idea what to get her. Maybe it was time to pop around for a friendly visit and do some sneaky recon at her place, get a sense of what she

was into. Or I could grill her on the drive to the Christmas tree farm to pick out our shared tree on Friday. She'd said I should get to know her so I'd know what to buy her, right?

Pete arrived just after five thirty to collect Chloe, and I'd barely said hi to him when I heard the building door opening downstairs. I tried to school my expression into something that wasn't too eagerly anticipatory. It could be any one of my neighbors, but based on the time, it was probably Annika. And, based on the look Pete gave me, I was absolutely certain I was failing at the "acting casual" thing. She appeared at the top of the stairs, a smile lighting up her face when she saw us.

Annika looked great in clothes (and undoubtedly out of clothes too) but there was something about her work outfits that made my heart beat just a little faster. Today she was flowing instead of fitted— low-heeled boots under loose eggplant-hued wide-legged pants, and a cream-colored flowy silk blouse under the long gray wool coat she was unbuttoning as she walked.

She shifted her handbag to the crook of her left elbow. "Hallo, Pete. Hallo, Chloe," she said, waving cheerfully. Her expression softened as she looked at me. "Hi, Evie."

That glance in my direction was enough to send a rush of joy through me, and I managed a quick, "Hey" in response.

Pete's smile for Annika was wide and genuine and made my stomach churn. An annoying tinge of whatever I felt that I was trying to ignore but if I stopped to really think about it, was totally jealousy, flared. I hated jealousy, especially in myself, but there it was. Actually, maybe it wasn't jealousy so much as a type of wishful thinking.

Whatever it was, it was stupid because Annika and I had spent time together and Pete was not my competitor. If she decided she wanted to ask him out and by some miracle he accepted then I was happy for them both. Pete was my best and oldest friend and if he was good enough for my sister then he was certainly good enough for the woman I had a crush on. I should have been happy for Pete, jumping back into the dating pool. I *was* happy for him. Ecstatic even. But why was he jumping in with the woman I wanted to maybe date? The only woman I'd wanted to be with in a long time.

"Annika, hey." He stepped in behind Chloe, resting his hands on her shoulders. "So I checked out McCartney's guitar. His first bass, the one that was stolen, *was* a 1961 Höfner."

She tsked him teasingly. "What did I tell you?"

"You were right and I'm a dumbass for even questioning your wisdom," Pete said somberly.

Her laugh burst out. "I do love to hear that I'm wise." She moved to stand by me, gracing me with a warm smile and a lingering back touch. Her expression softened as we made eye contact, before she turned back to Pete. "Are you still okay with sharing your truck for the tree?"

"Course I am," he confirmed brightly.

"Thank you. That's very helpful." Annika's focus moved to me. "And we're still buying a Christmas tree on Friday, when I come home from work, aren't we?"

I nodded. "Yep. All set."

"Good." Her hand slid down to just above my waist and I felt the gentle press of her fingertips before she moved away. "I'll see you later then." She gave Pete's shoulder a quick pat, said something under her breath to him, which made him laugh, and then walked up the hall, opened her door, and disappeared.

I turned back to Pete and Chloe when I realized I'd just dumbly watched my neighbor walk away. Thankfully Pete was preoccupied and didn't catch my obvious staring. Chloe, on the other hand, had definitely caught it and I shook my head at her wide-eyed expression.

After a quick search through his daughter's backpack, Pete turned to Chloe. "Where's your math book? And aren't you missing your basketball bag?"

Chloe's expression turned comically confused. "Uh…yeah."

He turned her around and gave her a gentle push toward the door. Once she was out of sight, he sighed and pulled the door mostly closed. "Is forgetfulness a puberty thing?" he muttered.

"Maybe. You were pretty dumb as a teenager." I dodged his playful arm punch.

"You're lucky you're my best friend."

"I am," I agreed. As soon as I'd said it, an uncomfortable sensation wriggled under my skin. "And have you made a new friend, Pete?"

"Huh?"

I lowered my voice. "Annika."

Understanding finally dawned on his face. "Oh. Yeah. She's great."

Every muscle in my body suddenly felt as if it was contracting. "Yes, she is." I glanced up the hall to confirm her door was closed—unless we shouted, Annika shouldn't be able to hear us. Still, I grabbed his arm and dragged him toward the stairs, further away from her door. Quietly, I asked, "So, how *was* your date with her last night?" Good job. That sounded interested and caring, and totally not at all jealous. I wasn't jealous. But I was something I didn't have a word for yet.

"Not a date," he answered automatically, matching my voice for volume. "And it's lucky I love you so much and don't mind talking about you, because she kept asking about you last night. Kept bringing you up. Not in an obnoxious way, but in a way that made me think that *maybe* I wasn't the person she wanted to be out having dinner and drinks with…"

"What do you mean?"

He rolled his eyes expansively, exaggerating his exasperation. "I have no idea how someone can be so aggressively clueless about something right in front of them. She's *into* you, Evie. Big time."

I crossed my arms over my chest, feeling oddly defensive about his expression. "Yeah, well. I'm into her big time too."

"So, why haven't you done anything about that?"

"Because…for one, I'm her landlord." It sounded lame, even to my ears.

"Only technically. Do you even know what goes on in this building?" It was a pointless question to which he already knew the answer. No, I didn't. "So, try again."

"Because…because…" I exhaled loudly. "What if we hook up and then afterward it's horrible and awkward and we have to interact because we live across the hall from each other?"

"What if it's not horrible and awkward, but amazing? What if it leads to something lasting?"

It couldn't lead to something lasting because Annika wasn't lasting. She would be leaving once her work project was done. I flailed for more reasons to not act on my attraction, because admitting that I couldn't deal with someone leaving me felt too raw. "I like her, Petey, a whole lot. She's becoming a friend and I don't want to ruin that for an—" I lowered my voice again in case Chloe overhead. "Orgasm or two."

"I think it'd be more than one or two," he said, his twitching mouth making his mustache jump.

I sure hoped so. "Look. She's easily a ten and I'm just…like, a really fun seven. Maybe an eight on a good day and if the light is great and I'm wearing makeup."

"God, I do not know where you and Heather got this faux modesty thing you both have. That Heather had," he corrected himself after a moment. "It's not from your parents."

Probably both of us trying to blend in instead of standing out when we already stood out so much. I gestured up and down his exceedingly tall, muscular frame. "I don't have the hot single dad hipster lumberjack thing going on like you. I'm just me." And *me* came with so much emotional baggage I needed a porter to help carry it around.

"For good reason," he deadpanned. "You've got your own thing going on, and your thing is great."

"My own thing." I snorted out a laugh, because if I didn't laugh I might cry. "Emotionally stunted and riddled with abandonment issues is a thing?" Abandonment… Sure, Annika wouldn't be abandoning me exactly, but she'd still be leaving once she'd finished the work she'd come here to do. "I'd have to be a fifteen to get her over all the behind-the-scenes shit I come with."

"Ah." Pete steepled his fingers in front of his barrel chest. "Ladies and gentlemen, we've arrived at the truth portion of the conversation."

"I hate you," I mumbled.

"Sure you do," he laughed.

"Look. I just…I don't know if I can do unattached. And I don't know if I can do attached, but only for short term. So I think it's better to just do nothing."

"Stop it." He pinched my lips together and I blew air between them to make a *pffthhhppfttt* sound, which did the trick, and he let go. "You've never just done nothing, Evie. Doing nothing is the opposite of what you do. It's like you're physically incapable of just sitting there, watching things go by. So why don't you just admit the truth?"

"And what's the truth, Dr. Minogue?"

"That you're afraid. Afraid to love someone so hard in case they don't love you back, and love you for you. Afraid to lose something."

"Exactly. And I'm absolutely going to lose her. She's not here for long, remember? And I know myself well enough to know that being with her a little will make me want to be with her a lot. And when I can't have that, then what will I do? Also, how am I supposed to have a relationship? I'm a side-mom for my niece, which I adore being, and you and Chloe are the most important things to me. I don't know how to fit someone else into that."

"That is the stupidest, lamest excuse for something I've ever heard. So be with her a lot. Figure it out. Anyone you deem worthy of allowing into your bubble with me and Chloe will fit. You're just too scared to examine your own bullshit to work out how."

I glared at him, infuriated that he was pushing my buttons and even more infuriated that he was right.

Chloe barged out through the door, holding both math book and basketball bag. She paused when she noticed we weren't right by the door anymore, then came right over. "Got 'em!"

It wouldn't have taken this long for her to get her things, which made me suspicious she'd heard us talking before I'd dragged Pete down the hall, and dawdled to let us have a conversation. "So you do," I agreed with too much cheer, glad my niece had interrupted a delve-into-Evie's-issues session.

Pete checked the stuff Chloe had just collected, then looked back to me. "Just think about it."

"Think about what?" Chloe asked.

"World peace," I said. She gave me a dubious look, but rather than get locked into another impromptu therapy session, I stretched up to hug Pete. Chloe consented to a hug, and I made sure to give her an extra-hard squeeze, which she tolerated without a single grumble. "Catch you guys tomorrow."

I waited until they were out of sight to go inside. But not before I'd stared for way too long at Annika's closed door. The stuff Pete had said about Annika being into me had stuck in my head. I'd kind of thought she was. Okay, I was sure she was. But she'd also been giving mixed signals, and she hadn't outright declared to me that she was into me.

Were they really mixed signals, though? Or was I so afraid of the intensity of my attraction, and what seemed to be the intensity of hers, that I was purposely ignoring what I thought I was experiencing?

Fuck it. I mean, fudge it. I grabbed my phone and my keys, and before I could second-guess myself, I locked my door and went up the hall to Annika's. She didn't respond to my knock, and the second-guessing I probably should have done earlier rushed at me. I waited for a minute and was preparing to do an abrupt about-face and pretend I'd never knocked when I got a text from Annika.

Shower. Ten minutes.

That gave me enough time to run back to my apartment and check my appearance and brush my teeth, which I should have done before knocking on Annika's door. What was I thinking, rushing over there wearing sweatpants and a hoodie that were absolutely due for laundry? I yanked off my outer layers and pulled on a pair of joggers and a long-sleeved blue Henley. And I knew myself well enough to know the only reason I'd changed was because I cared about what she thought.

Annika answered my second knock immediately. Her hair was down, wet from her shower. It smelled like she used a shampoo called Cool Forest Breezes or something. She'd changed into faded sweats which were tight enough to make me tell myself I needed to not stare, and a maroon hoodie. "Sorry, I was in the shower when you were knocking." She rubbed her phone against the leg of her sweatpants. "And I got my phone wet texting you."

"Oh." I swallowed the juvenile thing that'd come right to mind. But I left it in there, content with just thinking about how I'd like to make her wet in the shower.

"You changed your clothes?"

"Oh, yeah. It felt weird to come over wearing sweatpants."

"Why?" she asked, her eyes sweeping slowly over my body. "I'm wearing sweatpants."

"Well yeah, but you're in your own home."

"It's only me, Evie. So, why *did* you come over?" she asked, in a way that made me think she knew the answer.

"I haven't eaten yet and thought maybe we could grab dinner?" My voice rose hopefully at the end. "If you didn't have plans."

She laughed. "I do not have plans. I do not have plans most evenings. Do you like Mexican food?" Annika asked, arching an eyebrow. "Pete said the Sabroso Taqueria is good."

Funny, now I was with her, just the two of us, with her focus all on me, the mention of her closeness with Pete didn't spark discomfort the way it had before. "I do, and it is. I'm happy with that if you are. I'll eat anything on the menu, so go right ahead and order."

"Great. He also said you do not like cilantro and that you have to get the guacamole without it."

I wondered how much they'd talked last night if they'd reached "these are Evie's food dislikes" stage. And I also wondered why they talked so much about me. Because, like Pete had said, maybe "she's into you, Evie, big time."

While we waited for dinner to arrive, Annika poured me a glass of white wine, teasing me about the fact Mexican should really be accompanied by beer, which she poured into a glass for herself. She ushered me to the couch and dropped heavily onto it, exhaling a satisfied sigh. "Pete said you and he became friends in high school?"

"Yeah. We became friends pretty much instantly, thankfully with zero romantic interest between us." I smiled. "Even if I had been interested in dating guys, I don't think he would have even looked at me twice, romantically. Heather was the year above us and he had the biggest crush on her. It was hilarious. They started dating midway through our tenth grade and were together until the second she died." I tried to swallow the lump in my throat and failed, so I tried a mouthful of wine to help budge it. My words still came out tightly. "They were so in love, you could feel it just by being near them, they radiated it."

"That's amazing," she said, gushing a little.

"It really is. Of course, my parents didn't approve. Pete's family is wealthy, but nowhere near 'Phillips wealthy.' And they're originally from California but moved here for his dad's business, so that was against him as well." I shrugged, aiming for nonchalance. "But if you're…looking for someone to date, I don't think you could go wrong with Pete. He's a total dweeb, but he's the best, kindest man I know, and he gave me a niece who is one of my favorite people in the world, so for that, I love him more than almost anyone."

Her expression had softened as I professed my platonic love for my brother-in-law, and then it turned confused. "Dweeb?"

"Oh, uh—" I needed to start carrying an urban language dictionary around with me. "Not good with social situations, boring, nerdy."

"Oh." She laughed. "He seemed very competent in our social situation, not boring. *And* he was very helpful, telling me what kind of gifts you like."

My mouth fell open, then I spluttered, "That's cheating!"

Annika look utterly angelic. "Is it really? I don't recall discussing anything about reconnaissance. I was utilizing tools available to me."

I snorted out a laugh. "I'll tell Pete he's a tool."

She frowned, clearly trying to figure out what I'd meant. So I clarified, "A tool is a jackass, a stupid guy with a big ego." I shrugged. "Not sure where it came from. Pete's not really a tool in that etymological sense."

"Oh. No he is not a tool in that context. You're right, he's a really nice guy."

My heart dropped down past my stomach. "Yes, he is." My smile faltered for a moment and I forcibly pasted it back onto my face. "And he's single, as you know. I've tried to get him back out there on the dating scene, but he is staunchly resistant."

"That's nice to know, and yes, he did mention that you try to be his wingwoman."

"Mhmm. My sister was very clear that she didn't want him to be romantically lonely after she died, but that's obviously easier said than done when you're still madly in love with your wife who died of cancer seven years ago. You could do far worse than Pete." I felt the desperate urge to swallow nervously but managed to suppress it. "Assuming you're even interested in him. Or…in…dating someone."

"Oh. Ja, okay. I see. That would be hard for him. But," she said gently, "I do not want to date him. You are right, Pete is great, such a nice guy, and he is…very good-looking. I hope we can be good friends. Nothing more," she added, a hint of firmness in those last two words.

"Oh. Okay." Annika hadn't clarified with "I want to date you instead," so I just left it. But I didn't want to leave it. I wanted to do whatever the opposite of leaving it was. Picking it up and carrying it around with me?

"You have Chloe with you every weekday?" she mused, moving past dating to something deeper. "Do you want children of your own?"

"I don't think so, no. I mean, I have Chloe. And that pregnancy was so unpleasant that I never, *ever* want to do it again."

Annika's face went through a classic range of confusion, from *what the heck?* to *what the actual fuck?* "I don't think I understand," she said slowly. "Chloe is your niece? Not your daughter?"

I nodded. "That's right."

"But…*that* pregnancy? Yours? But Chloe? Sorry, I'm very confused."

"Mhmm." After a moment, it twigged. "Oh!"

I was acting as if Annika already knew my life story. We'd shared so many things, things that felt intimate for me, things that I'd share with a friend or partner. "I was the surrogate for Heather and Pete. They'd always wanted kids but Heather's super-aggressive breast cancer kind of threw a spanner in the works. But she was adamant she wanted a child and it was either refuse all cancer treatment so she could get pregnant and safely carry, which meant she'd likely only spend a few months with their child before she died of that super-aggressive cancer, or start treatment ASAP and have a surrogate carry for her. We all agreed that having her around to spend time with her child was the thing to do. It was a no-brainer for me to do it."

It'd taken some wrangling, because there were very few fertility specialists that were comfortable with me, never-had-a-kid Evie, being a surrogate, even if we avoided agencies and did it privately. But my parents' wealth, resources, and influence sat right alongside their desperate desire to have a grandchild, and here we were. They made it happen because the thought of an outsider carrying their grandchild wasn't "acceptable," and neither was airing our "dirty laundry" to a stranger. Luckily, I offered to do it before they'd thought of it because those would have been some awkward conversations with my parents and things were plenty awkward enough.

Annika brushed her fingertips over my forearm. "I think that is the most unselfish thing I've ever heard. You did that for your sister?"

"Of course. Being their surrogate meant I got both a niece *and* almost six more years with Heather."

"Does Chloe know?" She paused, her whole face screaming "I can't believe I just asked that," and hastened to add, "I'm sorry, that is none of my business."

"It's fine," I reassured her. "I'd be curious too. Yeah, she knows. We told her last year, much to the horror of my parents who felt it should be kept a secret, like it's dirty or something. She totally understands, doesn't seem at all weird about it." I laughed. "Now, when she's feeling like a little shi—like a little brat, she even calls me Aunt Incubator."

Annika laughed so long and so loud, I thought she might stop breathing. "Aunt Incubator," she said, still chuckling. "I love that. I love it a lot."

I grinned and leaned in, lowering my voice to conspiratorial. "Honestly, I kind of do too. But no, pregnancy and I were not friends at all. I felt so…wrong. Like I wasn't sick, there were no complications, it was just not a nice feeling. I love Chloe more than anything and I wouldn't take back what I did but I wouldn't want to do it again." Sighing, I added, "And my mother would probably start interfering in my life again, just because I had her grandchild in my uterus, again."

"Again? Was your mother interfering with your pregnancy?"

"No," I said tightly. "We only spoke about it a few times. She called when I was about four months along to berate me because she didn't think I was taking pregnancy seriously and that I might be harming the fetus, possibly their only chance at having a grandchild." My laugh caught in my throat. "I said sorry, couldn't talk, my skydiving plane was about to take off, and hung up on her. That was the last time my mother spoke to me. That night she sent a lengthy email which would have made me cry if I wasn't already expecting it." Instead of crying, I'd had a tantrum, and had only stopped because her words about harming the fetus had somehow penetrated—not that I'd been doing anything that would harm my sister's kid. I'd always treated Chloe like the precious cargo she was.

Annika's nose wrinkled like she'd smelled something foul. "She thought you were harming the baby…how?"

"By breathing. Eating. Exercising. Working. Just normal things. But I did all those things as a *lesbian*. You know, lesbian breathing. Lesbian eating. Lesbian attending prenatal care. And so on. So even though I helped provide their only grandchild, I'm still a lesbian. They just couldn't get past that. Actually no, it's my mother who can't get past it. I don't think my father really cares as long as I'm not actively disgracing the family name, but he just does whatever my mother tells him to."

"I see," Annika said carefully.

"Yeah, and then there was all the other sh…tuff around the pregnancy that just added to the unpleasantness. My girlfriend dumped me because of the surrogacy. Said she supported my 'journey' and that it was 'so noble,' blah blah bullshit, but she couldn't be with me while I was pregnant. And she got most of our friends in the divorce." Shrugging, I added, "And after Heather died, I just…retracted further into myself I guess. It was easier to just exist in my new normal than expend mental energy trying to change it." After Heather died I didn't feel like doing things. Eventually my friends stopped asking and then eventually they weren't my friends anymore. If they ever really were.

"Divorce?" The word rose an octave on the second syllable. "Also, that was a *shit*. Swear jar."

"I should never have told you about that." As I added yet another thing to my away-from-the-jar tally, I said, "And divorce is a figure of speech. We weren't married."

"Oh. Well, it sounds like she wasn't a particularly nice girlfriend then," Annika said, and I loved her for not mincing words.

"Not at all nice. She was vapid, intolerant, and I learned she was more interested in my family's assets than in me. It felt like she hated everything I did, even before the surrogacy." I frowned. "Now that I have distance and a little more wisdom under my belt, I honestly don't even know why I dated her, and for so long." Probably because she was part of the circle and I felt like I should. It was fine in the beginning, but it hadn't taken long for the cracks in her personality to show. I clamped my molars together, trying not to think of her voice.

You're not worth it…if you weren't a Phillips, nobody would date you…if your family wasn't rich you'd be nobody…you're an emotionally stunted idiot.

"She hated everything, like what?" Annika asked.

"Like…the way I drop my clothes on the floor instead of taking them off neatly and turning them the right way immediately before putting them in the hamper." My eyes widened. "I mean, I put them in the hamper after showering, I don't just leave them lying on the floor for hours or days."

The faintest blush dusted her cheeks, and she filled her mouth with beer like she was trying to smother a thought, or prevent it from escaping her mouth. Maybe she was thinking the same thing I was. That I would like to pull her clothes off and drop them onto the floor. I should really just kiss her. No, I shouldn't kiss her. She's technically my tenant. "So…yeah," I said hoarsely. "That's another chunk of my life story that you absolutely did not ask for."

"No, I didn't ask for it," she agreed. Her eyes softened at the edges, and after a long pause, Annika reached out and took my hand, squeezing gently. "But I'm very glad you decided to give it to me."

CHAPTER TWELVE

Annika

Tonight was all about self-care. Long relaxing bath, skincare mask, manicure, pedicure, soothing music, and a large glass of red wine. I'd probably switch to beer and order pizza, because I'd yet to try Boston pizza. Finding a nail place was also on my list of things to do, as was finding a hair salon. I'd probably just ask Rachel. She always looked great.

I'd briefly considered calling Evie to ask if she wanted to do something tonight, but a niggle of self-doubt gnawed at me. We'd spent a lot of time together in the ten days since we'd met, and I didn't want to come on too strongly. Especially when I was aware of my attraction to her, and was trying to balance that with all of my self-imposed rules about relationships. But I wanted to spend time with her, and the thought of spending the evening alone, even if I was doing something as relaxing as self-care, made me feel a little bit flat.

After our conversation last night, I was extra curious about her, especially after her revelation that she had carried her niece for her sister and Pete. She was right—it was noble and brave. And honestly? It made me fall just a little bit in love with her. Early, shallow love, just a fraction past attraction. Nothing that would break the rules of being in Boston.

I hadn't told Rachel that the woman I was attracted to was apparently very wealthy and owned the building in which I lived, and that I worried something might happen between us and I'd find myself apartment-hunting. Not that I *really* thought Evie would evict me if we had a fight or something—she'd confirmed she wouldn't. But it felt weird knowing that she owned the building, and who knew how many more around the country and maybe even in other countries.

But I understood why it had never come up in conversation before. We barely knew each other. Revealing private details about family and financial status didn't usually happen in just a few weeks. And yet, she had revealed it.

Once I'd painted my toenails, I hobbled into the bathroom to put on a facemask. I had at least ten minutes before I'd need to wash it off, so I hobbled back to the couch and settled with my feet propped up on the coffee table. All I could think about was what Evie had said about her family: That I could just Google. So I did.

I typed in "Phillips family Boston" and was flooded with results. Information about the early Phillips family, right through to their current business and charitable dealings. I kept scrolling. Apparently Evie was somehow related to the guy who started the internationally used, multi-multi-billion-dollar software company StartLine, if Wikipedia was to be believed.

I opened another tab and typed in "Evangeline Phillips Boston." There was nothing about her graphic novel publishing at all, which made sense given she used a pen name. That made me pause. I hadn't really thought anything of it before, but now it made me wonder. Did she use a pen name because she wanted to remain anonymous, or to separate herself from her family? And if it was the latter, was it Evie's choice or her family's?

The Phillips-Hale Group had Evie listed as a board member. The philanthropic organization gave away…oh. Wow. "Very wealthy" was a big understatement. Medical research, social housing and healthcare grants, education, nonprofit venture capitalism, and also something called blue-sky science. Then there was the E.S. Phillips Foundation that listed Evie as the board president. If she was the president, maybe this was her own personal foundation for charitable endeavors? And, oh, that foundation had given away…

Scheisse. That was also *a lot* of money. More than a lot. Objectively I knew money could have that many zeros included, but seeing it right there was something else. And if that's what they'd given away, that meant Evie had—

I dropped the phone on the couch beside me.

Okay, she had said as much but now I knew that Evie was rich. Really *really* rich. Rich as in, "we've passed millions and we are into billions" rich. I wasn't struggling financially, and had never given much thought to my social status as it related to my financial status. But now? Now I felt a little bit uncomfortable.

And that felt ridiculous. If Evie hadn't told me, I wouldn't have known. Sure, there were hints she wasn't struggling financially, but nothing about her screamed that she was so wealthy she could probably buy a country if she wanted to. I picked up my phone again, and Googled "Billionaires in America." Okay. So she wasn't on the Wikipedia list of top 25 richest people in America. Nobody with the surname Phillips was. So she wasn't *that* rich then. Just a little baby billionaire. I snorted at my qualifier.

She was down-to-earth, kind, funny, and someone I liked being around. The wealth thing wasn't an issue before she'd told me, so why should I let it become an issue now? She was exactly who she was when we'd first met.

Knocking on my front door pulled me out of my introspective spiral. The only person it could be was someone I wanted to see. I just didn't know if I wanted Evie to see me in a clay mask, but I couldn't ignore her. I hobbled off the couch, trying not to dislodge my toe separators, and waddled to the front door.

I peeked through the peephole and, as expected, saw my friendly neighbor holding a pizza box. The fact she'd basically read my mind added another point in the column of pros about Evangeline Phillips.

I raised my voice so she'd hear me through the door. "Hallo, Evie."

"Hey. I…" She cleared her throat. "This is silly, and I should have checked, but do you want to have dinner with me? I went out and got pizza." Evie raised the pizza box level with the peephole. And every thought about her money fell out of my head. She was just a woman. A fun, thoughtful, sweet woman.

"I do want to have dinner with you. I love pizza, but I'm…I'm wearing a mask."

"Like a Covid mask? Are you sick?" The concern seeped from her. "Is that why you're not opening the door? Do you need anything?"

"No, not a sickness mask," I hurried to reassure her. "A skincare mask."

"Ohhhh, gotcha." There was a long pause before Evie asked, "Is it one of the skin-melting-off ones or…? Because those sheet ones freak me out, even when they're on my face."

Even though she couldn't see me, I shook my head. "It's a clay mask."

"Okay. I'm totally okay with that, if you're okay with that, because this pizza is going to get cold. It's from Coppa and it's really better hot. How much longer do you need to have the mask on?"

I checked my watch. "Three minutes."

"I'm not going to run screaming if I see you in a mask."

"You say that now…" I teased, but I opened the door a crack. "Come on in, but be warned."

Evie faked a gasp, then grinned. "Just kidding." She stepped into the apartment and somehow managed to not touch me, which was impressive given the tiny gap I'd left for her. "You've done something with your face. I like it."

I lightly slapped her arm. "You promised."

"So I did," she said, smirking now. She stared at the assortment of nailcare tools and polish on the coffee table. "Nice colors." After a quick glance down at my toes, still ensconced in separators, Evie mused, "It looks like I'm interrupting something."

"Not at all. It is just a 'me' night. Self-care."

She took a half step backward. "Then I'm definitely interrupting. By definition, *me* nights are for yourself only." Evie raised the lid of the box and the teasing hint of pizza aroma burst forth, making my stomach growl. "I'll just leave half of this here for you to eat at your leisure. Every good self-care session needs pizza."

"Evie. Stay. I mean it. But I do need to wash this mask off." I pointed to the kitchen counter. "That's probably the best place for the pizza until I clean up."

She slid the box onto the counter. "What can I do?"

"Sit. Relax. Not be horrified by my mask."

She nodded decisively. "Done, done, and done."

After I'd pulled down two plates, I turned back to her. "Beer? Wine? Something else?"

"No beer, ever, thanks. Don't like beer, remember? Ejected from a beer hall."

"Jaaaaa, I know, but…beer and pizza," I spluttered. "It's like… Mexican food and beer. Münchner Weisswurst—white sausage— and sweet mustard. The combination just *works*. It's nonnegotiable." Grinning, I leaned toward her, then immediately felt self-conscious. Which was dumb, because there was nothing about Evie's expression or body language that suggested she was anything but open, even with me wearing a face of clay.

Evie smirked. "Well, I negotiated it. Wine, or full-fat Coke with pizza works just fine for me."

"Wow. I didn't even know people could do that. Eat pizza without drinking beer, I mean." As well as a can of Widowmaker Double IPA, I pulled out a bottle of sauvignon. Yes, I'd put it in the fridge in case Evie happened to come by, though I hadn't expected her so soon. The bottle was nowhere near as expensive as the ones she'd provided—I'd Googled and then gulped, hard—but it was still a quality wine. "And what is full-fat Coke? Coke doesn't have fat in it?" Or maybe it did in America, I had no idea.

"Not diet or zero sugar. Regular Coca-Cola, chock-full of sugar. It's the only time I drink it, and it gives me a sugar zing for days."

"So, if you have something you need to stay awake for, you drink… 'full-fat' Coke?" I could think of a few things I'd like to keep her up all night doing. Maybe I should load her with sugar and suggest we burn off some energy together.

"Mhmm." Evie accepted the glass of wine with a murmured, "Thanks."

"You're welcome. Okay, if you serve up some pizza, I will wash this mask off so you no longer have to stare at my clay face."

"Deal." She smiled lazily. "And I like your face, even with clay."

She was making it *very* hard to not act on my feelings.

By the time I'd finished with my face and toes, Evie had set a few slices onto plates. "Tell me about this pizza," I said.

"Tomato base, Italian sausage, shishito peppers, roasted onion, ricotta, and chili." She passed me a plate. "I know it sounds a little odd with the peppers and chili, but trust me. And after seeing you pouring spicy salsa on everything, I'm sure you'll be fine. All their pizzas are great, though. Some people say Coppa is too fancy and it's not really a Boston staple. And I agree, if you're just craving a regular pizza. But if you want some woodfired amazingness, then you can't go past this." She pressed her mouth together and two dull pink spots dusted her cheeks.

Her rambling about pizza was cute and I had to resist the urge to tease her. "What is the Boston pizza staple?"

Evie looked up. "I mean, Boston isn't like New York or Chicago for pizza, but I think Regina in the North End. It's been around forever. It's not fancy, but it's kind of…like a comfortable blanket."

"Well. This is very good." After a long swallow of beer, I bit off another big mouthful. "But I love pizza enough that I will have to sample many pizzas while I'm here."

"Primo's is like three seconds down the street if you're desperate for pizza fast. But I'd be happy to take you on a Boston pizza tour."

"I'd be happy to go on that tour." I finished the slice of pizza and my beer, then stood up to get another beer. "I realized that I never asked you what you like to do when you're not working. What kind of hobbies do you have?"

Evie turned to watch me. "I like anything that's being away from my desk, outdoors if I can. I love to move. Doesn't matter what season, I want to be outside."

My eyebrows shot skyward. "Even *this* season?"

"Yep! I love winter. I don't even mind Snowmageddons, though I'd prefer one where I could ski instead of being holed up at home all cozy. But I'm just as happy grabbing my snowshoes and cold-weather gear and heading out on a trail."

"You know, I don't like the cold very much. I simply tolerate it. Where do you ski?"

"Colorado. Every January and February I have four weeks or so there. My grandma left Heather and me a house in Vail, which is now just my house. Heather was a speed demon on any run, was on the college ski-racing team."

"Not you?"

"Not me," she confirmed. "I don't mind the steep or rough, but I like to chill down the run or spend a day playing in pow. I don't like getting hurt trying to go as fast as I can, so I don't. I'm definitely more afraid than my sister ever was."

"Afraid? You? I don't see that," I mused. I brought my fresh glass of beer and the bottle of wine to top up her glass back to the table.

Evie thanked me as I refilled her glass, and picked it up immediately, drinking deeply. "I'm afraid of a lot of things. I never used to be but it kind of crept up on me as I got older and realized things hurt."

"Like what? Hurts, that is."

"Most sports. Relationships."

I smiled at the second noun, which felt like a careless add-on. "Ah."

"I still do all those things. Just cautiously. Except relationships."

"You're not cautious with relationships?"

She laughed. "No, I don't do them at all. How about you? Do you ski? Even though you don't like the cold. But, you know…there's warm clothes and mulled wine for that."

I shook my head. "Snowboarder."

"I forgive you," she said seriously.

My smile started slowly, then bloomed as realization dawned. "Oh, I see. You're a ski snob. I never would have picked that."

Evie grinned cheekily. "Nope, not a snob at all. I just really like my tailbone. I tried boarding once and broke my tailbone about fifteen minutes after I first strapped my feet to that demonic device. Never again."

Nodding, I wiped my mouth with the paper napkin Evie had supplied. "I have to apologize."

Her eyebrows rose quickly, then settled back down. In exchange, her forehead crinkled. "Apologize for what?"

"For completely making you wrong in my mind. I had you as an indoors person, a gamer, an Anime nerd, tabletop roleplaying games and all that."

Evie expelled a loud laugh. "I see," she drawled. "I suppose I could see why you might think that. Sitting in front of those monitors, inside, for hours on end is the one thing I dislike about my job."

"Oh? That's a shame."

"A little. Luckily I'm not tied to my desk." She finished her slice of pizza and delicately wiped her fingertips on the paper napkin. "So… if you're not interested in dating Pete, are you interested in dating someone else? Do we need to hit the bars and clubs? I'll drag my old as—butt out and be your wingwoman too if you want."

Inside, I was almost crying in frustration. Did she really not see it? No, she didn't, because I hadn't come out and explicitly said that I was so attracted to her that when we were together all I really thought about was dragging her to bed. And why couldn't I make myself just say it now? What exactly was holding me back? I didn't think she'd reject me, so it wasn't that fear. Which meant it was another fear. "Serious relationships aren't really on my list of things to do while I'm here," I said carefully.

"I see. What about not-serious, no-strings-attached relationships?" she asked. The question came out casually but her face was *not* casual. Evie shook her head. "I can't believe I just asked that."

"I'm glad you did ask it. No strings attached is probably more what I'm looking for right now," I said, aware that my heart had started beating fast.

"Okay, sure." She looked devastated yet trying to hide it.

I should just kiss her. Explain that by confirming I wanted no strings attached, I meant I wanted *her* with no strings attached. A little voice in my head asked if strings would be such a bad thing. Yes, they would be a bad thing. Because strings could only stretch so far, and certainly not from Boston to München. But if I could cut the string before we left… I'd done it with Sascha, why not with Evie?

I didn't want to ruin a nice evening, especially one that was designated as self-care, with forcing Evie to talk me through my conflicting feelings. It definitely felt like something had shifted. And I blamed myself. But I didn't know her well enough to have the strategy to get over this social speedbump without potentially ruining our tentative friendship.

Once the pizza was gone, Evie drank the last of her wine, and stood. "I should go and let you get back to your self-care evening."

"You don't want to see me in another mask?" I deadpanned.

"Oh I do, for sure. But one is enough for today." At the door, Evie stuffed her hands into the pockets of her jeans. "Well. Good night."

"Good night." It felt natural to hug goodbye, and Evie relaxed, melting into our embrace. "Thanks for bringing dinner, and for your company." After a little squeeze, I relaxed my grip, not wanting to make things awkward.

"Any time. Thanks for having me around."

I caught the unmistakable expression in her eyes, the slight flick of her gaze to my mouth before she'd hugged me. I was both relieved and disappointed that the telltale "I want to kiss you" didn't result in a kiss.

"It was my pleasure. Sleep well," I said, smothering my disappointment with extra cheer.

"You too."

Something heavy hung in the air between us, but it seemed neither of us were able to pick it up. I'd never been this indecisive before. I suspected why, and it scared the shit out of me. Evie nodded, then slipped out of the door as quickly as the opportunity had slipped through my fingers.

Less than a minute after I'd bolted the door behind her, there was a persistent knock. After checking it was indeed Evie back again, I flung the door open. Laughing, I asked, "Forget something?" I glanced behind myself, trying to see the coffee table and if anything of hers was on it.

"I did," Evie confirmed. She took a deep breath and let it out slowly. "I forgot to kiss you. I was second-guessing myself. I'm still second-guessing myself." She opened her mouth, then closed it again. Her lips worked as if she was trying out things to say and not liking any of them. "About that no-strings thing. Would you consider it with me?"

I had to swallow before I could answer, though I didn't need to think about that answer. "Yes." My pulse was hammering and butterflies began flitting around in my stomach.

"Good. That's really good." Her mouth twisted into an approximation of a smile. "And, I'm sorry."

Frowning, I asked, "What are you sorry for?"

"For not kissing you before and now we have to talk about it and I've made it totally weird."

I bit my lower lip. "We don't have to talk about it. Do you usually talk about kissing before you kiss someone?" I teased, trying to lighten the mood.

"Sometimes. Most of the time we kind of just…agree to it mutually. By kissing, when the moment presents itself, which it has a few times with us. But I've been too stupid or afraid or whatever to just make the move."

"Ja, me too," I murmured. I wondered if now was the time to bring up the no-strings-attached qualifier again. It wasn't that I didn't want to kiss her—I did, desperately, and in more places than just her mouth. But could either of us do casual sex or whatever this might end up being? My libido decided for me—we could talk about that later. I could worry about that later. Much later.

I moved into Evie's personal space, lightly gripped her hip, and pulled her into me. I lowered my head until my mouth was near her ear, and murmured, "And it is anything but weird."

Evie grabbed a fistful of my hoodie, her fingertips digging into my waist as my lips grazed the soft skin underneath her ear. "You're right," she said hoarsely. "It's not weird." She reached for my face, guiding my lips down toward hers. Evie paused for the briefest moment, a teasing breath passing between us that had me reaching my hands to her neck to bring her the final, minute distance.

The kiss began slowly, tentatively, almost a little awkwardly and out of sync as we tested this new dynamic. I kept one hand on the side of her neck, my other moving instinctively to her waist to bring her closer. The smallest touch of her tongue against my lips made me exhale an involuntary groan. Evie's hand tightened against my waist, her hips pushing into mine. Her lips were so soft, plump, luscious, and intoxicating and I could have easily spent hours enjoying her kisses.

Evie broke first, but only just barely. Her breathing was quick, a little rough. "I've been thinking about kissing you from the moment I saw you," she said, her voice having taken on a new huskiness that sent a small thrill of excitement through me.

"Then I am very glad you stopped thinking and started acting."

Evie's tongue swiped along her lower lip and I wondered if she knew how much the action teased me. "Is it okay if I act some more?" she asked coyly.

"Ja, it is." I tilted her face up and leaned in, bringing my lips within a whisper of hers. "In fact, I think I will have to insist upon it." Though if we kept going the way we were, I might combust.

"Good," she said, and moved in to do just that.

I lost track of time as I lost myself in kissing her. Evie pressed herself to me until my back was against my door, and we ended up with hands under tops. I delighted in the shiver that went through her as I stroked the soft, warm skin of her lower back, and then delighted in the way her fingertips brushed lightly over my ribs.

I was seconds away from moving her hand up to my breast when Evie pulled back with a soft groan. "I should really go," she mumbled, her voice trailing off like she hadn't quite convinced herself that this was what she wanted to do.

I was about to suggest that she could come inside, come into to my bed, but there was something in her expression that stopped me. I took in a deep breath to settle my simmering arousal. "Ja, okay. I'll see you tomorrow after work?"

"What for?" she asked, feigning ignorance. I narrowed my eyes at her, and Evie laughed. "Don't worry," she said. "I haven't forgotten tree shopping day." She paused, then stretched up for another quick kiss, lightly tracing the edge of my jaw with her fingertips. "Wow, that mask has made your skin so soft."

That was not what I thought she was going to say and apparently my expression gave away my confusion.

She grinned. "Good night, Annika. Thanks for"—Evie gestured vaguely between us—"that."

"I think I should thank you…" I murmured. "And, good night. Sweet dreams."

"Oh, you can bet on it," she said breezily.

I held a tight handful of my hoodie as though I could forcibly stop myself from following her. Evie waved from inside her doorway, then closed the door. And I fell back against my doorframe. Scheisse. My entire body was humming with excitement and unresolved sexual tension.

Though I had work tomorrow and should really start preparing to go to bed, I had another more pressing need. I didn't even make it to my bedroom. I didn't even take off my clothing. I sat on my couch with a hand in my pants and thought about fucking her right here. I imagined the weight of her on top of me, Evie writhing underneath me as my fingers drove deep inside her, and my orgasm came upon me with explosive impact. Unfortunately, masturbation didn't blunt the edge of my desire for her, and I readied for bed feeling sexually frustrated and annoyed with myself for not just suggesting we sleep together.

I gathered Evie's Saint Nikolaus presents and opened my front door, intending to sneakily leave the box by her door. I nearly tripped over the small black-painted box in front of my door. I crouched down to look at it, noticing first that there was a painted boot on the top, with ANNIKA written underneath.

I should have known Evie wouldn't need to be reminded about something. Not only had she beaten me to setting out "boots," but she'd clearly spent time and effort on creating mine. I gathered it up and walked quietly to her door and set down the brown paper bag, on which I'd drawn a very clumsy boot in Sharpie pen.

Then I rushed back into my apartment to see what Saint Nikolaus had brought me. After all, hadn't I been a very good girl?

CHAPTER THIRTEEN

Evie

I'd driven to Pete's and left my car there, swapping it for his "I'm a manly man who needs a pickup to buy a bag of birdseed every three months or help a pal move furniture once a year" vehicle to carry Annika's and my shared-custody Christmas tree. Thankfully we'd drawn the line at calling it a mash-up of Christmas tree and Weihnachtsbaum, though we both burst into laughter when I'd said Christmasbaum as a joke to test out the portmanteau.

We could have had a tree delivered, but Annika insisted she needed to choose "her tree," that part of the experience was spending time walking amongst the offerings and making the selection.

"How far away are the Christmas trees?" she asked once she'd settled in the passenger seat.

"About a ten-minute drive," I said, glancing over at her. Of course every time I looked at her now I thought about our kiss. The way I'd pushed her against the door, the casual exploration of her tongue, how her hands had roamed, how my hands had roamed. It was problematic to think about those things when we were trying to do things other than kissing. Things that required my concentration, like driving. "Full disclosure, I've never actually been there. I had to ask Pete where to get a tree. I'm honestly not sure of the steps for purchasing a Christmas tree."

"What are your criteria for the perfect tree?" Annika asked, fiddling with the heat vents.

"This year, my only criteria is 'not too heavy.'" I leaned over to help her with the climate control and on a whim, snuck a kiss—which Annika returned—when she turned her face to look at me. "It's been so long since I had a tree that I really can't think of my must-haves. My parents' trees were always just…huge, almost touching the ceilings which were ridiculously high to begin with. And they always felt so overdecorated. Like bigger was better somehow."

"That is *definitely* not true," she confirmed, letting a hint of innuendo through.

I laughed. Rolling my hands forward over the wheel, I asked, "How about your criteria?"

She held up a hand, folding fingers down as she ticked off, "Alive, never plastic. Kind of, emm…poofy, you know? It has to look like a Christmas tree, a good shape, in proportion."

"I see. You're one of *those* people."

She turned sideways in the seat to face me. "What's a 'those people'?"

"The kind of person that's going to make me walk every single row of the farm until she finds the tree that matches the aesthetic in her head. The aesthetic she can't actually describe, because she just *knows* what it looks like."

"Ja, that's me," Annika confirmed cheerfully. "If you're going to get a tree, then why not get a great one?" She shifted uneasily. "You're not going to kill it before Christmas Eve, are you?"

I flashed a toothy smile. "Not intentionally. You're welcome to come over every day to check on it and make sure it's okay."

Annika's laugh filled the cab of the truck. "I know you were just being silly with that offer, but I think I might do that."

I enjoyed the flood of pleasure at the thought of a daily visit from Annika and moderated my response so it sounded pleased but not over-the-top excited. "Well, you know I'm home for most of the day. It'd be nice to have a visitor to break up the tedium."

"Then you should expect a daily tree-checking knock on your door. It will be the first thing I do when I come home from work." She hmmed. "Or maybe I'll come before work."

"I'll be ready for you, whenever you decide to come," I said seriously.

"We need to buy the decorations too," Annika reminded me.

I'd suggested we could go before getting the tree, but Annika "needed to see the tree" so she could get a vibe or something for which kind of lights and other decorations we'd need to buy to supplement those she'd brought with her.

She touched my shoulder. "I keep forgetting to thank you, in person, for your Saint Nikolaus gifts. So, thank you. It was such a thoughtful gift. And you beat me to it last night!" She had texted me this morning to say thanks for the gift and thanks for the kissing.

"You're welcome. And thank you for mine. It was kind of fun to have a Santa visit this morning."

She held up a forefinger. "Nein, nein, nein. Not Santa. Heiliger Nikolaus."

I grinned. "Sorry. Saint Nick."

Annika sighed. "You're so naughty, I'm surprised Saint Nikolaus didn't leave you a bundle of sticks."

I winked. "How do you know he didn't?"

Annika just rolled her eyes, but there was a hint of amusement in the expression. "Come on, we need to leave or someone might take our perfect tree."

The drive was quick, and made easy by our casual chatter. We exited the truck, and I went around to her side where Annika was already waiting for me. "Ready to purchase your first American Christmas tree?"

She clasped her gloved hands together in front of her chest. "Yes! I have been looking forward to this all week."

"Me too," I admitted. There was something about being with her that made doing the things I usually had no interest in feel special.

"You look very cute in a beanie." Annika tugged it down over my ears then kept her hands there, gently cupping my face.

"I know. That's why I love winter so much. Beanies, staying inside and being cozy and warm, big roaring fires, skiing, good whiskey, hot chocolate, lying in bed when you're supposed to get up and do something."

"Ja, I can see the appeal." Still holding my face, Annika kissed me, staying close to my lips as she murmured, "You might convince me to like winter."

I asked a dangerous question. "If I let you lie in bed, you mean?"

"If it's with you, then yes." Annika let go of my face, her fingertips lightly trailing downward until her hands gripped the front of my puffer jacket. Annika took the half step necessary to eradicate any space between us completely. "Why haven't we done that yet?"

I swallowed hard. "I honestly don't know. I mean, aside from the fact we only just decided we were kissing one another like…yesterday?"

"Aside from that," she echoed. "And me neither. It's not that I don't want to," she said hastily, like she was afraid I might think there was no attraction. I didn't think that at all—she'd made it very clear that there was attraction.

"Same. I want to a whole lot." I licked my lower lip. "Okay, I lied a little. I think I might know." After inhaling deeply, I just said it. "I'm not good in relationships, Annika. Not that I'm saying that's where we're going. I just, I don't think it's fair to treat you like a test, to see if I can sustain a relationship, because that's what it would feel like for me because you'll be leaving at the end of next year. And I think I'm worried it might make things weird between us if it doesn't go well, and we have to live right next to each other. And maybe it feels a little like…rushing? We've only known each other for a few weeks." A laugh rose up my throat, and I pushed it back down. Annika and I were outliers—most other queer women with the level of flirtation we'd been engaging in would have fallen into bed with each other within minutes.

"Rushing," she mused. "I suppose you're right. And we agree that neither of us are ready to be in a relationship right now."

"We did agree that. And if I'm honest, I'm regretting it a little."

"Why?"

"Because I really want to sleep with you," I admitted in a surge of confident honesty that was so unlike me when I was around a woman to whom I was attracted.

"The feeling is mutual, Evie," she said in a low, husky murmur.

And in another surge that was so unlike me, I said, "We *could* just do that. Sex. No strings. We mentioned that, right? I mean, what could go wrong?" I only just held back my nervous giggle at the thought of everything that could go wrong.

Annika laughed, and echoed my thought. "A lot of things. But let's not think about that right now."

"Good plan," I agreed. After an eternal pause, I quietly asked, "Are you saying you still want to try something with no strings?"

"Yes. I think I am saying that."

My heart rate tripled. "Okay. Good. So…should I get a bikini wax?" My esthetician would probably fall over in shock if I contacted her in winter for a wax, because there was only one reason for it.

"Why would you need to get a bikini wax, Evie?" she purred, feigning innocence.

I swallowed hard, and my answer came out hoarsely. "In case someone happened to spend some time around my bikini area."

"Mmm. I know someone who would like to spend time in that area, and she does not care if that area is waxed or not waxed."

"Fuck. Okay, mercy," I begged, taking a step back.

"That's one blue slip for the swear jar," Annika pointed out, biting back her smile.

Grumbling under my breath, I opened my swearing note and added to it.

Annika touched my arm lightly. "Listen. We don't need to plan anything. If intimacy happens, then it happens and if it doesn't then that's fine too. And if intimacy doesn't work out for us, then we can just go back to spending time together the way we have been. There's no pressure to be anything or do anything."

"That's a good point. Okay," I breathed. "Let's talk about it. Later. Because right now we have to buy a Christmas tree."

She kissed me again, thankfully just a quick peck on the lips. "Yes. We do."

After perusing the entire lot of balsam and Fraser trees, Annika decided on a six-foot balsam. I personally thought the Fraser was a nicer tree, but when I said so, I was treated to a discussion—if you could call a one-sided lecture a discussion—that was basically how wrong I was. She'd clearly Googled American Christmas trees extensively.

I stood with my mittened hands tucked into my armpits, nodding as she gave me an oral presentation about balsam versus Fraser. It was all about the overall image, and she preferred the shape and general vibe of the balsam. Yes, the balsams had softer needles and more flexible branches, but Annika didn't subscribe to the heavy Christmas ornament club so that didn't matter, and yes, balsams dropped their needles more than Frasers (so far she wasn't doing a good job of convincing me balsam was best), but all those things were unimportant attributes in the face of The Most Important Christmas Tree Attribute after the shape—the balsams smelled better. She'd know, she sniffed most of the trees which made her shortlist. I mean, they all looked and smelled like Christmas trees to me.

Once she was done with balsam and Fraser, I received an oral presentation about Nordmann fir versus blue spruce, which were the two tree variants in Germany.

She paid for the tree, and directed the young guy who'd wrapped it up back to the truck, charming him with her happy chatter the whole time. He remained charmed, even as she bossily asked him to not damage the tree while he put it in the bed of the pickup and secured it.

"We have an amazing tree," Annika said gleefully. "I love this tree."

"I'm glad you love it. It's a good tree."

It was only when I'd put the keys in the ignition that I realized I didn't have a tree stand and had to run back to purchase one. When I returned, the cab had warmed a little and Annika was smiling at something on her phone.

"Are you staring at photos of our tree?" I asked.

She glanced up, still smiling. "Ja. I think my father will be very relieved that I have a tree. Or rather, that *we* have a tree. I'm sure he will approve of this one."

"Did you send him a picture of our tree?"

"Yes. He's asleep—it's past midnight in Germany, but I'm sure he will be very pleased to see the tree when he wakes up."

"Then I'm doubly glad we got that tree. I thought we could take a detour on the way home and check out some of the over-the-top decorations on the houses in the burbs." It'd been a while since I'd been to Somerville for their Christmas lights, but a quick Google had told me they now had an official online self-guided Illuminations Tour.

A smile lit her face. "That sounds wonderful."

It took just over twenty minutes to drive to Somerville, and I cued up the Google Maps route so thoughtfully provided by the Illuminations organizers, and also put on the suggested Spotify playlist titled "Happy Holidays," turning the volume down to low background noise. As expected, there was a throng doing what we were and we joined the slow procession of other lights-gawkers.

Most of the houses had pretty standard decorations—lights, candy canes, stars, Santas, baby Jesus and his posse, snowmen, reindeer and sleighs, elves, and trees. But some houses had tweaked the theme a little. I saw some light-up palm trees (wishful thinking), and some that had no theme except "garish."

"Ha! Look at that *Die Hard* one." I pointed out the printed image of John McClane in an air duct from the movie, bordered with flashing red and green lights.

Annika laughed. "That is amazing. I love the *Die Hard* movies."

I smiled over at her. "Same."

The overall vibe of the tour was "bright," a sentiment Annika echoed. She also observed, "Can you imagine the electricity needed to run all of these lights? Then the time and effort to put them up and pull them down?"

"It's a whole thing, isn't it. But, neighborhood spirit and all that."

"Ja, I suppose so. How did you know about this?" Annika asked when I stopped to let a family cross the road in front of us.

"Heather and I used to come here to look at the lights together, and then when Chloe was little, the four of us would do the trolley tour." I paused, thinking I should probably check she knew what I meant. "You know what a trolley is, right?" When she nodded, I continued, "Then we'd go out for desserts afterward. I came with Pete and Chloe a few times after Heather died but…it just didn't feel right."

"How does it feel now?" she asked gently, reaching over to stroke the back of my neck.

"Pretty good, actually," I said honestly.

Annika's expression softened. "I'm pleased."

"You want to go to another suburb, or are your retinas sufficiently burned by over-the-top Christmas decorations?"

"I think I've seen enough for tonight."

"Do you mind if we stop for coffee or hot chocolate on the way home?" I didn't need either, but I just didn't want the evening to end.

She grinned. "Zwei Doofe, ein Gedanke."

Frowning, I tried to figure out the words from the little German I knew. "Two somethings, one something else?"

"Two stupid people, one thought."

Laughing, I asked, "Are you calling me stupid?"

She raised an eyebrow. "I called myself stupid too. What I meant is I had the same thought."

"Ah. I think the English equivalent to that saying would be like 'great minds think alike.'"

Annika nodded. "I'll try to remember that." She glanced back into the pickup's tray. "Will someone steal our tree?" she asked fretfully.

"They'd better not." I puffed myself up jokingly. "I will defend our tree with my life."

Annika exhaled loudly. "Okay. Let's stop for coffee. Maybe some waffles too?"

"Oh, yes," I agreed, embarrassed by the sensual purr I'd just emitted. "Waffles or pie."

"Both?"

"Why not?"

"I see no reason why not." Annika reached over and rested her hand on my thigh, gently squeezing.

I took her fingers and brought her hand to my mouth, lightly kissing her knuckles before I put her hand back on my thigh. The sensation of her hand was both comforting and teasing.

The South Street Diner was technically on the way home if I made a detour, and given I'd already detoured for lights, what was one more? It also wasn't too far from our place. Our place? No, Evie, it's not our place, it's our place*s*. You're rambling because you've imagined moving in with her and now your brain is thinking whatever it wants.

The parking on Kneeland near the diner was all permits, but I found limited meter parking on South Street. I reverse-parked Pete's Beast like a pro, earning a clap from Annika. I gave the reversing camera screen a loving pat before turning off the car. "Time for pie. And waffles."

Annika fretted. "Is this place safe for the tree? The parking isn't in view of the restaurant. Anyone could steal our tree."

"Okay. Firstly, it's a diner. Calling this place a restaurant is generous. And secondly, no problem. One of us can just go in for takeout. Or if the tree gets stolen, we'll just go back and get another one."

She pouted. "But this is *our* tree. It's the best one."

I was sure most people thought the tree they'd chosen was the best tree, but I didn't argue. Instead, I leaned over and kissed the pout off her lips. "You're right. It is the best one. I'll go in and we can either take it home or sit and eat it here with our tree."

I fed the meter in case parking-meter gremlins were about, and jogged the short distance to the diner. The line wasn't too horrendous and I was back at the car within fifteen minutes, juggling a tray of coffees—I'd recalled our discussion about Annika drinking lattes—and a bag containing two boxes with hot desserts, a tub of ice cream and whipped cream to go on top, as well as cutlery and napkins. Annika had turned on the interior light, and I could see her watching me approach.

I set our coffees in the cup holders between us then passed her the bag containing the rest. "You're in charge of keeping these safe."

"I will guard this with my life," she said jokingly, echoing what I'd said earlier.

The feeling I'd been trying to ignore for days rose up. The feeling that I wanted to be near her constantly, that there was something between us, something beyond a simple attraction. "Do you want to eat here, go home, or go somewhere?"

"Go somewhere," she said instantly. A few minutes into driving, Annika asked, "Where are we going?"

"It's a surprise. I wish Boston had more green spaces and stuff open at night where we could just park the car and sit, but they all close after dark. So…how do you feel about a mediocre nighttime city view?"

"I feel good about that."

It was less than ten minutes from the diner to the Museum of Science, and we were silent for most of the drive. Annika stared out the window at the city lights passing by, holding the bag with our desserts on her lap like it was a precious newborn. She peered at the exterior of the building as I pulled off to the parking garage. "I love museums."

I smiled. "Same. It's been ages since I came here. I need to find time to visit more."

I wound my way up floor after floor until we were on the rooftop. At this time of night, it was almost empty and I parked facing the lit-up MoS sign, with the Lechmere Viaduct on our left. I left the car running with the heat on. The noise of Pete's man-truck in exchange for a warm cab was worth the annoyance.

Annika unbuckled her seat belt and leaned forward to peer out the windshield. "How do you know about this place?"

"Heather and I used to come up here. It was just a…normal place, you know? We could just sit here and talk. Or not talk. Sometimes one of us, whoever wasn't driving, would smoke a little weed and we'd just hang out together, like normal people."

"I see. Do you still smoke?"

"Nah. I quit cigarettes before Chloe was born. And weed before that." I laughed. "It makes me dumb."

"Interesting," she mused. "It makes me horny."

I cleared my throat. "Noted." I passed her the takeout cup closest to her. "Here's your coffee. Why don't you give me that stuff and I'll get these treats served up."

She handed everything over and watched as I assembled the segments of our desserts. The waffle and pie were still warm, and the ice cream and cream still cold. So far, we were winning. I scooped ice cream and cream on top of the waffle and pie. "Which do you want?"

Annika laughed. "I want both."

"Share?"

"Yes."

I handed her the apple pie—the better of the two offerings—and got to work on the waffle. After a big mouthful, I declared, "I've just realized that there are not enough desserts in my life."

"That's so sad." Annika pointed at the stone arches to our left. "What's that?"

"The Lechmere Viaduct. Trains go over it."

She pointed toward the Zakim, lit up, the cables looking like rays of light in the dark. "And that bridge with the…strings. What's that?"

"Officially, it's the Leonard P. Zakim Bunker Hill Memorial Bridge, or 'the Zakim' if you don't have half an hour to say its full name."

She laughed. "Zakim it is." Annika licked the plastic spoon, and I was sure she knew exactly how sexy she looked. "So…what other 'normal' things did you do, aside from sit here and smoke?"

"Honestly? Not much. Sometimes I still just want ordinary things like…mowing a lawn. You know I've never mown a lawn? We had groundskeepers for our holiday homes when I was a kid and I got in trouble with my mom when I asked some of the staff if I could try it. You don't do that if you're a Phillips."

"A guy at work complained about mowing his lawn. He said how much he loves winter because there's no mowing. I don't think mowing is an enjoyable task."

"Probably not. But I still want a lawn to mow and the chance to complain about having to do it."

Her eyes softened. "You want…middle-class normality?"

"Yes." That had never been an option for me. Being disgustingly wealthy has a lot of benefits. But there's always a flipside.

Annika scooped up a large chunk of pie then we swapped desserts. "Middle-class normality like mowing and smoking weed on the roof of a museum car park. Though I think weed is for all social classes," she clarified.

"That's true."

Nodding slowly, she got to work on the waffle. "Do you know where we can get some weed?"

Her "it makes me horny" rang in my head and I had to collect myself before answering, "Unfortunately not."

"That's a pity. We could do some really fun *normal* things. I guess we'll just have to do them without weed." She licked her lower lip a second before biting it, and I wondered if she was being deliberately provocative.

"You can't do that," I murmured. "Not here."

I didn't need to elaborate, tell her that she was driving me crazy. She smiled gently. "I'm sorry."

"I get it. So far this has been…flirting without consequences. And I'm just as guilty of doing it as you are."

A crease appeared between Annika's eyebrows. "I think that is a good description."

"Yeah. But now it feels like there are consequences."

"Ja. And…I don't think either of us are ready for those consequences."

I wished I could be ready, but the niggle of fear was screaming in my ear. I blew out a loud breath. "Should we get the tree home? You have to work tomorrow. And I need to take this truck back to Pete's and get my car." And if we stayed here, things might get sexy. Sexier.

"Okay," she agreed quietly.

I drove home with Annika's light hand on my thigh, realizing as I turned the corner onto our street that we'd basically done a big circle around Boston. I took the chance that there'd be no parking permit checkers around and parked near my building—my car was at Pete's so it wasn't like I was taking up a space I wasn't paying for. Loophole.

After we manhandled the tree up the stairs and cleaned up the needles that'd rudely disengaged themselves from the wrapping, Annika dictated where to put the tree in my living room. She was the perfect amount of bossy and I let her tell me what to do, then remained quiet as she supervised while I tried to straighten the tree in the stand. After almost ten minutes of her "A little bit left, no that's too much" and "It's tilting to the front, no, now it's too much to the back" I finally got it to stand in a way that pleased her.

"Okay, let's unwrap it," I said. I left her eyeing up the tree—which was as straight as it was going to get because I was done with tree wrangling—while I went to fetch scissors. The moment we'd pulled the material holding the branches against the trunk free, I froze. "I've just realized a major issue."

"What?" she asked with a hint of panic, as if the thought of an issue with Christmas was unbearable.

"How the heck are we going to get it out of my door and in yours?" Laughing, I spread my arms wide. "This is one bushy-ass tree. We're going to lose half of it on the journey."

Her face fell. "Oh no. Oh…no. I did not think of that." Annika crossed her arms, one hand coming to cover her mouth. She stared at the tree like she could somehow will the branches to tuck themselves back in against the trunk.

I stared too, but as much as I wanted to stay there with Annika and puzzle out the tree problem, I really had to get Pete's truck back. "Well, we'll just have to figure it out in a few weeks."

"Yes," she said. Finally, she looked away from the tree and when her eyes fell on me, they were warm, bright with excitement. "Trying to figure it out together gives me more reasons to see you. And that is not a bad thing, Evie."

"No," I quietly agreed. "It's not."

CHAPTER FOURTEEN

Annika

I'd slept fitfully on Friday night after we'd collected our Weihnachtsbaum. I wasn't too hot, too cold, hungry, thirsty, or anything that should have interfered with my sleep. But I *was* completely and utterly charmed by Evie, which was enough to keep me awake, thinking of her and fantasy what-if, long-term scenarios. My what-ifs were pleasant, but in this case they were unrealistic. I kept reminding myself that I needed to focus on the reason I was here in Boston.

Work.

I'd had a busy, productive week at work. We were still in the early stages, and while the design team had already started the artwork and layouts, most of us still planning timelines for each stage of development, testing, and rollout. This new project was interesting, but challenging, and the balance between my working and nonworking time made me happy to go in to work, rather than dreading it as I had been for the past year or so. This change of scenery had been exactly what I'd needed to break out of my stagnation.

Change of scenery.

That was one way to refer to the person who lived next door. Speaking of that person… Before Evie left to return Pete's truck, we'd made vague weekend plans, simply along the lines of "let's do something," and we'd already agreed that we'd light our Advent candles together each Sunday. I teased her that she was more excited about my baking than spending time with me. And Evie had given me a slow, smoldering look that made my skin feel like it'd caught fire.

"No," she'd murmured. "It's definitely spending time with you that I'm most excited about…" Then Evie had leaned in, and after a maddeningly long pause, kissed me.

After the initial fumbles during our first kiss, every kiss since had felt like we'd been kissing each other forever. But still, all I could hear in my head was the question I'd asked her last night. *"Why haven't we done that yet?"*

And her hoarse reply, *"I honestly don't know."*

I spent my Saturday running errands, buying groceries, doing housework, and FaceTiming with my parents. I'd been through Evie's Saint Nikolaus compilation—a "Boston pack"—many times, and every time I felt a rush of joy at her thoughtfulness.

I hoped she would like my homemade cookies, the tiny plastic ski I'd found in a thrift store, the braided leather bracelet that I'd made, and my amateurish drawing of Saint Nikolaus. I'd really wanted to splurge on her, buy her something a little bit more expensive as well as thoughtful, but what did you buy a woman who could buy herself literally anything she wanted?

I made it through most of the day before my need to see Evie overwhelmed me. Just before dinner I stripped out of my old sweatpants, pulled on leggings and an oversized cable-knit sweater, then crossed the hall and knocked on her door. I'd deliberately not brought a bottle of wine or dinner because that would only tempt me into staying. But knowing Evie, she'd offer either or both and I'd end up staying anyway. Staying felt dangerous, especially after last night.

Last night…

Every time I thought I'd stopped thinking about it, I thought about it again. I'd wanted to prolong the evening, and would have happily spent hours sitting in the car on that rooftop parking lot, just talking. And perhaps making out like teenagers. The more we'd talked, the more she'd shared, the more I wanted to dive into her life and know more. I wanted to know what made her angry, what made her happy, what her dreams were. Evie was so easy to talk to, so easy to be around. And I wanted to be around her as much as I could.

But the wanting was dangerous. The undeniable fact was that nothing between us could last—I was leaving in a year and starting a relationship would be unfair to both of us.

Evie opened the door shortly after I'd knocked, pulling it wide to admit me into her apartment. "Hey," she said softly, her expression relaxing into pleasure.

I was certain my expression matched hers. "Hi." I glanced around her, relieved to see the tree still standing and alive. "How is our tree?"

"I'm great and I had a good day, thanks for asking. How about you? Excited for the rest of the weekend?"

My shoulders dropped, my mouth twisted into a grimace. "I'm sorry. That was very rude of me." I moved closer to rest my hands on her hips. "Hallo, Evie. It's wonderful to see you. How are you?" When she smiled, I brought my hands up, one of them on the small of her back to pull us together, the other resting lightly on her neck. Our eyes met, and I waited a few seconds before kissing her. The kiss was slow and unhurried, gentle yet passionate and I welcomed the rush of warmth. She smiled against my mouth before pulling away, looking at me intently as I answered her. "Yes, I had a nice day, and I'm very excited for the rest of the weekend." Specifically, spending time with her. "How was your day?"

"Very productive, actually. I got a lot of work done, which was nice." She stretched up to give me another quick kiss, then took my hand and led me to the tree. "And as you can see, the tree is perfectly fine. If I had to describe it, I'd call it 'happy.'"

"It does look happy," I agreed, lightly pulling one of the soft branches. "You're a very good Christmas tree caretaker. For someone with no experience," I added teasingly.

She smirked. "You're damned right I am." The smirk faded. She sighed. With her mouth set in a thin line, Evie pulled out her phone and I knew she was making a note for her swearing jar. "Have you had dinner?"

I hesitated for a second. "Not yet. I—just wanted to see how the tree was." I smiled sheepishly, knowing how transparent I must seem.

Evie grinned. "Should I set up a camera so you can check it from work during the day? Or check in in the middle of the night when you're thinking about the Christmas tree?"

"The tree isn't the thing in this apartment that I think about in the middle of the night," I said before I could stop myself.

Her lips parted. "You're really naughty, you know that?"

"Yes, I have been told that before…"

"Mmm." Evie inhaled deeply, then, perhaps wisely, redirected the conversation. "Are you hungry?"

"A little bit, yes." I knew exactly where she was leading, and assured her, "But it's fine, I can make myself dinner."

Her expression fell. "Are you sure?"

"No. I'm not sure. But I don't want to interrupt you and take over your evening any more than I already have."

"You would never do that," she assured me. "If I'm asking you to come around, or to…stay around, it's because I want to hang out with you. So, do you want to have dinner with me?"

"Yes, I do."

"See? Wasn't that easy?" Evie wandered into her kitchen, and I followed. "So I know we were thinking of doing something aside from lighting Advent candles tomorrow, but what do you say to an outing. A Christmas outing," she added hastily.

I raised an eyebrow. "I say I'm very interested."

"Good, because Chloe sprang wanting to go to the Snowport Christmas markets at the pier tomorrow. I know you and I were talking about Christmas markets, but we haven't organized that. Do you want to come with us?" Her voice rose hopefully with the question.

I didn't even think before answering, "Yes." Christmas markets were quite possibly one of my favorite holiday things, and I'd been excited about Boston's. "But are you sure? That's time for you to spend with your niece."

Evie's eyes creased at the edges. "Yes, I'm sure. Chloe suggested I invite you, actually."

"Okay, then yes, let's do it." I'd been missing the overall feeling of Christmas, and even though the season was permeating Boston, it just didn't really feel the same. Christmas markets would certainly help. "What time will we leave?"

"I thought around three? That gives us time to look around before it gets dark. And we can have dinner there. Pete's going to drop Chloe off here, and we'll just drop her home when we're done."

"That sounds perfect." I kissed her pleased, smiling mouth.

"That's exactly what I thought. Now, let me grab you a drink and then we can think about dinner? Did you have anything in mind?"

"I was going to make myself a sandwich."

"Oh." She frowned. "Well, if that's what you want, I've been told I make a great PB&J."

Raising my eyebrows, I asked, "Told by who?"

"My niece. So I'm not sure it counts."

"I think it counts. I'm sure you make excellent sandwiches."

Evie batted her eyelashes. "You do know that flattery will get you anything you want, right?"

"I did not know that, but I'm glad I know it now…" Oh the things I could do with flattery if that were the case.

She looked as if she knew exactly what thought had just come into my head, and a smirk quirked her beautiful mouth before she said, "How's a cheese et cetera platter to start while I think of something else to cook or we decide what to order. Or, we just have more cheese." She pulled a bottle of white wine from the wine fridge and set it on the counter.

Cheese et cetera… Oh. Right. That was a perfect way to describe charcuterie. "That sounds great."

Evie uncorked the bottle and poured two glasses, passing one to me. "Give me a few minutes to put these clean dishes away and then the best damned et cetera platter will be coming your way."

"Swear jar," I said as I clambered up onto one of the high stools by the counter, on the other side to her.

"Thanks…" she said dryly, tugging her phone from her back pocket again.

"You're welcome," I said sweetly. "Is there anything I can do to help?"

Evie glanced over her shoulder, an eyebrow arched. "Aside from looking gorgeous and keeping me company? No, nothing."

"I can do both of those things," I deadpanned.

She winked. "I thought so."

I spotted the notepad she'd used to make her Merry Weihnachten list during our first planning session on her counter. A few things had been crossed off, like *Saint Nikolaus Day* and *Advent candles*. I knew I shouldn't snoop, but I picked it up and, on a whim, turned back one page. And found myself looking at a pen drawing of my face.

Evie turned around and stopped dead, making a sound like a strangled mouse. "That's um, that's just…"

"It's me?" I said, unable to take my eyes from the page.

"Yeah."

Finally, I looked up. "This is what I look like to you?" It was obviously me, but it was also…a better version of me. It was a physical representation of rose-colored glasses. I could almost feel the attraction, the desire, the…love in every line. And she'd drawn this less than a week after we'd first met. She'd felt that then?

Evie bit her lower lip, then nodded. "Yes."

"It's incredible. I can't believe you drew this." Couldn't believe one drawing could convey so much emotion.

"It's easy when you have good source material," she said. The words triggered a blush, and she turned back around and quickly began pulling clean items from the drying rack by the sink. Perhaps too quickly, because when she went to grab a mug, she knocked her coffeepot off the drying rack. The metal coffeepot hit the floor with a light clang that was quickly smothered by Evie's, "Fuck!"

Smiling, I automatically admonished her with, "Swearing jar." But when that first "fuck" was followed by a half-dozen more, I decided not to tell her she owed a lot of blue slips to the jar. Instead, I hopped down from the stool and went to her side. "What's wrong?" I asked gently.

Evie tensed when I rested a hand on her back and I pulled it away immediately. She didn't respond to my question, but it was obvious that her entire mood had changed from the light, easy teasing of seconds before to something darker. Finally, she turned to me, holding up the top half of her stovetop espresso maker.

I could see right away that the handle had snapped off near the hinged lid. "Oh, no," I murmured. I moved to touch her again but held back because of her earlier incongruous reaction. "That's unfortunate."

Evie burst into tears. My stomach clenched. I'd messed up my response to her somehow. So, I did the best thing I could think of. I took her by the shoulders, pulled her close, and hugged her. And she hugged me back.

I held on to her as Evie wrapped her arms tightly around my waist. She pressed her face against my shoulder and sobbed like her entire world was falling apart. I rubbed gentle circles on her back, remaining silent as she cried. There was absolutely nothing I could do except wait for her to either tell me what was wrong, what she needed, or to settle herself down.

"This was Heather's," she said around heaving sobs. Evie inhaled a handful of long, stuttering breaths, and seemed to get the oxygen she needed to keep talking. "I've used it every day since she died, and now I've broken it."

"Oh, Evie, Schnucki, I am so sorry."

Her voice still trembled and broke, her words tumbling over one another as they rushed out. "It's annoying and I don't know why she bought it because most of the hotels didn't have stoves, so she bought this little camping burner with disposable gas cannisters. I don't know why she didn't buy a mini electric hotplate. It was a pain in the ass the entire time we were on our Europe trip, because every time we used planes instead of trains she'd have to dump the gas and buy more when we landed. And she complained constantly because I made her use it outside our room because I'm paranoid about carbon monoxide poisoning. But it really does make great coffee. It's the only thing of hers

I have, the only thing I wanted after she died. This stupid coffeepot. And now I've broken it." Evie broke into fresh tears. She pressed the butts of her palms into her eyes, gulping in deep, shuddering breaths.

I lightly held her shoulders, just letting her know that I was there with her. When she'd dropped her hands again, I took one of them and brought it to my mouth to kiss her palm. "Do you need help?"

Evie nodded, her tear-filled eyes never leaving mine.

"Okay, well. Let's fix it."

She leaned over and tore a square off the roll of kitchen towel to wipe her eyes and blow her nose. "How?" That single word came out so broken and childlike that I just wanted to gather her in my arms again and somehow wish it all better. But that wasn't going to fix the broken pot.

"I'm sure there are replacement parts online. I don't think this is the first time someone has broken their pot. What is the brand?"

"Bialetti. She bought it in Italy like…eighteen years ago."

After a moment of Googling, I asked, "Do you know the size? In cups?"

"No." Evie pressed her lips together, but not before I saw the tremble in them.

"Okay. Then let's find out." After another quick kiss to her hand, I let go to Google "how to find your Bialetti size," and had an answer in seconds. "Do you have a measurement tape?"

"No." She smiled crookedly. "But I do have a measuring tape."

I took the teasing because it wasn't cruel, and more importantly—it was Evie being more like herself instead of this distraught shell. "Okay, then I'll take your measur-*ing* tape, please."

Evie produced one from a drawer, watching me as I measured twice then checked the measurements against a moka pot size chart. "It's a two-cup pot." From there it was simple to search for a replacement handle and order it. I paid for express shipping and set my phone down with a flourish. "Okay, we have a replacement handle kit coming. It will arrive on Monday. You can come to my apartment and I'll make you coffee in the mornings until then. And as soon as the handle arrives, I'll fix the pot for you."

"How do you know what to do? I can find someone local to fix it. Or send it to Bialetti. Or…" She inhaled deeply, forcing a brave smile. "I can just get a new one. Maybe it's time for a fancy automated machine."

"*Or*, I can fix it for you," I said gently. "My father is an engineer, do you remember? And he loves to fix things. The smaller and more—"

I frowned and twiddled my fingers like I was working on something. "You know…ähm…little and hard to work with."

"Fiddly?"

"That sounds right. Ja. The smaller and more *fiddly* they are, the more he loves it. He taught me some things about repairing household items and broken things in your home like pipe and tiles. And we used to build small models of machines."

"Wow. The only thing my dad taught me was how to run a board meeting, that every transaction in life—and he didn't just mean financial—should result in a break-even or net gain, and also don't let anyone know you have money or they will try to take it away from you."

I pressed my lips together. When she shared things like this, I didn't know how to respond. "Those are useful skills to have, for you," I said carefully.

"I suppose they are, if I want to be a horrible caricature of wealth." She frowned. "Sorry. You know what, I'm not going to be one of those people who pretends they hate having money. I don't hate it. It allows me to do things I want, live in a way that's comfortable, and help as many people as I can. I've never had to budget or worry about affording something. And I recognize my position of privilege. I just wish it came without family bullshit." Evie's face scrunched up, and she blinked rapidly, her teeth scraping her lower lip. "I'm sorry. I ruined the mood by talking about my family. More than I already did with my tantrum."

"You haven't ruined anything," I assured her.

"Thank you." She took a deep breath, squaring her shoulders. "You know, I'm feeling a little out of sorts. I know we were having dinner and all that but…Would it be okay if—" Evie stopped suddenly, as if she'd just realized that she was in her own home and couldn't ask if I minded if she left. Which meant I had to leave. I didn't want to leave her, but I did want to respect her wishes and give her whatever space she might need to work through her feelings.

I didn't hesitate. "Ja, of course. But you know where I am if you need anything."

That elicited a small smile from her. "I do."

I leaned in, then paused, giving her every opportunity to back away from a kiss if she wanted. Evie did anything but. She wasn't as enthusiastic or passionate as she usually was when kissing me but for some reason, this soft, emotional kiss made me feel even more connected to her.

"Thank you," Evie said again, the words stronger this time. "For listening. And for…helping."

"Of course. Any time," I said, meaning it.

She looked so pained that I wondered if she was going to be able to say what she was clearly trying to. "It's…I'm not good with…help. Asking for or receiving it."

My whole body ached with sympathy for her. I gently gripped her biceps. "I understand, and it's okay. You can take whatever you need from me."

"Okay. Thanks." She exhaled a loud, relieved breath. "I'll text you tomorrow morning to confirm the time and stuff for Snowport?"

"That sounds good." I chanced another quick kiss, then reluctantly left her. Reluctantly because I wanted to soothe her hurts, gently pull down all the walls she'd built. But if I couldn't pull them down, then hopefully Evie could show me a way to climb over them.

CHAPTER FIFTEEN

Evie

When I heard the knock followed by the sound of my front door unlocking, I knew Chloe had arrived for our Christmas markets outing. And she was early. I popped my head out of the bedroom in time to see her practically skipping into the living room with Pete following at a more sedate pace. There was no greeting, no preamble, just an excited, "You're doing a date thing! It's a Christmas miracle!"

I held back my eye roll. "If this were a 'date thing,' would I be bringing my favorite niece along with me, or would I be doing something private?"

"That's exactly what I told her," Pete said.

Chloe sighed expansively. "Whatever. I'm gonna go see if Annika is ready."

"Okay," I agreed. "But you're early so if she's not ready, don't hassle her."

"I won't," she said, exasperation leaking from those two words.

Pete came into my bedroom, leaning against the doorframe to watch me pull on a pair of knee-high brown leather boots over my jeans. He had a pinched sort of expression that demanded I ask, "What's up?"

"Your mom called me today."

"Oh wow. Lucky you. I'm jealous," I deadpanned. "So…so…jealous."

"Yeahhh."

I raised an eyebrow when he didn't say more. "And what did she berate you about this time?"

Pete sighed so dramatically I felt the rush of air. "The nanny thing. And she's still pushing me to talk to Chloe about changing her surname to Phillips, so she can"—a raised voice accompanied his air quotes—"'truly embrace her role in the Foundation.'"

"Oh, Christ. She has no shame, does she? God, maybe you and I should make an IVF baby just to shut them the fuck up." I mentally added a blue slip to the swear jar. "Or better yet, I'll just give them some of my eggs and they can make themselves another grandchild with some good-ol'-boy sperm and raise it however they see fit. And then maybe, just maybe, they'd lay off my niece."

He adopted a faux scandalized look, the same one he'd given me all through high school when he'd come to me with a particularly juicy piece of gossip. "You'd really split the inheritance and trusts that are supposed to be all Chloe's with another kid?"

I matched his expression. "With my biological child? Damned straight I would." Laughing, I patted his arm. "Don't worry, Petey. You know how I feel about having a kid of my own."

"I know, peanut," he said, serious now. "But you know I think you'd be a great mom, and the world would be lucky to have your genes in it."

"My genes are already in the world because I'm still alive. And technically some of my genes are in Chloe. Besides, I'm almost thirty-seven. And as much as I hate to place the burden of carrying on this branch of the Phillips line on my darling niece, I'm going to do just that because I have zero desire to have a child of my own. How long did my mom rant for?"

"Two point three Stairway to Heavens. Not so bad." He'd been in a band in college and had learned to deal with my mother's tirades by tuning out, and singing songs in his head. The longest rant she'd ever done, according to Pete, was "an excruciating five point six Bohemian Rhapsodies."

"Wow. Is that a new record for shortness of rant? And just think, in a few weeks you can be ranted at in person." I clasped my hands together and batted my eyelashes at him. "Oh what a wonderful way to spend Christmas."

"Tell me about it." Pete's forehead wrinkled and I knew exactly what he was going to say before he asked, "Are you sure you'll be okay?" He reached out to squeeze my shoulder.

I patted his hand. "You ask me that every year, and what do I say every year?"

"You *say* that you're totally fine and don't worry about you and who cares about Christmas. But saying it doesn't make it true."

"It is true," I asserted yet again.

Pete sighed. "Yeah, I got it. But I'm still going to ask."

"I appreciate that. But it's old news, Pete. I'll manage the same way I do every year."

"I'm sorry." I had no idea how he managed to articulate around his hangdog expression, but he did.

"And you say that every year. I know, and it's fine. You've got Chloe to think about." Until my niece was twenty-one, my parents held the purse strings for Chloe's beyond-substantial trust fund, and I understood Pete's reluctance to rock the boat. I didn't *really* think my parents would jeopardize their relationship with their only grandchild, the last link to Heather, but who knew what they might do in a fit of capriciousness. "And she *should* know her maternal grandparents." Even if they were bigots. Well, one bigot and one weak-willed person.

"I agree. And she loves them. But she *is* starting to ask me more questions about why you're never there. I mean she knows things between you and your parents aren't great, but…"

I shrugged. "You can tell her why if you want. Explain it however you think best."

He rubbed his mustache. "I might have to. Sorry, Evie."

"Whatever, it's fine. And if she wants to talk to me about it, she can. It's only for another five and a bit years until she's eighteen and can access the trust Heather set up for her, and eight and a bit years until she's twenty-one and she can access the big fund. And then you can give them double middle fingers if you want. Or…you can let it go and keep doing what you're doing now." I squeezed his arm. "It's okay if you don't hate them, Petey."

Though my words sounded convincing, a tiny irrational part of me kind of wished he did hate them. I wished someone would go to bat for me, and rage against my parents' ridiculous behavior. But I understood his position. My self-righteousness felt better when I didn't think about the fact I'd stayed in the closet until I was twenty-one, just so I could access all that money.

"I adore you, my little bean." He opened his arms and I went to him for a hug. Pete kissed the top of my head, gave me an extra squeeze, then let me go.

"And I adore you too. Besides, Annika and I are doing our Merry Weihnachten, remember? I won't be alone for Christmas this year."

"Yeah, of course I remember. Why don't you bring her to our place for our early Christmas celebration? It's easy enough to add another person for dinner."

It wasn't the worst idea he'd ever had. And now that we'd tentatively admitted that we were attracted to each other, that uncomfortable jealousy about Annika being into Pete had disappeared. "Sure. I'll ask her."

"Check in with her about gifts. I'd like to get her something so it's not strange when we're exchanging things."

"Okay. I mean, knowing how much she loves Christmas, she'd probably be happy with that and want to reciprocate for you guys."

"Got any ideas? I know she likes music. And you."

I blushed. I'd give myself to Annika as a gift any day. "Ummm. She had to leave a bunch of books in Germany. She likes to travel, likes good food and wine and…beer." I was uncomfortably aware of how generic those interests were, because the truth was that after only two weeks of spending time with her, I still didn't know Annika all that well. "So, I don't know. A book? Voucher for a travel accessories store or dinner?" God, what boring ideas.

"What kind of books?"

"Based on the few tattered ones she deemed special enough to bring with her, I'd say romances about ladies who like ladies."

"Has she read your stuff?"

I gaped for a moment before spluttering, "Don't you dare." It wasn't like Annika didn't know my titles—she could buy my work herself. But the thought of actively pushing it at her made me feel beyond embarrassed.

"I'm just saying. I could give her signed copies because I'm a cool guy who knows a graphic novel artist."

I rolled my eyes at him and turned away to pull out my scarf rack. Before I could pick one from my admittedly way-too-large scarf collection, Pete pushed past me into the walk-in. "Wear the different-shades-of-blue one. Makes your eyes really blue."

"That makes no sense. Color can't make other colors change. My eyes are the color they are."

"Trust me." He pulled the scarf down and wrapped it around my neck. "You need to look your best, my dearest friend, because regardless of what you told Chloe, this is kind of a date."

"It's not a date. We're not in a dating zone. I don't know what zone we're in, but it's not dating."

"So why not ask her what zone you're in? Or ask her out on a date that doesn't include taking my daughter along?"

"Right. That would be the mature and rational thing. Yes. I should do that." Except for my problem of being a little afraid of relationships after all my shitty ones.

"You know," Pete mused. "Last night, Heather visited me in ghost form. She said you need to get over it and start doing more shit, stop hiding from your life. She knows you started doing that after she died and she's super mad at you."

"I can't believe you're throwing my own Ghost Heather joke at me."

"You threw it at me first," he rebutted. "And aren't you doing exactly what you tell me not to do? Avoiding life because Heather's gone?"

Before I could rebut his rebuttal, my front door opened again. The sound of Chloe and Annika chatting filtered through my house, growing louder until Chloe barged right into my bedroom. But Annika paused near the doorway. "Klopf klopf."

I smiled and beckoned her closer. "Come in." I noted the disciplined way her eyes remained on me after an initial look around the room.

"Oh, Evie. You look great." Annika glanced down at her own outfit. "I'm glad it seems I got the American Christmas market clothes right."

"You sure did," I agreed, annoyed with myself for how breathy I sounded. Why not just hang a sign around your neck that screams "I'm so into you I can barely breathe," Evie? She wore a red-and-green button-down under her thick black puffer jacket, and tight black jeans tucked into well-worn, black Doc Martens boots which were so hot and so at odds with her usual image that I almost forgot to breathe for real. A gray scarf and matching beanie made her outdoors-ready. "You look…really good."

Chloe snorted. Pete cleared his throat. I glared at both of them before looking back to Annika. After last night and my emotionally stunted reaction to breaking my coffeepot, I didn't know how she'd react to seeing me again. I didn't know how I'd react. I'd hated that I couldn't open up and let her be there for me the way she obviously wanted to. But now it was like nothing had happened. And the fact she didn't hold my outburst against me made me like her even more.

Pete interrupted my internal hyperventilation and self-flagellation to give Chloe some cash. "Please try to limit your sugar consumption just a little. Aunt Evie will bring you home after, okay?"

"Okay." She hugged him around the waist. "Enjoy your man-night, Dad."

He chuckled. "I will. You guys have a great time." After kissing Chloe's forehead and hugging Annika and me, he left.

"You guys all set?" I asked.

"Yup." Chloe grabbed Annika's arm and led her to the door.

Annika patted the hand Chloe had linked through her elbow. "I am ready to see how your Christmas markets compare to ours. There may be some arguments. And perhaps lists laying out the pros and cons of each, though of course the Christmas markets in Germany have no cons." She said this with a sly glance at me, as if she expected me to defend the Snowport Markets.

As I locked the door behind them, I protested, "Hey, I have no allegiance to these markets. You know my stance on Christmas. So I'm going to stay out of it."

"Sure you are," Chloe laughed.

I kept silent for the drive. Mostly because there was little room for me in the conversation as Annika and Chloe chatted about their favorite Christmas things. Annika had to keep twisting around to talk with Chloe, and each time she did, she flashed a shy little smile at me. I miraculously found a parking space at Seaport and after snugging on my beanie, and checking Chloe had all her warm stuff, we made our way to the market. "Oof," I said, zipping up my down vest before buttoning my coat. "It's brick out."

Annika paused pulling on her gloves. "Brick?"

"Cold," Chloe supplied. "You need a Boston pocket dictionary. Haven't you given Annika a translation guidebook, Aunt Evie?" she said innocently.

"No," Annika said for me. "She hasn't." She gave me a quick kiss on the edge of my mouth then tucked her arm into my elbow, leaning into me as we walked. Chloe, on my other side, had her fingers nestled in the pocket of my peacoat. She used to do that when she was younger and had outgrown hand-holding, but still wanted to make sure we didn't get separated. And something about the fact she was doing it now made my chest feel a little tight.

"So, if it's 'brick,' does that mean it's going to snow soon?" Annika asked warily.

"Maybe?" I said. "Last year was a bit of a snow dud."

"I hope this year is also a snow dud," she deadpanned.

"As long as it buckets down in Colorado, I don't care," I said, laughing.

As we approached the entry—bright and cheerful with two columns of foliage lit with twinkling lights and strings of lights leading into the market space, which was rows and rows of upscale tent structures—Annika disengaged herself. "Oh! I want a photograph of this." She handed me her phone. "Could you please take it for me?"

"Sure." I pulled off my mitten. Annika jogged over to stand in front of the entryway, looking around to make sure she wasn't blocking anyone from entering. She flung her arms out wide and smiled so hugely that I smiled at her smile.

After I'd taken a few photos, Chloe nudged me in the side. "Let me take one of both of you." She took Annika's phone before I could say anything. My niece nudged me again, harder this time. "Go," she said, and I had no choice but to comply.

Annika's whole face brightened as I approached. I moved in beside her and we stood close, hugging each other around the waist. She turned to look at me, a gentle smile curving her lips. "I'm so glad I'm here with you, Evie."

I smiled back. "Me too."

I was just about to kiss her when Chloe skipped over to us and handed Annika her phone. "You guys. So cute."

Cute was edging into me having feelings and I was taking the path of if I didn't think about it then they weren't real. I fought down a blush as I asked Annika, "Where do we start? Is there a Christmas markets protocol?"

"Ja, of course. Look at everything, purchase everything, eat everything."

"Okay. Let's do it. But first, hot drinks." I bought Annika and I coffee, and a hot chocolate for Chloe to keep us warm while we browsed. Neither of them seemed hungry yet, though with the food aromas pressing in around us, I wondered how long that would last. The markets were bustling without being oppressively busy.

Annika was obsessed with Betty the Yeti—a person in a bright pink…creature costume, because who could say for certain if she was really a yeti, considering such things didn't exist. The sound Annika emitted when she spotted Betty made the person inside the costume fling their arms wide and dance a funny little jig. After more photos and a conversation with Betty that was just Annika gushing, we continued.

We spent an hour browsing the stalls, and I bought a few things—a special Snowport Markets mug, another scarf to add to my already-too-large scarf collection, some funky notebooks with animals painted on them, and a blue-and-white flannel shirt. Chloe bought a leather wallet (probably Pete's Christmas gift) and some bodywash. Annika purchased a mug like mine, a wool wrap, hand cream, a puzzle, socks, a bracelet, some earrings, and a candle. And it looked like she'd been severely restraining herself.

Once we were sufficiently laden with stuffed cloth bags slung over our arms, I asked, "Are you guys hungry?" Because I was approaching really hungry, which would be a recipe for grumpiness disaster.

"Yes," they said in unison, though Annika's answer was an enthusiastic "Ja."

There were so many food options, from a taqueria to crepes, Italian to cheese-wheel pasta. And I wanted to eat it all. "Okay," I said. "I need to pace myself. Maybe we need to come back another day so I can try everything."

Chloe doubled over, feigning side-splitting laughter. "Now who loves Christmas?"

"I love *food*," I said indignantly.

"Oh! Look at this one," Annika said, pointing to a stall. "Baked Cheese Haus?"

I watched the vendor heating the flat surface of a half-wheel of raclette cheese and then tilting it until the gooey, delicious top layer oozed onto toasted bread. Sold. "Haus? Surely this isn't a German national dish?"

She laughed. "No. But it looks very good."

"Agreed. Chloe, you interested?"

She wrinkled her nose. "Nah."

I turned to Annika. "Want to share one?"

"Ja, please."

We decided on the Jambon Cru with cured ham, baby gherkins, and Dijon mustard, though Annika did mull over the one with a bratwurst. "If we're still hungry, we can get that one later," I pointed out, ever the voice of gluttony reason.

"That is a very good strategy."

Annika offered me the first taste, holding the baguette up for me. I held her wrist to keep it steady, and took a huge bite. "Oh my god," I mumbled once I'd swallowed. "God I love cheese."

Annika's eyes widened. "Is it that good?"

"Better than good," I assured her.

Chloe made a noise of exasperation. "While you guys are…doing whatever it is with that cheese, I'm gonna go get tacos."

"Use the hand sanitizer before you eat, please." I'd been militant about making sure all three of us sanitized at regular intervals.

Chloe handed off her bags to me, then pointedly walked to the sanitizer station to do as I'd asked her. Annika and I moved out of the way of the flow of people to eat and wait for Chloe to get her tacos. I stared after her, and kept staring until Annika nudged me to tell me it was my turn for the baguette. Once I'd had my mouthful, she quietly asked, "What's wrong?"

"Nothing," I said, surprised she'd asked.

"Are you sure?" She gestured toward Chloe standing in line at the taqueria stall.

"Oh. It's just…she's growing up I guess, and it's hard. Soon she won't need to come to my place after school, she'll be able to go home and organize her own dinner. Technically she's old enough now but I lobbied Pete to let her keep coming." He hadn't been hard to convince. He wasn't an overbearing dad, but he was protective. "I'm scared she won't want to hang out with me if she doesn't have to." I wasn't sure if it was because I'd been pregnant with her, or because Heather was gone, or just because she was my niece, but I loved Chloe with every cell in my body without feeling any sort of "mom" type bond with her.

"Evie," Annika said gently. "I can't think of anyone who wouldn't want to spend time with you. I know that I do."

"You're so sweet. And the feeling is mutual. Me spending time with you, I mean."

"I'm glad to hear that. And Chloe is really a very good kid. And she seems very emm…well-adjusted."

"I think she is. Despite everything me and my family seem to do to try and screw her up."

Annika frowned. "Like what?" She held the baguette out to me and I bit off another delicious, oozy mouthful.

Once I'd swallowed, I answered, "My swearing, for one. And…I don't want my parents influencing her, trying to turn her into something she isn't just because she's a Phillips. They seem to be trying to force her into a box because of her genes."

"What is it about your family that's so awful? Aside from not accepting you. That is awful, but I feel like there's more than that."

"There is. But now's probably not the best time to start a conversation about it."

"Okay," she said amiably. "If you do find the right time for the conversation, I'm here."

"Thank you." I paused to collect my thoughts. "Hey. Listen. About last night. I shouldn't have asked you to leave, especially not after I'd invited you for dinner, and you were so sweet. I was embarrassed about my reaction and just…I was just embarrassed."

"I understand," Annika said, her tone gentle. "And it's okay. Really."

"It was just a lot. That's all. And I—" I inhaled deeply. "I really appreciated that you didn't ask if I was okay, because obviously I wasn't. You asked if I needed help, and even when I said I did but I didn't know what I needed, you knew. It was just what I needed in the moment, thank you."

"You're welcome." Annika leaned down and kissed me softly on the mouth.

"Will you come home with me?"

Her eyes widened. "Of course." A sly smile made its way across her lips. "You live in the same place I do, and you drove me here, so I have to go home with you."

Laughing, I nudged her. "I mean, back to my place. I still haven't lit my second Advent candle."

"I'd love to." She turned slightly to face me front on. "Evie. I'm so glad I met you. I was…struggling, wondering if I did the right thing, moving here, especially for such a short time."

"What do you mean?" I asked quietly.

Annika's forehead wrinkled. "Before I moved it felt like everything was just on the edge of falling into place for me, but then it was like nothing would work out. It was hard." She laughed quietly. "But with you, there is nothing but easiness. And I feel like I should be more upset about ending my relationship back in Germany, but I just don't care at all. Especially not now with—" She cut herself off. "Does that make me a monster?"

"Not at all," I said emphatically. "I've learned not to allocate care to things that don't deserve my care. For a while I worried what people thought, especially after Heather died, like was I grieving too much or not enough. Nothing felt right. But I knew Heather would have told me, if she was still around, to not overthink it." She would have told me to not overthink my feelings for Annika too. I shrugged. "Sorry, it's not exactly the same and I didn't mean to drag my stuff into this. I think what I was trying very clumsily to say is that there's no right or wrong way to feel."

"No right or wrong way," Annika mused, nodding slowly.

Our conversation was halted by Chloe returning with her tacos. We resumed our Snowport excursion. More browsing, more photos—Annika's next obsession was the fifty-foot-tall Christmas tree—until around seven thirty when we agreed we'd seen all that could be seen and bought everything we wanted. Annika suggested some dessert before we left. Chloe and Annika did rock-paper-scissors to choose waffles or crepes and Chloe won with crepes. I was still full from the raclette…s, and the cheese-wheel pasta and the roast pork—all shared with Chloe and/or Annika—but I ordered a plain butter and sugar crepe, while Chloe and Annika both went with Nutella. Annika paid for the desserts, I made both of them sanitize their hands, and we ate as we walked back through the rows toward the exit.

Annika licked oozing Nutella from her thumb and when she caught me watching her, winked. I swallowed hard, trying to ignore the slow trickle of heat running down my spine. I moved closer and was just about to grab her hand and pull her closer for a sneaky kiss, when Chloe, somehow the master of both putting Annika and me together and pulling us apart at the most inopportune times, butted in. "Give me your trash and I'll dump it."

"Okay," I said, trying not to make it sound like a sigh. "Thanks."

Annika and Chloe were chatting like old friends as we walked back to the car. I stayed quiet and listened, enjoying the sensation of Annika's body pressed against me, the feeling of her hand gripping mine.

I was just about to pull out of the parking space when some idiot in a souped-up sports car came speeding around the corner and cut me off. I braked hard and, in my head, let loose with a stream of screaming expletives.

Though it was mumbled, I still very clearly heard Chloe's "Scheisse!" from the back seat.

I wasn't fluent in German by any means, but I knew what that word meant. "Chloe, fuck. I mean, fudgesicle," I hastily corrected myself. "Swearing is swearing in any language."

Annika suddenly seemed very interested in her phone.

"Just for that German S-word, Chloe, I'm pulling one of my S-words out of the jar. So think about that. That's two dollars less you'll be getting, kiddo." The swear jar had already reached $127, so those few dollars meant nothing in the scheme of things.

"What about the F-word you just said?" Annika pointed out, all interest in her phone gone now she could shift some blame.

Whose side was she on, anyway? I narrowed my eyes at her, though I smiled so she knew I wasn't pissed. Then I turned around and narrowed my eyes at my niece.

Chloe's casual look was worthy of an Oscar. "Annika taught me some German."

"Did she now?" I glanced at Annika who had grown very still and very quiet. "And when?" I tapped Annika on the forearm. "Here I am trying my best to not use curse words and you're just teaching her all the German ones."

She raised her hands. "I would like you to know that I did not teach her expletives, just some easy phrases. And as for when. Tonight while we were buying things."

I'd totally missed that. And I totally loved it. The teaching, not the missing.

"Hey, Annika," Chloe said, snatching Annika's attention. "I was wondering. Do you think in German or English?"

"If I'm speaking English, English. German, then it's German."

"Yeah but what about your private thoughts that you're not going to say aloud in English *or* German, like 'Evie is hot'?"

Annika grinned, shooting me a quick glance before looking back to Chloe. "German."

"Chloe!" I interrupted. "Please stop. I'm begging you."

She spared me a look before turning back to Annika. And thankfully, she switched topics away from torturing her aunt. "I have French class, and I think in English first then translate in my mouth." Chloe frowned. "I feel like you're supposed to think in the language that you're speaking, but…I'm not there yet. And I keep forgetting things in French and just saying them in English."

"I think once you are fluent, you'll probably think in whatever language you're speaking. And forgetting words is normal. I still do it." She laughed, and the sound of it filled the car and warmed me through. "I once forgot the word *legs*. I just could not think of the word, such a simple one. So I called them *walking arms*."

Yeah, okay that was funny. I laughed with them. "Can we leave now?"

"Okay," they said, again in unison.

They were ganging up on me, and it didn't bother me one bit.

CHAPTER SIXTEEN

Annika

After an early-morning text informing me that there was an issue with power in the Pyramid building, I sent out a message on Teams to let everyone on the project know we'd be working from home today. Other than setting up a time for a group video meeting, I wouldn't speak with them unless they needed me. They were adults with good work ethics and I wasn't going to badger them about their hours.

And I wasn't going to badger myself either. I'd been too hyped up to go to sleep after the Christmas market and then spending time with Evie after we'd lit her second candle, and I'd been awake until the early hours. A day working at home was a gift from the universe.

In between work tasks, I'd baked all the gingerbread slabs I needed to construct my Lebkuchenhaus. I was about to set aside work to begin the construction when someone knocked on my door. My mood soared, because it could only be Evie and time with Evie was always preferable to being alone. A quick peep through my peephole made me step back in surprise, but I opened the door immediately. "Chloe. Hallo. Is something wrong?"

"Nope, all good," she said cheerfully. "Can I come in?"

"I—" What was the right answer here? Was it odd for me to let Evie's niece into my apartment? She'd lingered at the open doorway yesterday when she'd come over to check if I was ready. Of course *I* knew I wasn't a creep, and I was sure Evie and Pete did too. And it wasn't like I was a stranger to her. We'd had a great time at the markets yesterday, but why was she here, asking to come in to my apartment? "Is Evie with you?"

"Nope." She popped the P sharply. "Aunt Evie isn't home. Which is why I'm here."

I peeked out the door and toward Evie's, which was closed. "Did you lose your key? Or forget to bring it today?"

"Nope. Just don't wanna hang out there alone. And I don't have much homework, so…" She shrugged.

That was a fair point. "Okay. Have you called your aunt?"

"Yep. No answer." She shrugged again. "Dunno where she is. She's usually home. But I can just go hang out at Aunt Evie's until she gets back."

I weighed the options. Chloe wasn't a kid-kid, but it felt weird to leave her alone, even if she was in a familiar, safe space. I opened the door fully. "Ja, okay, of course, come in."

"Thanks!"

"How did you know I was home?"

"Your music."

Oh no. "I am sorry about that." Evie had never mentioned anything about being able to hear my music. "I didn't know it was that loud."

"It wasn't." She grinned. "I'm a Swiftie, so I've got a radar for her music, at all volumes." After looking around my living room, Chloe said, "Smells really good in here." Then, "Why don't you have a TV?"

I went over to my laptop on the kitchen table and logged off the office server. I still had a little bit more work I wanted to do, but it could be done later. "I don't really need one. I can watch movies or television shows on my iPad or laptop. A TV is just one more thing to sell when I leave."

"When are you leaving?" she asked casually.

"The end of next year, unless the project I'm working on is finished early." My answer came out easily but inside, I felt a tiny panic. I didn't want it to finish early. I didn't want to leave Boston. I didn't want to be apart from Evie.

"Think it will be? Finished early," she clarified.

"I don't know. We've only just started it."

"I hope it doesn't finish early," she said airily. "My aunt really likes you."

This kid was confident, I'd give her that. I hadn't had much to do with children, but Evie's niece was very easy. I didn't really know what age-appropriate thing to say in response to her statement, so I settled for a neutral, "I like her too. Do you want a drink?" But what did I have in my fridge that was suitable for a preteen to drink?

Thankfully Chloe's request was simple. "Just some water please."

"Are you hungry?" I asked as I pulled out a jug of cold water.

"Nope, but thanks. I made a sandwich at Aunt Evie's."

Again, there was that strange expression. But I wasn't fluent enough in twelve-year-old girl, and she wasn't my relative, so I let it be. I filled a glass and left it on the kitchen counter for her, and while Chloe drank her water, I texted Evie.

Chloe is here. I'm not sure why. But it's all fine, just so you know when you get back.

I stared at the screen for ten seconds, but there was nothing, not even typing dots. Chloe brought her glass over to put it in the sink, then paused to study the things I had stuck to my refrigerator. It was mostly menus from Evie's "Boston pack," but I'd also stuck some of the sentimental cards I'd been given for my farewell and a couple of birthday cards from friends and family.

She touched the card with a hot-air balloon on it that my brother had drawn, very badly. "Who drew this?"

"My brother. As you can see, he is not good at art."

Chloe snorted. "Nope. But it's still cool he did that. My aunt draws me a birthday card every year, of us doing something crazy like deep-sea diving or going to space or mountain climbing. I love them. She gives sympathy cards to my dad for his birthday."

From what I knew of Evie, that seemed right and I laughed. "That sounds very cool. When is your birthday?"

"April third. When's yours?"

"The eighth of October."

"Just so you know, Aunt Evie's is February twenty-ninth. She was born in a leap year. 1988. So we do two birthdays for her, the twenty-eighth of February and then the first of March."

How interesting. "Oh? What about in leap years when her actual birthday happens?" Like this year.

"We just have one day on her real birthday." Chloe made it sound as if it were obvious. "Dad says the extras is something my mom made up, because otherwise Aunt Evie would only have a birthday every four years, so they needed to add in more celebration days for years that aren't leap years." She shrugged. "Doesn't make sense. She gets more birthday days than a regular person."

Smiling, I agreed, "Yes, she does." But Evie was worth it. We could have sat there all afternoon just chatting about random things, as we had yesterday, but I had a flash of inspiration. "Have you ever made a gingerbread house?"

She shook her head.

"Do you like eating gingerbread?" When she nodded, I asked, "Want to help me? I need to start on my gingerbread house. Lebkuchenhaus."

Chloe mouthed the word a few times before trying it out. "Lebcoooken-house." I smiled at her close-enough pronunciation as she asked, "How long will it take?"

I pointed to the table where I'd left my house pieces to cool. "I already baked the gingerbread into its shapes. So now it's just making the construction and decorating." Smiling, I added, "But once the house is built, it needs to set at least until tomorrow. So there will be no decorating today."

"Oh. But that's the part I really want to do." She side-eyed me cheekily. "Can I get time off school to help?"

Laughing, I told her, "You will have to talk to your dad about that. I think school is more important than decorating a gingerbread house. And I don't think I could stay home from my job to do it either."

The look Chloe gave me made me think I'd misallocated the order of importance of decorating and work. "I will," she assured me. "How hard is it to build a leb-coooken-house?"

"Hard enough. But don't worry, I'm an expert Lebkuchenhaus builder *and* decorator."

Chloe's gaze was unwavering. "Expert builder," she said, drawing the words out as if she was turning them over in her head as she spoke. "And you're fixing Aunt Evie's coffeepot." Chloe pointed to the replacement moka pot handle kit, sitting on the counter where I'd left it after unboxing the parcel that had been delivered that morning. Then she stared at me again. "You don't look like someone who can build or fix stuff." Chloe flushed. "Sorry, that sounded mean. I didn't mean it like that. No offense."

I smiled. I wasn't offended. Though I *was* curious about what a person who builds or fixes stuff looked like. "It's all right. My father taught me how to fix a lot of things. It is quite a useful skill to know, don't you think? Because now I can fix your aunt's coffee maker."

"Yeah. It was my mom's." Chloe's nose wrinkled. "Aunt Evie called my dad on Saturday night, crying about breaking it."

"Ja, she was quite upset. I understand it's very special to her."

"It is," Chloe agreed. "I get it. But also…not really. Like, it's just a coffeepot thing, but I know it was my mom's coffeepot thing and Aunt Evie is super sentimental about it." She played with the small bag containing the replacement handle and pin. "I have a few things Mom gave me but they're also just *things*, you know? They aren't my mom. I don't know if I'd be upset if they got broken or lost." Chloe looked up. "Does that make me a bad person?"

My heart hurt for her losing her mother. For Evie losing her sister. For Pete losing his wife. "I don't think it makes you a bad person at all. You feel the emotions that you feel. It makes sense to me." I hoped that was the right answer.

Chloe nodded slowly but didn't seem to want to talk any more about her mother. Instead, she pointed at my table. "Aunt Evie has a wreath like that. It's cool."

I smiled. "I know. I gave it to her."

The smile she shot back was far cheekier than mine, as was her echoing of my words. "I know." She looked around my apartment again before finally bringing her gaze back to me. "So…how do we make this gingerbread house?"

"With gingerbread," I deadpanned.

Chloe rolled her eyes, but she was smiling.

I pulled out the container of gingerbread offcuts. "I'll teach you."

Chloe helped me clear and clean the counter, and set out ingredients to make the icing "mortar" to hold the house together. She ended up doing most of the mortar mixing and building under my instruction. It made sense—I was a project manager after all—and I was happy to guide her and hold the pieces in place while she laid the foundations.

As we assembled the wall and roof panels of the house, Chloe and I nibbled on the gingerbread leftovers I'd baked to fuel me through the building process. The house looked pretty good by the time we'd finished construction, and I moved it to the side of the counter where it could set without being in my way.

We were partway through cleaning up when there was another knock on my door. I glanced at the time. Almost five p.m. Though I was sure it was Evie, I still checked the peephole. My mouth went dry. I flung the door open, and then my brain stalled.

If I didn't know her face so well now, I may not have recognized Evie. She was dressed in a tailored wool pantsuit, dark gray with a subtle check, paired with a white silk blouse that showed just enough cleavage to tantalize. Her hair was down, falling to brush her shoulders. She wore makeup. And perfume. And heels. She looked like a businesswoman, or lawyer, or…something that was melting my brain. Something very *very* hot. The look seemed to change her, make her seem more confident and commanding, and I could see who she might be in her other life, regularly dealing with hundreds of millions of dollars like it was just another day. This new aura was super sexy.

Evie gripped my upper arm, leaning in for a quick kiss. She pulled back, smiled warmly, then came in for another, longer kiss. "Hi."

In her heels, and me barefoot, we were the same height and the new dynamic startled me out of my stalled state. "Hallo," I managed to say.

Her forehead wrinkled. "Are you okay?"

I nodded a little bit too enthusiastically to cover up the fact I was having a hard time focusing due to how hot she looked. "Ja. I'm fine. You…look really good."

Evie glanced down at herself, then back up to me, her mouth quirking into a knowing smile. A single eyebrow rose slowly. "I'm glad you like it. You should see me when I'm *really* dressed up for galas and fundraisers." She lightly touched my hip. "I kind of like what you've got on too."

I thought about her being "really dressed up," and my voice was a little rough. "I didn't know you had a thing for old sweatpants."

Evie bit her lip, and I was sure if we were alone, she'd have already been kissing me until neither of us were capable of thought. Instead, she shot me a pained look, squeezed my hip and took a step backward. Keeping her voice low, she said, "I'm sorry about not being here. And sorry Chloe came around to bother you." She reached back and pulled her hair up, then let it fall free again. And I tried, and failed, to not think about running my hands through it. "She would have been fine alone at my place, but thanks for hanging out with her."

"It was my pleasure. And she was not a bother at all. She was a very good assistant."

Evie leaned around me to peer into my apartment. "So I see. Is she assisting or hindering?"

I grinned. "Definitely assisting." I stepped to the side to let her in.

"Good." She smiled, lightly touched my cheek, then slipped into my apartment. "Smells amazing in here." Evie bent to kiss the top of Chloe's head. "Sorry, sweetie, the beneficiary meeting ran a little later than I thought." She frowned. "Did you get my text?"

"S'okay. I *am* old enough to hang out by myself." I noted she didn't acknowledge Evie's question about receiving her text. "Did you see Grandpa?"

"Let's talk about that some other time," Evie deflected. She unbuttoned her suit jacket. I closed my gaping mouth. Turning to me, she asked, "So, are there any gingerbread failures for me to try?"

"No failures. I never fail when I'm making gingerbread. But there are leftovers."

Chloe agreed, "Annika is right, Aunt Evie. This is really good. I can't wait to eat the actual house with all the frosting."

"You don't eat the gingerbread house," I said.

Chloe's face morphed into a horrified expression. "What? But… what's the point of making it then? And why make good gingerbread if you're not going to eat it?"

"You do it because that's just what you do for Weihnachten." I held up my hands. "Don't ask me, I don't make the rules. But most importantly—do you *really* want to eat something that's been set out for days, weeks even? They get stale."

Chloe persisted. "But can you eat it?"

"Of course you *can*; it's made of food. But why would you want to?"

"Because it's delicious."

"Okay," I conceded. "If you want to eat the stale house, I'll give it to you on the twenty-seventh and you can eat as much as you want." I glanced at Evie, who had a mouthful of gingerbread. She smiled around it, and shook her head like she wanted no part of the transaction. I turned back to Chloe. "But I take no responsibility for stomachaches."

"Deal. But we'll be at Grandma and Grandpa's then. Can you keep it until we get home?"

"Ja, of course. It will be safe here until you return."

Evie gently butted in. "Okay, Chloe, let's leave Annika alone, and you need to have dinner."

Chloe nodded, then turned to tell me, "Make sure you keep that gingerbread house safe. I'll be here tomorrow after school to help out again."

Evie swatted her. "Oh sure, who cares about homework, right?" She took her by the shoulders and turned her toward the door. "Go back to my place, and I'll be there in a minute."

Chloe nodded. "Thanks for hanging out, Annika."

"It was my pleasure. Thank you for helping with the Lebkuchenhaus."

She gave me a thumbs-up. Just before opening the door, Chloe paused and picked up the Rubik's Cube on the bookshelf. "Annika, did you know Aunt Evie can solve a Rubik's Cube in under a minute? That's fast."

Evie interjected, "No it's not. The world record is like four seconds."

I winked. "Three point one three four seconds, actually. Set last year."

"I stand corrected," she said. Then to Chloe, "What are you doing?"

Chloe laughed. "Talking you up. Duh." She disappeared with a cheerful wave.

"I'm sorry about her," Evie muttered. "She has this idea that—never mind."

I did mind a little bit, because I wanted to know what idea exactly Chloe had that required "talking her aunt up." But I let it go. "I have those parts for your coffeepot. So I'm ready to repair it whenever you are."

"Oh, great. I'll come by once Chloe goes home?"

"That is perfect. I can finish cleaning up. See you soon."

"Yes you will," she murmured, leaning in for a quick kiss. She pulled back first, and I sensed her reluctance. "But not soon enough…"

Evie returned an hour and a half later, and unfortunately she'd changed out of what was one of the sexiest outfits I'd ever seen. Never mind. I'd be thinking about her in it, and then imagining taking her out of it when I went to bed.

"Have you eaten?" I asked.

"Uh, yeah." She frowned. "Actually, no. Not since lunch. I'm not really hungry." The frown transformed into a grin. "I had some of your gingerbread notfails before."

Gingerbread notfails made me laugh. "Okay. I've been eating them too so I'm not hungry for now either." I glanced at her empty hands. "Do you have this pot for me to fix?"

Evie's eyebrows shot up. "F—ruit. I forgot it. Back in a sec."

She practically sprinted out of my apartment, and was back in less than a minute. As Evie handed me the moka pot, the sleeve of her Henley pulled back to expose her wrist. The wrist where the thin bracelet I'd created and given her for Saint Nikolaus now resided. It made me smile.

I turned the pot over to study the handle connection. "My ex-girlfriend had one of these," I mused. "Just a cheap one, I think. She never made coffee as delicious as yours. And my ex-boyfriend didn't have the patience for anything more than an automated coffee machine. Sit down while I get my tools."

"You brought tools with you from Germany?"

"Ja. Just a couple of essentials. My father gave sets of tools, big and small, power and manual, to me and Markus." I shrugged. "He likes to know we can take care of things ourselves. And I can, mostly."

Once I'd settled beside her at the table, Evie asked, "So, your ex… boyfriend? *And* your ex-girlfriend?"

"Technically the ex-girlfriend was the ex before my ex-boyfriend. My ex-ex." I glanced up and smiled patiently. "Yes. I'm bisexual."

"I'd gathered." She smirked. "You checking both Pete and me out gave it away."

"I was *not* 'checking Pete out,' not in a romantic or sexual way." I used pliers to work the pin holding the handle to the pot free. "You, however," I said as I dropped the pin to the table, "I *was* checking you out in a romantic way and a sexual way. I thought that might have been obvious, because it's you that I'm kissing."

Evie was silent for so long that I looked up. She was watching me, her cheeks a gorgeous pink. I smiled, pleased that my comment had hit its target. Finally, she said, "I suppose you're right. Sorry, I'm still getting used to the idea of you. Wanting me that is." She cleared her throat. "Do you…like men and women equally? Like the whole world is a buffet for you?" Evie pulled a face, sticking out her tongue. "Bah. Sorry, that's kind of offensive."

It was probably one of the least offensive questions about bisexuality that I'd been asked. "Oh god, no, not at all. It is barely a meal, definitely not a buffet. I prefer women. In relationships. In bed. Outside of bed." I shrugged. "In general really."

She grinned. "Me too."

I laughed. "I had noticed that." As I pulled the new pin and handle from the packaging and eyed both to make sure they were right, I thought about how to better answer her question about equality. "I find it easier to connect with women. But every now and then I'm attracted to a guy, usually only physically but sometimes emotionally. And it is very frustrating to only find one part of the connection that I am looking for."

"Was that part of why you broke up with your ex? The guy? The one you broke up with just before you came here? There was no connection?"

"Ja, that was part of it. But it was really that we were incompatible. And incompatible relationships are a chore, everything in them feels like a chore, and I don't like doing chores. I felt like I constantly had to defend my time from him." I frowned. "Is that right? Have I explained it correctly?" I went over it in my head, trying to parse what I'd just said. "Do you understand what I mean?"

"I do, yeah." She exhaled loudly. "I've had relationships like that. Actually, most of my relationships have been like that. They always want all of me all the time. That's why I've never had a lasting relationship, I think." Evie laughed dryly. "Well, that's one of the reasons."

"I've had some long relationships with men and with women." I got to work fitting the new handle, talking as I did so. "They were good in their own ways. But there's always something that makes me realize it's not going to work and that is *not* gender specific." It was about my expectations—there was always something that made me want to pull away. Sometimes obvious things, sometimes less obvious things that were nothing more than annoying niggles that I couldn't explain. Not even to myself.

"Define 'long,'" she said.

"About six months." I frowned, wondering at her questions. "Are you freaked out by me being bi?"

Evie recoiled a little bit. "Not at all," she said emphatically. "Just trying to understand. Of course I have bi friends. But I've never dated a bi woman so I'm just not sure how your brain is working. And I like to know how things work." Her eyes widened. "Not that you and I are dating, but…you know."

Dated. Dating. I mulled over her fumbled words. Did I want to date her? Yes. But *could* I date her knowing I would fail at yet another relationship because I had to leave? "I think, at the moment, what's important for you to know is that I'm very interested in you. For friendship. And more than friendship. But not a relationship. I'm not staying in Boston, and…" I trailed off, hoping she understood my *why* from that one reason. I could have delved into the other reason why—my resolution, which at the moment felt like nothing more than a flimsy thought—but I didn't think it was the right time, especially not if we weren't dating. And Evie had just confirmed, rightly, that we weren't.

Evie's mouth twisted, and I couldn't quite decipher the expression. That twist of her lips turned up into a smile, but her eyes didn't join in with her mouth. "Then I guess it's agreed. Because I'm okay with a friendship slash more than friendship slash not a relationship too."

"That sounds good. Should we shake hands to seal this deal?"

She shook her head. "No. But we can kiss to seal it."

I held up the repaired moka pot. "I feel like I deserve more than a kiss for fixing this."

"I think you might too," she murmured. Evie met my eyes, and the raw desire in them made my stomach curl.

"If I didn't have my period, I might ask you to pay up in full." I took a deep breath to steady the butterflies in my stomach, the butterflies that were thinking of exactly how she might "pay" me, when I wasn't feeling completely unsexy. "So, a kiss will do. For now."

"For now," Evie agreed quietly.

She leaned forward, and settled her debt. And while her payment was thorough, it still felt entirely unsatisfying.

CHAPTER SEVENTEEN

Evie

My artistic inspiration was still surging through me, thank the universe, and aside from dinner Wednesday and Friday, and collecting Chloe on Tuesday after she'd gone to help decorate the gingerbread house, I hadn't seen much of Annika. Knowing she was right there across the hall felt almost worse than if she were in another city, because our dinners were followed by us making out on the couch like a pair of horny teens. Yet…despite that horny-teen vibe, for some reason, neither of us had suggested going any further, even though we'd hinted at it plenty before.

I wanted to suggest it, and every time we parted, it was on the tip of my tongue to ask her to come to bed with me. But every single time, fear squashed my words. Fear of what it would mean if we took that step, fear of the fact it already felt too late and too inevitable to stop it, fear that it had been so long since I'd been intimate with anyone, and fear that it would change everything between us and send me tumbling over the edge into loving her.

A little before five p.m., I'd heard Annika leave for her work Christmas thing and had resigned myself to a boring Saturday night of scrolling through streaming services before going to bed. She'd been apologetic, pouting as she told me "I wish you could come with me.

But it will be boring for you. And I didn't know I might want to take someone when I, emm…RSVPed to the event."

And I'd told her I'd be okay. But being alone at night made me realize how much I'd started to rely on being with her. I was clearly falling for her. Exactly what I didn't want to happen. And we hadn't even slept together, though it wasn't for lack of desire from either of us. More like…it seemed we were both aware of what it would mean for us when we were trying to keep things casual.

Sleep would not come, mostly because I kept thinking about Annika. Eventually I just gave in and grabbed my vibrator. I was asleep within minutes post-orgasm.

I was jolted from that sleep by my phone ringing, and fumbled frantically for it. Nobody ever called in the middle of the night with good news. Instead of Pete's or, even worse, Chloe's number on the screen, it was Annika's. My heart rate slowed, and my panic was replaced by pleasure. I smirked to myself. There was only one reason for her to be calling me at one a.m.

A drunk booty call.

Well, I was all for it. I tried to inject suave casualness into my, "Hello?" Nope, I just sounded like I'd eaten a bag of sand.

"Evie-Evangeliiiinnne," Annika said, her voice a curious mix of excitement, relief, and a kind of growly sexiness. Oh she was definitely intoxicated.

"Hi. What's up?" Aside from the concentration of alcohol in her bloodstream.

"I have a *big* problem."

I rubbed my face. A big problem was way less fun than a booty call. "What problem is that? Can I help?"

"Ja. That's why I made a call to you." My drunk booty call was looking less likely by the second, and probably for the best. She sounded really drunk. And very very German. In the background, a woman was talking loudly and to compete, Annika raised her voice to a level that made me hold the phone slightly away from my ear. "The Fahrdienst isn't here. We can't find *any*," she whined. "None. Kein Fahrdienst."

What the fuck? "The *what* isn't there?"

"The *car*. You know. Uber! Über." She laughed, and a hilarious snort crept in. "This car is not here, so it is *not* über. It ist un-über. The worst. Not best."

"Right. Okay. Have you reloaded the app? Restarted your phone?"

"Jaaaaa." She drew it out and even in German, the "Of course I have, you idiot" indignation was there. "No Uber. Can you come and us rescue, please?"

I threw back the covers. "Sure. Of course. Where are you?"

There was a scuffling sound and a long pause. "Emm, South Street. Near the trains."

At this time of night—this time of early morning—traffic wouldn't be too heinous. "Okay. I'll be there in fifteen minutes. Don't go anywhere, okay?" The last thing I felt like was a worried wild goose chase all over Boston.

"I will promise it you. We're sitting right here and going not away."

"Good. See you soon." I ended the call, flung myself out of bed, and pulled on sweats and a warm hoodie. Who needed a bra at this time of night? Not me. I stuffed sockless feet into Skechers, grabbed a couple of buckets from the laundry, and left the building. At any other time, I might have paused to enjoy the cold stillness of the night, but I had people to rescue. I unlocked my Mercedes SUV and put the buckets on the passenger side floor. I liked my car detailer enough to not want to make him clean up alcohol-soaked vomit.

Annika was leaning against rough-wood planter boxes, next to another woman. I was glad I got to witness her Christmas party outfit, even if it was a little rumpled. Adorably so. I jumped out of the car just as Annika jumped away from the planters. Sort of. I caught her arm before she toppled over.

"You are a knight with shining armors," she declared. Annika leaned into me and kissed me lightly on the cheek. With an expansive wave, she indicated the dark-haired woman standing unsteadily—even more unsteadily than Annika—by the planters. "Evie-Evangeline, this is my friend. Rachel. Rachel, this is my Evie-Evangeline."

Rachel straightened up in a perfect impersonation of a drunk person trying to act sober. "Oh god. You're right. She's fucking *cute*." She fell against the side of my car. "Hello, Evie. Thank you for coming to rescue us. Fuckin' Uber is fuckin' fucked."

"You're welcome."

She patted the door gently. "This's a really nice car. I love nice cars. Isits a AMG G 63?" she slurred. "China blue?"

"Yes it is," I said, surprised she'd picked both model and color. "Do you both have everything you need?"

"Ja," Annika said. She touched my face with her fingertips. Her mouth formed a lazy smile, which was so kissable that I almost did just that. Except the drunk and not really able to consent kind of put a dampener on the thought. "You *are* fucking cute. Fucking sexy," she murmured.

"Thank you." The sentiment was nice, and I was sure she meant it even if all her filters were drunkenly absent, but at the moment I was more focused on getting them into my car and home. And if we made it with no puke in my vehicle, I was going to count it as a win. "Let's get you home and into bed."

"Oh no. Did we waked you?" she asked in a loud whisper, her eyes widening.

"Yes, but it's totally fine." I didn't know where Rachel lived, and hoped she was lucid enough to give me directions or an address.

Annika and Rachel climbed up into the back seat and once I made sure they were both belted in, I passed them a bucket each. "Right, here's something for you guys in case you need to hurl. Please aim for inside the buckets. I'd be grateful."

"I never barf when I'm drinking," Rachel said imperiously.

"That's lies," Annika rebutted. "In München…" She paused and I braced myself for puke. Nope. Annika stuck her hand through the gap in the front seats. "She hat gebrochen after going to bars. I witnessed it."

I turned around and nearly collided with Annika who'd unbuckled and was leaning forward. "How long have you guys been friends?"

She grinned and kissed my nose with ninjalike quickness. "Since three years."

Rachel filled in a bit more of the story. "A couple years ago, I worked in the Munich office for eight months."

"München," Annika corrected. She pushed herself back in the seat and refastened her seat belt.

Rachel slapped Annika. Or tried to. It was more of a limp-wristed pat. "I told you I'm not speaking German when I'm not in Germany. I'm bad at it."

"No you're not," Annika said fondly.

This little friendship lovefest was cute, but the longer we lingered, the higher the chances for this funny drunk interaction to turn into an unfunny drunk interaction. "If I could just interrupt for a moment. Rachel, where do you live?"

"Oh. Ashhhmont. Y'know, Dorchester. One minute."

"You can just tell me. I'll put it in the GPS."

"Nah, here. My phone'll navigate." She tapped me on the shoulder and when I turned around, she shook her phone until I took it.

She'd brought up Google Maps. I checked the address, put it into my GPS and handed the phone back. Apparently the issue of me navigating using her phone had left Rachel's brain the moment she took the device again, and now it was just magic that'd get her home.

"Evie-Evangeline is a very good driver. Sichere Fahrerin," Annika said emphatically. I wondered why she was so emphatic about that. Hopefully it was something good like "Smells nice" or "Great ass."

"Great driver, and cute," Rachel declared.

Oh boy. Time to go. I cracked the back windows an inch to give them some fresh, cool air, and pulled out.

The drive with both of them was…an adventure. Thankfully they were cheerful rather than obnoxious. The main point of conversation seemed to be whether or not Annika and I were dating. I was curious about that one too, but Annika somehow managed to deflect Rachel's probing. She did let slip that I was a fantastic kisser—even I could decipher the "fantastisch" that slipped into the sentence. I kept my mouth closed, though I was definitely thinking she was also a fantastic kisser.

I slowed to a crawl then pulled over where the GPS told me to, cutting Rachel off in the middle of her argument to Annika that she *really* needed to date me. Perhaps for the best.

She tapped the window. "Oh! I live here!" Rachel undid her seat belt with a flourish and while they hugged their goodbyes, repeatedly, I jumped out to open the car door for her.

Annika waved. "Byeeee, Rachel. See you am Monday Morgen."

I took the car keys and left Annika in the car while I helped Rachel to her door, checking repeatedly that she'd be okay once she got inside. Leaving a wasted person alone made me feel uneasy, but I had no idea how I could deal with her *and* Annika. Rachel would be fiiiiine, she assured me. Apparently her roommate was home and would take care of her.

Annika had moved from the back seat into the passenger seat and before I started the car I made sure she'd buckled herself in and had her just-in-case bucket. Yes to both. She turned to look at me then leaned her head back. "You are so hot. I would like to touch you," she said dreamily.

"I'd like that too. But not right now." Not while I was driving and also not when we got home. Consent and full participation were sexy, and she was currently completely incapable of both.

"Okay." She snaked a hand toward me and after lightly touching my shoulder, broke into a fit of giggles.

Annika napped for the rest of ride home but snapped awake when I shook her gently. "Annika? We're home. Can you walk up to your door?"

"Ja, I stand up," was her response. She let me help her out of the car, and wrapped an arm around my waist while I guided her inside and up the stairs to her door, my other hand carrying the two buckets stacked inside each other. The walls were helping her walk.

"Okay, let's get you inside. Got your key for me?"

"I can do it," she insisted. "I have keys."

"I know you do, sweetheart, but why not let me do it for you? Let me help."

"Ja, you can help," she agreed. "You're so great, Evie-Evangeline."

Grinning, I said, "I know."

Finally I got her inside, and the door secured behind us—no easy feat given I was practically holding her up and moving her around. We'd made it halfway across her living room, heading for the bedroom where I was still trying to figure out how to tuck her into bed, when Annika paused. "I am feeling a little bit…Brechreiz." At my raised-eyebrows look, she stuck out her tongue.

That action didn't need a translation. "Sick? Are you going to hurl? Ohhhkaaay, let's get you into the bathroom." I had the buckets in case she didn't make it.

Thankfully we made it into the master bathroom in plenty of time. Annika smiled at me, raised the toilet seat, carefully pulled her hair back, gracefully sank to her knees, then not so gracefully threw up. Also thankfully, between taking care of Heather during her chemo, and watching over Chloe when she was sick, I was immune to vomiting.

I helped Annika hold her hair back, and she gripped the sides of the bowl with both hands and got rid of at least some of what she'd had to drink. Hopefully she'd feel a little better in the morning if she puked up some of the booze tonight. Annika reached up and back, fumbling around until she found my arm. She held on to my wrist while she emptied a little more of her stomach.

When she was finally done, I left her sitting on the bathroom floor while I went to get her some water. She drank the glass slowly, then pushed herself to her knees and used my legs and the sink to stand. "I wasche my face and I go in bed." Apparently all that alcohol had stolen some more of her English aptitude. It was both amusing and adorable. I had no idea how someone could be so sexy they made my brain melt, and yet so adorable I just wanted to hug her. But Annika managed it.

"Good plan. Do you need help?"

She sighed. "No. Danke."

"Do you want to brush your teeth?"

"Ja." She picked up a tube that was most definitely not toothpaste. I carefully took it from her hand. "Annika, I think that's moisturizer. Here's toothpaste."

Annika raised the toothpaste tube up close to her eyes. "Oh. I mistaken that tube for this one."

I stood by while she brushed her teeth, then stepped out of the bathroom while she used the toilet. Leaning against the wall, I looked around her bedroom properly. I'd caught glimpses into it before but I'd never paid much attention. The bed had a light-colored wooden frame, her bedspread a muted blue and green pattern with a thick gray blanket across the foot of the bed. The entire vibe was calm, yet still conveyed Annika's warmth.

Annika flung the bathroom door open. "I am ready for bed." As she wobbled across the room, she pulled her top off and dropped it on the floor, and when she started fumbling with her belt, I froze. I didn't want to be a lech and stare at her undressing while she was obviously far too intoxicated to consent to my staring. But I also wanted to help if she needed it. I settled for turning side on and periodically asking, "You okay there?"

And every time I asked, she answered, "Ja."

I had no idea how undressed she was, and thankfully Annika stumbled to the bed and got under the covers before I discovered she was too undressed for my comfort. I saw an expanse of skin, but nothing I shouldn't see without at least asking first. She made a noisy show of trying to get comfortable and I helped her with the covers that seemed to be arguing with her. Or she was arguing with them.

"I'm going to leave a bucket next to the bed, okay? So if you can't make it to the bathroom, use the bucket."

"Ja. Okay. Thank you." She flailed an arm out from under the cover and draped it over the edge of the bed.

I was sure she'd be okay; she wasn't pass-out drunk. But I didn't want to leave her. I was pretty good at sleeping anywhere, and her couch would do for the short remainder of the night. I refilled the glass of water and left it on the bedside table, along with a bucket on the floor.

I pulled the blanket from the end of her bed, stole a pillow from the stack against the headboard, and went to keep guard on her couch.

* * *

I'd been woken a couple of times by the sound of Annika throwing up or dry heaving, and had gone in to check on her each time. She'd wordlessly accepted my help, downed the glasses of water I forced on her, gargled sloppily with mouthwash, then stumbled back into bed. Thankfully Annika had kept her underwear and bra on, because helping her puke while she was naked wasn't high on the list of things I felt like dealing with.

The interrupted sleep definitely weighed me down. I struggled awake around eight and went in to check on Annika. She lay on her stomach, face smashed against the pillow, her right arm hanging off the bed with her fingers touching the bucket. I checked to make sure she was breathing, then turned to leave.

A garbled "mmphingskkgg" sound made me turn around.

"You alive?" I asked.

Another indistinguishable sound made me smile.

"Do you want coffee?"

Her right hand formed a weak thumbs-up.

Laughing, I backed out of the room. "Call me if you need anything." I found a container of pods and started coffee. From the bedroom came the sound of someone moving unsteadily around, then the bathroom door closing before the shower turned on. When I heard the water shut off, I put on more coffee. Annika emerged when I was halfway through my second cup of French roast.

She pouted and with a quiet sandpaper voice declared, "I am having a very bad hangover."

I held in my laugh. "I'm not at all surprised."

"This is not usual for me. I am not liking it."

"I don't know anyone who likes hangovers."

She grunted. "Thank you for last night. And I'm sorry. So so sorry. And I'm also very, very embarrassed." Annika lowered herself so slowly to the kitchen chair it would have been hilarious if it wasn't so adorably pathetic.

"It's okay, really. I'm glad to help out."

She dropped her head into her hands. "I have never been so sick."

"Are you feeling any better now?"

"Ja. I think. I haven't made emm…How is it called?" She wrinkled her nose and apparently just gave up trying to find the right English grammar. "I haven't done vomiting for a few hours."

"I know," I said, laughing at what she said, and the way she'd said it. I cut myself off at her wince. I wanted to hug her but she looked like she might shatter or hurl if I touched her. "Here. Drink this." I handed her a glass of water. "Then take two of these." I passed her a bottle of ibuprofen. "And then, drink this." I set the mug of coffee on the table.

"Danke," she whispered. After a careful sip of water, she opened the bottle of pills with shaking hands. "I'm scared to think about how much I drank last night. I should make sure Rachel is okay."

"Do you want me to go around and see if she's all right? Her address will still be in my GPS." She had a roommate, so I was sure she was fine. Relatively speaking. Based on how Annika looked, her coworker was probably wishing she could die.

"No, I can't ask you to do that. You did so much. Thank you for staying last night." A trembling hand raised the mug halfway to her mouth. Annika set it back down on the table and instead, leaned forward and sipped her coffee. "And thank you for driving to get me. And taking Rachel home. Thank you for all of the things."

"You're welcome. So you couldn't get a, um fahrd…whatever, but what about taxis?"

She looked up, blinking slowly. "Fahrdienst—Uber, rideshare. And a taxi? I…well…I don't know. I didn't think of it. And Rachel never said anything. I think maybe we were too focused on the Uber app not working."

"What were you drinking?" I already knew the quantity—lots—but was curious about what had induced such a hangover.

"Red wine with dinner at the steakhouse." Her forehead wrinkled, and after a moment she mumbled, "Then Champagne. And then…" She held her thumb and forefinger about an inch apart. "A lot of little Wodkas."

I bit my lower lip. She was so adorable. Hot, obviously. But also adorable. It was a dangerous combination. "Vodka?"

Annika nodded. Just once. Then winced. "Mm. Wodka."

"Vodka?" I asked again.

"That's what I—" She cut herself off and looked up, grinning shakily. "It's unfair to tease people who are suffering as much as I am suffering."

"You're right. I'm sorry. You're just really cute when you're speaking Germish."

"Germish? Oh…German-English." She managed another smile. "It's a portmanteau. Brangelina," Annika added as triumphantly as someone suffering a heinous hangover could.

"That's it. And it was correct English mostly. But with some German mixed in. I learned some words." And learned that I was really, really into her. Not that I'd had any doubt, but seeing her vulnerable like that, having her trust me enough to call me for help had cemented it.

"I'm sorry. I hope I didn't say anything embarrassing? Or *do* anything embarrassing. Except for calling you. And getting sick."

I'd hoped she'd follow the W-for-V rule again and say "womiting." I shook my head. "No, nothing to be embarrassed about. And just think, you can now add getting drunk with your coworkers at your American work Christmas party to your traditions list."

She didn't look like she was happy to add that one.

"How do you feel about eating something?" I asked.

"I feel very bad about that."

I coughed out a laugh. "I get it. But some toast might help. Why not just try a little and see how it goes down."

A wobbly smile broke through her misery. "Evie, I am sure it will go down, but I am very scared it might come up again."

CHAPTER EIGHTEEN

Annika

The combination of mortified embarrassment and my hangover did not feel good at all. My workplace Christmas party had been fun—dinner, drinks, a little bit of dancing. Then everyone had split apart and some of us had ended up at another bar. And that is where things got a little bit fuzzy.

When I'd texted Rachel to check she was okay—she was, relatively speaking—she'd reassured me that I hadn't done anything embarrassing. Unless I counted constantly telling her how hot Evie was and how much I liked her. I *did* remember parts of Evie coming to get us, mostly that when I'd seen her I'd been overcome with two feelings that battled with each other. Arousal and gratitude. Both enjoyable sensations, but one was very much at the forefront.

Evie was apparently still concerned about my pitiful state and even after she could have left me, she didn't. We lounged about my apartment, lit my Advent candles—both coffee and the bland toast that stood in for Weihnachtsplätzchen stayed down—and watched an episode of *Dr. Who* on my laptop. Around ten a.m., Evie said she was going to leave me with my misery, mumbling something about needing a shower and a long nap.

My stomach sank and for a moment I wondered if I was going to be sick again. No, that was just my disappointment. Of course I didn't expect her to stay here with me all day and babysit my self-inflicted misery, but even if I hadn't been suffering the worst hangover of my life, I would have wanted to spend my day with her.

Evie's eyes brightened as she continued, oblivious to my pathetic longing, "But…I'll see you later to light my candles?" Her sweet hopefulness made me smile.

"Ja, of course you will. I'll bring cake. By that time, I might even be able to stomach it." I hoped I'd be able to stomach the smell of baking it.

"And I'll provide hot beverages." She bit her lower lip. "Will you stay for dinner? Maybe we could chill with a movie or something before. Or…after?" She wasn't tense exactly, but there was a definite sense that she was feeling a little bit needy. If she was desperate for my company, I wasn't going to deny her. I was desperate for her company.

"That sounds good. When should I come around?"

"Uh, maybe just give me until like three p.m. to nap and then get ungroggy after?"

I wilted at the fact she needed a nap because I'd kept her up. And I hadn't kept her awake the way I really wanted to keep her awake. "I'm sorry," I said, hating how pathetic my apologies still sounded.

"I know. And it's okay." She took my hand, leaning in as if to kiss me. Then she paused.

"I brushed my teeth." I grinned to prove it. "Fresh and minty."

Evie's return grin made my stomach flutter with excitement and something else that was too scary to name. "Well that's a relief," she said teasingly. "I like you a lot. Vomit breath, not so much." Her kiss was gentle and sweet and far too short. "I'll see you in a bit."

All I could do was nod dumbly.

Mama FaceTimed me while I was wallowing on the couch staring at my laptop, which had finished playing another episode of *Dr. Who* and was waiting for me to cue the next one. And instead of sympathy, she teased me about being hungover. She casually asked how work was going, how our Merry Weihnachten—said with a grimace—events had been to date, asked to see my completed Lebkuchenhaus, and then…she'd asked about Evie.

"What about Evie?" I said, trying to hide my surprise. I'd sent my parents pictures of the Snowport Markets, including one of me and Evie at the entrance, along with a description of my visit and how I thought they compared to the Christmas markets back home—they didn't but it was still good. Mama had been suitably interested in the pictures and then more than interested in the one with Evie.

"How is she?" Mama asked.

"She's good."

"Are you two still getting along well?" she asked, her tone a perfectly curated mix of "I'm curious but I'm trying to seem casual."

"Yes, we are."

"That's wonderful. Your father and I were talking and we thought we might come visit you in Boston in February. We can meet your neighbor, and your other new friends, of course."

"Really?" My mother wasn't known for being subtle, but this was beyond obvious.

"Yes, really. It's not exactly difficult to come see you, Anni."

"No, I know that, it's just…" I shook my head and smiled. It would be wonderful to see my parents, and so soon. I'd planned to go back for a week during the summer. "It's just nothing. I would love to show you around my new city."

Her eyebrows shot up as soon as I said "my new city," but instead of interrogating me about it, Mama said, "Oh, I have to go. Your father wants me to drive him to the chess club." She turned the phone so I could see him.

"Hallo, Papa!" I said. He waved and blew me a kiss, then tapped his watch and disappeared, muttering about his games. Chess was important. More important than his daughter, but thankfully only on Sundays.

As she signed off, Mama echoed what Evie had been saying. Drink water, and eat if I could. And then she said something Evie hadn't. "Have a shower, Annika, put on some actual clothing, and be productive. Have you baked something to eat while lighting today's candle?"

When I shook my head, I received the expected maternal disapproval. "Well, stop indulging in misery. You'll feel better if you *do* something. I love you."

"I love you too."

She blew me a kiss and ended the call. I was actually surprised that had been the extent of her admonishment about me lying around. As if the fact it was the weekend and I was entitled to do absolutely nothing, especially when encumbered by a hangover, mattered to my mother.

I cued up the next episode on my laptop. Just another hour of feeling sorry for myself. Then I'd get up and be productive. Maybe.

On the dot of three, I knocked on Evie's door. As prodded by my mother, I'd baked a fresh apple cake, and I'd also baked some snowflake cookies as a thank-you and peace offering in one for Evie.

"I just wanted to say thank you, again. You didn't have to come and get me last night, and you didn't have to help us, and you didn't have to stay with me to make sure I was fine, and you didn't have to stay in the morning to take care of me. But you did."

Her eyebrows shot up. "Of course I did. If you ever need something and I can do it, then I will."

I grimaced. "I really don't know how we got that drunk, but…it happened. And I am still feeling regrets."

She ate a cookie, and made a sound of enjoyment that had my stomach twisting into knots, in the good way, not the hungover way. "I'll bet. Have you been staying hydrated? Have you eaten anything else?"

I nodded. "I drank electrolytes and ate more toast. Did you have your nap?"

Evie shrugged. "Not really. Maybe thirty minutes or so. My body is tired. My eyes are exhausted. But my brain is wide awake."

"Oh, ja, I know that feeling very well." I'd been struggling with that feeling for a couple of weeks now. Mostly because I was awake thinking about her.

The silence stretched for a few moments more than was comfortable, as if Evie was thinking about her response. What she said was completely unexpected. "So…did you have a hot make-out session with anyone last night?" She sounded too casual, too indifferent.

The question had arrived from nowhere, and I reeled back, startled. "What? No! Why would you ask me that?"

"Because part of a Christmas party is picking up a hot stranger," she said matter-of-factly.

"We have very different ideas of what happens at a work Christmas party," I said dryly.

"Maybe," Evie mused. "Though, to be fair, I've never actually been to a work Christmas party."

"Well, the only hot person I want to make out with is you, so…we should probably make out."

Evie smirked, but underneath the cockiness I saw relief. "We probably should."

But instead of grabbing me and pulling me to her couch or somewhere else equally as comfortable to do just that, Evie glanced at her watch. My stomach sank, and not from being hungover. How many more hints did I have to drop? When she looked up again, I noted the faintest blush dusting her cheeks as she asked, "Do you want to go for a walk before dinner? Some fresh air might help. Maybe grab a coffee, and we can pick up something to eat? Or eat out then come back here? Whatever you're feeling up for."

I consulted with my body. I no longer felt sick, but I still had a little bit of the hungover tired shakiness that I recalled from my university days of too much alcohol. On second thought, Evie was smart. I wasn't feeling my best, and I wanted to enjoy making out with her and anything that might come with it. "That sounds like a good idea. Let me just get changed into something warm and for walking."

I met her outside my door and took her hand, holding it as we left the building. We made our way toward Beacon Hill Books & Cafe because I could not abide Starbucks. I'd had enough coffee for one day, and after buying a hot chocolate for myself, and a decaf chai latte with lavender syrup—Americans' bizarre culinary tastes amazed me—for Evie, we walked down Charles Street toward Boston Common. I was becoming quite good with my directions and street names, though if I left my little section of Boston I sometimes still had to consult Google Maps. We walked side by side, hands brushing, through the black wrought-iron gates into the Common. I peered up at the huge decorated tree. "That Christmas tree is a lot bigger than ours."

She laughed. "Just a little. We really need to come look at it properly one night."

"Mmm," I agreed. I wanted to stand arm in arm with her, huddled together in the cold night air, staring up at the tree the way I used to when I was a child.

"Did you know it comes all the way from Nova Scotia? Canada. It's a weird tradition to thank us for helping their city with some explosion in the early 1900s. And what's even weirder, is they don't come from a farm. They're like…some person's private tree on their property that gets cut down, like it's some great honor to send Boston your tree." She sniffed. "I don't know why they don't just plant a fu—fun tree here and let it grow to fifty feet."

"Because that's not the tradition," I argued. "And Christmas is about traditions, even if it's creating new ones because you moved across the world."

Smiling, Evie raised an eyebrow. "Ah yes. Traditions. Do you ice skate?"

"I can, yes."

"Well, when it's cold enough, you and the rest of the city can skate on the Frog Pond." Evie turned and pointed across Charles Street. "Have you been into the Public Garden yet?" she asked.

"No," I said, embarrassed by my admission.

"Let's go," she enthused. "And we'll have to come back when the flowers are blooming."

We.

"I would enjoy that very much."

"Me too," she said. Evie took my hand, and we strolled slowly through the gardens, quietly enjoying the walk, until something horrible broke through my peaceful enjoyment.

"What is that awful sound?" I muttered. It wasn't exactly fingernails on a chalkboard, but it was pretty close, and in my current state, the noise was beyond my tolerance.

Evie laughed. "That's Erhu Guy." She pointed to an older gentleman sawing away at a standing violin-looking instrument. "He's here pretty much every day, for hours, been doing this for as long as I can remember and yeah, it seems musical improvement isn't his goal." She shrugged, nose wrinkling. "His 'Twinkle Twinkle Little Star' isn't half bad. But…it's definitely not half good." Evie held out her coffee to me and I took it. She jogged over and dropped some money into his jug then jogged back.

Once we were out of earshot of the guy, I asked, "Did you give him that money to make him stop playing?"

She laughed again. "No, sorry. It's actually a really pretty instrument in the right hands. Unfortunately, he's got the wrong hands and is kind of a bad-music staple around here. Now I think we should seek out other erhu musicians and you can hear how beautiful it's supposed to sound."

"Should I trust you?" I said, feigning wariness.

Evie's coffee cup paused. Her mouth twitched into a smile as she said, "Yes."

"I do," I said.

"Good," she murmured. We held eye contact, and Evie's softened. "You hungry?"

"Yes, I think I am."

"Pizza? We can stop by Primo's for an early dinner on the way home?"

What better way to finish off a day of hangover misery than with some greasy, cheesy food. "That sounds very good."

We made our way back to the park entrance, still hand in hand, and then walked slowly toward the pizza restaurant. I was thrilled to discover that, like me, she thought pineapple was an acceptable pizza topping and after ordering we waited inside Primo's at one of the small wooden tables. Evie pulled up a video on YouTube of a skilled erhu musician. She was right that the erhu was beautiful, in the right hands. Evie took the pizza and I carried the garlic bread and Caesar salad. The walk home was quick, and cold.

We collected water and napkins, and had set the pizza on her coffee table when Evie backed away. "Get comfortable," she said. "I forgot forks for the salad."

Instead of sitting down, I decided to check on the tree. The needles were all springy and none of them had turned brown. Something new on Evie's bookshelf caught my eye and I stepped over to look. "Oh! You have a Christmas card." I leaned close to study it, obviously handmade, elegant and refined.

Evie made a disgusted sound, which made me turn around. "Mmm. I got my annual impersonal Christmas card from my parents yesterday. Their mass-produced, Happy Holidays from the Phillips Family, except Evie, thing. Hand-delivered, as always. No USPS for my mother." She shrugged and preempted my question by saying, "It feels like shit. It always has. But now, with our thing, it feels even more shit. Because it doesn't need to be this way."

"So why are you allowing it to be this way?" I asked quietly.

"I'm not *allowing* anything," she said flatly, dropping the forks onto the coffee table. They landed with a sharp clang that made me wince.

"I'm sorry," I said instantly. "I should not have pushed you. And I'm sorry that I keep doing things that I need to apologize for."

Evie sighed, sitting heavily onto her couch. "You don't need to apologize. I know my family situation seems weird to you, but I just…I don't know how to make you understand it. And I feel bad for telling you to just accept it, but—" She shrugged, her teeth worrying at her lower lip. It was clear she wasn't going to elaborate, that her "but" meant "but you just have to accept this thing that affects me and maybe affects my relationships with others."

I almost told her that I didn't want to just accept it. I wanted to tell her that I really wanted to understand, wanted to help her with something that was obviously upsetting for her. But it was like she'd stacked even more bricks on top of her walls to keep me from getting to the core of her. Was it even my place to try to climb those walls? We weren't a couple. We were just friends who were attracted to each other and expressing that attraction by kissing.

I crossed the room and sat beside her. But Evie had pulled her knees up to her chest, her arms loosely slung around her shins. I leaned over the barrier of her knees to get closer to her. She didn't budge, or resist. I rested my hands on her shoulders, lightly stroked either side of her neck. "Evie-Evangeline. From the moment you stumbled and fumbled into my life, I knew I wanted to get to know you better. You arrived at the perfect time, like a real Christmas angel, when I was struggling with my huge life change. I just want you…" I frowned as I thought about what I needed to say. "I want you in my life, and I want you to know that I am here for you if you need to talk about anything."

She said something so quietly that I couldn't hear it clearly, but it sounded like she may have said, "I want you to know everything." She looked slightly to the side to avoid my eye contact. After what felt like an uncomfortable eternity, she finally met my eyes and said something I did hear clearly. "I'm sorry. Insecurity isn't very sexy."

"Maybe not, but that doesn't mean you're not sexy," I countered.

Her mouth quirked. "Do you use *sexy* when you're talking about all your friends?"

The change in her expression made me bolder. Intimacy felt like such a logical progression to our attraction, but it seemed neither of us wanted to be the one to put our hand up first to initiate it. "Only the ones I really, really like."

Evie lightly brushed her thumb over my lower lip. I bit teasingly before she bopped my nose with her forefinger. She leaned forward enough to dislodge me, and I fell back onto the couch. Evie followed until she lay half on and half off me, the body contact intimate enough to set my pulse racing.

She held herself up, her mouth a whisper from mine, teasingly close as she murmured, "So what I'm getting here is that you really, *really* like me."

I closed the gap between us and let my lips answer the question. Evie made a little throaty sound when I kissed her, and did the thing that I loved—placed one hand on the side of my neck, the other cupping the back of my head as if she was trying to hold me there, kissing her. We parted for a breath, enough time for me to answer, "Oh, no. I really, really, *really* like you."

My stomach growled loudly and Evie laughed, pulling back. "I think you also really like pizza."

Screw pizza. Right now, I just wanted to take her to bed. To discover everything that made her squirm and scream. To share in her pleasure. But there was something in her expression that stopped me. Underneath Evie's clear desire was something that looked like fear, and the moment I saw it, I felt the same emotion dig its way into my belly. And it made me pause.

Why was I giving her mixed messages?

I dug deep for the answer. The truth was uncomfortable, but important. I was holding back because I was afraid. Not of being with her. Not of maybe falling deeper for her. I was afraid of my past, of fulfilling the criticism Sascha had thrown at me as a parting shot.

"You don't know how to be alone, Annika."

I was so desperate to prove that he was wrong that I was denying myself the chance to be with a woman I wanted to be with, desperately. Hadn't I said I needed to prioritize myself? Wasn't me being happy doing just that? And being with Evie made me happy.

So I had to move past my fear. Because this thing between Evie and me was *not* just simple attraction. It was connection. It was real. I knew it was real because I had never felt this before. And that's how I knew it was right. But knowing it was real and right wasn't going to make it easier for us to overcome our fears.

CHAPTER NINETEEN

Evie

It was just dinner with Pete and Chloe. And Annika. No big deal. I'd had dinner with all of them heaps of times. Just not all together at once. I changed my outfit three times, and after checking it and deciding I wanted to change again, realized I was going to make us late if I didn't get over it. It was just Annika, who'd seen me in all sorts of clothing, from the most casual old house sweats to my board-member fancy-ass shit. And if I wore something too over-the-top, Pete and Chloe would tease me mercilessly.

I looked fine in my loose button-up blouse and slim-fitting black pants paired with low-heeled ankle boots. I'd even put on dangling candy cane earrings I'd purchased especially in a bundle of Christmas-themed earrings for Merry Weihnachten. I'd just locked my door when I realized I'd forgotten something very important and rushed back to my bathroom, then rushed back out and across the hall, the bags filled with gifts and wine bumping against my hip.

Annika opened her door and I blurted breathlessly, "Sorry I'm late. I forgot to put on deodorant."

She tilted her head, a frown edging the corners of her mouth. "Is that important?"

"I get sweaty when I'm nervous, so yeah, it is."

Annika looked me up and down, the frown twitching into a smile. "Why are you nervous? Also, you look very nice."

"Thank you. So do you," I said, still breathless, only now it was because I'd finally twigged to what she was wearing. A dress. A dark-green maxi dress with a fitted smocked bodice, long sleeves and a gently flowing skirt. Silver jewelry and simple pair of white heels completed the outfit. I finally managed to get some words from my brain to my mouth. "I don't know why I'm nervous. Maybe having you come to Christmas dinner with Pete and Chloe?" And maybe because I was so attracted to her that some days I felt like I could barely function.

Last night when she'd come around for dinner after work, we'd been *this close* to going to bed. We'd even reached the "Evie has her top off and Annika's top is unbuttoned" stage of making out. And then I'd yawned. Really *really* yawned. Like an "I'm going to swallow the world" yawn. Annika had laughed and pulled back, but not before she'd cast a lingering look at my bra-encased breasts. And then smothered her own yawn. I'd flung my arm over my eyes and groaned as I apologized for ruining the moment.

But…it hadn't been the worst thing. After my last relationship, which felt like a lifetime ago, I'd had a few casual encounters and none of them had been good. Not in the "this sex is bad" way, but in the "I'm so tense I can't relax and climax" way.

And that shit was messing with my head.

But Annika was so different. For one, I had feelings for her. And I trusted her, and was sure it would be different. But some tiny stupid part of my brain was still whispering "What if it's not? What if you've forgotten how to enjoy intimacy?"

As if she had known what was whizzing through my brain like a high-octane race car, Annika had taken me by the hands and looked into my eyes, her expression so open, so honest, so…wanting, that some of my fear melted away. "I want *this*"—she squeezed my hands—"when we do go to bed, to be special. When we're not exhausted. When we're both sure. Because, Evie…" She licked her lower lip. "I am going to keep you awake for many hours."

And that low, sensual, matter-of-fact declaration had almost completely smothered my fears. Almost.

Annika's touch on my arm brought me back from my introspection. "Don't be nervous," she said, her voice warm and soothing. "It's just dinner. Think of it as a practice for our Merry Weihnachten celebrations."

"You're right," I agreed, even as I knew it was so much more than that. "Anyway, our car should be here any moment so we should probably go downstairs and wait."

"Are you certain it is coming?" she asked dryly. "I'm not sure I trust the Uber here."

I laughed. "I promise. And if it isn't, then I'll drive."

"Okay. Because I do not want to walk in this cold, carrying these gifts."

I'd told her about the gift-giving, and that it was not expected to be reciprocal, especially with such short notice. But as I'd thought she would, Annika carried a couple of elegantly wrapped gifts. I held them while she put her coat and scarf on, hooked her handbag over her forearm, and locked up. Annika took her gifts back, but not before cupping my face between her hands and kissing me softly.

The ride to South End only took ten minutes, which made me feel ridiculous for not just driving. But I wanted to relax and enjoy dinner and a couple of drinks, and more importantly? I did not want to deal with parking. Pete and Chloe lived in a condo overlooking Peters Park—a source of great teasing because Petey had his own little park— that he and Heather had bought just after they'd married. Going to the Minogues' place still pierced something inside me, because there were shades of Heather everywhere. Not so much that they had photos of her strewn on every surface, but more that her touches saturated the space. A rug. The throw blanket. The handcrafted kitchen table she'd commissioned from a single huge piece of redwood.

Chloe flung open the door. "Merry almost Christmas!" she hollered.

Laughing, Annika echoed the greeting, emphasizing the "almost," as I hugged my niece. Pete appeared, and we were greeted with hugs and cheek kisses before he left again, promising drinks and appetizers. After I'd helped Annika out of her coat and shucked out of mine, we set our gifts under the Christmas tree. Annika lightly touched one of the branches, trailing her fingertips over the lights which were blinking on and off.

I was watching her obvious enjoyment of the tree when something caught my eye. "Peter," I called out, and when his head popped back into the room, I drawled, "Why is there mistletoe in your house?"

"Oh, that old weed?" he said airily. "No clue."

I narrowed my eyes at him. "Nice try."

He grinned and I looked to Chloe, who was kneeling under the tree, arranging the gifts we had brought. Checking them out, more accurately. "Did you hang it?" I asked her.

Her face was impressively impassive. I held back my sigh.

"It *is* a tradition," Annika mused. She took my hand and pulled me to the doorway of the living room. Her eyes widened slightly as she took my face in gentle hands, then bent her head to kiss me. The kiss was soft, sweet, and perfectly appropriate for in front of my brother-in-law and niece.

When we'd separated, I turned to Pete. "I thought maybe there was someone you wanted to kiss, Petey. Got anyone else coming around?" He showed me exactly where Chloe had learned her impassive expression from, so I turned to Chloe. "Or was it for you?"

Her reaction was exactly as I'd expected. She screwed up her face and muttered, "Gross" before she spun around and went into the kitchen.

Annika laughed and gave me another quick, chaste kiss. She remained close to whisper, "Or perhaps it was you who asked for the mistletoe to be placed there…"

"I don't need mistletoe to kiss you."

Her eyes sparkled, but before she could answer, Pete and Chloe came back, each holding a tray. "Time for drinks and predinner eats," he declared cheerfully.

Chloe had some fancy mocktail thing Pete had whipped up, while he had a whiskey sour and Annika and I had Champagne to start, but with the promise of cocktails of our choice when the bottle was done, as was his custom. It was nice to not have to try and finish the whole bottle myself for once. I supposed that was a tradition of mine. Look at me, indulging in Christmas traditions.

While we snacked, we handed out gifts, swapping them all at once so it wasn't like having an audience of three watching in anticipation, which was always so fuc…awkward.

I'd expected Annika to be neat with wrapping paper, carefully sliding her thumb under the tape and folding the wrapping paper to be recycled. But no, she tore into Pete and Chloe's gift like a two-year-old, a look of pure delight on her face. "Oh, this is the new Leigh Winters book! I have been meaning to buy this." She flipped it over to read the back, then glanced up again, grinning widely. "Thank you!"

"You're welcome. And thank Evie," Pete said. "She helped me."

"Oh, the tables turned about," Annika drawled, glancing at me. She winked. I gulped. "See, Evie," she said, "it's normal to ask people for help."

"So it seems," I said.

As well as the book, Annika had been given a CD (how retro) and an ugly Christmas sweater that matched mine—it was tradition for

Pete to gift the three…now four…of us the garments—and she put it on immediately. This year's design was a Tyrannosaurus rex dressed as a decorated Christmas tree, with LOOK I'M A TREE REX above the cartoonish drawing. She'd burst into giggles as she'd read the caption. "This is wonderful," Annika enthused. "Thank you both so much."

She'd bought Pete a book on the Beatles, and a beanie with foamy beer glasses on it. Chloe got a book on German grammar, which she was so genuinely enthused about that I wondered just how much German Annika had been teaching her, and a Taylor Swift tote bag that she clutched to her chest with glee. Part of my gift to her was an "IOU 1 T. Swift VIP concert ticket for her next tour" that I'd printed out. I'd taken Chloe to the Taylor Swift concert in Vegas in March and survived, and I'd survive again. The rest of her gift contained a small Pete-approved makeup kit, an Apple watch, and a purse.

Pete was thrilled with his new bison-leather duffel and long-sleeved cashmere polo top that I hinted was a nice date shirt, to eye-rolling effect.

In addition to my ugly sweater—which I put on after Annika's goading encouragement—I had a massage voucher, socks with tacos on them, a mug captioned with "World's Okayest Aunt," which made me laugh for a good three minutes, and an Exploding Kittens card game.

The four of us sat around in our ugly Christmas sweaters, which were actually awesome Christmas sweaters. Pete left sporadically to pull the chicken out to rest, and check on the status of food until he declared it was "Eatin' time!" as if we hadn't just spent an hour snacking.

Pete was an excellent home chef and he'd gone even more all-out for the not-Christmas dinner than usual. The food was fabulous, the company and conversation even more so, and by the time dessert rolled around, I was happily tipsy but not drunk, as was Annika after we'd consumed a couple of French 75s.

We wound up the evening a little after nine thirty, declaring that more family dinners including Annika—and the nuance in Pete's words was not lost on me—needed to happen. After effusive good night hugs and kisses and promises to travel safely and talk soon, we bundled ourselves into the Uber who had been waiting patiently downstairs for us to emerge. Big tip for you, sir.

For the short ride home, Annika had her hand stretched across the back seat, her fingers lightly brushing my thigh. It was the barest touch, but it had my nerves firing, my insides twisting with want. We exited the car, and Annika took my hand, walking slightly in front as if leading me. She held it all the way up the stairs, then let go when I paused by my door.

As I unlocked and opened it, I asked, "Do you want to come in for a nightcap?" I didn't want a nightcap, but I didn't know how to just come out and say "Do you want to come in so I can fuck you until we're both screaming?" A little of my fear was still there, but desire was pushing my apprehension aside.

She shook her head. "No."

My heart sank at her blunt refusal. "Okay. Another time then?"

I saw something naked in Annika's expression. Something hungry. Something that made excitement stir low in my belly. "I don't want to come in for a nightcap," she murmured, her eyes on my mouth. "But I *do* want to come in for…" She ran the ball of her thumb slowly, softly, over my lower lip. "You."

I didn't get the chance to respond before her mouth was on mine and she was pushing me backward through my open door. She kissed me like she'd been starved for kisses, and I responded enthusiastically to her hungry lips and searching tongue.

We didn't break the kiss while I turned the lock. We didn't break the kiss as we offloaded our gifts onto the floor by my kitchen counter. We didn't break the kiss as we yanked off our coats and flung them in the direction of the couch as we moved toward my bedroom. And we didn't break the kiss until we'd helped each other shed all our clothing onto the floor near my bed and we were naked.

Annika growled, a low, throaty sound that felt almost possessive. "Let me look at you," she purred as she put a little space between us. The loss of contact felt awful. The way she looked at me felt anything but. Annika knelt in front of me, her hands on my ass holding me against her mouth as she placed hot, wet, open-mouthed kisses over my belly and thighs. "You look just like I imagined you would. Sleek… sexy." She pushed me gently backward and I dropped onto my bed. Her gorgeous mouth quirked. "Perfect."

I would have returned the sentiment, but "perfect" didn't quite do her justice. If I were drawing a naked woman, I would want her as my model. Slender but soft with full, high breasts, luscious curves, and the most incredible legs. I swallowed. My desire was a low simmer, easily controlled for now, but waiting to boil over. "I don't even know what to say. How to tell you how gorgeous you are, how much I want you."

"You just did that," she said smugly.

"I suppose I did." An uncomfortable sensation rose up beside my excitement, and I fought with whether or not to share. But Annika seemed to pick up on something from my face or body language.

"What is it?" she asked.

"I'm nervous," I admitted. "About…being naked in front of you." Which was ridiculous, because I was already naked. It'd been over a decade since I'd been intimate with a woman I had feelings for and I wasn't quite sure how I'd respond to her touch. And I had all the feelings for Annika.

"Why?" Her eyes softened, then lazily traveled the length of my body. "You really shouldn't be."

"I've been pregnant," I said quietly. "My C-section scar. And… stretch marks."

"Do you think that would make me think you were any less sexy?"

She definitely had never given me the impression that she would be bothered by scars and stretch marks. "No, it's…it's me."

"I understand," she said, nodding thoughtfully. "Would you like me to turn the light off?"

"No," I said instantly. "I want to see you."

Annika smiled indulgently. "And I feel the same way." She dropped onto the bed, crawling toward me like a big cat stalking something. Annika paused, hovering above my body and I pulled her the rest of the way down until the full, naked, glorious length of her was pressed on top of me. As we kissed, our legs tangled, and I felt the heat of her arousal against my skin. Annika made a small noise of desire, and broke the kiss to lavish attention on other parts of my body.

I gripped the back of her head. "In case you're wondering, I don't have any STIs," I muttered, trying to get the pleasantries out of the way, which was incredibly hard given what her mouth was doing to my nipples. "That's sexually transmitted infections. STD, diseases, sounds so…gross, doesn't it?" Oh fuck, and we've reached the nervous rambling portion of intimacy. I drew in a deep breath, trying to calm myself.

She stopped her thorough attention to my breasts. "I know the acronym STI, but thank you for clarifying." Annika paused, her mouth quirking. "And I wasn't wondering. I assumed, knowing you, that you would have been courteous enough to tell me before we went to bed. And you said you haven't been in a relationship for a while."

"And I assumed the same. I feel silly for bringing it up, it's just… you were in a relationship recently, and…"

Annika's eyebrows shot up. "Oh. Ja. But there was no unprotected sex. And he didn't like going down on me, and I saw no reason to do something he wasn't willing to do, so there is nothing to worry about in that department."

My voice cracked in disbelief when I confirmed, "He didn't like going down on you?"

Annika rolled us so I was on top. "On anyone." She pulled my face down and after her tongue suggestively slid along my lower lip, she kissed me.

"He's a fucking idiot," I declared once we'd separated for air. "Is that something *you* like?" At her raised-eyebrows silent question, I elaborated, "Someone going down on you."

Annika inhaled shakily. "Ja. I like that a lot. And I really enjoy doing that for those who…deserve it." Her tone made it absolutely clear that she thought *I* deserved it, and my abs clenched in anticipation.

"Good. So do I. He really is a fucking idiot." I kissed her neck. "Because you're delicious." I peppered her collarbone with kisses, then slid down the bed, marking a path with my mouth as I told her, "Gorgeous." I licked her hip. "Intoxicating." I tasted her upper thigh. "Sexy." I pushed her legs apart. "I can't wait to taste you," I murmured. Her arousal was so close I could smell it, and my throat felt tight with anticipation.

Annika's thighs quivered under my hands. "Then you should put your mouth on my clit," she said hoarsely.

"Should I?" I asked innocently.

In answer, Annika pushed my head down firmly, but not roughly. I didn't need any more encouragement, and I was done teasing her and myself. I paused for just a second before slowly dragging my tongue through her arousal. Annika jerked underneath me, her fingers coming to my shoulders, her nails digging in sharply. She couldn't know it, but a little pain always spiked my arousal and I barely suppressed a moan.

She didn't suppress anything, loudly crying out, "Oh…oh my… that feels so good, Evie. Please keep…yes…oh my god…oh yes."

It was the sexiest fucking thing I'd ever heard, and I had to take a moment to settle myself before I came right then and there. I inhaled a long breath through my nose in a desperate attempt to control myself. She cried out again, and a hoarse string of German followed. And though I had no idea what she was saying, I got its basic gist. But almost as soon as she'd verbalized, Annika tensed, and not in the good way. I tensed too and pulled back, propping myself on my elbows to look up the glorious, naked length of her body.

Before I could ask what was wrong, she blurted, "I'm so sorry."

Oh. That was not what I was expecting. "For what?" I asked gently. Very delicately, and very reluctantly, I withdrew my touch.

"For speaking German." She reached down and took my hand, bringing it to rest just underneath her belly button. Annika put her hand on top of it and our hands rose and fell with her breath. "It is a rule I have, to not exclude people from a conversation by speaking a language they don't understand. I…have never had to apply it in bed before, and I forgot myself."

"Were we having a conversation?" I asked innocently. "Is that what they call this in Germany?"

A flush spread up her chest to her neck. Annika laughed, and the light tension in her body eased. "I suppose we weren't. And no, of course it's not. But I excluded you from my pleasure." She bit her lower lip.

I laughed and crawled up the bed to kiss those pouting lips. "Trust me, I did not feel excluded."

"But…you wouldn't understand what I was saying."

"Not the exact meaning, no. But I knew. You're telling me exactly how you feel. With your body." I licked a slow line up the center of her torso until I came to her breasts. "With your nipples, they're so full and dark." I took one, then the other into my mouth, sucking lightly before biting firmly. Annika moaned, her hands coming to my hair. "And sensitive," I added, lingering a little longer to feast on the plumpness of them before I kissed my way down her ribs and belly. "With your breathing, it's ragged and desperate." She inhaled sharply when I kissed low on her hips as I settled my shoulders between her spread thighs. "And you're telling me with your arousal." I dropped my head and slowly drew my tongue through her slick labia. "It's so thick…so wet. And you taste *so* fucking good."

She groaned, fisting a hand in my hair. Annika guided me and I complied, but before I dove in fully, I murmured, "So…say whatever you like, baby, in whatever language you want."

And she did.

It was almost like she was seducing me with her words, telling me what she wanted and where, how much she was loving it. And that accent begging me to finger-fuck her deeper and harder, to not stop licking her, to make her come, that she was so close and so ready and please…please…*please*, had my stomach in knots and my clit throbbing so hard it was almost unbearable.

She was a little bossy, borderline demanding, and I fucking loved it. Being with Annika was unlike anything I'd ever experienced in bed before, and I realized that she was pressing buttons I hadn't even known I wanted pressed—and she hadn't even touched me. I relished the arrival of her climax, the way her body arched, the way her skin glistened with sweat, the way she vocalized exactly what I was doing to her and how much she wanted it, how much she wanted *me* as she came with a hoarse cry.

It took a few moments for her to catch her breath, then Annika propped herself up on an elbow, glancing down at me. "You might regret teasing me and making me wait like that."

"Good," I said, my whole body tingling with anticipation. "Then punish me for it."

"How much do you need to be punished, Evie?" She took my chin, holding it firmly without being uncomfortable, forcing me to look at her.

I held her gaze, but didn't answer. So Annika decided for me. She rolled me onto my back and pressed me into the bed as her hands and mouth traversed my body. She used her nails and teeth, but not painfully. Perfectly. She pushed my legs apart, and made me wait for an eternity before her hot, wet mouth covered my arousal. Fingers paused at my entrance, and I emitted a sound somewhere between a whimper and a demand before she entered me.

"Tell me what you like," she said, the command clear in her tone.

I could barely get the words out, but I forced myself to say something so she wouldn't stop. "Exactly what you're doing right now. That's what I like."

Annika laughed, low and amused. "I can see that." She groaned, a throaty, hoarse sound, and slicked her tongue through my heat. Then she turned my own actions back on me. "I can taste that…" She lightly sucked my clit. "I can smell that…" She thrust deeply. "I can feel that."

"Jesus…fuck," I hissed. My abs clenched as Annika's tongue worked magic on my clit and her fingers worked magic inside of me.

"Fuck?" she said as she slowly stroked her fingers in and out. "Yes. That is what we're doing."

I moaned. "Oh god. Why are you teasing me?"

"Am I? I don't think I'm teasing you." Everything ceased—her fingers, her lips, her tongue. "Now, *this* would be teasing, wouldn't it? If I just stopped." I felt her breath against my swollen flesh. "What do you think? Is this…teasing?"

"Please don't," I begged in a hoarse, breathless whisper. Payback was not fair. My entire body was about to explode, and I needed her to keep touching me, to keep licking me, to keep her fingers inside me.

"Please don't…what, Evie?" The lightest kiss touched my hip, burning the skin with heat.

"Please don't stop fucking me," I gasped.

"It doesn't feel good, does it? Being teased?"

Actually, it felt really fucking good. But I couldn't say that because she put her mouth back on my clit, and the slow stroke of her tongue took my breath away. Two fingers entered me again, her thrusts increased in speed, pressing deeper and harder with every stroke until I was almost seeing stars, it was *so* fucking good. Heat bloomed between my thighs, my clit pulsing hard with arousal. Annika's mouth and hands worked in synchronicity, until my climax rose hard and fast. I cried out loudly, my entire body tensed and shuddering as I came. There was no thought, only pleasure. The heat and arousal surging through me made it hard to breathe, and once I'd come down the other side, I had to concentrate on just inhaling and exhaling.

Annika leaned over me, a finger tracing the line of my collarbone. "In case you forgot to count"—her lips followed the path of her fingers—"you owe your swearing jar approximately three thousand dollars…"

"Activities that occur within my bed, or yours, are exempt from the swear jar. Actually, words that occur anywhere while one or both of us are naked are exempt."

"Mmm. Then perhaps we should get a few more of those words out of your system." She kissed me hard as she slung her leg over my hip to straddle me. "Think of them as…free words. I will not remind you to put them in your jar."

It was very hard to concentrate with her arousal against my belly, the expanse of smooth, sweat-slick torso right there. All I managed was a hoarse, "Thanks."

"You're welcome." Annika's teeth brushed against her lower lip, which was quirking at the edge. "You called me baby."

I'd said a lot of things, most of which I didn't remember in my current blissed-out state. I raised myself up slightly, gripping her hips for balance. "I did?"

"Ja, you did."

"Oh." I couldn't decipher her expression, so I decided to hedge my bets and say nothing.

Thankfully she let me off the hook. "Nicknames are really fucking hot. Especially during sex." Annika leaned down and kissed me, her tongue playing lightly against mine. She pulled back a fraction to whisper, "Especially coming from your mouth."

"That's good to know."

She braced her hands on my shoulders and began to rock forward and back, grinding herself against me. "I would like to hear some more…"

"Okay, baby," I murmured, my abs tensing at the sensation of her wet clit gliding over my skin. "Whatever you want."

She groaned and pulled my hand between her thighs.

Annika was right when she'd said she was going to keep me up all night fucking, and I lost all sense of time as we lost ourselves in each other. The only thing in my consciousness was her, and me, and this pleasure. When we were both sated, she pulled me against her, wrapping me in her embrace. She murmured something I didn't quite hear, but it didn't matter. I felt what she meant.

I partially woke a few times because of the strange and unfamiliar sensation of someone in my bed. Annika slept pressed against my back, a heavy, comforting arm over my waist. And as if she sensed in her sleep that I'd stirred, that arm would tighten almost imperceptibly then slacken again.

But when I woke at my usual time, indignant at the morning light, I was alone. And it felt so awful, so empty, that I almost wanted to curl into a ball and cry.

CHAPTER TWENTY

Annika

Leaving warm, naked, and tempting Evie in bed while I took my pleasantly sore body to work was the last thing I'd felt like doing, and not only because it felt a little bit like sneaking away from a one-night stand. She'd been blissfully asleep and the temptation to stay, to wake her with teasing touches and demanding kisses, had been so strong that for a moment I'd considered canceling my morning team meeting. But then I reminded myself that there could be other mornings just like this one, but where I could stay. I hoped.

I contented myself with watching her for a few minutes, studying her features: the neat lobe of her ear, the full softness of her lips—slightly parted now—that small bump in the bridge of her nose, the fine, fair, downy hairs along her jaw. The covers had slipped to expose the smooth, soft outer curve of her breast and an expanse of skin on her back. I longed to touch her again, to crawl in behind her and kiss my way from her neck, down her back until I woke her with my touch.

But instead of doing what I most wanted to do, I carefully extracted myself from behind her, slipped from her bed, and gathered my clothes. I dressed in her living room and as I crossed the hallway to my front door, I texted Evie in the hope the words would fill in where my physical presence couldn't. *Sorry I couldn't stay, I have a meeting this morning. Last night was incredible.* I added a mind-explosion emoji and a monkey covering its face emoji, and left it at that.

After taking a long, hot, revitalizing shower, I caved and ordered an Uber so I could linger with coffee and fried eggs and toast while I dealt with some important emails from the München office.

Evie's response to my text had excitement curling through me. *Mind blowing indeed. Thanks for the text. I thought you'd panicked and fled.*

I hastened to reassure her. And myself. *Not at all. Are you panicked? I know we had been drinking…* Drinking but nowhere near drunk, and our intimacy was the natural progression, the thing we'd been moving toward almost since we'd met.

No panic. I have the opposite of panic. I wasn't drunk and was perfectly capable of consenting to tit.

I snorted out a laugh at the autocorrect. A second later the typing dots appeared and then a text that felt indignant, even though it was just words with no tone context, landed. *Consenting to IT. IT.* Then after a few more seconds: *Though I did consent to tit.* Wink emoji.

A soundtrack of Evie from last night ran through my head, stalling on her begging me to suck her nipples as I fucked her. Not surprisingly, the nervous butterfly flutter started up again as I replayed those incredible hours. The relief of us being sexually compatible as well as all the other ways we seemed to fit together outside of the bedroom was immense. The butterflies eased a little bit, but were unfortunately replaced by anxiety.

I knew the source of it, even as I told myself I was jumping ahead by imagining the future with her in it. The future where my role in Boston would be over and I'd move back to München. Alone. Back to the office where Sascha worked. I tapped my thumb against the side of the phone. I didn't want to think about this, especially not now.

I knew I would have to face up to this issue at some stage. Some stage later. As I ate the last mouthful of toast, I responded to Evie's message. *You certainly did. I hope you'll consent again sometime.*

Undoubtedly. Likely very soon…

I am looking forward to that. I'll talk to you later. Have a good day.

You too. The typing dots appeared and disappeared a few times and then a heart emoji next to an *xo* appeared on my screen.

I closed my eyes, holding the phone against my chest.

God, this was going to end badly. So why didn't I stop it now, before I got even deeper in and lost a way to get myself out? For the simplest reason there was. I didn't want to.

I managed to focus enough to do some work. In the last week or so, I'd finally felt settled into the role and new location, that my team and I were in sync, and that they'd reached the trust and respect stage. It was a nice feeling, and coupled with the lingering high from last night and the promise of more intimacy with Evie, I felt like my life had settled nicely.

A little bit before lunchtime, Marty, a member of the Global Connect project team, knocked on my door, holding up his tablet. "Annika? I have a few front-page mockups for you to look at. Just primary artwork."

"Great, thanks." I motioned him in, and we spent the next forty minutes going through the designs, figuring out which theme fit the app best and playing with the layouts. I tried to remain focused, but my mind wandered. Evie, with all her artistic talent, would know at a glance what worked and what didn't.

Evie. A warm flush started at my throat and spread upward, and suddenly all I could think about was how my body felt—the pleasant sensation of muscles used, the lingering sensation of having been fucked hard, and fucking someone hard, for hours. Scheisse. I hoped Marty didn't notice that I'd gone suddenly silent, or that I was undoubtedly blushing.

Movement caught my eye, and I glanced up to see Rachel hovering by my open door, her expression making it clear she needed to talk with me. I wound up with Marty. He gathered his tablet and left, smiling widely at Rachel on his way out. Everyone in this office was so happy and upbeat, with just a touch of carefree attitude, and it was both wonderful and a little bit unnerving. The work was done and it was good, on time, and on budget. It was just…relaxed. The office culture in München was a little bit more rigid. Not somber or rude, but just…German.

I smiled at Rachel as I waved her into my office. "Hallo. How may I help you?"

Apparently with nothing, because she blurted, "What's up with you?"

"Nothing is up with me." Except for everything…

Rachel indicated my face. "You're blushing. You got a little crush on Marty?" she teased, though her expression made it clear she didn't *actually* think that, and was just making fun at me.

I shook my head, and indicated she should close the door. Rachel did so, then came back to sit. "Closed door? It's about to get scandalous! I love it."

"Sorry to disappoint you, but I'm not sure this is a scandal. I just… have a problem."

"Work or personal?"

"The second," I said, leaning back against my desk with my hands resting lightly in my lap.

"Let me guess." She tapped her chin, pretending to think it over. "The problem's name is Evie."

"That is a very good guess," I said glumly.

Rachel's expression turned incredulous. "How the heck could she be a problem?"

"You should make another guess. I'm sure you will figure it out."

I fidgeted as she stared into the distance, her expression blank. Finally, she looked back to me and the understanding that was teasing at the edge of her expression blossomed. "Oh. Riiiight." Rachel grinned, shrugging carelessly. "I don't know that I'd call falling in love with someone a *problem*."

"It is when I'm not supposed to stay in America. It is when neither of us wants a relationship." I bit my lower lip, which felt like it was starting to tremble. "Well. I did not want one before. Now, I…" I threw up my hands then let them fall back to my lap with a heavy slap. "I want it. I want all of it. And it's not going to work."

"There are solutions to every problem. Fixing problems, finding workarounds? That's kind of our job."

"My dating life is not software," I said indignantly.

"It'd be a lot easier if it were."

I couldn't disagree. I'd love a troubleshooting guide for me and Evie. A thought I'd been trying not to have muscled its way to the front. There *was* room for more permanent project managers in the Boston office. I held back a sigh and changed the subject. "Do you want to eat lunch and buy Christmas tree decorations with me?" I had everything I technically needed, but I wanted to check once more in case something amazing jumped at me.

Rachel's eyes widened. "Five days before Christmas, you haven't decorated your tree yet, and you think you're going to get decorations now?"

"We don't decorate until Christmas Eve," I pointed out. "And I have some decorations."

"Still. Girl, you are living dangerously."

"In more ways than just Christmas decorations," I said seriously.

* * *

I was far too old for playing it cool, and whatever this was between us, I wasn't going to pretend that I didn't want to spend all my free time with Evie. Or pretend that I didn't want to sleep with her again tonight, and tomorrow, and all the days after. We hadn't made firm plans, but it seemed obvious that we'd see each other tonight. Pete and Chloe had left for their Christmas with Evie's parents at their holiday home in…Greenwich I think she'd said, so I knew she'd be free.

I texted her while standing naked in my bedroom after my shower. *I'm home from work. I'd like to see you. Are we spending tonight together?*

Thankfully Evie seemed to be on the same "let's be honest" wavelength as me. *Yes. I don't want to have dinner without you. I don't want to go to bed without you.*

The admission made my chest feel tight. *Dinner? Drinks? Dessert…?* I knew exactly what I wanted for dessert.

All of it. was Evie's quick response.

I'll be there soon.

I'd had an idea while riding the T home, and instead of pulling on just any old panties and bra, I rummaged in my underwear drawer for something a little bit special. Then I put on ordinary sweatpants and a long-sleeved tee over the top. God I loved being able to be comfortable around Evie. Getting dressed up together was nice, and I was sure we'd have more of that, but for now, I just really loved being able to relax with her.

I grabbed something from my closet and stuffed it into a tote bag. The best thing about living across the hall from my girl—from the woman I was sleeping with, was that I didn't have to pack anything for overnight. I could just walk down the hall to brush my teeth if I wanted to.

Evie opened the door seconds after I'd knocked and a rush of emotion hit me when I saw her. I didn't want to waste time with greetings, so I took her face in my hands and bent to kiss her. Evie met me halfway, one hand on my waist and the other coming to tangle in my hair. It had been far too long since that beautiful mouth had been against mine. The moment we kissed it felt like I hadn't taken a full breath since I'd last kissed her, but could now breathe again.

"Hallo," I said, kissing her again.

"Hi." She tucked a piece of hair back behind my ear. "Good day?"

"It's better now. How about you?"

"Same." She grinned, gave me another quick kiss, then disengaged herself. "Drink?"

"In a minute." I toed out of my slippers and left them by her door. I was bursting with my idea and had to tell her. "So. I had this idea on my way home from work. I don't know whose Weihnachten gift it will be, but we can decide that later."

Evie's eyebrows arched slowly. "You have my attention. What's your idea?"

"I want to pose for you. Like…" I frowned. "In the movie. Oh, scheisse, what is it?" Evie was watching me trying to figure out what I wanted to say. I gestured frantically, as if that might shake loose the words. "The big sinking boat. *Titanic*!" I finally said triumphantly.

Laughing, Evie clarified, "You mean instead of drawing you like one of Leo DiCaprio's French girls, you want me to draw you like one of my German girls?"

I laughed at her adaptation of the line from the movie about drawing naked women. Leaning forward, I traced a forefinger along the edge of her jaw and down her neck. "I would hope that I'm your only German girl."

"You're my only girl, period," Evie said seriously, without hesitation.

"Very good answer." I kissed her, hard, and Evie's hands came to my ass. She pulled me into her, and I let her. But only for a moment. I pulled back to set a little bit of distance between us. "No," I said, impressing myself with my restraint. "Drawing first."

She groaned. "No…"

"It will be worth the wait, I promise."

"I know it will be," Evie muttered. "Why do you think I'm agreeing?" With a sigh, she took a full step backward. "Just let me grab some stuff from my office."

While she jogged upstairs, I took the time to compose myself. I'd been suppressing my desire for her all day and was reaching my limits. I pressed my hand hard to my stomach, trying to slow my breathing.

Evie came thundering back down the stairs, holding a large sketchbook and a small rolled-up canvas case. She paused by the couch. "My tools are at your disposal, ma'am."

That could be taken a few ways, but I chose to behave. "I see. How do you want me?"

"Right here and right now," she said huskily.

I chuckled. "I know. I also know you know that I meant, how do you want me for this portrait?"

Despite my words throwing cool water on her libido, Evie's expression was anything but cool. It was sensuous, inviting, wanting… Her response was tight. "However you feel comfortable. Clothed or… unclothed." She licked her lips. "Seated, reclining."

"Hmmm." I eyed the couch and then the few comfortable armchairs that were dotted around her living room. When I indicated the couch,

Evie nodded and went to collect a chair from the kitchen table for herself. She fidgeted with its placement, standing beside it and looking up at the couch, then adjusting the position.

She settled herself and unrolled the canvas case, pulling out a couple of pencils. "Ready when you are."

Where to start? Top…or bottom? I eased my long-sleeved tee off and took my time folding it before I set it on a chair. Evie went very, very still. Her eyes never left my body as I slowly shimmied out of my sweatpants, folded them and left them with my tee. Okay, so my clothing was pretty unsexy, but my lingerie—black bra and thong with red lace edging—made up for it.

Evie met my eyes. "Is this for me?"

"Yes. Well not for you to have but I wore it for you."

"Is this the gift you were talking about?"

"Part of it," I murmured, teasing a finger around the curve of my breast above the cup of the bra.

Evie studied me like she was appraising a work of art. "It certainly is a gift," she said, and I only just heard the words she'd mumbled under her breath. Evie opened the sketchbook and flipped through it. "Are you ready?"

"No, I am not." I reached behind myself and unhooked my bra. I heard her sharp inhalation. "Should I stop there?" I asked.

She shook her head.

I pulled the bra off and let it fall. Evie's eyes followed my movements as I hooked my thumbs in the waistband of the panties. Before I slid them down my thighs, I asked, "Now? Should I stop?"

"No," she said roughly.

I bent to step out of the panties and collected the bra. Instead of placing the lingerie with my other clothes, I set them on her lap, slipping to the side when she tried to touch me. If I let her touch me then it would be all over. I'd fuck her right there where she sat in the chair. And I wanted to tease her by making her wait, by making her see me as she drew me. I wanted to tease myself.

"Now are you ready?" she asked, her voice hitching at the end of the question.

"Almost." I went to the fabric tote I'd left by the door and collected a Santa hat. I popped it on my head and took up a reclining position on the couch. "It *is* the Christmas season, after all."

She blew out a loud breath. "That it is," she said hoarsely. "Merry Christmas to me."

"And to me also…" I dropped one leg off the side of the couch. I knew the position would give her a view between my thighs.

"Are you warm enough?" Evie asked thickly.

"Very. The way you're looking at me is making me very hot."

Evie cleared her throat again, fidgeting with her pencil. "It's been a while since I drew from a naked live model…"

"Oh?" I began stroking my breasts. "Is it harder to draw someone who's naked?" I asked innocently.

"It depends on the person." Evie chuckled, though it was strained rather than amused. "It *is* very hard to concentrate when you do that. Also, you may end up with six right hands because it keeps changing position."

"Sorry," I said, only meaning it because it was making her task harder. I was not sorry for touching myself.

She smiled as if she knew what I was thinking, then got to work.

I was utterly transfixed watching her, even though I couldn't see what she was creating. The little crease between Evie's eyebrows had deepened, and I watched her eyes flicking from me to the page over and over. Her expression was intense, concentrated, yet soft and relaxed at the same time. I studied the graceful length of her neck. The smooth, strong line of her jaw. The shape of her ears. The freckle on her left cheekbone. Staring at that freckle made me think of the one on her hip, the one under her breast.

I watched her drawing and imagined that hand caressing my body. My skin heated as if it were actually happening. My breathing quickened and I fought the urge to squirm, to get up and go to her.

After about forty minutes, Evie stopped drawing. Forty torturous, teasing minutes. "Okay," she said, her voice a little bit breathless. "That's enough."

I stretched then stood. "Can I see it?"

She closed the sketchbook and set it and the pencil aside. "Not until Christmas. I need to fill in some of the details."

My pout had no effect. "My Christmas, or yours?"

"Let's split the difference and you can see it at midnight between Eve and Day."

"Mmm." I closed the space between us. "I had no idea someone drawing me could be so…erotic."

"I had no idea drawing you could be so erotic," she answered, standing up. Evie took my hand, turning it over before she playfully bit my thumb, sucking it into her mouth. She kissed the tips of each of my fingers before gently placing them on my lips. "Are you hungry yet?" Her gaze strayed down, eyes searing my bare skin.

"Yes," I whispered. The unrelenting throb of my clit made it hard to think. "But not for food."

She pushed her hips forward into mine, her hands snaking around to grab my ass. She kissed me, lingering long enough to make me want more—much, much more—before she pulled away. "Good. Let's go to bed."

I nodded.

But we didn't make it to her bed.

CHAPTER TWENTY-ONE

Evie

I still hadn't found anything to give Annika for a Christmas Day Merry Weihnachten gift, and I was starting to panic. And now we were sleeping together and not just friendly, sometimes-kissing neighbors, I felt like I should get her something better than just some nice-but-bland gift. Somewhere along the way, it'd become less about sharing our Christmases, and more about sharing ourselves and I really wanted to give her something special.

Drawing her on Friday night had felt so intimate, as intimate as sex, and it had given me an idea. Not the drawing of her. But I could draw something else that might be meaningful to her.

While Annika had been dressing after we'd fucked on the couch where she'd posed for me, I'd snuck another peek at the drawing. And even though she'd just licked me to climax, arousal still stirred. I had no idea it was possible to want someone so much. To want them with a depth of feeling that seemed endless, like it would never be fulfilled, only temporarily satiated. She'd made a playful grab for the sketchbook and I'd lightly slapped her ass as I said, "Nuh-uh." Something flashed in her eyes, and I made a mental note—more ass slapping.

Of course, to create this gift for her, I'd have to go through my photos, which meant seeing Heather. I smiled. It'd been too long since

I spent time with my sister. It was a poor substitute for actually being with her, but preferable to having nothing.

I wondered what Heather would say if I told her that I'd developed some pretty serious feelings for Annika. She'd probably make a joke about the lesbian tendency to fall in love at the drop of a hat, get defensive when I reminded her how quickly she'd fallen for Pete, grill Annika about everything from her favorite childhood memory to her preferred moisturizer, and then invite us both around for dinner and drinks so she could grill us about how we'd fallen in love.

How *I'd* fallen in love. I really didn't know how Annika felt.

It was too soon to be in love with Annika, wasn't it? Well… Rationally, I knew it wasn't too soon. But emotionally? Yeah. Way too soon.

We spent the rest of Saturday mostly together, though Annika went back to her apartment for a few hours, grumbling about housework, which gave me some time to work on her gift. We cooked dinner together—a simple pasta meal with a cucumber salad that Annika admitted she sometimes made and ate on its own when she was feeling too lazy to cook or even go to the trouble of ordering dinner. It was basically lazy pickles, and I was totally down with it. We shared a bottle of wine. We talked about weekend plans and confirmed food for Christmas Eve and Christmas Day. We watched a movie that I didn't really watch because I was too busy thinking about her and us, thinking about the fact that we were…*we*. A thing together. Her and me.

I still didn't know how to label us. But did we need a label? Heart, stop being dumb, and listen to Head. If only my head and my heart would get in sync. It wasn't that my head didn't want Annika as much as my heart did, it was that my head remembered what it felt like when my heart was broken.

Annika's fingers lightly brushed my thigh. "Do you want me to stay tonight?"

I looked up. We'd already had sex. There was no reason for me to say yes other than I wanted to fall asleep wrapped up in her and wake with her face pressed to my neck. "Yes."

Her eyes softened as she smiled. "Good. Then I will go home and brush my teeth. And collect my pajamas."

"You won't need pajamas."

Someone was calling me in my dream. Just a telemarketer. I let it ring. And let it ring. Until something permeated my unconscious brain and I woke with an uncomfortable rush of adrenaline. Annika was in bed beside me, which meant it couldn't be her asking for another post-party rescue. If it wasn't her, it could only be Pete or Chloe. My stomach dropped. I fumbled for my phone, my stomach dropping further when I saw Pete's name on the screen. There was only one reason he'd call at midnight. "Petey," I said, my voice a breathless, panicked whisper. "Are you and Chloe okay?"

"We're fine," he said soothingly. Thankfully he got right to the point. And the point made my breath catch. "Peanut, it looks like your dad has had a heart attack. He's alive and conscious, and he's in the hospital."

I sat up, running a hand through my hair. "Oh shit. Is Chloe okay? Did she see it?"

"No, she was in bed." He didn't say it, but the "thankfully" was threaded through every word of that sentence. "It was during after-dinner drinks and cigars. He just…dropped to the floor." Pete exhaled loudly. "It was pretty fucking scary."

"I'll bet," I said. Annika stirred, the arm around my waist tightening. She mumbled something incoherent as she struggled with the sheet. I patted her hand as I asked Pete, "Are you okay?"

"Yeah, I'm fine." Pete offered information I didn't ask for. "He's at the Greenwich Hospital. Uh…Your mom went with him. As far as I know, he's going to be okay. Or, as okay as you can be after a heart attack. I don't know the treatment details yet."

Annika rolled over and turned on the bedside lamp, then sat up, pulling the covers over us as best she could. She rested one hand between my shoulder blades, the other on my thigh. I turned to her and smiled to indicate everything was fine. "Okay, well, thanks for letting me know. Are you guys staying in Greenwich or coming home?" They'd only been there since Friday afternoon, but if things were all ass-up, who knew what was happening with Christmas.

"I'm not sure. I'll talk to your mom when she gets back and see if she wants us here or if we'll just come home, but I'll let you know. She may even want us to stay for longer, but I have to think of Chloe going to school and me at work and all that stuff."

"Sure. Just let me know."

"Yep. I'll text you if I have any news." He didn't need to say that he'd be texting me because my own mother wouldn't even contact me to let me know my father had had a medical emergency.

"Okay, sounds good. Talk soon."

Annika rubbed my back, her hand moving up to massage the back of my neck. "What is happening?"

I loved that she didn't ask if everything was all right, because it was fairly obvious from my side of the conversation that it wasn't. I turned on my bedside lamp and shuffled to face her, leaning my shoulder against the headboard. "Looks like my dad has had a heart attack. He's in the hospital. Apparently he'll be okay."

"Oh, Schnucki," she murmured, cupping my face softly. "I'm sorry. Are you all right?"

"Yeah, of course," I said.

"Are you sure?" she asked gently.

"Yes," I answered, irrationally annoyed by her pushing, gentle as it was. "Of course I am. Why wouldn't I be okay?"

"Because your father had a heart attack."

"And he's fine."

"Jaaaa," Annika said, drawing the word out in a way that made me think she didn't really agree with what I was saying. "I'm just saying… if one of my parents had a medical event, I would be devastated, even if they were going to be okay."

"I know you would. Because you're close to your parents. But I'm not, and I haven't been for a long time. And I've accepted that. I really wish you would too." I knew she understood what I'd told her about my relationship with my parents, so why didn't she *understand*?

"Have you accepted it, Evie?" she asked evenly. "I don't think you have."

"They made the choice, not me. I never wanted this, but I'm stuck with it because my mother can't stand who I am. And my dad is just a spineless coward who goes along with it because he can't be bothered standing up for me." I felt mildly ashamed at laying into him when he could have died, but the truth was the truth.

"What about Chloe? Shouldn't she see you reconcile with your parents, her grandparents? Wouldn't it be nice for you to be there at Christmas with your whole family? To share other important events with them?"

I gripped the sheets so hard that the skin of my knuckles felt like it was going to crack. "Chloe wasn't even born when my mom all but disowned me. She's never known anything except this with regard to me and my parents. She's never seen me interact with them, and I've never said a bad word about them in front of her because she deserves to have an unsullied relationship with her maternal grandparents. So Chloe doesn't give a shit what I do with my parents."

"But I'm sure she knows that—"

I cut her off. "Look, Annika, I know you're just trying to help. But you don't really know anything about my family. I don't need to have a relationship with them to fulfill my duties with regards to the Foundation. My father is going to die eventually. So is my mother. That's just life."

"Wow. That's…that is very cold." She pushed the bedcovers back. "I am going to go back to my apartment."

I stretched to touch her, but she was already out of my reach. "Annika…"

She started getting dressed with short, jerky movements. "I think you need to be making time to think. And I am a little bit frustrated with you right now." She didn't need to say it. I could hear it in her voice.

"Yeah, well. I'm frustrated with you too," I said, unable to prevent my peevishness. I sat up, pulling the sheet up over my breasts. "You can't just waltz in and tell me how to interact with my parents when you've never seen the aftermath of your mom telling you she dislikes who you are and your dad just saying well I guess that's just the way it is, sorry."

"And you can't invite me into your life and then"—she clapped her hands together—"just close the door on all the parts you don't like and tell me they are off-limits. That's unfair. And I am sure that it was awful for you, but you are treating me like an idiot. And you're not letting me support you."

"I don't *need* your support with this. I've lived with *this* for fifteen years. It's my thing, not yours."

"Your thing. Ja, you have made that very clear. But if you want more with me, Evie, then you are needing to learn to share your feelings, the good and the bad."

Words fell from my mouth before I could think. "Maybe I don't want that." The moment I'd said it, I wanted to grab the words back. But I couldn't. They were out in the world, hurting both of us.

Her nostrils flared. "Right now, that is a feeling of mutual."

Well. She'd just launched a perfectly sharpened arrow, and it'd hit its mark. So I did what anyone who's been wounded would do. Anyone who didn't have healthy ways to deal with their emotions, that is. I fought back. "You just need to back the fuck off about my family, and everything will be fine. Please," I added through gritted teeth.

Annika inhaled deeply. Her eyes never left mine, but her jaw worked like she was chewing on something foul to say at me. But she didn't. Instead, she calmly said, "Ja, okay, Evie. I will back off."

And she did. She backed off so much that she left me. The quiet snick of my front door closing echoed through the house. I fell back onto the bed and covered my eyes with my forearm. Tears pricked at my eyes, but I couldn't even cry. That's a ten out of ten for a complete overreaction. Well done, Evie, you've shown her what a complete and utter pile of garbage you are.

I had no idea what I should do.

So for a while, I just did nothing. When I felt like I could stand up without my legs quitting, I went to lock my front door behind her. Then I took myself back to bed and dove underneath the covers, pulling them up over my head.

I curled into a ball and pulled the other pillow closer, desperately hoping to catch a trace of her scent. For an hour I tried and failed to make sense of what had happened. I should go knock on her door or text her. Great idea, Evie. Wake her up. That'll make her even happier to speak with you. Not that I even knew what I would say. My emotions were all over the fucking place. I was utterly furious with her for pushing into my personal life, for trying to force me to do something when she had no idea of the situation. And I was upset with myself for handling it like an emotionally stunted idiot, which, yeah…I was, but I didn't have to fucking act like it all the time, did I?

Annika was wrong to push, wrong to say what she did. But, I was wrong for reacting the way I did. I just couldn't help it. My relationship with my parents was such a raw spot that every time I thought about it I wanted to scream. Unfortunately this time, I had screamed. At Annika. No, not screamed exactly, but I may as well have.

I felt nauseated, that trembly churny icky feeling where I knew I wasn't going to hurl but that felt uncomfortable and all wrong. I'd ruined everything. And for what? Because I didn't like someone telling me that my relationship, or lack of, with my parents wasn't healthy. Someone who obviously cared about me. Someone who liked me for me. It was self-sabotage.

At that thought, another niggling one took root. A thought that surprised me. I should probably go see my father. It'd take around three hours to drive to Greenwich and maybe the drive there and back would give me some breathing room. I checked the visiting hours for the cardiac unit and decided to leave after I'd been for a run this morning.

But if I was going to make a six-hour round trip and talk to my dad for more than a minute about something other than perfunctory conversations about foundation stuff, I needed to sleep. I punched my pillow into submission, then rolled over, facing away from where Annika had been lying, and closed my eyes.

But I couldn't sleep. Eventually I decided to channel my emotion into work, and went up into my office to draw. I sketched the outline of an eight-panel scene of a fight between Harper and Thea, letting my frustration and upset guide my hand. It was great art, and a mild catharsis.

I watched the sun rise and set down my stylus. Aside from the few hours before Pete's call, I hadn't slept at all and could unfortunately add nausea from exhaustion to my nausea from being an awful person. But I knew moving my body somehow would help. I already risked running into Annika when I left, so decided on a lazy—and cowardly—treadmill jog.

While I was working off some cortisol, Pete texted to let me know that my dad was still okay, and they were doing more tests, but it looked like the angioplasty had been successful and he should make a full recovery. He'd be spending the morning at the hospital with my mother and would bring Chloe—who was hanging out at the house with my parents' staff keeping an eye on her—for a visit in the afternoon. I wondered if my parents knew he was keeping me informed.

After stretching, breakfast, and coffee made in the moka pot Annika had mended which did not make me cry at all, I showered. Instead of pulling on jeans, a Henley, and a pair of sneakers or something equally as comfortable, I dressed rich-person casual ready for the Greenwich crowd. Locking my door, I stared at Annika's and wondered if I should go see her. I didn't even know what I'd say. "I'm so sorry" would be a good start, but I was too scared she'd tell me to fuck off.

I made a mental note to put an IOU for $100 for all the verbal and mental expletives of the past eight hours and slunk out of the building. The gray sky and chilly drizzle matched my mood perfectly, and I inhaled deeply, letting the crisp air into my lungs.

Ordinarily I loved long drives, tuning out with music, an audiobook, or a podcast, and taking in the scenery. But this time I drove in silence, not really paying attention to the surroundings. The silence gave me three hours to think about what I'd done. It was a very uncomfortable time alone with my thoughts, because it didn't take long to conclude that I'd probably ruined any chance of ever having something more with Annika. I'd sabotaged everything before she could leave me and return to Munich. Typical avoidance behavior. My therapist would be so proud of me. For my self-realization. Not for me acting like a bitch.

It was almost a surprise when I realized I was approaching Greenwich, and I sat up a little straighter and paid more attention to where I was going. I hadn't been here since I was twenty, before Heather's cancer, before Chloe, before everything went to shit. As soon as I'd parked at the hospital, I grabbed my phone from my handbag to text Pete.

There were two texts from Annika sent a little after I'd left. *I'm at your door and you're not answering. Are you ignoring me?*

Then ten minutes later. *If you need some time and don't want to talk to me, that's okay but please let me know you're okay.*

A simultaneous rush of relief and anxiety washed through me. It was more than an olive branch, not that the branch was hers to extend—it should have been me first—and I grabbed it like it was a lifeline. I tapped my thumbs against the phone case for a few seconds, then typed out my text. *I'm sorry. I left early this morning. I'm fine. Can we please talk about this?*

It took barely any time for her to respond. *CAN you talk about it, Evie? Because I don't feel like you yelling at me again.*

A fair response, but it still stung. God I was fucking this up so badly. *Yes I can. I want to. I'm out of town until later this afternoon. I'll let you know when I'm home.* Thankfully she didn't ask where I was, though I was sure she could infer that I'd skulked off to see my father after her admonishment.

Okay. Be safe. Thankfully, she didn't gloat. A few seconds later, a heart emoji came through.

I exhaled loudly. Maybe we'd be okay. I really fucking hoped so. I wasn't ready to let go of her. I didn't want to push her away. I let my head fall back onto the headrest and sat in my car for a minute until my heart rate had settled down.

When I could breathe fully again, I texted Pete. *Petey, I'm at the hospital, just sitting in my car in the parking lot. Can you tell me when my mom is gone so I can come see how Dad is doing?* Because I saw my dad sporadically for board things, visiting him was within my comfort tolerance. But seeing my mother, especially when she'd be upset about Dad's medical event, was beyond my emotional abilities right now.

Pete responded almost instantly. *Sure. I think she was talking about trying to find a doctor to talk to soon.*

I sent back: *Thanks, let me know when the coast is clear.*

He responded with a thumbs-up emoji.

And now, to wait.

I reclined the seat and lay back, eyes closed, waiting to sneak in like a bandit to see my father. I'd dozed for maybe twenty minutes when my phone sounded a text alert. *We're leaving. I should be able to keep her occupied for half an hour. Come now.* He added details of my dad's room number and how to find him.

I sent my own thumbs-up emoji and sprang out of my car. I power-walked to the building, rushed inside, and after finding a bathroom to deal with my traveler's bladder I made my way to cardiac care.

As I strode briskly down the hallway, I silenced my phone so as not to disturb the heart-attacked, and dropped it into my handbag. I hated hospitals. I'd never had much to do with them. Until Heather's cancer. Then I'd had as much to do with them as I wanted for my whole lifetime.

Of course Dad had a private room—though given the financial status of the population of Greenwich, the hospital probably only had private rooms—and I found myself sweating and dry-mouthed at the partially open door. He had his eyes closed, but I knew he wasn't asleep because Pete and my mom had just been there. I knocked lightly, and Dad's head snapped up. His eyes lit up the moment he saw me, and I felt a little better about my decision to visit.

Dad was clean-shaven, his thick salt-and-pepper hair neatly combed. He seemed…shrunken somehow, even though I knew he couldn't be—I'd seen him only last month at a board meeting. But he was definitely subdued. Maybe it was that he was quiet and that made him seem littler. It was so weird seeing this behemoth of a man made small by his health scare, and I was alarmed to find my eyes prickling with the threat of tears. "Hi, Dad."

He smiled, reaching for me with an unsteady hand. "Evie. Thanks for coming."

I pulled the door mostly closed before I moved to his bedside, took his hand and lightly squeezed it. I didn't know what else to say, so I mumbled, "You're welcome."

Once I'd taken a seat in the bedside chair, he said, "I'm surprised you came all this way." The unspoken "because you haven't voluntarily seen your parents in more than a decade" lingered in his statement.

"It's a three-hour drive. Not exactly around the world."

"Still, it was just a little heart attack. It was minor, barely even a heart attack."

"Oh right. Collapsing on the floor, being unconscious, and requiring a medical procedure is no big deal," I deadpanned.

He impatiently waved the notion aside, and I left it because my father was a lawyer. You could not argue him down. He always won. "So. You know what's happening in my world. What's going on in your life?"

It was so casual, so conversational that I was momentarily stunned by his question, by the fact that he was acting as if nothing had happened in our family. So I answered him like I would a dad I hadn't talked with properly for a few months, not many years. "Not much. I have a new volume out soon so I'm busy with that."

"That's great. Are you…seeing anyone?" he asked.

He seemed like he actually wanted to know because he was my dad, not because he wanted to hold it against me. Maybe having a near-death experience had made him rethink things. I paused for a few moments, and decided I'd play along. "Sort of. I met someone and she's amazing but I'm pretty sure she thinks I'm a heartless bitch now. So, thanks for that." I tried very hard to keep the frustration from my voice, and rated my success at about twenty percent.

Dad picked up on the frustration, and the nuance. "Thanks? Why is that my fault?" he asked indignantly, his face morphing into confusion.

I adjusted my tone, not wanting to upset him and give him another heart attack. "Because you had this heart attack and I wasn't suitably upset."

"Were you upset at all?" I knew from his tone that he wasn't bothered that I wasn't very, or at all, upset.

I shrugged. "Not really. If you'd actually died then I would have been a little upset. But you didn't, so I wasn't. But, I figured I should come say hi before you died."

"Well that's good to know. I would have had a heart attack years ago if I knew you telling me something personal was the reward." I'd forgotten his dry sense of humor—it'd been so long since we'd talked beyond the superficial interactions that related solely to the Foundation. I had a sudden, sharp pain behind my breastbone (hypochondriacal heart attack because I was in the cardiac ward?) at the fact it was so easy to sit here and banter with him. We'd missed out on so much because we were all so fucking stupid.

"I'm glad you consider seeing me a reward," I said.

"Of course I do."

"And you know, if you wanted to know personal things before now, you *could* have just asked me."

"I know. But…" I could tell by his expression that he was fighting with himself and after a few moments, he changed course. "Do you want me to die so you can reconcile with your"—he cleared his throat—"girlfriend? Because I can do it." He pretended to take a deep breath and hold it, and out the side of his mouth, muttered, "Just gimme a minute."

"Dad!" I said, swatting his arm. And I couldn't help it—I laughed.

Thank fuck he didn't say something corny like "I've missed the sound of you laughing." Instead, he leveled a look at me, one I'd forgotten. It was his lecture look. And he didn't disappoint. "If you know what you did wrong, and you're sorry, then you should apologize." The words felt weighted. And also completely incongruous coming from him. I didn't even think he knew what "sorry" meant.

"I suppose I should," I agreed. No, not suppose. I knew. I'd been cruel, and unfair, and short-tempered, and a bunch of other negative adjectives. And I knew why I'd immediately gone on the defensive. Annika had touched a raw nerve. Because no matter how much I tried to tell myself that my parents' stance on my sexuality didn't hurt—it did. A lot. And having the woman I was intimately entwined with, the woman who I'd let see parts of myself I let nobody else see, tell me that I was not being a nice, or smart, person stung. A lot.

After a sigh, I added, "I will apologize."

"Good." He cleared his throat again, and I wondered if he was going to sling an apology my way. Thankfully he didn't, because my emotions were about as raw as they could get right now. Instead, he went to a comfortable topic. Business. "Just so you know, when I do decide to die, I've already nominated you as the Foundation's board president." And then, damn him, he went to personal. "And I know you were probably wondering about my will—"

"No, I wasn't," I interrupted.

"Still. You should know that you're well taken care of, especially now with…Heather gone. You're my daughter, Evie. I love you. I know it hasn't seemed much like it lately. Or, for a while, perhaps. But I do. And your mother does too. This whole thing is utterly absurd, isn't it?"

Oh screw him for telling me this now. I took a deep breath and mastered my emotions before I broke down. I'd half-expected his board nomination—my mother didn't want anything to do with the Foundation beyond the social events—but it was still a surprise. As was learning he hadn't cut me out of his will. Not that I needed more money and assets. It was the principle of it that mattered. "Good thing you and I have the same vision for the family's foundation then, isn't it," I said. I couldn't comment on our rift. I didn't have the mental bandwidth right now to dive into it.

He chuckled. "I suppose it is."

A knock on the partially closed door made me tense, before I realized my mother wouldn't knock—she'd barge right in like she owned the place. Which she actually might. Whoever was at the door waited for my dad to tell them to come in, then a midforties woman, presumably a nurse, came in and cast a practiced eye over the monitors.

"Thomas," she said warmly, "how are you feeling?"

He glanced at me before speaking. "Tired, but otherwise fine."

I nearly fell over at his admission that he wasn't invincible, but held my tongue.

The presumably nurse looked to me. "If you're tired, then some rest might be in order. You've had a lot of company today."

My father acquiesced—acquiesced!—with a nod. Once the woman had exited, pulling the door mostly closed again, I stood. "Well," I said. "I guess that's my cue."

"I'll see you at the next board meeting," Dad promised.

"Only if you don't overdo it and kill yourself with another cardiac event before then," I said dryly.

"I'll try not to."

I hesitated, then leaned down and kissed his cheek. "In that case, I'll see you in a few months."

"I look forward to it," he said quietly. "Take care of yourself, Evie."

"You too." And then I left before I did something embarrassing like cry. Geez I was a mess. It wasn't his health scare that had upset me. It was reexamining all the feelings about my parents that I'd tried to throw overboard.

And yeah, we hadn't reconciled exactly—that would take more than ten minutes, if it happened at all—but maybe at the next board meeting, we might make conversation instead of our usual polite "How are you?" where we weren't actually interested in the answer. And then maybe one day, we could go for drinks or something like a normal father-daughter get-together. I held no illusions that I would move back into my family the way I had before I'd come out, but it would be nice to not feel so on edge all the time around my dad. And maybe one day, I'd speak to my mother again.

Unfortunately, that day came far sooner than I'd anticipated or wanted. I'd walked barely ten steps down the hall, trying to sneak away, when Pete's distinctive height caught my eye, coming toward me. And in front of him, striding in that way she'd perfected—economical and purposeful all in one—was my mother.

Pete, you traitor. Our ideas of "thirty minutes" were vastly different. Though he seemed alarmed rather than smug. Okay, so maybe he hadn't orchestrated a little family reunion after all. His eyes widened and, safely behind my mother, he mouthed, "Sorry."

My whole body had reacted and the weird mix of anxiety, anger, shock, fear, and frustration made for an interesting combination of shaky and sick and tense. My heart raced. For a moment, I thought my legs might quit. I should have known this was a possibility, but I'd really thought I could just sneak in to see my dad and sneak out without seeing her, trusting Pete to run interference.

My mother looked almost exactly the same as when I'd last seen her, a few years ago at a gala, from a distance, though her coiffed hair was a little shorter. I'd always marveled that she never seemed to age, though I suppose a dedicated team of antiaging doctors and beauty therapists were responsible. Her eyes, the exact dark blue as mine, yet—I always fancied—far more cool and aloof, softened fractionally when she saw me. That softening sent a simultaneous wave of panic and relief through me. Not that I thought she'd make a scene, because if nothing else, Margaret Phillips would never air private family business in public.

I took a moment to compose myself and make sure my voice wasn't a, trembly, b, shouty, or c, squeaky. "Hello, Mom."

And her voice was the same cool, modulated tone I recalled when she answered, "Hello, Evangeline. It's nice to see you. You look well."

"Thank you, I am well," I said, hating the reversion to the stiff formality of my early years. At least I hadn't called her Mother.

"I'm pleased to hear that." There was no trace of disingenuity in her response. "Thank you for coming to see your father."

"Of course." I stared for a few moments and when it was clear that would be the extent of this conversation, I turned to Pete. "You'll keep me updated?" At his nod, I exhaled loudly. "Great. I'm sorry, but I need to get home."

I had a huge apology to make.

CHAPTER TWENTY-TWO

Annika

When I'd woken up alone in my own bed, I had to blink away tears. People had arguments. It was a normal part of any relationship—romantic, friends, family—and it certainly wasn't the first I'd had with a partner. But the argument with Evie was so short, yet so sharp that I felt cut to ribbons. It had taken a lot of self-control not to lose my temper. But, as much as I wanted to fight back, I knew that wasn't going to help at all.

She'd said some horrible things in anger, but I didn't think she'd actually meant them, because in that moment I'd seen just how vulnerable she was, and how much she needed someone to tell her that she was loved and accepted for who she was. Vulnerable people threw up defenses to protect themselves, and it was cruel of me to be so antagonistic about what made her feel so vulnerable: her family.

I'd knocked on her door, and when she didn't answer, I'd sent a series of texts, none of which were answered. Then finally, not knowing what to do, I'd pulled on a cardigan, and winter boots over my leggings, and gone outside to check for her car.

It wasn't on the street. I'd walked up and down to check if she'd parked further away for some reason. There were a lot of very expensive cars, but hers was the only Mercedes SUV and there was no way I'd miss it, especially not the bright blue color. No—she wasn't there. My stomach had sunk. So she'd run away. This really did not bode well for us. I did not like dancing around a subject, especially one that had caused an argument.

Not everyone was like me though, and I knew some people needed space after a fight. And space was fine. If she wasn't ready to talk about it, then I would wait until she was. But refusing to talk about it was not a good way to have a relationship. And I desperately wanted a relationship with her. I clumped back up the stairs and shut myself inside my apartment.

When my phone had alerted me to a text a little after eleven a.m., I'd grabbed it like it was an oxygen mask in a crashing plane.

Evie. I closed my eyes, but it didn't stop the few tears from leaking out. I swiped at my eyes and opened our texting chain. *I'm sorry. Can we please talk about this?*

Though my relief was so palpable I felt it as a rush of adrenaline, my fingers had flown so quickly over the screen I didn't even have time to think. And perhaps my response was a little bit blunt. *CAN you talk about it, Evie? Because I don't feel like you yelling at me again.* Maybe I didn't need the capitals to emphasize my point, but despite feeling bad for what I'd done, I was also frustrated by her reaction.

If the underlying snideness bothered her, she didn't react. *Yes I can. I want to. I'm out of town until later this afternoon. I'll let you know when I'm home.*

Okay. Be safe. I added a heart emoji and put my phone down before I said something I didn't want to say over text.

What did this mean for us? Yesterday I would have said that I could see a future for us. I'd been considering maybe asking about permanent project-manager positions in Boston. Or failing that, asking about extending my assignment and visa. But now I didn't know. Did I want a relationship with someone who wouldn't admit to herself what this rift with her parents had done to her?

I was certain there was more to the story. But how could I have a relationship with someone who didn't share my feelings about the importance of family? How could I build a family with someone who didn't have the same values that I did? And was it even fair for me to hold that against her?

I decided I'd had enough of moping around my house, worrying about Evie and her father and us, and texted Rachel. *Meet me for lunch?*

Shouldn't you be spending time with your hot girlfriend?

Yes, I should be. If she was even my girlfriend. *She had something to do today.* It wasn't a lie. Evie did have something to do today. People had something to do every day. I just had no idea what her something was.

Rachel texted me the name of a café not far from the office, and after checking the T timetable, I texted I'd be there in an hour. Some time with a friend, and a little bit of distraction was exactly what I needed to sort through the mess in my head.

The weather had turned and I was not enjoying the cold drizzle one bit. Though I supposed feeling miserable in my body matched feeling miserable in my emotions. Rachel was already inside the café, studying a menu and she grinned as I approached. "I beat you!" she said triumphantly. "For the first time ever."

It was true. I was usually punctual. "Ja, you did." I unzipped my jacket and loosened my scarf before I sat beside her.

As if my lateness somehow meant something was wrong, Rachel studied me, her eyes narrowed. After an eternity of uncomfortable scrutiny, she finally asked, "What's wrong?" She touched my shoulder, her entire face scrunching up like she thought that might help her decipher my expression.

Well. I had fallen over at the first hurdle. I tried to protest that nothing was wrong, but Rachel just sighed. "I look at your face five days a week. I know when something's not right."

The waitress interrupted the interrogation, and I ordered coffee and eggs benedict with smoked salmon because I needed something comforting. The moment we were alone again, Rachel covered my hand with hers. "Seriously. You okay?"

I gave up trying to pretend. "Evie and I had a terrible fight early this morning and now she's…gone. I am not sure where she is."

I'd had a small idea that maybe she'd traveled to see her father, but had dismissed that immediately. The utter vehemence with which she talked about her family, the disregard she seemed to have for the fact her father had suffered a serious medical event made me wonder if I really knew her. It was like she became a completely different person when she spoke about her parents. I'd finally understood, after hours lying awake, that her cruel indifference was probably just part of her walls. That she had to act that way, to protect herself.

But it was still very hard to listen to her speak like that to me. I wasn't a saint, I had absolutely said cruel and hurtful things during fights just to make someone feel as bad as I felt. But for some reason, hearing it from Evie had hurt more than anything that had ever been thrown at me in the heat of an argument.

Rachel paused as our coffees were delivered, but as soon as she'd taken a sip of her Americano, she dove right back into my issues. "Did you break up with her?"

"You can't break up with someone if you're not dating them, so no, we didn't break up. We just had a disagreement. About her relationship with her family. She doesn't seem to care that she is…entfremdet"—I twinkled my fingers, trying to get the word in English—"*estranged* from her parents." I explained what had happened to her father in vague terms. I wasn't sure if Rachel knew who Evie was, as in Evangeline Phillips, and I didn't want to share something that wasn't really mine to share. "And you know how important family is to me."

"Then isn't it nice to get all the kinks out now before you start dating her? Assuming you *are* going to date her."

"Ja," I sighed. "Dating feels…inevitable, I suppose."

"Wow, first off, I can't believe you didn't make a joke about kinks. And secondly, 'dating feels inevitable'? Now that's some downer wording if I ever heard it. You don't want to date her?"

"Of course I want to date her. I want more than just dating her, but—" I huffed out an exasperated breath. "What happened to working on myself and being comfortable with being alone?" It felt silly to even say it. The resolution had been shoved into a deep dark corner of my mind for weeks, ignored and collecting dust.

"Why the fuck do you need to be comfortable being alone? It's not like you're chronically codependent and need to figure out how to be alone when your partner isn't there for a few hours. If you're a person who enjoys being in relationships, then that should be where you're at."

I sipped my coffee, stalling to gather my thoughts. I was in love with Evie. I knew it with as much certainty as I knew my name. And now it was all dangling over the edge of a cliff and I was desperately trying to figure out how to pull it all back. "I know it's stupid, but it has been stuck in my thoughts ever since Sascha mentioned it."

Rachel pursed her lips. "Mhmm. And I bet that's exactly what he wanted. To make you think of him every single time you think of a relationship with someone else, his stupid voice is in your head telling you lies. And he thinks you'll go back to him because of that."

I scoffed, "There is no chance of that." The thought of seeing him at work again when I went back sent dread through me. Maybe he'd quit, or move to the Paris office or something before I finished in Boston.

"Oh I know. But you're still letting him win."

I turned that over in my mind for a minute. She was right. My ex was wrong. "I really like her, Rachel. And I more-than-like her too, which is also ridiculous because we haven't even known each other a full month." But it was undeniable. My feelings were there and were not going away, not even after this fight.

Rachel shrugged. "Hey, if you know you know. I've fallen in love in less than a week." She grinned slyly. "And I've fallen in lust in less than a minute."

I held in my sigh. "I think I know that feeling," I finally admitted. "But how can I be in a relationship with someone who doesn't value family the same way that I do? Even if we're not looking at long term, because I'm leaving."

"Do you *have* to leave?"

"Well, this project is only for twelve months. Or maybe a little bit more if we run over time, which I refuse to do, even to spend longer with Evie." It was tempting but completely unprofessional.

"You know…I bet if you ask, there'd be a job opening in the Boston office for you. Turn your temporary relocation permanent. We definitely need more project managers now that Kim's gone full stay-at-home mom and David decided on a career change."

"I have thought about that already," I admitted, embarrassment heating my cheeks—who plans a permanent move to another country after knowing a woman less than a month? "Visa issues aside, I have to think of my family. And Evie is committed to her niece and brother-in-law here. Being in a relationship in two countries would not work."

"How often do you see your parents and brother? Do they live in Munich?"

"No. They live in Hamburg."

She made a "go on" gesture. "Which is where? Compared to Munich? And where's Munich? My geography sucks."

I rolled my eyes. She'd lived in the city for eight months and I knew she was aware of the general location. "Hamburg is at the top of the country. München is down the bottom."

"And how long does it take you to drive to see your parents and brother?"

"Train," I corrected. "Six hours." Her raised eyebrows had me adding, "Seven or eight when I factor in delays."

"And how often do you take the train to see them?"

The conversation was running away, and I didn't like feeling I was chasing after it. Especially because I had a very good idea about the destination Rachel was leading me to. "About once every four months or so, for birthdays and that sort of thing. And for Christmas of course. And they also come to see me."

"I'm not going to ask about flight times, because I've taken a direct flight from Boston to Munich and it only took seven and a half hours. So…" She trailed off, eyebrows raised pointedly.

So Boston to Hamburg would be comparable. I held up my hands to forestall any more of Rachel proving her point. "Okay, all right."

Rachel folded her arms, smiling smugly. "All I'm saying is, think about it. You know we're short of project managers here, which is why they dragged you from Germany in the first place. I bet you could name your salary and they'd transfer you here in a heartbeat and deal with visa extensions and all that shit."

She had another point. Instead of fighting amongst the managers for projects to lead in München, I could be assured of heading plenty in Boston. And if it didn't work, then it wasn't like I couldn't get another job, or even start my own small development company. But did I want to leave my home? And for what? A woman who'd proven that she didn't care about family.

But… Was that really true? I'd seen the way she treated Chloe. She'd carried her sister's child. And her relationship with Pete was a perfect example of sibling love, even if they weren't blood relations. So maybe her interactions with her parents weren't what I would class as "normal," but to say she didn't value family was plain wrong. *I* was wrong.

I held back my sigh. I'd smothered our relationship before it even had a chance. I realized then just how judgmental I'd been.

Rachel barreled on, "And you know the best way to deal with visa issues? Marry someone…"

Grinning, I said, "Halt die Klappe."

"I'm sorry, was that German for 'I'm already planning my wedding, will you be my bridesmaid'?"

Still smiling, I rolled my eyes. "No, it's German for shut up. And I am *nowhere* near thinking about a wedding. I am still trying to decide if I'm brave enough to just…stay. Anything that happens after that decision is too far ahead for me to think about now."

I was thinking of staying in Boston because I was falling in love with Evie. But was I only thinking that because I was unable to be alone? No, that wasn't it. I didn't need to stay in Boston to be "not alone." I could be not alone in Germany just as easily. Perhaps more easily. But who knew what the next year might bring? What if I committed to staying, and things between us didn't work out?

"How many thoughts have you just had in the last thirty seconds?" Rachel asked.

I glanced up. "Approximately five million."

"Not many at all." Smiling widely, she held up her hands. "Enlighten me?"

"I was just thinking, what if later me and Evie are having some more arguments?"

Rachel snorted. "Then you'll be like every other couple on the planet. Arguments don't end relationships, Annika, unless you don't deal with the cause of the arguments."

I nodded slowly. "That is a good point."

"Look," she said matter-of-factly. "Every problem comes with multiple solutions. You just gotta find which ones will work for you and Evie. Maybe it'll be easy, maybe it won't, but worrying about it isn't going to help."

"You're right." I leaned over and hugged her. "And you're a good friend."

"Backatcha, pal." Rachel squeezed my forearm. "I think you know what you want to do. You just have to be brave enough to put that on the table as a possibility." Her smile was gently encouraging. "You don't need to commit to anything now, but you do need to commit to being open about all the options, and commit to doing some work to make it work. And that's both of you, assuming Evie is on board with whatever you guys have now turning into something permanent."

"Ja. Perhaps that is where I should start before I get myself worried about things I might not need to be worrying about."

"Exactly."

We lingered over lunch, and our conversation meandered. We parted around three p.m., and I took my time walking back to the station, pausing to look in shopfronts, popping into a few to browse. Mostly, my strolling was to give myself some more time to process everything. One question kept pushing its way into my brain and I decided to stop ignoring it.

Did I want a relationship with Evie?

And as soon as I'd answered myself with an emphatic *Yes*, the next question barreled into my consciousness.

Did I want a long-term relationship with her?

Yes.

I wanted all of it. The family dramas, figuring out work and my visa, maybe separating for a little bit of time for those visa requirements, any arguments that might arise in the future. Because all of the undesirable stuff was nothing compared to the possibilities that being with her would bring me. The joy, the security, the love…

When I turned onto my street, I was relieved to see that Evie's car was back. I walked over to it and touched the hood, noting it was still a little bit warm. I decided to give her some time to relax before I texted. I needed to apologize for forcing my feelings onto her, for not being supportive.

Because if I didn't apologize, then it was possible I would be ruining something that could be the best thing in my life. It was possible I was going to break my own heart.

CHAPTER TWENTY-THREE

Evie

I stayed under the hot shower spray far too long, trying to slough off the emotion dredged up by my day. Who knew that going to see my father would result in so much clarity? The drive back to Boston had been just as revelatory as the drive to Greenwich. Thank god for the lessons I'd learned in therapy, right?

I'd decided three things, unequivocally. One, I wanted Annika—romantically, as a friend, as a partner in all ways. Two, I was as to blame for the rift between me and my parents—they had started it, but I'd kept it going. Three, what Annika had said was right—I hadn't accepted what had happened between me and my parents.

Instead of texting Annika that I was back, asking if we could talk and if she'd come around, I decided to go to her place. It was a strategic decision, one my dad had told me many years ago: being in unfamiliar territory automatically put people on the back foot, even if they didn't realize. Being in Annika's apartment would make her feel more comfortable, though I knew by now that she was also comfortable at my place, as I was at hers. But she deserved the upper hand for this discussion.

What should I bring as a peace offering? Another bottle of the 1986 Château Lynch-Bages Bordeaux? I only had two bottles left, so that was a pretty good grovel. I set the bottle on the counter, but then rethought. Drinking wine was a great icebreaker, but I also wanted to say what I needed to say without a whole bottle of wine getting in the way. Hot chocolate first, then maybe wine.

And no powdered hot chocolate mix for this apology; it was time for Heather's fix-anything hot chocolate. She'd made it when I was sad or angry about important and unimportant things. She'd made it during our big travel adventure whenever we were tired or hungover. She'd made it after I'd come out to my parents, after I'd told her that my mother had said of course I wasn't gay, to stop being so ridiculous, that I was just confused and trying to rebel against the family and I needed to stop being such a petulant child and what would people think of us.

I mixed milk, double cream, and some Swiss (sorry, Annika) chocolate in a saucepan, and watched it carefully, stirring until it was ready. After a taste-testing sip or three, I poured it into a thermos. Now for the extras. I dropped mini marshmallows into a small container, and pulled out a bottle of Courvoisier XO cognac, just in case we wanted to adult it up. Probably a little wasteful to put that cognac in hot chocolate, but who cared?

When I was trying to juggle the bottle of wine, liquor, thermos, and marshmallows to get out the door, I realized maybe I'd gone a little overboard. I used the bottom of the bottle of Courvoisier to knock on Annika's door.

She opened it within seconds, her eyes lighting up when she saw me, then lighting up more when she saw what was in my arms. "Hallo, Evie."

"I come with a peace offering." I looked down at my cargo. "Or, offerings?" I amended with a nervous smile.

She took the wine and cognac and left them on the kitchen table. "Thank you for coming over," Annika murmured. "With your offerings," she added, a smile teasing her lips.

"Well I had to, because I need to apologize because we've planned this Christmas stuff and I've already got your gifts. *And* I have this goose being delivered tomorrow and I have no idea how to cook it and it's too much for just me. So, I thought I'd better say I'm sorry." I took a deep breath, relieved Annika was still smiling and seemed to have taken my ice-breaking joke as I'd intended it.

She nodded slowly. "Those things seem like good reasons to me."

"I thought so." Holding up the thermos, I said, too brightly, "Hot chocolate? It's so miserable outside. Or wine? Or cognac? Or hot chocolate with cognac?"

"Cognac in hot chocolate sounds wonderful, thank you." Annika turned away to collect mugs, and I busied myself opening the thermos and container of marshmallows.

"This is Heather's special fix-anything hot-chocolate recipe. I really need to teach Chloe so when she's older she can make it for her boyfriend, or girlfriend, or her kids or her friends, or maybe even me, or she might just want to make it for herself." I was aware that I was babbling, but the words just kept spilling out of my mouth until I noted Annika's expression. Patient, expectant, amused.

"What are we fixing?" she asked steadily.

I had to take a breath before I could answer, but the single word still came out tremulous and questioning. "Us…?"

"Evie…" she murmured.

"Yeah?"

Annika said nothing more. Instead, she closed the space between us and pulled me into a hug, her embrace tight and comforting. I melted into her, wrapping my arms tightly around her back, burying my face in her shoulder, breathing in the warm comfort of her.

"Evie," Annika repeated, pulling back a little. "We are not broken. Maybe a little bit…" She mimed wringing out a towel, then hitting something with a hammer. After another few moments, she said, "Dented. But not broken."

A rush of relief flooded through me. I hadn't completely fucked everything up. But I needed to make sure Annika knew how much I regretted what I'd said to her. My heart thumped hard against my ribs, the beat quickening with my rising anxiety. I needed to apologize before I got too overwhelmed and couldn't. I sucked in a deep, ragged breath and let it out in a rush along with her name. "Annika. I'm sorry for how I acted. I'm sorry for what I said. I'm sorry for the way I treated you during our fight. I was wrong, and I was cruel, and I'm sorry. Obviously my parents and my lack of relationship with them are sore points for me. My parents never apologize. To us. To each other. To our staff. To the public. They think 'sorry' is weakness. It took me a long time to learn how to apologize and sometimes I'm still not good at it. So, I'm sorry."

"I know," she said quietly. "I'm sorry too. I said hurtful things. And I pushed you when I should not have pushed you."

"I said hurtful things too. *Really* hurtful." I felt my lower lip quiver and pressed my lips together in an attempt to stop myself from crying. "But unlike you, I said them because I wanted to hurt you for hurting me. And there's no excuse. I lashed out at you when you didn't deserve it. And I'm so sorry."

"I know you are," she said gently. "It was just…I was upset that you didn't seem to care about your dad, and I made that about me and how I love my parents, not about you and what has happened with your parents. In my head, I was accusing you of not caring about family when I know family is not always about your parents."

"Just because my parents did a terrible thing and I don't have a relationship with them doesn't mean I don't know the importance of family. Actually, I think it means I know even more how important it is."

"Ja, I realized that too. You with Chloe and Pete, the way you love them, I know you know what family is. And I'm sorry that I took your…" She frowned, gesturing the way she did when a word was stuck. "Unconventional family as a meaning that you don't care about family the way I do. I was very caught on that thought last night, and I could not free myself."

"I know. And I knew exactly where you were coming from. I think it hurt me so much because you were right." Her eyebrows shot up at that. "I knew what you meant, I know what you wanted for me, and I just didn't want to admit that I was wrong."

"How were you wrong?"

"My lack of a relationship with my parents *does* affect me, and I didn't have to accept it." I exhaled tremulously. "And the worst thing is that I'm just as much to blame as my parents. Seeing my dad made me realize that. I could have reached out to them sooner. I could have tried to mend fences, or just…tried harder to fight to be seen and accepted. I could have tried to help them understand, held their hand and shown them how to do it. But I didn't. I've been so focused on what they did and not what I did in return."

She stroked my cheek with her thumb. "What did you do, Evie?"

"I…it's…my mother never said she didn't love me, she never said I couldn't be part of the family. But her disapproval and disbelief just fueled my self-righteous indignation about not being supported unconditionally when I came out. My mother's views on my life are fucking shitty and my father's weakness is fucking shitty. But *I'm* the one who chose full nuclear warfare on them, and I'm the one who let it be a red-hot exclusion zone this whole time instead of attempting to clean up the fallout."

Annika smiled. "That is a very clever analogy."

"Thanks." I sighed. "The problem is she's too proud to beg me to stop this whole thing, and I'm too proud to tell her that sometimes I miss my parents, so we've just been at an impasse all this time because neither of us will budge. I'm not diminishing what she did, and I'm not saying everything will suddenly be hunky-dory, but I feel like I'm going to step away from my stash of indignant-outrage fuel and let the fire just die out. I don't know if we'll ever reconcile to a point where our relationship is fully mended, but I hope we can at least reach the 'being around each other for important things and being civil' stage. I think that might be in the cards."

She took my hand, holding it between both of hers. "If it is, I hope you get what you need. And I will support you."

"I would like that, so much. I lost my parents. And then I lost a girlfriend because I wanted to give my sister what she most wanted. And then I lost my sister. I know my family doesn't look like most families, but it's the one *I've* chosen." I inhaled a shuddering breath, and tried to speak, but kept failing around my tears. Eventually I managed to get out, "I don't want to lose you too because of this. Because of me. Because I'm so fucking emotionally stunted."

Annika gripped my upper arms. "You are not emotionally stunted. You are having emotions right now and you are sharing them with me. And you haven't lost me, Evie-Evangeline." Those warm, strong hands moved to cup my face, her thumbs lightly wiping the tears from under my eyes.

"I really hope not," I choked out.

"You haven't," she repeated.

"Thank you. For...staying." My eyes felt puffy and were undoubtedly red. I wiped them on my sleeve. "Well this is me. I'm a mess, in so many ways." And she was still here.

Her expression softened as she gently assured me, "No, you're not." Annika pulled me into another tight hug, kissed my temple, then gently guided me to the couch, fix-it-all hot chocolate forgotten for now. "Sit down and let's relax for a little bit."

I dropped heavily onto her couch and leaned against the arm. Annika sat beside me, pulling a fuzzy woolen blanket over both of us. She fussed with it, tucking it in and smoothing it down, and I recognized the fussiness was nervousness.

I exhaled shakily. "I think maybe I didn't trust you to not hurt me. Because that's just what happens to me. Every single fucking time. It's like a curse, to be hurt. So I was trying to push you away before you could." I bit my lip. "Maybe I wanted to push you away and make it easier for when you do leave."

"How did you know you were doing that?"

I managed a little smile. "I've had a lot of therapy over a lot of years."

She blinked hard a few times. "I am not going to hurt you, Evie. Never. Not intentionally."

"I know that. I do. Deep down. But you're leaving. That's going to hurt, whether or not you meant it to."

"It's going to hurt both of us if I leave." Her voice cracked up at the end of her sentence. But it wasn't the emotion that caught my attention. It was what she'd said.

If.

If?

It *could* just be Annika's English. Sometimes she got words just a little wrong. But…what if it wasn't? I was too scared to ask.

She squirmed from under the blanket, stood up, and started pacing, gesturing expansively. "Evie, I do not want to leave. I want to stay with you, but that has so much confusion with it. Sometimes you are making me crazy. You are all I think about. Every nights. All of the days. I am going over every possibility, stay or go, together or not together." She stopped pacing long enough to look at me. "And I am having all of these feelings."

"What kind of feelings?"

"Even though I knew why we made a fight, I was very mad with you. Frustrated and annoyed at you. But I still love you."

My eyebrows went up so quickly I would have laughed if I wasn't about to cry. "You love me?"

Annika didn't hesitate. "Ja, I do." She came over to the couch and dropped to her knees in front of me. "I don't know *who* told you that you are emotionally stunted, or that you're a bad girlfriend or lover, but they were so wrong, Evie. You are not. And you deserve to be loved for who you are. Not what your surname is."

Well. That did it. I bawled. For a while. And she did nothing but sit with me, comfort me, soothe me, until I could speak again.

Inhaling deeply, I admitted, "So, I was in Greenwich today. I went to visit my father in the hospital."

Her eyebrows shot up. "Are you okay?"

"Yeah, I am. It was surprisingly painless, actually."

"I'm very pleased it was painless." Her tongue flashed out to swipe over her lower lip. "I hope you didn't go because you felt I bullied you about not seeing your sick father."

"You didn't bully me," I promised, "but you did make me realize my behavior was wrong. And I…I saw my mother at the hospital too."

I coughed out a laugh, wiping my eyes. "It has been a roller-coaster of a day."

"How was it? To see your mother?"

"Seeing her was fine," I said honestly. "It's not the first time I've seen her since we made our big separation declaration. I've seen her at events, but just not spoken to her. And seeing her made me realize something." I laughed again, a little less choked this time. "It has been twenty-four hours of realizations."

"Ja, tell me about it. What did you realize, Schnucki?"

I still had no idea what *Schnucki* meant exactly, but she always said it with such gentle fondness that the endearment just felt like love. "My mother always felt she had ownership over us because she created us, like my sister and I were her property. Proprietary over maternal. Everything in my family, between my parents and me, and my parents with Heather, it always felt transactional. That's what I grew up with, that nothing comes without getting something in return. That's how you operate in those circles. If something isn't giving you something, it should be cast aside."

I sucked in a ragged breath. "And that…that fucks with a person. It fucked with me. And I wish I didn't automatically react this way, but deep down, something in me probably thought that you wanted me to reconcile with my family because you wanted some of the wealth my family has. Not what *I* have to give you. It made me think I wasn't enough for you." I had to stop to take a few deep, calming breaths. "And that thought is on me, this is *not* you. I know *you* wouldn't. But… people have, and it's awful. And the fear it might happen again is so hard to set aside."

"People like your ex-girlfriends?" she asked quietly.

"Yes," I agreed in a whisper. My family, me, we have an obscene amount of money. It was an undeniable fact. And people liked that fact. "I'm not accusing you of anything to do with wanting the material things I have. It's just an ingrained fear and I hate it."

She stroked the back of my hands. "I can see how that would make it very hard for you to trust people."

"It does. But I trust you. You make me want to change, to be different. Being alone since my sister died, this thing with my parents, I've just gotten used to it. Comfort breeds stagnation. And I don't want to be stagnant. You've broken me out of this cloud of…whatever the fuck I've been in for the last fifteen years. I don't want our relationship to be anything like the relationships I had before."

"Then we will make sure it isn't. It's already different, isn't it? I'm the first beautiful German woman you've ever slept with, yes?"

I laughed through my tears. "You certainly are. You're *the* most beautiful woman I've ever slept with."

"I like how that sounds." Her expression softened. "What you admitted takes a lot of courage, Evie. First to say you were wrong, and then to say you are going to be the one to try and repair it."

"Mm. I don't know how it'll go, but I'm going to call my parents on Christmas Day and wish them a Merry Christmas, and check in on Dad. And then I guess I'll just see where things go from there. If it doesn't go anywhere, then I can say I've made an attempt." I glanced up and found her hopeful gaze fixed on me. "If you can just give me time to work through things. I mean, not…push at me about it because that makes me feel, I don't know, like, defensive. I'm going to do it, but I need to sort out everything that comes with that."

"Ja, of course," she said instantly. "Whatever you need."

I took her hands, squeezed gently, turned them over to study the delicate shape of her fingers, the smooth skin of her palm. "That drive was exactly what I needed to work things through in my head. I want you, I want *us*, Annika. I want us to date, for real. I want to tell you that it's you and only you, because that's the truth. I want us to live together, somehow. I want to do things with you. Things I haven't done in years. Concerts at Jordan Hall. BSO. The ballet. Travel." I inhaled quickly. "You need to watch some baseball, visit the aquarium, the *Constitution*, fuck there's so much. I want to show you all the Boston tourist things and then all the things for Bostonians that we hide from tourists. And it's terrifying, because I've never felt this way before and it's terrifying because you're not staying."

A thought flitted through my head. Could a relationship with her be like those wine vintages I enjoyed—all the more precious for knowing it's fleeting?

Her face had brightened more and more as I listed each touristy thing, and then fell at my final few words. "I don't know what I am doing. I don't want to leave. I don't want to spend a year with you, knowing it is going to end when I leave. But I don't know if I'm brave enough to move permanently. That's…that's very scary for me. And not just because of moving. It is—" She sagged. "It is me not wanting to put my emotional things onto you."

"What emotional things?" I asked. I'd never had any inkling of any emotional issues from her.

"My ex, he said…he said I do not know how to be alone. I know, inside of me, that he's wrong and that he was trying to hurt me. But *that* is why I promised myself that when I was here, I would be alone. It was maybe to prove him wrong, but I pretended it was for me, to work on my own self."

"Your ex said that? What a dick."

She laughed dryly. "Ja, well, we have already known that. I made a resolution to be alone, but then I forgot about it because of how I feel about you. I am…" Annika sighed deeply. "I am scared that I'm maybe moving too quickly because of me not wanting to live here alone. Me loving you so much because I need someone. And then I'm also scared that I'm not feeling like this just because of that. I'm scared that you are who I'm supposed to be with, because I have never felt so much love like this."

So much love…

I inhaled deeply. "I just think—do we have to decide right now? Can't we just *be together*, and say we're happy for now and we can figure out the future in the future?"

"I'm German," Annika deadpanned. "You want me to go into this relationship with you without having a plan?"

Grinning, I said, "Yes. I'm asking you to trust me."

"Well," she said, affecting an imperious tone. "You *were* right about the erhu in the right hands being beautiful to listen to." She sneakily wiped under her eyes. "So, maybe you are being right about this too."

CHAPTER TWENTY-FOUR

Annika

Though it felt strange, because it had come from an argument, it felt like Evie and I had grown even closer. She'd opened herself up to me, shown me her vulnerabilities, her desires, and asked me to not hurt her. And I had given, and requested, the same, and she had taken what I'd said and shown me the wonder of possibility.

With the exception of thirty minutes to light Evie's fourth Advent candle—she said she wasn't risking ruining Christmas by leaving it unlit—we stayed at my apartment for the rest of Sunday. Around nine p.m., she'd smothered a huge yawn. Without a word, I'd taken her hand, pulled her up from the couch and led her to bed.

We'd made love instead of fucked, reconnecting slowly, sensually, before falling asleep wrapped together. Evie loved to be the little spoon, which suited me perfectly—I loved the sensation of holding her, being able to press my face into her lemon-scented hair, the feeling of her smooth, warm skin.

Because the tree was "stuck" at Evie's, we'd decided to base our two-day celebration at her place. Some days it felt like I almost lived there anyway. Pyramid knew I wouldn't be working on Christmas Eve—it was not a vacation day in America—but I had to work on Monday. There was no question about where I would spend the night before Christmas Eve, and after work I took a fast shower and went straight to Evie's. Being with her felt so easy, so right, that I decided not to question anything and just enjoy it.

Tuesday morning, I woke before her. Until she began stirring, I lay still, enjoying the warm bed and the warm body wrapped in my arms. She squirmed, rolling over to face me, mumbling, "Morning."

I kissed her. "Guten Morgen und Frohe Weihnachten." After another kiss, I said, "Good morning and Merry Christmas."

She smirked. "It's not Christmas. It's Christmas Eve."

"Heiligabend. The Holy Evening. And yes, it's Christmas for Germans." I slapped her arm with the back of my fingers. "You really are a smart-ass."

"I know." Evie pushed herself up against the headboard. "Okay, just so I have this straight—"

"That is an interesting way to put it."

"Just so I have this lesbian and bisexual," she corrected herself without missing a beat, "we're going to eat, drink, decorate the tree, relax, and then eat more, and then it's gift time. Anything else?"

I raised an eyebrow. There was plenty else I could think of to occupy our time, but the focus was supposed to be on the Christmas events. "Ja, that's right. Don't forget to add Christmas carols to that list. And I have been working hard in my kitchen every free moment I have to provide you with a German Christmas food experience."

She traced light fingers up and down my bare arm. "What experience is that exactly?"

"A lot of potato salad. Sausages—"

"You made sausages?"

"No. But I searched many grocery stores to find the exact right ones. Are you going to allow me to finish, or are you going to interrupt me this whole—"

"No, I won't keep interrupting you," she interrupted with a facetious smirk.

I narrowed my eyes at her. "More cookies. Noodle soup for our dinner. Glühwein. Stollen." When I said I'd been working hard in my kitchen, I'd only been partially truthful. I hadn't made all of it. Some things, like the mulled wine were ingredients waiting to be combined. And I'd made the Stollen a few weeks ago so it could rest and be ready for Christmas.

"Sounds delicious." She glanced at her wristwatch. "Speaking of delicious, what's for breakfast?"

Breakfast for our respective main celebration days had been left to each of us—me for the twenty-fourth and Evie for the twenty-fifth—and I'd planned a scaled-down version of what my family would usually serve for Christmas or any special occasion. "You'll find out soon." I kissed her and reluctantly flung back the covers. Staying in bed was an appealing notion, but the thought of Christmas was too exciting to ignore.

We parted ways for half an hour to shower, and I went out to buy fresh provisions for breakfast before I'd meet her back at her apartment for a lazy breakfast—coffee, hard-boiled eggs, fresh bread rolls from the bakery down the street, some thinly sliced Gruyère and prosciutto, fruit, butter, and a couple of fruit jams I'd made, because I couldn't bring Mama's homemade jams with me to America. If I were back in Germany, there would be another dozen items on the breakfast table, and I resolved that no matter what happened between us romantically, I would take her to Germany for Christmas so she could experience exactly how my family did it—emptying the fridge to provide every imaginable thing to eat.

When I knocked, she called out that the door was unlocked. Evie was curled up in a chair by the window, drawing in a sketchbook. She glanced up, smiling when she saw me. "Get everything you wanted?"

"Ja, I did. What are you doing?"

She grinned. "People-watching."

I set the breakfast items on her counter and in her fridge, then crossed the room to her. "May I look? Please?"

"Sure." She paused. "You're also going to look at that nude drawing I did of you, aren't you."

"I am."

"It's a good thing I finished it, then. I still haven't decided what to do with it," she said, handing over the sketchbook.

I studied the pages. She'd drawn faces, hands, headless bodies in interesting poses. She'd captured the tiniest nuances of expressions, and again I felt awed at her talent. I flipped back a few pages to find the nude portrait of me. Like the pen sketch she'd done of me, this drawing made me feel like I was the most attractive woman on the planet. "This is beautiful. Thank you."

"For what."

"For seeing me like this."

"I'm just seeing what's there, Annika." Evie cleared her throat and took the sketchbook. She flipped back a few more pages and then turned the sketchbook around to show me. It was me again, a few iterations of my face. In the largest portrait, I looked like I was at the end of a smile, my mouth slightly quirked, my eyes laughing. And again, there was that soft, almost dreamlike quality to the drawing. At the bottom of the page Evie had written *Aphrodite/Artemis?* "I drew this minutes after we first met. I just…I had to draw you."

"A goddess?" I asked, my throat tight.

"Yes."

An indescribable feeling filled me, a burst of love so intense I thought I might cry. I leaned down and kissed her, gently sucking her lower lip before I pulled back. "I think you should put that book down," I murmured.

"Why?"

I straightened and pulled my sweater off over my head. "Because I would like to show you some more…'source material.'"

We lingered in bed after making love, then lingered over breakfast for an hour, before I could no longer contain my excitement and declared it was time to decorate the tree.

Evie nodded and I could tell she was hiding a smile. "Okay, Christmas Elf."

She had helped me transport boxes of things from my place to hers—my decorations, food and drinks, and my gifts for her. Evie collected the large cardboard box that I had labeled DECORATIONS, and pulled out new packages of tinsel, baubles, and lights. "Okay, solid start. And what decorations do you have from home?"

I preferred a tree with decorations that had sentimental value instead of uniform baubles, but unfortunately, I hadn't been able to bring all mine that I'd collected over the years. But I had the most important ones. I held them up. "My tree angel. Weihnachtsbaumengel. And, my pickle. Essiggurke." Evie's eyebrows shot up, and I laughed. "Don't ask, the pickle hidden in your tree is just a thing in Germany." This one had been knitted for me by Mama the year I'd moved out of my parents' house.

Evie held up both hands. "I wouldn't dream of asking." She plucked the pickle from my hands and studied it. "This is super cute." She raised her eyes to find mine. "*You* are super cute. I love seeing you so excited about this." Evie kissed me slowly, her free hand gripping the fabric of my sweater. "You're in charge of the decorating. Just tell me what to do."

I held her gaze. "Do you like it when I'm in charge?"

"Yes," she said instantly. Her voice was a little rough, and I hoped we would be able to get through decorating without interruption. Though, interruptions of the sexy type wouldn't be unwelcome.

"Good." I raised my chin. "Put on some music. If you can find a German Christmas playlist on Spotify, even better."

"Yes, Christmas Boss." She scrolled through her phone for a few minutes, then looked up. "The Best of German Christmas Songs?"

"That is perfect."

The sound of "Stille Nacht, Heilige Nacht" came softly through speakers from somewhere in her house. Evie nodded decisively. "I know this tune." She hummed along as she collected a chair and brought it over to help us reach the top of the tree.

Evie stood back, taking on the role of assistant. She handed me decorations, beginning with a light dose of tinsel, then the lights, then the baubles. I fussed with everything until I was happy with the look of the tree.

Evie held up the pickle. "I think pickle guy belongs front and center."

"Then you'll find it right away," I argued. "The whole idea is that whoever finds it gets a special present."

She frowned. "But that's skewed. I'm the only one who can find it because you'll know where it's hidden."

"Schnucki, do not question the process."

"I wouldn't dream of it." Evie gave me the pickle, then faced away while I placed the ornament.

Within five seconds of turning around again, she was pointing to the spot where I'd placed it near the back. "Found it," she said triumphantly.

"You win the special prize. Which you may collect later…"

Her look told me she knew exactly what special prize I planned to give her, but thankfully for the sake of finishing our decorating, Evie didn't verbalize her thoughts. Instead, she rubbed her fingers over the blush spreading across her cheeks. "I think it's time for the little… thingybaum angel." She passed it to me, and held out her hand to steady me while I climbed onto the chair to set the angel on top of the tree.

"I think it's crooked," she said, raising her voice over the sound of "Leise rieselt der Schnee."

I shifted it.

"Now it's crooked the other way."

I shifted it slightly back.

"No, that's still wrong."

I hopped down from the chair and moved away from the tree so I could check which way exactly it was supposed to go. It didn't need to go any way. I turned to her and folded my arms over my chest. "Is this payback for me making you straighten the tree over and over?"

She grinned. "Yes."

"That's not funny." I huffed at Evie, who just laughed.

"It's a little bit funny," she countered. "Okay, just a minute. Before you call the tree 'done,' I have something to contribute." Evie collected a small cardboard box from the bookshelf. With a flourish, she produced two baubles and held one out toward me. "Ta-dah!"

I froze, staring at the ornament. I blinked hard a few times but couldn't find the words.

Evie froze too, then seemed to reboot. "What is it? Shit…did I accidentally paint the wrong church?" Evie turned the ornament around and around, looking at it from all angles. "Is it wrong? Did I ruin Christmas?"

I cleared my throat and finally spoke. "No, you painted the right one. It's the Frauenkirche." I took it from her and stared at the delicately rendered painting of the towers of the Frauenkirche in München, with their distinctive clocks and green-domed roofs.

"Are you sure?"

"Absolutely." Finally I felt steady enough to meet her gaze. "This just makes me a little bit homesick, that's all. I'm not sure why. It's just a building. But it's perfect. You are perfect." I glanced at the other painted bauble depicting a ship, which had to be the *USS Constitution*.

Evie held it up. "Do you trust me to hang this Boston landmark on your carefully curated tree?"

"With supervision." I moved two baubles out of the way to make room, and we hung the Boston and München baubles front and center. "There," I declared. "That looks amazing."

Evie nodded. "We're all set. But, just one moment, wait, wait…" She picked up her phone and started scrolling. "One…moment, let me check something, I just…" After a few seconds, the volume of the music increased and "O Tannenbaum" came over the speakers. She took my hands and spun me around. "Now sing!"

I had no idea how we managed to finish the song, with me singing "O Tannenbaum" and Evie singing "O Christmas Tree" and both of us laughing through the words. But we did.

Evie wiped her eyes as she turned the music down. "Oh god, that was brilliant. This is a really great tree," she declared, relocating a bauble that had slipped. "It looks like Santa got drunk and threw up in my living room."

"He must have mixed red wine, Champagne, and vodka too…" I said dryly.

Evie bent double and wheezed with laughter.

After we'd set our gifts under the tree, we spent the rest of the morning on the couch, listening to Christmas music, reading, and just being with one another. The intimacy of the connection felt incredible, and I let myself imagine that we could have this every day for as long as we wanted it, pushing aside any negative thoughts about the logistics of my wish.

After a FaceTime call with my family at lunchtime—their dinnertime—we went back to relaxing, listening to music, snacking, playing cards and board games. Evie cheated at almost everything, though she did it sneakily, grinning at me when caught.

"There is one other very important Christmas family tradition for me," I told her, a few hours before dinnertime. "There is a movie on television every Christmas and we have watched it each year since I was a child. I didn't tell you about it, because I wasn't going to make you watch it all in German." I'd been planning on watching it alone, but had had a brainwave one night while I'd been trying to sleep. "But I found a German version with English…ähm, writing-over on it."

She smiled. "Subtitles?"

"Ja. That's it."

"What's it called?"

"*Drei Haselnüsse für Aschenbrödel*. That means three nuts, hazelnuts, for Cinderella. Like her three wishes. Do you have a DVD player?"

"I do." She raised an eyebrow. "Every year since you were a child? How old is this movie?"

"Older than us," I said, handing her the DVD. "I would watch it, and imagine marrying both Cinderella and her prince."

She stared at the cover. "I can see why you imagined that," Evie said, laughing. She pulled out her phone. "Ninety-one percent on Rotten Tomatoes. Wow, okay, clearly I've been missing something about Christmas all this time."

"Aside from me?" I asked, before I could help myself.

Evie grinned. "Yes, aside from you."

I poured us both a glass of mulled wine and we snuggled onto her couch to watch the movie on her huge television. The screen was wasted on the movie, which was still in the square format of the past.

It was a short film, just under one and a half hours, and I felt pleased that Evie seemed to be enjoying it, laughing at all the funny parts and remaining quiet for the serious sections. The English subtitles were…a little bit odd at times, but I thought that just made it funnier and didn't bother correcting them for Evie.

When the movie ended, Evie twisted to face me. "So, do you still want to marry both Cinderella and the prince?"

I shook my head. "No, I've found someone better." I knew how it would sound, and I'd said it anyway.

"I see." Evie glided her hand up the outside of my thigh. "Why is this person better?"

"She's hotter, funnier, kinder, smarter. Did I mention hotter?"

"You did," she said hoarsely. "How long until we have to have dinner?"

I groaned. "Too soon."

Evie inhaled shakily. "Later, then." It felt like a promise.

"Yes. Later," I agreed.

I was nervous about the food I'd prepared, even though I knew it was delicious. It was more that I wanted her to enjoy it, to enjoy these parts of myself. And if she didn't like it, I still had time to wow her with roast goose tomorrow.

Evie set the table with Christmas placemats, crystal wine and water glasses, and some fancy silverware and fabric napkins while I heated up the noodle soup and toasted the bread. She'd added candles, and was lighting them as I carried steaming bowls to the table. "This is my Oma's very special recipe," I said as I set the bowls down.

Evie made a little noise of appreciation as she tasted it. "Why is it so good?"

"Because it's made with love." I laughed. "Which really just means that she loves you enough to spend hours preparing it."

Her eyes softened. "I'm glad you love me enough to make this."

"I think I am glad too…"

We lingered over the rest of our dinner of potato salad and sausages, then dessert of Stollen and gingerbread cookies—I wasn't going to be able to look at gingerbread for at least a month once Christmas was over. As soon as we'd cleaned up after the meal, Evie asked, "Are you ready for gifts?"

"I have been ready for gifts since I woke up," I said seriously.

As agreed, we had bought ourselves new pajamas and wrapped them to swap. Finding pajamas had been a challenge, because I didn't know exactly what kind of pajamas were appropriate to wear around your maybe-girlfriend. If I were home with my family, it would have been a set of flannelette pajamas my mother had chosen for me, perfectly appropriate for a day with my parents, brother, and sister-in-law. But for being with Evie, I wanted to get something a little bit more enticing. Her house was always very warm, so I'd bought a satin set consisting of very short shorts and a tank top. Completely impractical for sleeping in as I didn't particularly enjoy the feeling of satin, but they looked incredible.

We'd settled on the couch for gifts and Evie feigned surprise when I passed over her pajamas gift to herself. "Whatever could this be?" she asked.

"I have no idea. But maybe it's something like what's in this gift?" I pointed to my self-wrapped pajamas.

Evie unwrapped gifts carefully, the complete opposite to my "tear it open" style. She held up the pajamas and enthused, "Thank you, these are great. Exactly what I wanted!" She had bought herself Rubik's Cube pajamas, the bottoms patterned with cubes all over them, matched with a tank top that had a completed cube on it.

I held my pajamas up, and Evie let out a low whistle before murmuring, "Merry Christmas to me."

We got to work on the rest of our gifts. Evie seemed delighted by the T-shirt I'd had printed for her. The front of it had MERRY WEIHNACHTEN and a cartoon Christmas tree.

My gift was a box filled mostly with red tissue paper, and I pawed through it to find a gift card for a local bookstore. With an apologetic wince, Evie told me, "There were so many options, and I panicked. I thought you'd prefer to pick one you want."

"This is wonderful, thank you. I know just the book I'm going to buy with it." Something small fell out of the paper, and I picked it up. A key attached to a Santa hat keyring. The implication flooded me, and my question escaped my mouth as a rushed, hoarse whisper. "A key?"

"Mhmm. For my place, obviously. You can come in whenever you want, go up to the terrace for some sun, use my gym—which you still haven't done—do whatever you want."

"Are you sure?"

"Yes, that's why I gave it to you. I—" She blushed. "I want you in my house, Annika. I want you in my life. For as long as we can make it work. I would like you to consider moving in with me in the future. We can keep your apartment for you, if you want some space or whatever, but there's so much room in my place for you. I know we've only known each other less than a month, and I know I'm being the epitome of U-Haul here, and it's not like we live far apart at all, and it doesn't have to be right now. This can be a 'just in case you need it' key."

I swallowed the tight lump in my throat. "I want that too."

Evie pulled me forward and I straddled her, settling myself on her lap. One hand slid up my back, underneath my top. She stroked her fingertips lightly up and down either side of my spine. "This is insane," she murmured against my neck. Her other hand was busy at the waistband of my pants. "I've never wanted someone as much as I want you. It's constant, like an ache if I'm not touching you."

"I know exactly how you feel," I agreed, tilting my head to allow her more access to my skin. I ran my fingers through her hair, lightly scratching against her scalp as she gently sucked my neck. My nipples hardened against her breasts, and the sweet pressure between my thighs grew so insistent that I couldn't ignore it any longer. "Let's move. Bed," I said hoarsely. "I want to spread you wide and fuck you hard."

When I moved to climb off Evie, she gripped my ass. "Wait," she said. "This is either going to be sexy as hell or a complete disaster." She tensed underneath me, and stood. Or…tried to stand while lifting me, then sat back down again. A loud laugh burst out of her. "Nope. Disaster."

I shimmied off Evie's lap, took her hand, and pulled her up. The moment she was on her feet, I pressed into her, wrapping my arms around her waist to keep her body against mine as we kissed. Evie arched into me, her mouth hungry, her tongue searching. Somehow we made it to her bedroom without breaking the kiss, and we parted to hastily remove our clothing before she guided me to the bed. Despite the desperation, our kisses turned languid, lazy. Evie's hands moved over my skin confidently, stroking my back, my breasts, my belly, my ass, my thighs, between my thighs.

I gently bit her lower lip as her fingers found my heat, and Evie groaned. We lay facing each other, kissing slowly as we lightly fingered each other's clits. The heat of arousal moving through my body was slow and soft, sensual. Evie spread her legs for me, and I shifted so I could push my fingers inside of her. She gasped, gripping my arm tightly as I thrust. Her fingers fluttered against my clit and I clenched my thighs against her hand.

I sucked her earlobe before murmuring, "The way you love my fingers fucking you, I am starting to regret not bringing some of my things from Germany."

She paused for the briefest moment before her fingers resumed their slow circling around my clit. "Things? What kind of things?"

"My harness, all my dildos…" I'd brought a vibrator with me and that was it. And now I was regretting my thought of *You won't need any sex toys except something to help yourself, because you're not going to sleep with anyone while you're in America*. I withdrew my fingers to pay attention to her clit.

Evie inhaled sharply. "You like to strap on?" Her eyes glittered.

The expression made my pussy clench. "Sometimes, yes…"

She rolled us so she was on top of me, and kissed my nipple. "Isn't it lucky America has places you can purchase those things." Evie moved to my other nipple, biting it gently. "If I'd known you liked strapping on, then your Christmas gifts would have been something different."

"I think that would be a joint gift," I said hoarsely.

"Mmm, yes…" She licked a slow path down my stomach. Evie's tongue paused as my hips bucked, then continued toward its destination. "I want you to tell me *exactly* how you'd fuck me if you had your strap-on."

"I would ask you to get on your knees," I said instantly. "To begin."

"Would you ask me to hold it while I sucked your clit?"

"If that's something you want to do, then yes." I caught her quick nod. "Mm. And then, I think I'd ask you to ride me, roll you onto your back to fuck you missionary, have you from behind with you on your hands and knees." I inhaled shakily, the anticipation of those things having made my breath catch. "I would fuck you until you lost your voice from screaming, until you came again and again."

She swallowed hard. "Would you let me lick you again once I'd come from you fucking me?"

"I would insist upon it."

Evie pressed my knees apart and dropped to her stomach. She kissed up the inside of my thigh, pausing for long enough that I was about to beg, before she slicked her tongue through my arousal. She lightly sucked my clit then raised her head just enough to murmur, "Like…this?"

"Yes," I breathed. "Just like that."

She licked me again, her tongue nothing more than a soft touch against my labia, and I bucked my hips up, trying to press my clit into her mouth. But Evie managed to keep her tongue light enough to hold me right on the edge.

"I am dying here," I muttered. "Can't you see you're killing me?"

She lifted her head, an eyebrow arching. "You are? I am? That would be a shame. I really don't want that. But…What if I want to play a little more?" she asked, pouting.

My desperation must have showed, because instead of teasing me endlessly, Evie bent her head and put her mouth back on me. There was no more teasing. Her tongue and lips did delicious things and I gripped a gentle handful of her hair as Evie licked and sucked me toward climax. She made little throaty noises of enjoyment, which only heightened my arousal. The pressure built and built until my orgasm came hard and fast, and I vocalized my pleasure loudly in German and English as the hot waves of my climax rolled through me.

Evie wiped her mouth delicately on my thigh, then kissed her way slowly up my torso until she lay on top of me. "Fuck, you are so goddamned sexy when you come."

I pressed my thigh between hers, delighting in the wetness that coated my skin. "So are you…" I said, shifting us so we faced each other again. Though I was desperate to fuck her, to hear her climax from my touch, I wanted to love her first. "Lie down, on your front."

Evie rolled onto her stomach.

"Spread your legs." I was unsurprised by the sound of my voice—commanding, yet tight, almost needy.

I heard her moan. Saw her ass and thighs tighten. Then she did as I'd instructed, moving her legs further apart. Evie brought herself up onto her elbows, her back arching. The muscles of her back tensed as I drew my fingertips down her spine, over her ass, between her thighs. Wetness coated my fingers and I indulged myself by bringing my fingers to my mouth. A surge of want rushed through me. I wanted to taste all of her arousal. But I also wanted to fuck her like this, and knew from her compliance, her expression, that she wanted that too.

I crawled behind her and bent over her to kiss her shoulder, down her back, over her ass. I kissed my way back up her body, pausing to lick or bite here and there, until I lay on top of her, keeping most of my weight on my hands. Evie pressed back into me, twisting her upper body around, and the expression of lust on her face made me quiver inside.

"Can I touch my clit?" she asked roughly.

"No. Get on your hands and knees."

She moved so quickly I would have been amused in any other circumstances. But now? A surge of raw desire flooded me. "Are you desperate for me to touch you, Evie?"

"Yes," she said hoarsely. "*Please.*"

I reached around and dragged my fingers through her wetness, pausing against her clit. I pressed lightly, played the engorged flesh with my fingertips. "Like this?"

"Oh god," she choked out. Her hips rolled with my movement, her breathing rasping out as I stroked her. I kept my touch deliberately slow and light, wanting to bring her up softly before I fucked her hard. Evie begged, "Please, please, that feels so good."

I sat back on my heels, pulling her with me. Evie was slick with sweat, her back sliding against my front. My mouth was against her neck, my teeth grazing her skin. She was the perfect height for me to fuck her like this, and the thought of what I could do to her if I had my harness made me shiver. I wrapped my left arm under her armpit, my hand cupping her breast, playing with her nipple, as my other hand snaked around to rest on her hip. Evie gripped my forearm with both hands, her nails digging into my skin.

"What do you want me to do?" I asked tightly.

She turned her head and found my eyes. "Fuck me. I want your fingers inside me."

I sucked her shoulder as my hand moved downward. Evie spread her legs wider, pressing harder back into me. I held tight to her, but my grip was also for myself—I wanted to feel all of her against my skin. Her breathing quickened when I found her arousal again. "Is this what you want?" I murmured, biting her shoulder now.

Her abdominals clenched under my forearm. "Yes. Please. Oh fuck, please," she cried out.

In this position I could only make shallow thrusts, but the access to her clit, the sensation of so much skin on skin made it worth it. She reached up and back to hold the back of my head, gripping a fistful of my hair. I kept my thrusts steady as Evie writhed, her ass grinding into me, and the light pressure against my clit was enough to send me toward climax again. "Oh god," she groaned. "That feels so good. I'm not…I can't hold on…fuck, baby, *please.*" She grabbed my left hand and brought it to her lips. She sucked my forefinger and middle finger into her mouth, her tongue playing over both fingers.

Evie's breath caught, a hoarse moan escaping her. I could feel the tension, the imminent arrival of her climax in the way she bucked back against me, her breathing ragged. She bit the side of my hand as a flood of arousal slicked my fingers. Evie shuddered, her entire body tensing as she came. When she finally stilled, I pulled my hand from between her legs and wrapped it around her waist, keeping her body tightly against mine.

Evie kissed each of my fingers, then dropped my hand. I immediately wrapped that arm around her waist too, and she sagged in my embrace. "Oh my god," she whispered breathlessly. Her chest rose and fell with deep breaths.

I swept her hair aside to playfully nibble her neck. "I love this…" I said against her skin.

Evie turned her head and met me for a deep, slow kiss. One hand held my wrist, the other tangled in my hair. "Me too," she said, her voice still hoarse and breathless. "And I love you."

I kissed every piece of skin I could access—the tops of her shoulders, her neck, her ears, her jaw—stalling until I knew I wouldn't cry when I said, "I love you too."

CHAPTER TWENTY-FIVE

Evie

    The first thing Annika said when I woke up was, "Guten Morgen und Frohe Weihnachten, Evie." She snuggled into me and kissed my chin, my cheeks, then finally my lips.
    "Merry Christmas," I mumbled, my voice rough with sleep. "Didn't you say that yesterday?"
    "Ja, but it's the American Christmas today, so I have to say it again. Are you ready for the day?" she asked brightly. Clearly she'd been awake and thinking Christmassy things for a while.
    "No," I said honestly, and Annika laughed. I wrapped my arms around her, pulling her even closer. "But ask me again when I'm properly awake."
    "I will. And…I might help you to wake up," she said, her hand sliding back under the covers to find my skin.
    "You want me to wake up so you can to get started on Christmas Day, right?"
    "Maybe. Or maybe I want to give you a Christmas gift now." She tugged me until I settled on top of her. We'd forgone our new pajamas, opting instead to sleep naked after we'd finally gone to bed around eleven p.m. for sleep instead of sex, and the lack of clothing made our quickie even quicker. This honeymoon period was amazing.

After we'd checked if Santa had visited—unfortunately not, getting old sucked, though to be fair, we hadn't left stockings out—Annika ducked back to her place to shower. I took one myself then started coffee so it'd be ready for when she got back. She'd put on the pajamas we'd "received" last night, ready for my American tradition of "nice pajama Christmas pictures." God, Christmas traditions were weird. A pickle in a tree? New PJs? Who thought of this stuff?

I poured coffee and added a little hot water to the espresso before doctoring the mug with Annika's milk and sugar. "Danke," she murmured when I passed it to her. After a small sip, she set the mug down on the floating counter and came back to me. She stood behind me, hands on my hips, her front pressed lightly to my back, her chin on my shoulder. "What will we be making for breakfast?"

"Okay, so when I was a kid, Christmas morning breakfast for my family was pretty extravagant. Think like…a full buffet spread."

"That sounds wonderful."

"It was. But I always just ate the pancakes. So, my American Christmas breakfast for you is pancakes. Syrup, fruit, and bacon if you want it."

"Yes, I want it. Do you need help?"

"Nope, it's all good. Relax and enjoy the morning, then we can get into those gifts. Are we talking to your parents again?"

The FaceTime with the Mayers yesterday had been wonderful, and thankfully in English, and I'd been included like I was part of their family. Annika had been teased about her "Americanized" accent while speaking English, we'd shown off our respective Christmas setups—ours was deemed acceptable—and her mother had grilled me gently about myself until Annika had told her to quit it. They were all warm, kind, and funny, and I could see where Annika got some of her personality.

"They might call us." Annika opened her mouth and closed it just as quickly. She bit her lower lip, then sipped her coffee like she was trying not to speak.

I smirked. "Say it."

She just shook her head, and kept her mug near her lips like a barrier to her saying what I knew was on her mind.

So I decided to just answer the unasked question. "I don't know if I'll talk with my parents today. I thought I'd call Pete, and if my parents are around and they want to talk, then we'll talk."

"Do you want me to leave?"

"No, of course not. But…I might just make the call myself? Introducing you might be a bit much for the first icebreaker." I smiled to soften the rejection. "But I told my dad about you, and I'm sure he would like to meet you. Once he's had time to…get used to the idea being right in his face."

"I would very much like to meet him too. And your mother."

"You say that now," I teased, though there was a large element of truth in the teasing. Honestly, I had no idea how my parents would react to meeting my partner, because obviously I'd never introduced anyone to them before.

"Ja, I do," she said seriously. "And I mean it. But there is no pressure. I hope you know that I'm here. I'm with you."

"I do. Thank you." I exhaled shakily, trying not to dwell on the nuance of that promise. "Okay. Pancakes."

"Ja," she agreed, smiling. "Pancakes."

Annika cut up fruit while I made a stack of thick, fluffy pancakes and kept an eye on the frying bacon. Miraculously, I didn't ruin a single pancake, which was a Christmas miracle in itself considering I hardly ever made them.

I set the warm plate stacked with pancakes on the table. "These are *not* a family recipe. I got it from the Internet, and let me say—these are made with love because I had to wade through a thousand-word essay about the recipe person's great-grandmother who was a milkmaid in Europe and how she wowed her prospective husband with these pancakes, and only ever used milk from three-year-old cows to make the butter and then she brought the recipe to America and passed it down to her children and their children et cetera, and they make their butter too but they don't have cows so use store-bought milk and… you get the gist, to get to the actual recipe. And, I have to say, those stupid recipe essays are one of my pet hates."

"Ah," Annika said as she sat down to my left. She frowned, her eyebrows creasing together. "Was it really an essay about a milkmaid and her three-year-old cows?"

I laughed. "No. But that's what those things are *always* like. Pointless."

She smiled. "Well, if the pancakes are good, then we can start calling them a family recipe."

I wondered if she knew what she was implying with these things. Talking to my parents, a family recipe of pancakes for us. She was implying that we would be together not only for next Christmas but for Christmases after.

Milkmaid-esque essay aside, the pancakes were really good. Once we'd finished breakfast and cleaned up together, I consulted my mental list of Christmas Day activities. "We need a Christmas-morning-in-pajamas photo. Of both of us."

"Who is going to see this photograph?" Annika gestured at herself, at the amount of bare skin on display in her satin pajamas.

"Just us."

"Okay then."

She arranged herself on the floor in front of the tree while I set up my phone with a mini tripod on the coffee table. After making sure the framing was right, I set it to a delayed burst. "Okay…get…ready. It's…time." I tapped the screen then leaped away from the setup.

Annika giggled as I ran back, hopping around the coffee table before diving onto the floor. She wrapped her arms around me, pulling me into her. "Say Käse," she whispered at me, which made me laugh.

She really was a certified Christmas Elf. If she was this excited about Christmas as an adult, I could just imagine what she'd been like as a kid, and there was something about her excitement that had mine building as well. Me, excited and enjoying Christmas. If you'd told me last year that this would be my attitude today, I would have laughed.

Annika ripped open the Rudolph-printed paper to expose the framed A3-sized drawing of the thirty-eight-meter-high gilded Angel of Peace and the surrounding Maximilian Park. I was suddenly so nervous about my gift that I started babbling. "I know it's lame giving you a drawing when I draw for living. But, I thought you might like a little picture of part of your city. I remembered my time there and what a beautiful city it is, so…" I cleared my throat nervously. Now I wondered if giving her this picture would just make her want to return to Munich. "I wanted to do a series of drawings, but I just didn't have enough time. But if you want more, I can do them."

"I do want more. This is a beautiful drawing of the Friedensengel. And *you* are beautiful." She said all of that without looking away from the vista of Munich but as soon as she uttered that last word, Annika looked up. "Maybe you could draw me a picture of you sitting outside of a beer hall?"

Laughing I agreed, "I'm into that. And I might draw you inside the beer hall, drinking beer while I sit outside."

She grinned. "Good." The grin faded, replaced by a serious expression that would have made me worried if not for her accompanying words. "Evie, I am so in love with you that you are the last thing I think of at night and one of the first thoughts that comes to me in the morning. I am so in love with you that being with you is the only time I have felt like myself in years. And I am so in love with you that it scares me."

I brushed her tight knuckles with my forefinger. "Scares you how?"

It looked like it hurt her to verbalize it again. "Because I don't know if I'm staying here. If I even *can* stay here. And these feelings are so intense and are only getting more intense."

"I know. And I know. Me too."

Her nose wrinkled. "I'm sorry to be making Christmas heavy."

I kissed her, then pulled her into a hug, kissing her neck, her ear, her temple. "I don't feel heavy at all. I feel weightless, like you've given me wings or something." I inhaled deeply as I pulled back. "Is Christmas always so emotional? I just remember arguments and stress, not like…extreme joy and stuff."

She smiled, quickly swiping underneath her eyes. "Christmas is whatever we want it to be. Maybe we're emotional because this time is special? Our first Weihnachten together."

"Maybe," I mused, trying not to wonder if it would be the only one. Forcing a smile, I changed the subject. "Let's get into the rest of these gifts."

"Oh," she laughed. "You mean, you want to open *your* gift."

"Mhmmm. Exactly."

"Now who is the Christmas Elf?" she teased.

Annika passed me an envelope made from wrapping paper. When I opened it, five small brown-paper packets fell out.

I turned one over and read the handwritten text. "Are these…?"

"Ja. Seeds," she said brightly. "For your roof garden. I'm going to help you plant them and show you how to not kill them."

This first packet was mixed wildflower seeds. "Because they are beautiful and will bring you bees for the other seeds," Annika explained.

"That's amazing." I checked the writing on the other packets—basil, cucumbers, tomatoes, and kale. She'd bought me something that would last, long after she'd gone, and the thought made me unexpectedly teary. I blinked a few times. "That would be really nice. Thank you."

"There is your other gift too," Annika said gently, thankfully ignoring my emotional response to seeds. But like the pancakes, it wasn't just about the thing—it was about everything surrounding it.

"Right, yes. Thanks." I carefully stashed the seed packets, then opened her next present. I could feel her restraint, the desperation for me to just tear it open. Inside was a royal-blue beanie knitted in a cool intricate pattern. I turned the hat over, trying to find the tag so I could go look at the store's other stuff. There wasn't one. "Where did you get this? I love it."

"From my fingers."

"You knitted it?" I asked, surprised by the answer. It was beautifully made, totally professional.

"Ja, I did. For your skiing, well, for après because helmets are for skiing. And I already have wool to make a scarf to match, but that's for your birthday and I'm sorry to spoil the surprise."

"Don't be sorry. These are so great. Thank you." I popped up onto my knees and crawled over to her for a kiss. "And I'm going to be so corny. You've given me more than just these presents. You've given me your love. Your trust. Your acceptance of who I am. Those things are so precious."

Annika cupped my cheek, her thumb lightly brushing my lower lip. "Thank you for accepting my things," she murmured, before she leaned in and kissed me again.

I hadn't planned a lunch exactly, and had thought we could just graze on snacks, yesterday's leftovers, and alcohol. But I *had* planned caviar for Annika. What better time than Christmas for her to try an expensive one for her first caviar experience? The big issue was that if she liked it, I'd be spoiling her for some of the less expensive stuff. I'd swallowed my pride and called my father to ask for help—to either ask his supplier to release some of Dad's stockpile for me, because I knew that shit was only ever available in limited quantities and most of it was preordered before it was imported, or I could buy a tin from him and pick it up from their house in Nantucket where at least one member of my parents' staff always remained over Christmas.

Failing all that, I'd been prepared to name-drop with a supplier or beg Pete to get his restaurant-owning friend to sell me a tin. But Dad had agreed readily and told me he'd call his supplier to deliver one of his two-ounce tins of Volga Reserve Royal Ossetra caviar—nice and mild to start someone on their journey, he promised. Who knew caviar could be the start of mending my relationship with my father? Technically, I supposed, the mending had begun with his heart attack.

I'd also procured some fresh blinis, organic butter (maybe from three-year-old cows), and crème fraîche to pair with the caviar. A bottle of Grey Goose would be the perfect accompaniment. The vodka had been chilling in the freezer, and shot glasses and a caviar serving bowl in the fridge since this morning.

I spooned enough caviar for a couple of reasonable portions into the chilled bowl and put the remainder into the fridge. Annika watched me approach with the tray, and apparently noted the amount of caviar I'd set out. "Are you having any?"

I sighed expansively. "Only a tiny amount to make sure it's fine to serve you. Because I am nothing if not a good caviar hostess. Beyond that, it's all yours. But I *will* drink the vodka and eat some of the blinis."

After a sniff that made my sinuses contract in horror, I determined the caviar smelled "good," as in not spoiled, not…good. I scooped out the tiniest portion I could and spread it on the back of my hand near my thumb joint. Bottoms up. I forced down my disgust and gently rolled it around in my mouth before gently squishing the roe against the roof of my mouth. The things you do for love. The caviar was fine. For caviar. Not for me. A hearty glug of icy vodka helped a little.

I ate a buttered blini to clear the residual taste. "Okay, first things first. Try not to chew it. Take your time and just let it melt, using your tongue to roll it around in your mouth, breaking it against the roof of your mouth. Unless you think it's disgusting, then chew it because that helps keep it away from your tongue so you taste it less."

"Okay."

"Second. No metal shall *ever* contact caviar. I'm no snob, but it really does fuck up the flavor." I sighed inwardly at my expletive slip and decided to give myself a break at Christmas.

"Okay."

"Third. Don't let Champagne snobs lie to you. Vodka is the best alcoholic beverage to accompany caviar and it *must* be ice-cold." I bit my lip, but my mouth rebelled and formed a huge grin. "Little Wodkas."

Rolling eyes accompanied this, "Okay."

"Are you ready?"

"Do I have to…make it like salt for a tequila shot like you did on your hand?"

Laughing, I assured her, "No. You can use the spoon. I just didn't want to stick that in my mouth and then put it back in the caviar."

"That is polite of you." She picked up the small caviar spoon. "What is this made of?"

"Mother of pearl."

Her eyebrows shot up, but quickly settled again. Annika shuffled forward on the couch. "Will you help me?"

"Of course." I scooped out a small portion and held it up for her. Annika leaned forward, held my hand steady, and ate the caviar.

Though caviar was the unsexist food I could think of, feeding her *was* sexy.

"It's good. I am not really getting any 'all of the dead creatures in the ocean' flavor at all." She scooped up a little more and ate it, rolling the roe around her mouth. "It tastes a little bit like…a nut?"

"Hazelnuts, yeah."

"Does all caviar taste like that?"

Smiling, I said, "No, it's like wine. They all have different tasting notes. I suppose it depends on where the fish live, their diet, the species. Now, try it with blini." I smeared butter thickly onto one of the small pancakes and set it on the plate ready for her to top with caviar. Then I poured us both ice-cold shots of vodka and drank mine, and then a second while she ate.

"Better," Annika declared once she'd finished. She sipped the vodka while I spread crème fraîche onto another blini, then nodded slowly as she ate it. "That one is my favorite."

"I'm glad you have a favorite. I'm glad you like it." I kissed her. "Sorry, you really do taste like you ate the ocean."

Annika grinned. "And you taste like you own a vodka factory."

"Maybe I do."

She pulled back, her eyes widening. "Do you?"

Laughing, I said, "I do not. A few wineries and a little craft whiskey distillery, none of which I have anything to do with because I know fuck-all about making alcohol." Christmas swearing freedom was in full swing and I was going to go all out with it. I ate another buttered blini.

"Are we adding caviar to future Merry Weihnachten menus? And also, we need to add fondue. Bringing my fondue set for just me seemed ridiculous, but I actually miss it."

I ignored the "future" and went for light and breezy. "Sure, if you want caviar, you can have as much as you want. And if it's fondue you want, fondue we shall do."

"You're very proud of yourself for that rhyme, aren't you."

"Intensely." I leaned over to kiss her again. "I know we don't have fondue, but we do have your goose."

As soon as Annika had mentioned goose was the traditional Christmas bird in Germany, I'd rung around to make sure we had one ordered for Christmas Day—organic free-range of course—and it had been taking up space in my refrigerator since its delivery Monday. I had no real attachment to anything as the main meal for the day, and was happy to let her add some Germany to America, because her joy gave me immeasurable joy. I'd eaten goose as a kid and could recall very little about it, but I trusted she knew what she was doing.

Annika had assured me, "I have the goose-cooking under control, but you need to prepare yourself, because my stuff inside made someone ask me to marry them."

"Stuff inside?" I'd almost bent double laughing. "You mean the *stuffing?*"

She'd thrown a dish towel at me. And then she'd kissed me in a way that almost made me propose right there, stuffing be damned.

My job was making sides, as "American" as possible, Annika had said. Mashed potatoes and gravy, roasted carrots and brussels sprouts, asparagus, and cranberry sauce (goose and turkey were close enough, right?). "Is that enough?" I'd asked when we'd gone over the list. "Too much? I feel like the timing of getting everything right is going to be hard."

"This is what Christmas cooking is about," she'd assured me. "Being"—twinkling fingers accompanied her—"a little bit frazzled."

"When were you going to call Pete?" Annika asked as I started putting away the caviar feast, with the exception of the vodka. The vodka had to stay.

I checked the time. "Whenever. Probably before dinner." I tried to remember my parents' Christmas Day routine, which I assumed was as rigid as I remembered from the last time I was in their house for the holidays. "Maybe I'll just do it now." I was surprised to find no negative emotions attached to my declaration. Maybe I was still in denial about actually speaking with my parents today. Who knew, my mother might decline my invitation.

"Okay. I'll…" She looked around.

"Stay right here," I said. "I'll go upstairs."

Annika nodded and poured herself a half shot of vodka.

I kissed her then left her to relax while I went upstairs. I decided to go out onto the terrace. Most people would be inside celebrating, so there shouldn't be too much background noise. I collected a blanket from the cupboard and unlocked the door to my wrought-iron-fenced terrace. It was brick out there, but the cold actually felt nice, bracing. The chairs were damp from the pitiful snow and not so pitiful rain, so I remained standing with the blanket wrapped around my shoulders and FaceTimed Pete.

"Eeeyello?"

"Hey, Petey. Merry Christmas."

"And Merry Christmas to you too!" he said jovially. Been getting into the good Christmas booze, there, Pete? "How's your Merry Whyyy-nack-ten going?"

"Fabulously. Hey, listen, shock and horror but…can you tell my parents I'm on the phone? And that I'd like to say hi?"

His mouth fell open. "Uh, sure. Let me just give you to Chloe while I go check with them."

My niece's face came into view. "Hey, Aunt Evie. Is everything okay?"

"Of course it is. Why?"

"You've never called us on Christmas before," she said matter-of-factly.

"I just wanted to wish you Merry Christmas. Did Santa visit?"

She nodded enthusiastically, but before she could give me a rundown on her gift haul, Pete came back. He looked both pleased and surprised. "They're into it."

"Great," I exhaled. "And, Pete? Can I talk to you after?"

"Sure," he agreed as he strode through the house.

Then, I was FaceTiming my parents. No time to dally, get right into it. I smiled, and it was only thirty percent forced. "Hello, Mom. Hi, Dad. Merry Christmas. Dad, you're looking good." He had good color and seemed comfortable.

"Feeling good," he said cheerfully.

"Thank you for calling, Evangeline," my mother said. Was that… emotion? "Merry Christmas to you too." She smiled, a genuine, interested smile. "Are you having a nice day?"

"I am, yes. Dad, thanks for that caviar. It was well-received." I didn't want to push by mentioning Annika by name just now.

He beamed. "I'm glad. Plenty more of it, if you need it."

"Thanks. I appreciate that."

"Where…*are* you, Evangeline?" Mom asked.

I glanced around. "Oh, just out on the rooftop."

"I see. Well, make sure you stay warm."

"I will." I had to hold back the surge of emotion at her concern, and cleared my throat so I could wind things up. "Okay, well, I'll let you all get back to your day. It was…nice talking to you." That sounded more like someone in an awkward social situation, but I supposed this kind of was an awkward social situation.

"You too, Evangeline," Mom said. She gave me a finger-wave and then I was passed back to Pete. I think. I heard Pete saying something to my parents and Chloe, excusing himself.

There. That was short and sweet. No vitriol. I'd call that a win.

The phone swung back and forth as Pete made his way through the house and out to the sunroom. It was a big house. It took a while. There was a contented huff as he settled himself, then brought the camera back up so I was looking at his face instead of receiving an inebriated tour of my parents' Greenwich home. "Okay," he said, raising his crystal tumbler to his mouth. "What's up."

"I really need you to talk some sense into me. You were right, I couldn't do it. I couldn't sit there and just let this thing with Annika go by. Petey, I'm in love. Like…really in love with her, and she's basically said 'ditto.' This whole Christmas thing has been incredible. We fought and made up, and it's amazing. The thought of her leaving makes me feel like I can't breathe. And I don't know what to do."

He laughed. "So first it was that you weren't sure she was into you. And now you're totally sure she is, and you're being tentative…why?"

"You know why! Because she's planning on going back to Germany at the end of next year. But then she keeps dropping all these hints like she wants to stay, but doesn't know what that looks like or if she can because of her job and visas and also just like, if she can emotionally because she'd be leaving her family. So it's like this…this tease."

"There's this thing, you might have heard of it, called a plane? It's a magic teleport machine. And I've heard it even travels between here and Germany."

"Smart-ass. Yes, *obviously* I could visit. And she could visit. But what about all that empty space in between those visits?" Empty, hollow space without her.

He rubbed his mustache. "Yeah that's fair."

"It's so new. And I don't know what's going to happen in the next year and I'm just not—"

"Shhhh. You're jumping ahead of yourself."

"Well someone has to consider the possibilities." I had, repeatedly for the past few weeks, and they were as terrifying as they were wonderful. "I haven't been in a serious relationship for over twelve years. I've got no idea what I'm doing. And adding something like long-distance into the mix? It feels like a recipe for disaster."

"Relationships aren't like fashion trends, Evie. They don't change what they look like every decade. You know what to do. And you're not stuck in Boston, you know."

"Okay, but I can't move to Germany and leave Chloe and you behind. I just can't. You're my family."

He rolled his eyes. "Has Annika mentioned anything about you moving to Germany?"

"Well, no, but—"

"But nothing. You're making up anxieties that haven't even happened. Why don't you just start at the beginning and tell her how you feel and what you want. For the love of all that's holy, just tell her. And then see where it goes from there. Be honest, and then you've done everything you can and the rest is out of your hands."

I sighed. "I hate that. I'm not good at just letting things happen." Maybe it was a lifetime of knowing that I had the means to make basically anything I wanted to happen, happen. But this wasn't something I could throw money at.

"I know. But sometimes you just gotta do that. Love you, my little peanut. I'm proud of you for calling."

"Love you too. Enjoy dinner."

Pete was right. Life was scary. But throwing away possibilities because of fear seemed really stupid. I was luckier than most, in that I had the means to make a relationship with Annika work even if we didn't live in the same country. Sure, it'd require some effort from both of us, but didn't all relationships need that? So, I was going to put all my cards on the table, and let the chips fall where they may. Nice mixed metaphor there, Evie.

Annika looked up when I came back into the living room. "Are you okay? Was your phone call okay?"

"Surprisingly, yes, I am okay. And the call was totally fine. I spoke to my parents for a minute."

Annika held my face in gentle hands. "You're cold." She kissed my forehead, each of my cheeks, then gently pulled my face up to kiss my lips. "I'm happy for you. And I am proud for you, that you did something very difficult."

"Me too," I murmured. "And…I have one more difficult thing, Annika."

The little crease between her eyebrows deepened. "What is that? Do you have more parents?" she asked dryly.

I laughed, grateful for the levity. "Fortunately not. It's…it's about us." That made the crease between her eyebrows approach Grand Canyon depths. "I'm going to be an adult and tell you how I feel."

"And how do you feel?" she asked quietly.

"I love you. I don't want us to break up. If we're even officially dating. I want you to stay in Boston past the end of next year, past when your project is done. But, if you can't, then I want you to know that we can figure something out. I just…I need you to know that I want us to work, however this *us* looks."

"Wait. Are we dating?" The tip of her tongue peeked through her lips.

"I think so, yes."

Annika smiled, her eyes creasing at the edges. "I think so too."

I exhaled loudly. "Glad we're on the same page. So yeah, obviously I want you to stay here, if you can, which I know is selfish. But if you can't then I want to figure out how to make it work. I'll come to Germany on the weekends and spend a very jetlagged day with you. I'll spend the whole summer, when Chloe is at camp and doesn't need me in the afternoons, with you. And…I mean, soon she won't need me at all." That day had been approaching and I'd viewed it with dread. I still dreaded it, but the thought of finding some other way to fill my time eased the upset. "I can move to be with you."

Her eyebrows shot up. "You'd move to Germany for me?"

"Well, yes. Not *right now*, but yes I would. If you asked me to later."

"That is interesting," she mused. "Because I…I think I would move to Boston, permanently, for you."

Hang on. "You…what?"

"I think I would move to Boston," Annika repeated. She pulled her lower lip between her teeth. "This is not a new thought for me, Evie. It has been in my head since you first kissed me, but I've been too scared to admit it. But, if you can be brave then I can be too. I thought I could ask if there is a job for me to stay in Boston when my project is finished. I know they need more project managers here. There will be a lot of things to figure out like visas and all that, but…" She shrugged, that simple gesture conveying that she thought we could figure it out.

"Do you *want* to stay? I know what that means. Your family is in Germany."

"I want *us*. And we can figure out the rest of the problems, like can I even stay in the Boston office and everything else, to make that work out. And if it doesn't work out, if I need to change jobs then I have skills. I can adapt. There are other types of visas that I can be on. It's not like it's that far or hard to go home to see my family."

"Even easier and more comfortable with a private jet," I pointed out.

"Do you have—" She shook her head and then, laughing, answered herself, "Of course you do."

"Actually, I don't have my own private jet," I corrected her. "I don't go anywhere to need one. But if we're going to be flying to and from Germany a lot, maybe I need to look into that. And if we do it, I may have to buy a zillion acres and plant trees to appease my carbon conscience."

Her expression softened. "I love you. Private jet or not. You know the things you have or could have is nice, but it's not what made me fall in love with you. *You* are what made me fall in love with you."

I moved to her so quickly she gasped in surprise when I kissed her, but in the next heartbeat, one hand was against my face, the other tangling in my hair. The kiss began slowly, a gentle reminder of what we were building, but when Annika's tongue swiped along my lower lip, I groaned. "What time does the goose have to go in the oven?"

"Two and a half hours before we want to eat it."

"We have a little time," I whispered.

"Ja. We do." She fingered the drawstring of my pajama bottoms. "These pajamas are so cute, I almost don't want to take them off."

"They aren't so cute that they need to stay on," I murmured. "And I can always put them back on again afterward."

"That is true," Annika mused, pulling at the drawstring until the knot came away. "But you wearing clothes is such a shame…"

CHAPTER TWENTY-SIX

Annika

Our Merry Weihnachten had been far better than I had hoped for. I'd told myself that if I could capture even just a little bit of my usual Christmas joy then I would be happy. I had, and I'd also captured something new and exciting. Something that made me crave more.

There had been mountains of leftover food but I decided we needed to make the mountain taller. Together, we made potato dumplings and braised red cabbage, bumping shoulders in Evie's kitchen and stealing kisses around molding the Kartoffelklösse.

I had to work as usual after Christmas Day, but every night from Boxing Day to New Year's Eve, we ate mixed German and American food for dinner, opened Champagne, made cocktails, watched television, played games, or very rarely because it was so cold—took evening walks around the Common under a light dusting of snow.

Each night we brushed our teeth and attended to our respective pre-bed routines at the side-by-side sinks in Evie's bathroom before going to bed. Sometimes we had sex, sometimes we just slept. The easy domestic normality felt so right that I knew leaving her really wasn't an option. It felt silly to be planning a move here permanently after only a month, with another eleven months or so stretching out before us. But I needed certainty about us. I couldn't have the shadow of my leaving following us about for the remainder of our time. So I would make sure there was no "remainder." The time we spent together from now on would be *our* time, for as long as we could make a relationship work.

We'd gone over options for New Year's Eve—party, stay home, part party and part home. We'd agreed we were too old for nightclubs or bar crawls, and while I'd had invites to a few parties from coworkers, Evie thought she could get us tickets to a party at SoWa Power Station, wherever that was, and I'd agreed right away. She'd told me it wasn't anything super fancy, just a regular NYE party, but that her foundation had held functions there before, and it was a nice space and shouldn't be full of twenty-one-year-olds puking all over themselves.

"Sounds like a good idea to me," I'd agreed. And then promptly began panicking. I panicked for most of the night before New Year's Eve until I realized I could just ask her. "What is the dress?" I asked her.

"Dress code?"

I nodded.

"Not black tie, not super casual. Like…formal-ish? But they're not going to refuse you entry if you don't meet a dress code."

"They won't refuse me if I'm with you, you mean…" I said. Evie grinned, shrugging instead of answering. "What are you wearing?" I asked.

"Not sure," she said distractedly. "Clothes."

"That is a coincidence because I also thought about wearing clothes." I hadn't really thought about having to attend any sort of fancy event while I was here, and hoped I had something suitable.

She laughed, and looked up. "Sorry. I was just organizing us a ride for tomorrow. Um, probably a dress, semiformal."

I exhaled. "Okay, thank you. I can work with that."

"If you're worried, I can call some people and they'll be here with a million options in your size before you can say *Pretty Woman*."

It took me a few moments to understand what she meant by "pretty woman," but I finally got it. "You know people who would come here with clothes for me?"

"I dress up at least once a month for events full of people who will gossip if you dare even wear the same piece of jewelry. I know *many* people."

"Okay. Let me go home and see what I have and then I will tell you if I need emergency help." I had an idea of what I could wear, but I needed to try it on and check shoes and accessories before I committed.

"Good plan. I suppose I should find something too." Evie grinned. "I hadn't planned on going out *at all*."

Back in my apartment, I pulled out a black dress and a red dress and decided the red silk midi dress looked really good. It only had thin straps, and I'd be freezing for a few minutes between the carpark and the venue, but it would be worth it. I decided to pair the dress with stilettos and masses of silver jewelry. I did not need any *Pretty Woman* help.

Pyramid had closed the Boston office a little bit early on New Year's Eve to give the employees time to get home and prepare for their celebrations. After stopping by Evie's for a quick hello and a not-quick kiss, I went back to my apartment to get ready. I left my hair down and styled it, made myself up for an evening out instead of a day at work, and was just grabbing my clutch when Evie let herself into my apartment with the key I'd given her a couple of days before.

My breath caught. "Oh my god," I murmured.

She wore a gown that made me desperate to take it off her. A long-sleeved, long black dress that looked like a slightly casual version of an evening gown fitted her body in ways that felt sinful. Drop earrings, a tasteful small diamond on her right ring finger, and heels that would have made her taller than me if I hadn't put on four inches of height with my stilettos.

"Jesus," Evie breathed, apparently having the same feeling I was. "You look incredible." She whistled. "I cannot wait to take you to a black-tie event."

"I cannot wait to go with you to a black-tie event." I traced my fingertips up her arm. "We look so nice." Wrinkling my nose, I asked, "It would be a shame to miss the party, wouldn't it?"

"It would…" she agreed, but it looked like it pained her to agree.

"So, we should go before we don't."

She'd declared that getting a rideshare on New Year's would be a nightmare, and had called a private car company she said her parents used when they were in Boston. The car was a limousine. I had never been in a limousine before. Inside was nice, spacious, full of leather and polished wood but otherwise unremarkable. Until Evie pressed a button and a compartment opened to reveal a bottle of Dom Pérignon.

Evie opened the Champagne and poured us each a glass. "We only have about ten minutes, so…drink up. Or," she added, "we can just drive around town and drink this instead of going to the party."

It seemed ridiculous to gulp down such expensive Champagne, but she did, so I did. "Will anyone you know be there?" I asked.

"Unlikely. My friend circle consists of one person. Pete. And anyone I know superficially will be in New York, Vegas, Miami, Paris, or somewhere like that. Or they're doing the Sydney-LA Double."

Frowning, I asked, "What is the…Sydney-LA Double?"

"Ring in the New Year in Sydney, Australia. Then on your private jet to Los Angeles to ring it in again, partying the whole flight across the Pacific of course."

"That sounds very tiring."

"It is," she assured me. "I've done it a few times, back when I could handle thirty straight hours of partying, and I nearly died from a hangover every time."

I raised my glass. "Champagne and lots of little Wodkas?"

She laughed. "Exactly."

The car pulled up outside the SoWa. The driver, a middle-aged man, held the door open and offered his hand, which Evie declined politely. After she helped me out of the limousine, she thanked the driver, confirmed she'd call when we were ready to be picked up, then, still holding my hand, led me toward the building. I paused a moment to take it in. A huge red-brick structure lit up like a Christmas tree. It looked like a renovated factory, with three pointed roofs edged with intricate brickwork detail converging on each other, so many windows—rectangular, big and small arch—that showed the brightly lit interior and exposed metal beams inside. It was gorgeous.

Evie squeezed my hand. "Ready to party like it's 1999?"

Laughing, I brought her hand up to kiss it. "Ja, I am."

We ate, danced and drank, spoke with strangers who were vibing the party as much as we were, and generally just had a very, very good time. The music was a good mix of old and new, some dance beats and some slightly slower but still upbeat songs. Watching Evie in public, surrounded by and interacting with all of these strangers was…a revelation.

The change in her was immediate, from the moment she'd walked into the crowd, like she'd put on another outfit. She was confident without being rude, almost commanding other people's attention. She paid attention when people spoke with her, remembered everyone's name, was polite with waitstaff. I'd always thought I was great in social situations, but she took it to another level.

And the whole evening, Evie made me feel so…*loved*. She made sure to include me in conversations, but it never felt forced, like she was struggling to work out how I would fit in. She was never far from my side and if we separated, I'd look around to find her and see she was already watching me, usually with an expression that was part desire and part pride. And none of it was overbearing or uncomfortably possessive. It felt like she wanted people to know I was there with her, but she wasn't monopolizing me or dictating how I enjoyed the evening.

As midnight approached, Evie made sure we each had a full glass of Champagne, and guided me to a spot near the edge of the crowd but not on the outskirts. The party was approaching the familiar hum of excitement, and we stood close. Evie carefully tucked some hair behind my ear. "I'm assuming Germany has the same superstition for kissing on New Year's?" Smiling, she raised the flute to her lips.

I decided to play dumb. "What superstition is that?"

"That whoever you kiss at midnight is the person you'll be kissing for the rest of the year."

"Oh, ja, of course. And then there is my own personal favorite superstition." I leaned down to speak near her ear. "Whoever you're fucking until dawn of New Year's Day is the person you'll be fucking for the rest of the year." I grinned, and sipped my Champagne.

Evie's tongue swiped out to wet her lower lip. "I see," she said hoarsely. "Then I guess we need to go home soon so we can make sure to fulfill that particular tradition."

"Yes, I think we should…"

The room quieted, then the countdown began. But all my attention was on Evie. Her eyes were bright, the blue darker in the warm lighting, and they watched me with a quiet intensity I'd never seen directed at me by anyone before.

"Happy New Year," she murmured, pulling me down for a kiss. Just before our lips touched, she smiled. "I cannot wait to spend this year with you."

"Me neither," I whispered, and closed the space between us to kiss her. The kiss was unhurried, gently passionate. Evie wrapped her free arm around my neck, forcing us closer together. My nerves ignited. "Let's go home."

* * *

I'd decided as soon as I returned to work on the second of January, I would speak to Nate regarding a permanent transfer to Boston. Evie seemed as happy, excited, and on board as she had been when I'd first mentioned staying in Boston as a possibility, but still, she had asked me a few more times if I was certain this was what I wanted. I knew she wasn't trying to make me reconsider; she wanted to be sure that moving, uprooting my life and being away from my family was what I really wanted, what would make me happy. One thing she'd said over and over again was that it was important to her that I knew she supported any decision, and that we could make it work no matter what.

But I didn't want the hard "no matter what." I didn't want long-distance. I wanted what we had, right here and right now, with the endless possibility of building our relationship stretching out before us. Being with her was my decision. I'd known it was the right choice for me but being out with her on New Year's Eve, and then New Year's Day which we'd spent cocooned in her apartment, watching movies, playing games, making meals, and making love, had cemented it. Evie made me a priority the way nobody I'd dated had ever done before.

I had made a mental "yes and no to staying in Boston" list and weighted each item according to importance. The only real reason I had to go back to Germany was my family, and as Rachel had reminded me, the travel time was comparable regardless of whether I was in München or Boston. There was no contest, my brain and my heart were telling me I needed to stay. And, if things didn't work out with my relationship or my job, I wasn't stuck in Boston or at Pyramid, though I didn't really want to quit this job. But I had moved from city to city in Germany, and from Germany to America, and I could move again.

Early Thursday morning I slipped out of bed, kissing a sleeping, mumbling Evie goodbye, then went back to my apartment to get ready for the day. But before I went to work, I needed to call my parents and tell them what I was considering. I'd never been nervous about telling my parents anything, but for some reason, this made me nervous.

They always took vacation time at the start of each year, so I knew they'd be home. But Mama took a little while to answer my call, and when the video connected I could see she was in the kitchen. She waved. "Hallo, my darling. Happy New Year."

"Happy New Year." I squinted. "Are you cooking?"

"Yes, baking, but of course I have some time for you."

"I won't take too long." I wet my dry lips. Why was I so nervous? My parents had never been anything but supportive. "As a hypothetical question, what would you say about me staying here for a little bit longer? Or…permanently." Aside from a slight lift of her right eyebrow, there was no change in Mama's expression. "I'll visit of course," I added quickly. "As much as I can. And…so would Evie. And of course, you're always welcome here."

"Evie is just a neighbor, is she?" Mama said dryly, her mouth twitching in amusement.

"Well, yes she is."

"And the rest of it," she laughed. "I knew from the moment you first mentioned her that there was something special about her."

"How did you know?"

"Oh, Anni, the way your face lights up when you speak about her, when I ask about her. It's like sunshine on gray winter days. I love that she makes you so happy," Mama enthused. "You must be in love."

"I am, yes." It wasn't the first time I'd admitted it, but it always felt so good to say it.

"Good. So, I say do what makes you happy and if that is staying in Boston, then that is what you need to do. International travel is so easy now. A plane trip isn't exactly a difficult undertaking."

"No, I know that. It's just…I—" I huffed out a loud breath. "I think I'm a little bit scared."

"Scared of what?"

"That I'm moving too quickly. That I might be making a mistake. That I might ruin this relationship."

Mama's expression softened into one I knew well—maternal kindness mixed with worry. "Oh, my darling. If it didn't mean anything to you, then you would not be so scared of making a mistake."

"I think it might mean everything to me," I said quietly.

"Then you know what you should do."

After half an hour catching up with everyone's New Year's Eve party stories and New Year's Day hangover woes, my team split off for a meeting to go over the plan for the next week, then separated into their respective workstations. And I went to find Nate.

He was in the break room making himself coffee and greeted me with a warm smile. "Annika. How did America live up to your New Year's expectations?" He'd asked the same question after Christmas.

"It lived up very well. Do you have a little bit of time for me to talk?"

"Of course." He made an expansive waving motion. "Come into my office."

Once we'd both sat down, I decided to not dance around the topic, and jumped right into the reason for my discussion. "Nate. Even though I've only been in Boston for a little bit over a month, I have enjoyed my time in this office very much. So much that the thought of going back to München is not appealing to me at all. So I have decided not to. And I would love to stay with Pyramid, so…is there a project manager position here for me to move into at the end of the year? Fulltime?"

I'd expected him to take some time to think about my request, but Nate took no time at all. His smile was so broad that his cheeks stretched, and he looked like he wanted to dance a little excited jig in his seat. "You know, I was just thinking before Christmas how great it'd be if you stayed. I've never seen a team working so cohesively or so enthusiastically. I would say there's *definitely* a managerial position for you here."

I exhaled a long, relieved breath. "Thank you. That would be wonderful."

"Let me talk to the bosses and set up a call with Munich and we'll go from there. But honestly, I see no impediments from our end." He grinned. "A little bureaucratic nonsense with the visa, but no impediments."

Smiling, I said, "I like the sound of no impediments…And I know the visa is a little bit of a barrier, once this one expires in three years, but if there is a way Pyramid would work with me to jump that barrier and help me move onto another visa, I would be grateful."

He waved dismissively. "With all the temporary relocations to fulfill project specs, we're old hats at it. You know you're not the first person to want to change locations permanently. I know Paris and Munich have had an exchange or two, and remember Mark went over to the Munich office from this office a few years ago and stayed there because he met his now-wife?" Nate laughed. "I'd consider you staying a more than fair trade. I don't recall the last time we had a project moving forward so quickly. You'd be an asset wherever you wanted to work, but I hope it's here."

Cocooned in the knowledge that my job was secure, and there was an easy enough way forward for me with my career at Pyramid, I floated along on a blissful cloud for the rest of the day. Even the ride home on the T didn't dampen my mood.

After I'd showered—no need to pack any overnight things because I already had most of my evening necessities at Evie's place—I let myself into her apartment. But she was nowhere to be found. "Evie?" I called. I heard the distinctive sound of the treadmill upstairs. Clearly her running motivation had kicked in late today. I took the stairs two at a time. I had never watched her running before, but like most things she did, she looked effortless, free and easy.

Evie raised a hand then pulled her AirPods out. "Hey, you. One sec." Evie stopped the treadmill and jumped off, wiping her face and neck with a towel as she came over. "I'm sweaty," she warned before leaning in to kiss me. "How was your day?"

I didn't mind her sweaty. The opposite, really. "It was very busy. But also very good."

"What made it good? Tell me about it? I just need to get a drink and stretch." She indicated that she was going back downstairs, and I followed her. As soon as she'd poured herself a glass of water, I answered her.

"I solved a problem."

She pulled a leg behind herself to stretch her quad. "Oh? That's great."

"Ja, it is. I solved the problem of us."

Her eyebrows crumpled toward each other. "You mean…?" She dropped her leg.

Nodding, I confirmed, "I talked to my boss, and I applied for a permanent transfer to the Boston office. He agreed that it should not be an issue."

Her mouth worked open and closed before she spoke. "It isn't? It's…happening? You're staying here for me?" Evie's voice broke at the end of her question.

I smiled, closing the space between us. "No. I am staying here for me. Because I need to be with you. In this case, for now, you are the immovable object. I can move. Literally. So I will move. Later, I may be immovable and you may have to do something. But whatever we do, let's do it together."

Her face lit up like a Christmas tree. "This is incredible, Annika. I'm so excited. I'm so happy and pleased and all those good words. But I want to be sure that you're sure."

I took her face in my hands. "I love how thoughtful you are. I'm sure. I have never felt this type of connection before, with anybody. And I would like to see if we can build it into something amazing."

She bit down on her lower lip, as if she feared asking me the question. "What about your family?"

"They are very happy for me. And I can visit and they can visit. We'll get a private jet…" I winked, and Evie laughed and gently pinched my hip. "But we will be required to spend some Christmases in Germany, that is nonnegotiable." Christmases. More than one. The years of possibility were stretched out before us.

"Deal. I'll start private jet shopping next week."

I wasn't sure if she was joking or not, but I kept the same light tone when I replied, "Good." I dreaded having to bring this up, but I knew it was important for her. "There is one thing we need to talk about."

She sighed and slumped against the benchtop. "Money."

"Ja. Money." Evie had started nervously chewing her lower lip. I closed the distance between us and gently tilted her face up. "I don't want you to feel that you have to spend money to make me happy. And if we move in together, or something more, then I want things to be equal." My visa was tied to a job for now, and while I made more than enough to be comfortable, I obviously had nowhere near what she had. "I want to help your brain learn that it doesn't need to worry about me and your financial status. I love you for you, not what you can buy. And I will do whatever I need to do for you to see that."

She exhaled loudly. "I already see it. So…what do you want to do?"

"For start, let's talk about moving in together. And we'll split every bill equally."

"Okay. But like, sometimes I'll pay for dinner or groceries or a coffee and lunch or whatever, and sometimes you will, right? Just like we've been doing already? That's not unfair, it's just us. And sometimes I *will* just want to buy you something because that's just me. And I kind of want that to be okay with you and for you to not feel weird about the cost."

"I know. And that is fine. But don't…buy me a country or anything, okay?"

Her face fell and she mock pouted. "Well there goes my idea for this year's Christmas."

"Fine, maybe just a small tropical island."

She grinned. "Deal." Her grin faded a little bit. "We can just assess how it's going as it goes, right? I know in my heart that you're not like anyone I've ever dated, Annika. And I know it won't take long for my head to realize that in its stupid memory banks too. I'm not worried."

"Good. Because neither am I. I love you. And I trust you to talk to me about things, even boring things like shared finances."

"I will." Her expression relaxed, and I could tell that despite her assurances that she didn't think I only cared about her economic status, her deep subconscious had still been a little bit focused on it, and I was glad I'd brought it up. "So when you say Christmas in Germany, do you mean like just Christmas, or Chrisssstmas." She drew the word out and indicated a huge, all-encompassing circle with her arms.

"The second one." I laughed. "Perhaps a slightly abbreviated Merry Weihnachten in order to accommodate my vacation hours. But

I really enjoyed combining things. And there is still so much we didn't do. So many foods we didn't eat."

"I loved it too," she said, smiling fondly. "If we only did *some* of the Christmas stuff then I suppose we'll need to start planning soon. Especially if we have to fit in your family and"—she grimaced—"maybe time with mine."

"Maybe we should try to combine everyone." I raised a querying eyebrow. "How do your parents feel about Germany?"

"How do your parents feel about Greenwich?" she shot back. Then she cringed. "No, sorry, I can't do that to them."

"We have to be prepared for the fact they might meet eventually, Evie."

"Sh—eet. Nope, I'm going to cross that bridge if we come to it." She shook her head like she was shaking the thought from it. "Right. This Christmas. I want to make and decorate cookies. I want more food. I want to nail down our menus early and try some new things. I want to figure out how to make a Santa visit happen in the middle of the night. Fondue. Did I mention more food? Germany. We have so much planning to do!"

I rubbed up and down her arms. "That all sounds wonderful." I knew it didn't matter what we did, as long as I was with her.

Her hopeful expression broke the last of my reservations, and I knew I had made the right choice. "So, you're definitely moving to Boston?" she asked quietly.

I took her hands and pulled them to my chest, holding them against my heart. "I already moved here, Evie-Evangeline. Now I'm just staying here."

She sniffled, her lower lip trembling. "You mean it? You're not leaving me?"

"No, Schnucki, I'm not leaving you. I am staying. For you. For me." I kissed her gently. "For us."

EPILOGUE

Evie

 Annika had asked to drive because she was taking me somewhere for…something. I'd discovered she loved driving, and given that she had no car in Boston, I often handed over my keys, which she took with great delight.
 I buckled myself in and asked again, "Where are we going? Are you going to give me any clue about this surprise?"
 "No. Because then there won't be a surprise." She input something into the GPS and I checked the screen. Framingham.
 "That gives something away. Are we going to see the wildflowers? Take a hike?"
 She remained silent, not even giving a subtle nod or headshake to let me know I was on the right path. She'd instructed me to dress for being outside and getting sweaty, so at the moment a hike was winning. The backpack she'd thrown in only made me more certain of my guess.
 The drive took about half an hour, though it felt interminably longer with me trying to pry hints from Annika and her staunchly resisting. The late-spring day was in the low seventies, the sky gently clouded with no chance of rain, and I had the window down to enjoy the fresher air as we left the city.

She pulled up at a set of lights. "I almost forgot. Mama booked their flights for my birthday. And she confirmed Markus and Sonja are coming too." The joy at having her whole family with her radiated through her voice.

I twisted to look at her. "Oh, that's great, darling."

Annika's parents had visited us in late February, not long after I'd returned from my yearly ski trip to Vail, which I'd shortened slightly because I couldn't bear being away from her for too long. She'd put them up in her apartment, because by then, she'd basically moved into my place. As soon as they'd left, she'd moved in officially. She'd asked if she could please, please cancel her lease, joking that she simply couldn't live there any longer. And I'd joked back that it was a good thing she asked, because I had new temporary tenants from Germany and I wanted to keep the apartment empty for their visits. My property manager had looked at me like I'd grown another set of ears, but was well used to me by now, so he just nodded, smiled, and told me "Sure."

Annika's parents had been here for my birthday, and had made it into a whole celebration week. Except for taking my birthday as vacation days, Annika had to work because she'd taken some time off to join me in Vail—like I said, being away from each other was hard—which meant it'd been on me to entertain her parents while they weren't off being tourists. And it had been utterly fabulous. We had cocktail hour every evening before either her mother insisted on cooking, or we'd go out to eat and drink the nights away. My parents had called for my birthday, and the card Mom sent was actually personalized and came with a small gift of jewelry.

Things between me and my parents were civil, though still infrequent, which was a big step up from basically nonexistent. We all seemed to be taking it as it came. Of course, at their first meeting—Chloe's birthday in April—Annika had charmed the pants off my father and the pearls off my mother. I'd joked that they liked her more than they liked me, which six months ago would have been no joke.

There had been no formal apology but then again, I hadn't apologized either. It was almost like this starting to move forward *was* the apology. My wounds hadn't fully healed, but maybe Mom's and Dad's hadn't either. Maybe they would always be there, but we'd managed to put a bandage over them so we could exist in some sort of a semifunctional relationship. Annika helped. I knew her opinions on the importance of family, and though she never pushed—she was on my side with all my remaining emotional baggage about the rift—she was a natural mediator.

I smiled over at her, and she glanced at me, smiling back. "What is it?" she asked.

"Nothing," I said quietly. "I just love you."

"That's good, because I love you too and otherwise it would have been *very* awkward for you to admit that."

I laughed as we pulled up to a gray wooden two-story and parked by the three-car garage. A middle-aged man came out the front door to meet us. I stretched, and checked I looked presentable for this stranger for whatever reason we were here. I met Annika by the rear of the car. "Are we buying a kitten or a puppy? Kitten and a puppy?"

Her eyes widened. "You want kittens and puppies?"

"Of course. Doesn't everyone?" I raised my eyebrows. "You know, Chloe's been bugging Pete about getting a pet. Maybe I should use the swear jar money and go to a shelter to adopt one for her." Pete might not talk to me for a week if I turned up with a puppy, but I needed to spend the money in Swear Jar #3 on *something* for my niece. We'd used the first two jars of swearing money to buy Chloe whatever frivolous things she wanted (and it was *a lot* of frivolous things once I paid out the chits in the jars).

The man met us on the drive, halfway between his house and my (though now it seemed more like *our*) car.

Annika rested her hand on my back. I loved how she did that, how the steady, supporting, loving touch always grounded me. "Evie, this is Carlos. He is one of my coworkers."

I held out my hand and as he took it, I said, "Great to meet you." *And why am I meeting you?*

"You too, Evie. Nice to put a face to the name finally." The reason for us being there became crystal clear when he gestured around us. "My kids were pretty happy to hear someone else would be mowing the lawn this week."

I looked to Annika, my eyebrows shooting up in surprise. "You got me mowing a lawn?"

She grinned. "Ja, I did. It is a late Weihnachten gift."

Carlos chuckled. "I'm not sure how much of a gift it is, but if you want to mow a lawn then I'm all for it." He eyed me. "You've never done it before, right?"

"Right," I confirmed cheerfully.

"Okie dokie. Nothing to it. Let me go get the machine while you put on your safety gear."

"I need safety gear?" I asked, looking between him and my girlfriend.

"You do," Annika said happily. She took me by the hand and led me back to the car. After rummaging in the backpack, she handed me sunscreen. "Put this on. I don't want you to burn your beautiful skin."

"Yes, ma'am." I diligently slathered my face, neck, and arms in the lotion, then put on the wide-brimmed hat she passed me. "This backpack holds a lot of stuff. What else are you going to pull out of there?"

Smiling triumphantly, Annika held out some brand-new earmuffs and leather work gloves. "Here. To protect the rest of you. And I have special sunglasses too if you don't want to risk yours."

"Good point. Thanks." They were surprisingly fashionable for safety glasses. Annika took my Ray-Bans and put them carefully in their case in my handbag, while I looped the earmuffs around my neck and pulled on the gloves. "How do I look?" I asked, striking a pose.

"Very capable. I would hire you to cut my grass."

I smirked. "Do you know what that means?"

Annika's forehead wrinkled. "Yes." She made a pushing motion like she was moving a lawnmower.

Laughing, I explained, "Well, yeah, but it's slang that means trying to pick up someone who's already in a relationship."

"Oh. Oh!" She frowned. "Well. Then…you can cut my grass but nobody else's."

"Deal." I leaned in and snaked an arm around her waist, pulling her close. "Baby, I'm gonna cut your grass all night long."

We burst into laughter, but before she could answer—probably for the best—Carlos appeared from the side of the house, pushing a bright-red lawnmower. Annika and I broke apart, still laughing. I indicated the front lawn. "How much grass is this?" I hadn't even seen the backyard, but I assumed it was about the same size.

"It's a half-acre block."

Goddammit. "I see, I see. Um, you don't have a ride-on mower?"

He grinned. "Oh yeah, of course I do. But Annika insisted on the push mower."

I turned slowly to her, drawling, "Did she now…"

She looked so innocent, it was adorable. "It's all about the experience of it. Isn't it?"

"Apparently so," I said dryly.

Carlos showed me how to start the mower and gave me a basic primer which consisted of "push it around until the grass is cut, don't stick any part of your body near the blades—those are under the mower, FYI—unless you don't like that part of your body and want it mangled or removed."

Mowing a lawn was easy. But it was also hot and tedious and it only took ten minutes before I was sick of it. Annika and Carlos sat on his front porch, drinking beer and chatting. Every now and then she'd wave cheerfully, then return to her beer and conversation. Occasionally, she took a photo of me toiling. On one pass, Carlos indicated I should throttle the mower back, and once I'd done so he yelled over the sound of the mower and my hearing protection, "You're lasting longer than I thought you would."

"I didn't know quitting was an option!" I yelled back.

I'd completed the front lawn, and really needed a break before I started the back. I'd experienced mowing, did I *really* need to do the back? Carlos had left five minutes ago to go collect one of his kids from a Saturday activity, after leaving another beer for Annika and a can of something for me.

After turning the mower off, I trudged to the house for a rest and a drink. I plonked down on the porch by her feet, unable to even make it into a chair. Annika passed me the water and once I'd drunk some, she swapped the plastic bottle for a can of black cherry White Claw. She pushed her sunglasses onto the top of her head. "I think it's a rule that beer is the drink of choice for physical activity, but I doubted even that would convince you."

"You doubted correctly." I cracked open the hard seltzer and drank deeply. Ohhhh yes. I shuffled so I could lean against her shins. "Okay. Mowing lawns sucks. I've experienced it and now I know I don't want that aspect of normality. Let's hire someone to do it when we get a place with a lawn. I am all about supporting small businesses, and now I am also all about not mowing lawns myself. Or we can stay in the city and just have a lawn for our vacation homes."

"Homes?" she asked, her voice rising an octave at the end of the word. "More than one? How…many of them?"

I ticked them off on my fingers. "Hamburg for when we visit your parents. Nantucket and Greenwich for if we ever visit my parents, because I love you too much to make you stay with them. The house in Vail for ski trips, but we already have that. Then a house on some nice tropical island for you to look forward to after winter."

She grinned. "Okay, I'm glad I moved in with you, because I can't afford rent in those places."

"You could if you wanted to marry me." I grinned. "But we'd never rent."

"Hmm," she mused. There was something that had sparked in her eyes when I'd said *marry me*, but she didn't comment on it. "So, you do not like my gift?"

"I love your gift. Well, the idea of your gift. The execution was… hard. Mowing lawns is really boring. It'd be better if I could listen to music or something, but the noise makes that impossible."

"So you don't like being normal then?" she teased.

I wrinkled my nose. "I suppose I don't."

Annika leaned down, and tilted my chin up for a kiss. "Good, because you, Evie, are anything but *normal*. You are so special." She kissed me slowly, thoroughly, and if we weren't sitting on a stranger's porch, things would probably have gotten pretty heated. When we separated, she said, "I have been thinking."

"What about?" I asked after a deep gulp of seltzer.

"I think we need a portmanteau of our own."

"Oh yeah? What did you have in mind?"

"Evika," she said triumphantly.

"Evika." Nodding slowly, I said, "I mean, it works…"

"It does. It was that or Annivie. And *that* is strange. As bad as Frohe Christmas."

Laughing I agreed, "Yeah. Evika. I like it." I relaxed back against her legs, looking around the front lawn, studying the trees towering above. "I've been thinking too. I want to buy a real Christmas tree, roots and all, and put it into a pot for us to use at Christmas. Then we can plant it in the yard of our own house someday. The yard someone else is mowing," I clarified.

Annika's eyebrows shot up. "Ja, okay, but until then, isn't it going to grow through the ceiling of the apartment?"

"It can live on the rooftop garden, and you can keep it alive."

"Oh, now I know why we're together. For me to care for your plants." She'd helped me plant the seeds she'd given me for Christmas, and they'd lived in small pots in my condo until it was warm enough, and they were strong enough, to go live out on my terrace. Annika checked them every afternoon, watering them as needed, and we'd often sit up there before dinner with a drink, enjoying the warmer evenings.

"Caught me." I twisted around and rested my arm across her knees. "So I was thinking, for this year's Merry Weihnachten, could we adjust the budget upward a little?"

"If you would like that. But you know it's not about what we spend for each other."

"I know. But…what if I wanted to give you a ring? A ring that came with a marriage proposal?" I clarified, in case there was any ambiguity.

She swallowed visibly, and I caught the slightest tremble in her lips. She set her beer down and took my face in her hands. "You've already given me yourself." Annika kissed me, and I responded enthusiastically. She lingered against my lips as she murmured, "And that is the best Merry Weihnachten gift of all. *You* are the only gift I will ever need."

I swallowed the lump of emotion that had welled up. "I feel like I used something like that line on you already."

"I am borrowing it," Annika said, kissing me again. When she met my eyes, there was the faintest hint of tears in hers. "And, Evie-Evangeline? If you want to give me a ring as a Weihnachten gift, or at any time before, I would say…*ja*."

Bella Books, Inc.
Happy Endings Live Here
P.O. Box 10543
Tallahassee, FL 32302
Phone: (850) 576-2370
www.BellaBooks.com

More Titles from Bella Books

Hunter's Revenge – Gerri Hill
978-1-64247-447-3 | 276 pgs | paperback: $18.95 | eBook: $9.99
Tori Hunter is back! Don't miss this final chapter in the acclaimed Tori Hunter series.

Integrity – E. J. Noyes
978-1-64247-465-7 | 228 pgs | paperback: $19.95 | eBook: $9.99
It was supposed to be an ordinary workday...

The Order – TJ O'Shea
978-1-64247-378-0 | 396 pgs | paperback: $19.95 | eBook: $9.99
For two women the battle between new love and old loyalty may prove more dangerous than the war they're trying to survive.

Under the Stars with You – Jaime Clevenger
978-1-64247-439-8 | 302 pgs | paperback: $19.95 | eBook: $9.99
Sometimes believing in love is the first step. And sometimes it's all about trusting the stars.

The Missing Piece – Kat Jackson
978-1-64247-445-9 | 250 pgs | paperback: $18.95 | eBook: $9.99
Renee's world collides with possibility and the past, setting off a tidal wave of changes she could have never predicted.

An Acquired Taste – Cheri Ritz
978-1-64247-462-6 | 206 pgs | paperback: $17.95 | eBook: $9.99
Can Elle and Ashley stand the heat in the *Celebrity Cook Off* kitchen?